Reviews

"I was instantly transported into the shoes of the adventurer, Carly, and her search to find the Holy Grail, the cup of eternal life. Could she be the one to uncover the connection between Stonehenge, King Arthur, and the Holy Grail? A modern-day Indiana Jones quest for the explorer in us all."

— **Courtney C.**, *Lipstick Hoarder and Avid Reader*
Follow Courtney on Instagram @the_pages_within

"*Etched in Stone* is such a unique and important read for all young women coming into their own, in a world full of contradicting messages about what women can, could, and should be! Galib has made it a must read for anyone who needs to be reminded that they are only limited by the barriers they accept, not the ones placed in front of them."

— **Tiffany J.**, *Administration and Communications MVP*

"Having grown up on Nancy Drew, King Arthur legends, and Agatha Christie, I immediately got wrapped up in *Etched in Stone*. Galib combines the talents of mystery writers of yesteryears and presents the twenty-first-century reader with a storyline that is both suspenseful and heartwarming as it follows the adventures of two freshmen students looking for the Holy Grail. As I was reading, I started longing for my college days and wondering why I did not major in archaeology! *Etched* was hard for me to put down, and as the mystery thickened, I was left smiling, surprised, and longing for more!"

— ***Grace G.***, *Reader, Medical Practice Manager, and Healthcare Provider*

"I really enjoyed that Lydia helped guide Carly throughout the story. They are both brave, intelligent women, so it was great to see that type of positive relationship between them."

— ***Avery F.***, *Reader who enjoys crime, mystery, and young adult literature*

"I love how this book is influenced by Tomb Raider and Indiana Jones, not just through references but through genre, style, and heart. It's refreshing to see more action–adventure stories starring female archaeologists. I appreciate the more serious, realistic take on this genre. Carly uses smarts (not guns) to solve mysteries and get out of tough situations."

— ***Charity L.***, *Renaissance Woman, Stargazer, and Collector of Video Games*

"Galib threw us right into an intense mystery. It was intriguing and the driving force that made me want to keep reading because I had to know who committed the crimes, why they were doing it, and if these freshmen really led a search that found the Holy Grail. This was really fun to read."

— ***Kaya S.***, *Believer in Magic, Devourer of Books, and Explorer of Worlds*

ETCHED IN STONE

THE KNIGHTS OF THE DAGGER
BOOK I

Dear Bob,
Be Brave! – and take that
leap of faith!

CHRISTINE GALIB

Christine Galib
(and Carly)

road less traveled
enterprises

Author's note: This is a work of fiction. Names, characters, places, and incidents are the product of the author's imagination or are used fictitiously.

ETCHED IN STONE

Editor: Kristen Corrects, kristencorrects.com
Typesetter & Proofreader: Kingsman Editing, kingsmanediting.com
Cover Illustrator: Giselle Harrington, giselleharrington.com

First edition published 2022
ISBN: 978-1-955824-02-6 (paperback)
ISBN: 978-1-955824-03-3 (e-book)
christinegalib.com

Published by road less traveled enterprises
roadlesstraveledenterprises.com

For Mom, Dad, and SMA

&

For every girl who has dreamed of filling big shoes,
wearing glass slippers, and shattering glass ceilings,
bravely taking the road less traveled
and creating her own path
with grace, courage, and faith

In memoriam:

SM and SHC

PREFACE

Beverly Cleary said, "If you don't see the book you want on the shelves, write it."

And so, I did. I wrote about strong female characters who bravely create their own path with grace, courage, and faith—and help strong female readers understand what being a trailblazer truly means. I wrote a book that doesn't depend on obscenities or lewd scenes to move the plot along. I wrote a book that inspires women to be themselves—even if that means getting nervous around their crush, not knowing how to apply eyeshadow before a date, and carrying around a journal so they can clearly and critically understand their thoughts.

I wrote a book that helps us fill big shoes and discover who we were created to be as our North Star guides us—even if that means taking the road less traveled and facing the facts with women's intuition and wits. Or, in this case, even if that means embarking on a quest for the Holy Grail itself.

I wrote a book that empowers women and men of all ages to handle whatever journey life takes us on, to find value in partnership, and to always take the leap of faith when presented with the chance to do so. I wrote a book that is, in short, the kind of book I hope moms (and dads!) will be proud to read with their daughters (and sons!).

I wrote the book I wished was on the shelves when I was growing up. And in doing so, I found the story needed more than one book to be told. So, I wrote a whole series of books.

Etched in Stone is the first book in The Knights of the Dagger series. It is the story of a girl who wanted nothing more than to fill her grandmother's shoes. It is the story of a girl whose quest for the Holy Grail helps her realize what being a knight is all about. It is a story that reminds us we are never too old, and it is never too late—or too early—to live our dreams, pursue our passions, and take evidence-backed leaps of faith into the unknown adventure ahead of us.

I hope you enjoy reading *Etched in Stone* as much as I have enjoyed writing it, and I'd love to hear your thoughts. Send me a note at christinegalib.com or find me on Instagram @roadlesstraveledenterprises. Use the hashtags #EtchedInStone and #TheKnightsoftheDagger and post your reactions, questions, and comments—and pictures—as you read!

ETCHED IN STONE

THE KNIGHTS OF THE DAGGER
BOOK I

I

I took a deep breath, tucked a loose curl behind my ear, and adjusted the strap of my leather satchel. It held everything I needed to start my first semester of college. With my course registration paperwork signed and submitted, I was officially a freshman at Nassauton College. Tucked away in an idyllic Northeastern town, between two cities and their airports, Nassauton had a close-knit community feeling but frequently drew international speakers. Nassauton boasted well-known faculty and facilities and was known for the rigor of its undergraduate education.

I applied to Nassauton to study with Dr. Sidney Hasserin, the rising-star archaeologist. He had studied under Dr. Allister Leith, a famous British expert on ancient relics. Dr. Hasserin was an expert on Stonehenge and the Holy Grail. I'd always been fascinated by the cup Christ drank from at the Last Supper, the cup He used for the Last Communion with His disciples.

Whenever I asked my grandmother—a world-renowned archaeologist and one of the few women who had risen to the top of her field—about the Grail, she'd always change the subject. I'd beg her to tell me about the Grail legends, but it was to no avail—that was the one topic Gran wouldn't talk about. This made me want to study the Grail even more. When I was accepted at Nassauton, I immediately signed up for Dr. Hasserin's freshman seminar, Grail Times: Understanding Stonehenge, King Arthur, and the Quest for the Holy Grail. Luckily, I'd finally gotten off the waitlist. I was awestruck that as a freshman, I could take a class with such a well-published professor.

In addition to its expert faculty, Nassauton boasted an expansive collection of artifacts. After I'd submitted my paperwork, I decided to walk down the hallway that had the best artifacts—the hallway with our professors' offices and portraits of former professors and deans, according to the Archaeology Department administrator.

"They did that on purpose," Joyce said as she reviewed my paperwork. "It's like they've got our department's faculty members guarding the artifacts—and keeping an eye on the new faculty and students." She looked over my papers a final time. "Carlyle Stuart, looks like you're all set, thank you. Welcome to Nassauton College."

I grinned as she handed me a copy and directed me to the hallway.

"Enjoy the collection!" she added.

"Thank you, Joyce. Have a great day!"

I headed to the hallway. Now, before the hustle and bustle of the semester, would be a good time to see the artifacts without the distraction from throngs of students passing through.

The artifacts had an ethereal and peaceful glow in the mid-morning sunlight. The light streamed in from the Gothic windows of the old stone building, adding to the eerie quiet of the empty hallway. I ambled down the corridor, looking at the delicate jewelry and well-used cutlery in the display cases. The rust on some of the cutlery gave it a reddish-brown tint. I stopped in front of an old, ornate kitchen knife with a wooden handle. *Who originally owned this knife—some chef, famous in her or his day? A maidservant who ran the kitchen, ensuring all dishes were prepared to the master of the house's liking?*

I kept walking, carefully placing one foot in front of the other. My moccasins made an occasional creak on the wooden floor. Every now and then, I'd glance up at the faculty members' portraits. The professors seemed to be peering at me, personally welcoming me to Nassauton. *Dr. Charlotte Stone-Robinson. Dr. Lola-Grace Paulman. Dr. Samuel Fuentes. Dr. Courtney Wessels. Dr. Lauren Tiffany Taylor. Dr. Brian Timothy Jordan.*

As I turned the corner, I saw another hallway of more display cases and office doors. I paused and gazed at the pottery and small bowls in the case closest to me. I squatted down to look at one of the bowls on the lower shelf when a man's voice from a few doors down the hallway broke the silence.

"You've been quiet for some time. Spill it, Lydia. What are you thinking?"

"Daniel, I think Sidney was murdered and I'm going to find out why."

I almost fell out of my squat onto the floor. *Sidney?* Were they talking about Dr. Sidney Hasserin? I could see his name on my course registration form. I bounced up and adjusted my satchel. Careful not to cause creaking noises on the wooden floor, I tiptoed to a case closer to the office with the voices. Even as I tiptoed, I felt Nassauton's professors staring at me from their portraits, telling me to be quiet.

Good call on wearing moccasins instead of heels, I thought. I looked at the larger bowls on the second shelf. The bowls were probably once bright and vibrant, but now they were a faded burnt orange. I listened as the voices continued from behind the half-open office door.

"Murdered? On what evidence? Plus, it'd be all over the papers!"

"Not if University Communications got there first and shut it down. I'm pretty sure only their team, the provost, you, and I know. I'm sure they haven't told our department staff. It's the new term. Everyone would be on edge with a murder, and of a favorite professor especially, to start the school year."

My eyes widened. Seeing the artifacts had turned into overhearing a conversation about the death—and potential murder—of Dr. Sidney Hasserin. I clutched my satchel's strap. I hoped no one else was around. Lydia and Daniel were certainly talking as if they were the only ones here. I quieted my breath, trying to listen more closely. If Dr. Hasserin really had been murdered, I had to know why. Was he involved in something illegal? What was he hiding? What had he found?

"Come on, you're a woman of evidence. You've got absolutely none here."

"Absolutely none? What about the notes Sid received—right after the conference, barely a few weeks ago. They were very similar to mine. Same double dagger marks, same style, and same phrases."

"Okay, so some notes, but even with your notes the police didn't find anything. They closed the case—if you can even call it that. Look, I know you're upset to lose your colleague and mentee—we all are upset to lose such a beloved professor—but things happen. This isn't a murder mystery. Maybe he had an undiagnosed condition."

I edged closer to the door, staying near the case with the bowls. I was eager to hear more, but careful not to be noticed—and terrified of what would happen if Lydia or Daniel walked out of the office.

"Undiagnosed? I don't think so. What are the odds? Where is the evidence for that? Sid didn't have any symptoms. Thirty-six and healthy as a horse. Always walked around with his monogrammed journal. Jogged the campus every morning."

"But that's how these things work. They can sneak up on anyone, healthy or not, at any time."

"Maybe, but I'm not buying it. At the conference, he hinted about what he'd discovered at Stonehenge. He wouldn't spill the beans—not even to me. Then he got the notes. And as of two days ago, he's dead. I'm telling you, I believe Dr. Sidney Hasserin was murdered."

I gasped and immediately covered my mouth. *What did Dr. Hasserin discover at Stonehenge?*

"I don't know what to say, other than we're all in shock and grieving our loss. You in particular must be devastated. I get it, trust me. But, you need to focus on finding someone to teach Sid's seminar, not on speculating theories about his death."

I heard Lydia sigh. I sighed too. I couldn't help but come up with my own theories, too, especially since I had come to Nassauton to study with Dr. Hasserin. I needed to help Lydia solve this mystery.

"I am. I posted the job description this morning. Worst case, we ask someone from the department to cover the course."

There was a pause, then the sound of chair legs scraping on the wooden floor. Lydia continued. "I'm sorry. I need to get back to my office so I can finish the email for University Communications. They want to announce Sid's passing."

Afraid Lydia would see me, I clutched my satchel strap, turned the corner, and darted down the hallway with the portraits. I exited out of the nearest door I could find. Chills ran down my spine as I ran back to my dorm room.

A murder to start the school year?

††

By the time I got back to my dorm room, I hardly had a few moments to wrap my head around my thoughts. I'd taken out my journal to write about what Lydia and Daniel said when I heard loud knocking on the door.

"Carly? Carly are you in there? I forgot my key!"

"Lara, I hope she's in there. The ice cream is going to melt. You can't let this happen again. You really need to make a copy of the key and leave it above the door."

My roommate's parents had descended on our room for move-in, ensuring their daughter had everything she needed for school—from bookcases to snacks to paper clips. They'd left suitcases and boxes piled up in our common area, accumulating more clothes, posters, or surge protectors with each trip they made.

The knocking continued. I sighed. I stuck my pencil in my journal and got up.

"Oh, Carly thank you!" Lara gave me a big hug as I opened the door.

"You're welcome," I said, a little intimidated by her energy and exuberance.

Lara walked into our room, her heels echoing on the floor as her golden-brown curls bounced around her face. She was willowy, and in her heels, she towered over me. Her parents marched in after her, lugging grocery bags from the town's organic market. As soon as her dad put his bags down, he walked to her desk and found her key.

"Lara, put this in your wallet and remember not to leave your room without it."

"Thanks," Lara said, taking the key from him. "I'll try." She turned to me. "So, how's your day going? I got us plenty of snacks." She paused, then added, "Oh, I love your moccasins! Look how cute they are with all those patterns!"

I smiled. "Thank you, they're hand-painted. They used to be my grandmother's."

"Come on Lara, help us put the food away. We haven't got all day and I'll need to be eating lunch soon since I'm following my clean eating plan."

Lara smiled, rolling her blue eyes a little bit, too. "Mom is on a strict schedule—and of course that means my dad and I eat when she says it's time. We can talk shoes when they're gone!"

If Lara wanted to talk shoes, she'd come to the right person. I'd brought fourteen pairs of my grandmother's shoes with me.

Lara turned around to help her parents unload their grocery bags, and I headed back to my room. I sat at my desk and picked up my pencil. *Stonehenge. The conference. Sid's discovery. The mysterious notes. His death. A murder?* I stared at the words I'd written on my page, twirling a loose curl and thinking. With Lara and her parents chit-chatting in the common room, it was very difficult to concentrate. Sighing, I put my pencil down. Now was as good a time as ever to finish organizing my closet.

I opened my closet to unpack my shoes. It might as well have been a small cabinet in a corner of my room. *What would Gran say if she saw me cramming all her shoes in a closet the size of a cupboard?* She had a walk-in closet the size of my entire bedroom, full of unending racks with boxes organized by country.

When I was little, I loved disappearing between the racks and admiring Gran's shoes. I was sure that for every city Gran visited—whether leading an excavation, giving a lecture, or attending a gala with dignitaries and scholars—she bought new shoes. A woman with a deep faith, a keen intuition, and an extraordinary shoe collection, Gran never let her fear of the unknown stop her from pursuing—and overcoming—any adventure. Gran always told me, *"All a woman needs to conquer the world are her curiosity, her research, and her faith—and shoes that make her smile dazzle like a thousand diamonds."* Every time I played dress-up in her shoes, I knew she was right.

I smiled as I opened the first shoebox. The red satin shoes had shards of mirrors scattered on them. In a nod to Greek architecture, they had onyx Corinthian columns for heels. As a six-year-old only child, I'd gotten hours of entertainment modeling those heels for Gran. The heels clacked on our hardwood floor as I imagined myself strutting around Gran and her partner's galas, inspecting relics recovered from Nazi hiding spots. She chuckled as she watched me, telling me she'd rather I shatter glass ceilings than wear glass slippers. I'd grin and tell her when I grew up, I would do both. I loved those shoes because Gran's specialty was Ancient Rome and Greece. I placed the shoes on the bottom shelf.

I opened the second box. Gran's Atlas heels had a world map sketched onto their sides, with gold compasses scattered across the countries. I traced my finger on the lines, feeling how smooth the material was, even after years of use. My favorite part of these shoes were the heels: mini gold figurines of Atlas, the man from Greek mythology condemned to hold the Earth. With his arms above him, Atlas held up the shoe's wearer.

"Where do you want the couch?" Lara's dad asked. Lara and her parents were chit-chatting outside my door. They'd unpacked all the groceries and were arranging the common room furniture.

"Doesn't matter, how about on the side wall?" Lara was apathetic. She'd lost interest a long time ago. I chuckled. Lara seemed like she would be a good roommate, and I could tell we shared an interest in fun, quirky shoes.

I picked up the third shoebox. It had Gran's black leather ankle-length boots, with big, silver studs on the heels. I laughed. As a little girl, I'd wear those boots—or Gran's knee-high, brown leather ones with passport stamps, or her gladiator sandals with real gold studs—when I felt daring. My feet in no way filled the shoes, but I loved slipping into them since they made me feel like I was a warrior. Channeling my inner Artemis or Hercules, and armed with Gran's cane as a sword, I'd jump off our living room couch and slash imaginary mythological monsters. My mom was usually the one to find me. "If you're going to wear Gran's boots, you've got to be brave enough to fill them," she'd say with a grin. I'd grin back, vigorously nodding.

When I was little, I couldn't wait for the day I would fill Gran's shoes. And today, as I looked at my moccasins—and started my first year at Nassauton—I knew I was taking my first steps to doing so.

I kept tackling the boxes, neatly organizing my shoes on the bottom shelf. When I opened the last shoebox, I gasped. There, tucked right alongside Gran's gladiator sandals, was a black velvet square box, about three-by-three inches. It had a Post-it note stuck on top, with my name scribbled on it. A small smile curled across my face as I recognized Gran's handwriting. Gran had never mentioned this box to me. I picked it up. It was surprisingly heavy. I felt the smoothness of the velvet fabric.

I popped the box open. Inside was a chain necklace with a gold pendant. The pendant was a horseshoe, with a gold dagger across the bottom. It looked regal and glamorous, like a necklace worn at very special occasions. I grinned. The dagger gave the pendant a bit of edginess, signaling its wearer was a strong and brave warrior. I picked up the pendant. It was heavy—heavier than I expected. *Is it solid gold?* The dagger's hilt had a little gap in it, as though it previously held something, maybe a gemstone, which had fallen out.

I studied the pendant more closely. I thought I'd seen it before, but I couldn't remember where. As I placed the necklace back in the box, I noticed a note taped to the inside of the top of the box. I carefully removed the tape and unfolded the note.

My Darling Young Explorer: I want you to have this. Wear it, hide it, keep it safe, and in your sight.

This pendant is part one of three
You're holding history in your hands
The gold dagger points to stones
Some standing, some fallen, in foreign lands

You'll need the missing pieces
To make this gadget whole
The second piece is not too far from home
Finding it first should be your goal

The third piece I cannot say
It's been lost for quite a while
There's no telling where it could be
On these shores or those of another isle

This gadget aligns with Stonehenge,
It must have been by design
When you have all the pieces
Stand at Stonehenge in the sunshine?

But in your quest trust no one
For there are evil ones all around
Warring knights seek this tool
They want what is lost to be found

P.S. Only trust the one who knows the answer to the Riddle of the Ages.

I looked up from the paper and gazed at my shoes. What were a mysterious poem and a gold pendant doing in my shoebox? I twirled a loose curl as I reread the poem, trying to understand what it could mean. *Why had Gran addressed this poem to me? Why did she want me to have a gold pendant?* I walked to my desk, bringing the box and paper with me.

Young Explorer. I smiled. I could hear Gran calling me by my nickname. I held the poem as I closed my eyes. If Gran had seen me discovering this pendant and poem, she'd say I was taking right after her. She'd be proud of me as I embarked on whatever adventure it would bring.

But Gran had passed away after my fifteenth birthday. *Here Lies Lyle Ainsley, Student of the Ages. Rest in Peace*. I'd sat by her gravestone, tracing my fingers over those words as though it would bring her back. A handful of people attended Gran's funeral. One woman stood out to me. She wore gold aviators and a wide-brimmed black straw hat the whole time. I thought that was tacky—to wear sunglasses and a straw hat to a funeral. But, I guess everyone handled their grief in different ways.

Gran's partner, Elkay, didn't even attend the funeral. I couldn't remember meeting Elkay—maybe she'd been around when I was younger. Did they have some type of falling out?

I opened my eyes and looked at the poem. *I want you to have this. Wear it, hide it, keep it safe, and in your sight.* I took a deep breath. As I reread the words, I could hear Gran saying them to me.

After the funeral, all the church ladies and J. Carmichael, one of Gran's closest friends, tried to console me. They assured me Gran was undoubtedly in Heaven. But I doubted Heaven was real: I couldn't see, touch, or experience it. I didn't have any proof for it. How could God want Gran there—and not here, with me? I was enraged at God for taking Gran away from me—an anger that was amplified when my dad passed away a few months later, after my church confirmation.

I'd never been able to forgive God for taking away two of my favorite people—and right after I had stood in front of my church and said I'd believed in Him! What kind of god would do that to anyone, let alone a teenager? I resented that God had woken up one day and disrupted everything that made my life safe and secure. *How could a god like that love me or claim to know my name and want a relationship with me?*

As I struggled with my doubts, I found certainty and comfort in my schoolwork. Pursuing knowledge—especially in archaeology—gave me an identity as a young scholar, explorer, and creative problem-solver. I liked applying my intuition and wits to finding evidence, creating solutions, and generating proofs. Every day, I relied more and more on what I could see, touch, and experience.

To help me cope with Gran's and Dad's deaths, I'd gone through our photo albums. I saw how much I resembled Gran. My mom always told me I had her mom's big green eyes and long, black curly hair. "You get it from me, and I got it from her, and she got it from her mom before her. You have generations of beautiful and strong women of incredible grace, courage, and faith watching over you, sweetheart," my mom would say while brushing or braiding my hair. "These women are always cheering you on, no matter what." I always knew I wanted to follow in Gran's footsteps and live up to her legacy.

I twirled a loose curl as I looked at the poem. With this poem, Gran was giving me my own adventure—a way for me to live up to her legacy and fill her shoes. It was as though she'd somehow known when the time was right, I'd find her pendant and poem. *I have to discover the poem's meaning. I have to find the gadget's missing pieces. I have to accept my quest.* I grinned. *Quest accepted!* I was not going to let Gran down.

My pendant—the horseshoe with a dagger on the bottom—was one piece of the entire gadget. *What are the other two pieces? How do they connect to my pendant?*

I started sketching what the complete gadget might look like and created something that resembled Stonehenge. Gran had written that the gadget aligns with Stonehenge, but judging from the question mark, she wasn't sure how. I wasn't sure either. *Maybe "stand in the sunshine" has to do with the summer solstice celebration at Stonehenge?* Thousands of people flocked to Stonehenge every year to celebrate the solstice, the longest day of the year. Experiencing this celebration was on my bucket list. Standing at such a historic and mysterious site, with so many strangers united in the same purpose at the same time, would be exhilarating.

The last stanza gave me chills. I wrote *quest*, *evil ones*, and *warring knights* in my journal, and underlined the words. *Is this for real? Or was Gran making up a riddle for me, like the riddles we'd solve when I was little?* She was always impressed by how I'd tackle riddles and solve them with little help. Where my mom thought I was precocious, Gran thought I'd make an excellent detective. In this poem, she'd given me several riddles, including the Riddle of the Ages, to solve.

I put my pencil down and gazed at my pendant. It gleamed in the sunlight streaming through my window. Against the box's black velvet, the gold pendant looked even more regal. I picked up the necklace and put it on, tucking it under my T-shirt. *Wear it, keep it safe, and in your sight.* The safest place would be around my neck.

I clutched my pendant through my shirt. "Be brave," I whispered, closing my eyes and inhaling and exhaling. I smiled. Gran might not have seen me move into my dorm room, but by wearing her necklace, I knew she was with me as I faced whatever adventures were ahead.

††

Later that evening, Lara and I were in our common room. Boxes were still piled up on our rug and in front of our couch, but the now-empty suitcases were stacked against the wall by the door. Lara was texting her friends and I was checking my email—most of them were about courses, club fairs, and upcoming deadlines. But one, from University Communications, caught my eye. It was the email Lydia had mentioned in the conversation I'd overheard.

> *Subject: Tribute to Dr. Sidney Hasserin, Member of the Archaeology Department*
>
> *Dear colleagues and students:*
>
> *We are writing to share the sad news that Dr. Sidney Hasserin, a professor in the Archaeology Department and one of the world's youngest experts on the British Isles, has passed away. He was thirty-six. Having contributed substantial research that advanced our understanding of British lore, especially the Holy Grail and its secrets, Sidney was an*

award-winning professor and steadfast supporter of his students at Nassauton.

He pioneered the class Grail Times: Understanding Stonehenge, King Arthur, and the Quest for the Holy Grail—unsurprisingly a popular freshman seminar that required students to go on a dig.

Grief counselors are available at the Boardman Clinic to support our community at this difficult time.

I looked up from my computer and stared at the wall. University Communications had said nothing about a murder. Was Lydia wrong—or right?

"I don't believe, it." I shook my head. "Dr. Hasserin passed away."

"Who?" Lara barely glanced up from her phone.

"The archaeology professor for my class!"

"What, you knew him?" Lara asked, still engrossed in her text conversation.

"No. But he was teaching my freshman seminar. And he was thirty-six! That's super young."

"That's sad," said Lara. "I remember that course now. You were excited for it. That's one of the only things you've talked about since I met you."

I smiled. Lara had remembered something other than her texts and the number of likes on her social media posts.

"I can't help it. I love this stuff. Archaeology is why I applied to Nassauton."

Lara looked up from her phone. "Hey, you want to come to this party? It's a few buildings over—in the junior class dorm."

"Thanks, but I'll pass. I need to work on a few things."

"Like what, party pooper? Debbie Downer!" she teased as she got up and headed to her closet. "Classes haven't even started yet! There's no homework! These are our last days of freedom! Plus, upperclassmen boys!"

She pulled three dresses out of her closet and hung them on her door. "Which one should I wear?"

I pointed at the middle one and smiled. "That one is pretty! And I'm good. Be safe and have fun." I paused and teased back, "Maybe you'll meet some smart senior guy."

Lara giggled as she reached for the middle hanger and closed her door. "Maybe I'll meet some hot soccer player!" she said from behind the door.

After Lara left, I decided to walk outside to clear my head. Nassauton was one of the oldest colleges in the country, and its buildings were beautiful testaments to Gothic architecture. As night replaced the day, the sunset's colors were the perfect background for Nassauton's old stone buildings. The twilight set a peaceful mood—a peace that, in the shadow of the potential murder of my favorite professor, his secret Stonehenge discovery, my discovery of the pendant and poem, and the start of the semester, I welcomed.

As I walked, I gazed at the pinks and orange whisps in the evening sky. I felt my pendant through my shirt, its horseshoe resting on my chest as I strolled along the walkway to our quad. Stonehenge was a link between Dr. Hasserin's death and my pendant. *Why is Stonehenge always associated with mystery? Where had I seen my necklace before?*

Maybe my mom knew something about my necklace. I decided to call her and ask, without telling her about the potential murder. She had enough on her mind with her work and didn't need to be worrying about me. And, at the slightest news, she'd become anxious and overreact. She picked up on the first ring, eager to hear about my day.

"You'll never guess what I found as I was unpacking Gran's

shoeboxes. I think Gran wanted me to have it. I think she wanted to send me on my first adventure!"

As I stepped over the cracks in the walkway, I described the pendant to her—and the quest Gran had sent me on. My mom's panicked reaction startled me.

"You found my mom's Henge Piece in a shoebox?"

"Wait, my pendant has a name? How do you know about it?"

"I told my mom I never wanted you to have it. Here she goes leaving it for you in a shoebox."

"What's so—"

"Destroy it immediately," she said.

"Wait, Mom, what? Why?" I couldn't believe her reaction. My mom wasn't even listening. She was trying to shut my adventure down before it even started. "What does the Henge Piece do, anyway?"

"I don't know what it does. I don't care to know. All I know is right after Lyle found it, she got these threatening letters. She and Elkay got the police involved. Carlyle Elizabeth Stuart, destroy that pendant immediately."

My mom's adamant stance only made me more curious about the Henge Piece. "Mom, please. I want to learn more about it. It was Gran's. I promise I'll be careful."

"I can't lose you too. Please focus on your schoolwork and getting settled at Nassauton." Her tone was firm, but I wasn't letting up.

"Mom, I can't pass up an adventure from Gran. I've been waiting for my first real adventure my whole life. This is it. You know how important following in Gran's footsteps is to me. Please."

I heard a pause on the other end of the line, then a long exhale.

"Carly." My mom's voice softened a bit as it trailed off. "Sweetheart, I don't want to lose you. You don't know what it's like to—"

"I do. I lost Dad and Gran, too, like you did."

I heard another pause.

"Please," I repeated. "I'll be very careful. I promise. I'm at Nassauton, surrounded by experts in archaeology and artifacts. They will guide me in my research and won't let me do anything stupid."

I heard another pause, then a sigh.

"Do you promise to go through the proper channels at Nassauton with every step you take?"

"Yes!"

"Are you sure?"

"Yes, Mom! I said I promised."

My mom sighed again. I could tell she knew more about my pendant than she was willing to tell me. I could also tell she was still balancing her own emotions about my desire for adventure and her desire for my safety. And it seemed like once I told her I'd involve Nassauton experts in my research, she'd let up a little. I was thankful I'd been able to convince her to let me pursue the Henge Piece mystery.

"I can tell you a little bit about its history. The Henge Piece was a very important artifact to Gran. She and Elkay never solved its mystery. It always bothered her."

"What do you mean, artifact?"

"They found it on some dig . . ." Mom's voice trailed off.

"Then what?" I asked.

My mom sighed. I could tell she was realizing the more information she shared, the more interested in it I'd become.

"It's okay, Mom, I promised you I would be safe. And I mean it."

She sighed again. "I know. And I know you're a freshman—not a gap-toothed girl jumping off couches slaying monsters. Here, give me a minute, I think I can find a picture of it."

The line went silent as my mom muted the call. As I was waiting, I clutched my necklace through my shirt. *This pendant—the Henge Piece—is an artifact? Shouldn't I turn it in somewhere? Or to someone? Should I not wear it?* I sauntered around, following the walkway as it brought me to the quad. I admired the detail in the buildings' stonework and grinned at the gargoyles in the archways. I'd arrived at the quad, with its volleyball court in the middle and picnic tables at one side.

A few students sat on the edge of the court, enjoying the end of the sunset in the balmy late August evening. Another group of students stood in an archway, practicing an a cappella song. I beamed as I listened to their close harmonies and laughter. With the upbeat melodies resonating in the archway and filling the summer air, Nassauton came alive. As I recognized the song, I hummed along and bobbed my head to the beat. Nassauton already felt like home.

Still humming, I paced around the quad, counting my steps and eagerly anticipating what my mom would find. To whom would I give the Henge Piece? I couldn't walk into the Archaeology Department and hand Joyce a priceless artifact. Maybe it was best to keep wearing it under my shirt for now.

"Are you still there? I found the picture!" my mom said as we resumed our call. "It was Lyle and Elkay, with their olive-green jumpsuits. They're both wearing gold-rimmed aviator sunglasses and their Atlas heels. They have the Henge Piece on display. It looks like a horseshoe inside a circle, with the gold dagger at the bottom—like what you described."

"Oh yeah! That one!" I'd seen that picture a few years ago. Gran and Elkay were surrounded by their friends at a gala.

"Yep, that's the one. Three years ago I think? It was one of the parties they had right after they came back from that dig in England—near Stonehenge—the one where Lyle hit her head when she fell. It was one of the last parties they had."

I paused. *Stonehenge, again!*

"Mom, she didn't fall. She said someone pushed her."

"Well, fell or pushed, she hit her head. That *was* her last dig. I don't think I'd even seen the Henge Piece until after she came back from that dig."

"Are you sure my pendant is the same one as the one in the picture?"

"Positive, from the way you're describing it. I've never seen any other pendant like it. It's got to be it."

"And that picture was taken right when Gran and Elkay came back from that dig?"

"Yes, pretty certain. Why, what are you thinking?"

"Maybe there's a connection between the Henge Piece pendant and that dig! Maybe they found it on that dig!"

"And if there is, and if they did, promise me you'll involve the Nassauton experts and you'll be careful! And if there is any danger, you'll stop your research. Do you promise me, sweetheart?"

"Yes Mom! I promise."

I hung up and walked around the quad to my dorm. I couldn't believe it: Stonehenge in Dr. Hasserin's latest discovery, Stonehenge in the mysterious poem, and Stonehenge near Gran's last dig. Had I stepped into an adventure far bigger—and more mysterious—than a pendant and a poem? Had Dr. Hasserin stirred up a secret that had led to his murder? What exactly did the Henge Piece do? Was everything connected—and why?

When I got back to my dorm, I noticed a guy walking from the driveway. He was carrying a big cardboard box. I opened the door and held it for him.

"Thank you," he said, his fingers slipping as he tried to keep his grip. He was lanky and tall—at least half a foot taller than me—and looked very fit. He was wearing a plain white T-shirt, gym shorts with *Nassauton College* written on them, and sneakers. His short brown hair was matted with sweat. His hazel eyes gleamed a little gold as they reflected the last rays of the setting sun. I could tell the box was getting the better of him.

"Need help?" I asked.

"Nah, I got it." He could hardly respond without exerting himself.

His fingers slipped even more as beads of sweat rolled down his face. The box started falling. I instinctively lunged forward and caught it.

He grinned. "Well, turns out I was wrong. If you wouldn't mind holding it so I can stretch my arms for a second, I think I'll be okay."

"Sure, no problem." I smiled.

He transferred the box to me, then stretched his arms above his head, wiping his forehead with his shirtsleeve.

"Nice shirt, by the way. I love Indiana Jones. That's my favorite movie."

I smiled, looking at my vintage *Indiana Jones and the Last Crusade* movie poster T-shirt. That shirt had seen countless weekend walks in the park with my dad.

"Thank you, it's one of mine too."

"I'm Blane by the way. Blane Henley. Good to meet you."

I waited as he finished stretching and wrapped his arms around his box.

"I can take my box back now."

"I'm Carlyle Stuart, but most people call me Carly."

"Well, thank you, Carly. I live a few doors away. See you around."

His eyes and mine met. We gazed at each other an extra two seconds before I smiled and waved goodbye. "See you, Blane."

Blane was handsome. Even in a T-shirt and gym shorts, Blane was very handsome. I grinned. I hoped our paths would cross again.

II

"Welcome to Archaeology 101, the Foundations of Archaeology."

Dr. Kells' voice was exuberant and affirming. She stepped from behind her podium, walked to the center of the stage, raised her hands, and spread out her fingers like she was casting a spell as she enunciated each word. "As you know by now, my name is Dr. Lydia Kells. I will be your guide throughout the adventure that is our course."

She wasn't all that tall or imposing, so when she said "guide" I imagined someone more like a fairy godmother. Her long, silver hair was arranged neatly in a bun at the back of her head. Could this be the same Lydia I overheard, hardly a week ago, speculating about Dr. Hasserin's murder? I didn't think the Archaeology Department had any other professors named Lydia. Dr. Kells paused. She glanced across the lecture hall. There were maybe a hundred or so students in the class. No one was sitting in the front row.

I sat at one of the little wooden desks a few rows in front of the podium, with my journal in front of me. I was pleased with where I sat: I could see everything, especially Dr. Kells' quirky attire—a flowy, long cotton skirt, riding boots, and a loose shirt tucked in—without feeling I was too close to the stage.

Dr. Kells took a few minutes looking each student in the eye before she continued. "I hope you all are ready to go on the ride of your lives surveying history as told by the artifacts themselves.

In this class, we will examine the evidence—not the words, not the stories, and not the pictures. Remember, there were no selfies, sorry! But my goodness, if there were, what stories would those pictures tell? As they say, 'Selfie or it didn't happen' and I say: 'Evidence or it didn't exist.' The evidence. Remember that word. *Evidence*. Find the evidence and let it be your guide."

Those phrases—*Evidence or it didn't exist. Find the evidence and let it be your guide*—stuck out to me. I jotted them down. They were similar to the phrases Gran said when she told me her stories. Finding the evidence was my approach to learning more about the Henge Piece. But, I'd found little evidence of it when I searched our library's database. I'd tried *Henge Piece*, *Henge Piece Lyle Ainsley*, and *Henge Piece Stonehenge*, none of which had returned anything.

Ten minutes into our first class, and I was enthralled by Dr. Kells. Not only did she look and sound like a great professor, but she used phrases that reminded me of Gran. *Did Dr. Kells know Gran?* She looked about the age Gran would have been. Dr. Kells inhaled, lifting her arms above her head, then bringing them back down. Her bracelets and bangles slid up and down her arms as she gestured.

"I'm not interested in what you feel. I'm interested in what you think and your supporting points for why you think it. I'm interested in the events that actually happened and the events for which we have the artifacts. The artifacts are your proof. The artifacts are your evidence. In this class, we will operate from evidence, not from emotion. The evidence is what matters, not how you feel about it."

Operate from evidence, not emotion. I wrote that down. I believed the evidence mattered much more than my emotions. My dad, ever the scientist, had taught me that: *Find the facts and let the facts speak more than your feelings.*

To my left, the door opened. I saw a student sneak in. It was Blane, the guy I'd helped with the box. At first, I barely recognized him. He was wearing black jeans, an untucked button-down shirt, and Top-Siders—and was carrying his laptop instead of a cardboard box. He cleaned up well.

He slid his backpack off his shoulder, sat down in the front row, and hastily opened his laptop. Dr. Kells looked at him, glanced at the clock in the back of the room, and shook her head. She walked back to the podium and picked up her glasses—big, thick, black-rimmed, rectangular glasses—and situated herself behind her laptop.

"Okay, class, make sure you have your smartphones or laptops out so you can access our course page. In an effort to go green, we will minimize what we print in our class. Everything is uploaded to our course page. So, let's find the syllabus and review it. Is everyone there?" The syllabus was on the presentation screen behind her.

I slid my laptop out of my satchel. Dr. Kells paused, picked up the remote, and clicked to her next slide.

"Let's start with the fun stuff. Your first major project will be a presentation on a famous archaeologist—and no, you can't choose Indiana Jones."

I was the only one who laughed.

"Your project will be due week after next. You'll take the podium and present, like you're giving a lecture. Take a moment to read the directions—and make sure you give yourself enough time to go to the library and do your research. Book an appointment with the staff, read a rare book or two. The books are important, too, you know. Don't run to the internet and cite the first link you get on Google. And remember, operate from evidence, not emotion."

Dr. Kells was definitely very intelligent and very quirky. She said what she needed to say, using each exact word to convey each exact thought. What adventures and excavations had she been on? She hadn't included her bio in the syllabus or in any course materials. On the Archaeology Department's website, under her name, it just said: *LK: Adventurer and Student of the Ages*.

After class, I walked up to Dr. Kells as she disconnected her laptop from the podium. I didn't have that much time. My next class, Chemistry 101, was in the science labs all the way across campus.

"Thank you for a great first class," I said, offering her a handshake as throngs of students streamed in for the next class. "My name is Carlyle Stuart, but most people call me Carly."

The professor of the next class, holding a Styrofoam coffee cup from the campus center's coffee shop, squeezed past the outgoing students and made his way up the stairs to the stage. He dumped his briefcase on the table near the podium and started setting up his laptop and notes.

"You're very welcome, Ms. Stuart." Dr. Kells shook my hand. Her bracelets and bangles slid around her arms. One caught my eye. It was a dainty gold chain with a simple gold charm. The charm was a black stone circle, maybe obsidian, with a small gold cross carved in the center of it.

"Beautiful bracelet," I said to Dr. Kells.

"Thank you, Ms. Stuart. It's an Ailm, which comes from the Celtic Ogham alphabet. The Ailm is associated with evergreens, which are symbols of surviving harsh conditions, and wisdom—the wisdom obtained through living through many years of experiences. It's also associated with healing and finding your purpose." She pointed at the cross and the circle. "It's kept me grounded through some of the darkest, toughest times in my life."

I smiled. "That's very poetic, Dr. Kells. It's amazing how jewelry can have such incredible meaning behind it." I took a deep breath as I thought about the Henge Piece around my neck, under my shirt. "I was hoping I could schedule office hours. I'd like to discuss our project with you."

Dr. Kells finished packing her laptop and picked up her leather satchel. "I'd be happy to, Ms. Stuart. Please email me and we'll set it up."

††

The rest of the morning, all I could think about was the Henge Piece. Chemistry class flew by, and lunch had been a blur. I spent my afternoon at the campus store. I had run out of shampoo and needed to buy some more snacks for Lara's and my stash. And, like every other student on campus, I had to buy my textbooks.

As I waited to check out, I kept thinking about what my mom had said about the Henge Piece. *If Mom had known about the Henge Piece, maybe she knows where the other pieces are.*

"Next in line, please."

I stepped up to the cashier and unloaded my shampoo and snacks. The cashier picked up each item, scanned it, and placed it in a plastic bag. Her pendant swayed as she moved. I felt my Henge Piece under my shirt.

"That'll be $18.97, please."

"Oh, did you get my textbooks?" I handed her a slip of paper with the titles and item numbers of my four textbooks.

"That'll be $588.99, please."

I grimaced. That was going to hurt my bank account. My mom had insisted every bit of proceeds from the estate sale of Gran's artifacts go to my college fund. Now I realized why. I stuck my debit card in the chip reader and paid.

As soon as I got back to my room, I called my mom. "What do you know about the missing pieces of the Henge Piece?"

"And hello to you, too, sweetheart. How was your day?" She chuckled. "I guess you're more excited about the Henge Piece than telling me how your classes went—or even giving me a proper hello."

"I had a great archaeology class. I really like my professor."

"That's great to hear."

I smiled. "But about the Henge Piece, what do you know about the missing pieces?"

"Well, I'm pretty sure Gran's partner, Elkay, still has one of the other pieces, and the ruby—that was the piece they lost. I don't think they ever found it."

"Are you sure, Mom? Do you think you can find that picture of Gran and Elkay and the pendants? Can you double check if the ruby is there? If it is, that would tell us that the three pieces were together after the dig."

I waited as my mom got the album and flipped through the pages. I could hear her sliding the picture out of the plastic.

"I'll text you a picture of this photo so you have it." There was a pause. "I noticed there's something written on the back. I'll text you a picture of that too."

It was hard to tell from the picture if the ruby was there. It was even more difficult to tell what Elkay looked like. The aviators really didn't help.

I took out my journal and pencil and jotted down my thoughts. I looked at my mom's text of the back of the picture. Inscribed in faded ink were the words: *LA and LK, Adventurers and Students of the Ages.*

I stared at the writing, reading *LA* and *LK* several times. I'd read *LK: Adventurer and Student of the Ages*—on the Archaeology Department's website. *That was all Dr. Kells had written for her bio!*

I looked at the back of the picture and gasped.

What if Gran's partner's first name wasn't Elkay? What if her initials were LK—and that's what Gran and Mom had been saying all along? I grinned as I looked at the front of the picture. There was Gran and her partner: Lyle Ainsley and "Elkay," also known as LK, also known as Dr. Lydia Kells!

"YES!" I fist pumped in elation. I had solved my first archaeological mystery, before I'd completed my first college assignment. Gran would have been proud of me.

In closing the door on one mystery, I'd opened doors on many more. I picked up my pencil and wrote questions in my journal. *If Dr. Kells was Gran's partner, does she still have the second part of the Henge Piece? How does the Henge Piece work? What else happened at the dig—was Gran really pushed? What about the conversation I'd overheard between Lydia—Dr. Kells?—and Daniel? How do the poem, the pendant, and Dr. Hasserin's potential murder relate to Stonehenge?*

With these questions on my mind, I emailed Dr. Kells to set up office hours.

III

Choosing a famous archaeologist for my presentation was easy. I was excited to share Gran's legacy as a trailblazer with my class. For my first trip to Rockfire Library, I'd worn my favorite Indiana Jones movie poster T-shirt and a pair of Gran's shoes.

With over seven million books and forty-eight thousand feet of manuscripts, Rockfire was one of the largest libraries in the world. I was proud to be a student at a college that boasted a collection of that magnitude.

"I'd like to see your archaeological books, please." As I waited for the librarian's response, I noticed a sign on her desk: *"The only thing that you absolutely have to know, is the location of the library."* It had Albert Einstein's name under it. I grinned, amused that the world-famous physicist valued libraries as much as I did.

"Ahh yes, you must be in Dr. Kells' class," the librarian said. She looked up from her computer. Noticing me grinning at Einstein's quotation, she added, "He used to have an office here, down the street, in the math department. Pretty cool, right?"

"That's so neat!" I loved learning more about Nassauton's history, and Einstein having a presence on campus was fascinating. "Also, how'd you guess I'm Dr. Kells' student?"

She grinned. "All the archaeology majors know exactly where the room is, so they don't come up to my desk. They go right to the room. So, I know you're not an upperclassman. And, every year Dr. Kells starts her class with the same project. I love it. It's a great way to get students engaged and for us to show off Nassuaton's library. Here, swipe in with your ID, then follow me." She pointed to the turnstile to my left.

We walked across the lobby, down a flight of stairs, and down a hallway to a room with a big metal door. The librarian opened the door and turned on the fluorescent lights.

"Here's the Archaeology Research Room, alphabetized by author and arranged by country and century. Students generally know the country and period they want to study, even if they don't know the authors."

The room smelled like it hadn't been opened all summer. I glanced at the big table in the middle with chairs neatly tucked under it. Floor-to-ceiling shelves surrounded the table, making walls of books that formed a perimeter around the table. A few aisles broke the perimeter, enabling students to walk up to the table to study or to veer right or left and get lost in the shelves.

"You can take the books off the shelves, use them in this room, and put them back without checking them out. Only if you leave the library do you have to check them out. Honor code kind of thing. We've found that system works pretty well, because no one wants to be stuck without a book they need."

"Sounds good," I said, looking around.

"And, if you come with me, I'll show you the Rare Books Room." She ushered me out of the Archaeology Research Room. "Most of our rare books have been donated or are on loan to us from museums," she said as we walked down the hallway. "Students are allowed to access them, but they have to wear gloves and handle them very carefully. There's a whole process. Students must have explicit permission from a professor, then they have to schedule their time, and they must be accompanied by a senior librarian. Not many other schools have it set up like we do. In most schools, the rare books are in a case and can't be taken out. But here, under supervision, students can use them.

It's great, really, when students have the chance to hold history like that."

We stopped outside a metal door that had a gold plaque in the center.

"Not much to see with the door locked," the librarian said. "But there it is. It's not that we don't want students in there—it's that the books are in temperature-sealed cabinets, and they are sensitive to light. So, we have moisture and humidity sensors and special lighting, which help the books maintain themselves."

She talked about books like they were people. I liked that.

"Thank you," I said. "I think I'll head to the Archaeology Research Room and get started."

"Great, and remember, you don't have to check out the books while you're in the library, only if you want to leave with them. Otherwise, put them back when you're done. Have fun!"

The librarian walked me back to the Archaeology Research Room and headed down the hall. As I walked in, a sense of pride and belonging flooded over me. Here I was, a freshman at Nassauton, about to start the first project of my college career.

I ran my fingers along the backs of several books on a shelf near the door, feeling the hard-back binding of each book and noticing the labels on the spines. Some of the books were older, with the labeling peeling off. Others looked like they were brand new. I slid one off the shelf. The glossy paperback cover felt smooth in my hands: *Siberia's Digs and Dolls: The Surprising History of the Dolls of the Bronze Age*. I flipped to the back cover and skimmed the blurb. It was about a doll and an animal figurine found in a child's grave in Siberia. The toys were 4,500 years old—some of the oldest toys in the world.

I slid the book back and continued walking, trying to look at all the titles. There were books on every subject. Several books in the British Isles section were written by Dr. Hasserin. *Was he really murdered?* I pulled a few books off the shelf. *What had he discovered about Stonehenge?*

In the Ancient Rome and Greece section, I found Gran's books. I grinned as I grabbed several, walked to the table, and started flipping through the pages. The smell of old paper filled the room. I loved that smell, since it reminded me of when Gran and I read my history books together after school. For every fact we read, Gran had a story from her own adventures. Now, instead of hearing Gran's stories, I was reading her books.

I looked at the cover of the first book: *It's All Greek to Me: A Study of Ancient Greek Customs and Traditions*, by Dr. Lyle Ainsley. I grinned, giddy. *The book I'm using for my project was written by Gran. How cool is that?* More than wanting to do well on my project, I wanted to honor Gran's legacy.

Lyle and Elkay—if I was right, Dr. Kells—were among the first female archaeologists to gain international prominence. That was a big deal, since it was very difficult to break into—and advance in—those circles as women who were not part of the old boys' club. Gran and Dr. Kells paved the way for younger women to follow in their footsteps—their careers in archaeology were groundbreaking.

With Gran as my inspiration, I knew I had big shoes to fill—and ever since my days of clomping around in Gran's boots, I was motivated to fill them. The significance of the moment hit me, overwhelming me with an intense feeling that I was exactly where I needed to be. I opened the book and started reading.

"Here's the Archaeology Research Room, alphabetized by author, and arranged by country and century. Students generally know the country and period they want to study, even if they don't know the authors." The librarian's voice filled the hallway as she showed another student around.

"Thanks!" the student said. "I appreciate your help."

"Did you want to see the Rare Books Room?"

"I'm good for now. I'd like to get started on the project."

The student walked into the room, his backpack straps flapping around as he disappeared into the shelves. A few minutes later, he approached the table.

"Mind if I join you?" he asked, placing his books down on the other side of the table.

"Not at all. there's plenty of table here." I looked up from my laptop. It was Blane. He took off his backpack and pulled the chair back. The metal legs dragged across the wooden floor, making a dull sliding sound.

"Thanks. Oh, hey, you're the girl who helped me with my box on move-in day. I remember your Indiana Jones T-shirt. Carlyle, right?"

I smiled and tucked a loose curl behind my ear. "Carly. But yeah. Blane, right?"

"Yep!" He reached into his backpack for his laptop.

"And you're the guy who was late to Dr. Kells' class on the very first day."

"Yep. Wasn't happy about that, but orientation for work study ran late. Made it as fast as I could—I don't want to miss a moment of Dr. Kells' class. But I made it in time for the best part." He opened his laptop and waited for it to turn on.

"What was that?"

"When Dr. Kells said 'No Indiana Jones' and out of a class of a hundred-odd students, you were the only one who laughed."

"Why was that the best?" I was surprised he heard me laugh, let alone remembered I had.

"Because at least someone other than me understands the greatness of Indy!"

I laughed. "You're clearly a fan of Indy's too."

"Yep, ever since watching the *Indiana Jones* movies, I've wanted to study archaeology. Wrote my college application essay on him—and somehow managed to tie in Nassauton and wanting to study with Dr. Kells."

"That's cool! I'm really into archaeology too. I'd pretend the sandbox was a dig and spend hours there. I'd mostly dig up everything everyone left behind—which pretty much was almost always other people's trash. But that never stopped me. My grandmother would always encourage me."

"Yeah, same. Well, not really about the sandbox part. Before he retired, my grandfather used to be an archaeologist. He went on many digs. I grew up around the artifacts he kept in our home. Some people's grandparents collect random garden gnomes or other little trinkets. No, I grew up with Ancient Egyptian urns right there on the shelf. My grandfather was the one who introduced me to Indy." He chuckled and flipped his laptop around. His desktop was a still from the "Leap of Faith" scene from *Indiana Jones and the Last Crusade*. "Indy is everyone's favorite archaeologist," he added, flipping his laptop back around. "I could quote you each movie line-by-line."

"So could I." I smiled.

"Is that a challenge?" he teased. "Careful—you never know if you'll find yourself in an *Indiana Jones* movie marathon with me." He laughed as he added, "You'd probably last longer than I would."

"Probably," I teased back. "But now," I said, pointing to the books on the table, "we should focus on our project for Kells' class."

"You're right, I gotta get at least some of this done before my next class." He opened his book. "King Tut, I'm coming for you, bruh."

I looked up from my book and chuckled. "Howard Carter already came for King Tut. Bruh."

Blane laughed. "So, all kidding about Indy aside, you're quite the archaeology nerd, right Carly? That's cool."

"You bet. It's all I've ever wanted to study. Nassauton has the best artifact collection—and professors, like Dr. Kells."

"Oh, she's an absolute legend."

"She is indeed," I said. "She has the best phrases too." As I shared Dr. Kells' phrases on evidence, and selfies, with Blane, we got back to our research. Every now and then, Blane would look up at me and grin. When he did, I couldn't help but grin back.

††

"How was your morning?" Lara and I were sitting in our dining hall, eating lunch.

"Got a lot done on my project! And you?"

"Oh great, class was fine. Get this, I think Jesse is going to ask me to be his girlfriend."

I smiled, picking up my sandwich. A tomato slipped out and landed on the plate. I picked it up and pushed it back in.

"That's so exciting, Lara. How can you tell?" I asked, taking a bite. Tomato juice trickled down my chin.

"He asked me to dinner on Friday at Winnie B.'s, that place off campus. The one my parents and I went to for lunch. It's like the perfect date spot."

I finished chewing and wiped the tomato juice with my napkin. The lettuce was extra crunchy today. "Aww, that's awesome! Do you think you'll say yes?"

"Oh absolutely. Jesse is such an amazing guy. I met him at a party the first week of school and we've been hanging out ever since. I want to see where this goes." Lara lifted a heaping spoonful of ice cream from her bowl to her mouth. "This is really good ice cream, wow. Want to try some?"

"I'm good, I'm lactose intolerant."

"Good to know. I'll make sure if I get snacks, they don't have dairy in them."

I smiled. Lara was very considerate. I was grateful I'd lucked out with a roommate who became a friend.

"Thank you. That's really nice of you. Also, I'm so happy for you—Jesse sounds like a great guy. Speaking of guys, I might have something to share too."

"Oh yeah?" Lara put down her spoon. "Go on!"

"Well, there's this guy in my archaeology class—"

"The one who was late on the first day? The one you told me about?"

"Yeah. He's cool. I think I kinda like him." I told Lara about seeing Blane in the library. "He's funny. And he's into Indiana Jones."

"Who?"

I chuckled. "Only the greatest archaeologist of all time."

"Well, your guy sounds like a huge archaeology nerd," said Lara as she slid her spoon into her ice cream. "In other words, perfect for you."

††

"Henley, Blane. You're up."

Blane walked to the stage and set up his laptop. He looked behind him to make sure his slide was visible. I was sitting in the front row, my eyes glued to the presentation screen.

"Hello fellow classmates, I'm Blane Henley. I'd like to start my presentation with an homage to the greatest archaeologist of our time." He paused, then clicked to the next slide. "Indiana Jones. In this picture, Indy needs to get across the ravine to find the Holy Grail. This scene is called 'Leap of Faith' since Indy must literally take a leap of faith. He can't see how to get across, and I'm not going to give any spoilers, so you're going to have to watch the movie to figure out how Indy does it."

Blane looked at me, and I smiled back.

"See, I was thinking a lot about what Dr. Kells said about evidence. She said: 'The evidence is what matters, not how you feel about it.' I was thinking about that later. While I think evidence is important—don't get me wrong—I think it's only a *part* of the picture. I think faith is equally as important. Evidence might get you to the finish line; faith is what gets you across. If there's anything simpler—and more complicated—than evidence, it's faith. I have faith, for example, that Dr. Kells finds the fact that I've incorporated Indy into my presentation humorous. She *did* say we couldn't present on Indiana Jones, but she *did not* say we couldn't have him in our presentation."

We all looked at Dr. Kells. She managed a wry smile. *Where is Blane going with this?* I wondered.

"I also have faith," Blane continued, "that the one person who laughed when Dr. Kells said we couldn't present on Indy, is finding this humorous, since she obviously understands that Indy was the archaeologist who made every kid think that they would be the one to dig up ancient treasure buried in their sandbox." He looked at me. "So, it's only appropriate that I start my presentation on Howard Carter with a dedication to my favorite archaeologist. Without Indy, I wouldn't have the faith in myself to even be here, in front of you, presenting on some guy who was a major Egyptian nerd. Without faith, I'm sure Howard Carter wouldn't have been able to keep going to find King Tut's tomb."

Blane clicked to the next slide, showing a picture of a young boy and his parents in front of a sign that had KING TUT ON TOUR in gold letters.

"That's me, right there, the day the King Tut exhibit came to my hometown. It was one of the best days of my life. I couldn't explain the feeling of seeing something so incredible, so wonderful, so historic. I ran around the whole exhibit from artifact to artifact, trying to see everything."

When Blane finished his presentation, our classmates applauded. Dr. Kells did too. And rightfully so: Blane had done a great job. He'd spun a story, captivating us in such a way that took us right there with Howard Carter as he uncovered King Tut's tomb in 1922.

Blane walked back to his seat.

"Great job," I said.

Blane grinned at me as Dr. Kells got up. "Well, we're out of time for today. Congratulations class, the first day of presentations is done! We'll pick up next week. Make sure you also keep up with your readings, because your first paper is due in a few short weeks at the end of September."

I packed up my laptop and joined the flood of students

heading out the door. Dr. Kells still hadn't emailed me back about office hours. With the start of term, and finding Dr. Hasserin's replacement, she probably had a lot on her plate.

††

That night, Lara was extra talkative. All she had on her mind was Jesse and their date. But tonight, I wasn't in the mood for constant chatter, so I packed my journal, books, and laptop into my satchel and went to the coffee shop in our campus center. A few groups of students were ahead of me in line, chit-chatting and taking selfies, but far more interesting to me were the posters of Nassauton's football games, mascots, and class pennants that covered the walls.

"Hey there, welcome to Café Naiviv, how can I help you?"

"Oh! Hi Blane!" I grinned.

"Hey, Carly!" Blane flashed a big smile at me. "Evening coffee break?"

"Yep, something like that," I said, looking at the menu chalkboard on the wall behind him. "I didn't realize you worked here."

"Oh yeah—work study; thought I'd pick working here so I could learn a thing or two about coffee. So, what'll it be?"

"Well, what do you recommend? There's a lot on this board."

"My favorite is the B-Side Special. If you've never heard of it, that's because I invented it. It's my specialty. It's half coffee, half hot chocolate, a dash of cinnamon, and a swirl of chocolate sauce. Whipped cream optional. Do you want anything to eat? All our pastries are half off after seven p.m."

"I'll pass on the pastries. But I'll have the B-Side Special," I said, reaching for my wallet. "But with no whipped cream. And with almond milk, please. And decaf or else I'll be up all night."

"Isn't that the point of an evening coffee break—to help you power through the night?"

I chuckled. "Nah, I'm not one to pull all-nighters. I like sleeping way too much for that."

Blane laughed. "Hey, I get you. I've never had a reason to pull an all-nighter. I've always tackled a little bit of work every day, and I'm fine."

"Mmm-hmm." I handed Blane my debit card.

"Oh, don't worry about it—on the house tonight."

I smiled. "You sure?"

Blane nodded.

"Well, thank you. That's nice of you. I appreciate it."

"Sure thing."

I went to a table, plopped my satchel down, and took out my journal, pencil, and a few books. One was a book for my literature class, one of the required freshman seminars. It wasn't too much of a page turner. But my paper wasn't going to write itself. Even though I should have started reading it, I couldn't ignore my thoughts on Stonehenge and focus on eighteenth-century authors.

I opened my journal and looked at my questions on the Henge Piece, the dig, Stonehenge, and Dr. Hasserin's death. Two weeks had passed, and the university still hadn't found anyone to teach his seminar. Feeling the weight of my pendant under my shirt, I picked up my pencil and opened one of my other books, one by Dr. Hasserin.

> *Stonehenge, in Amesbury, England, is a British cultural icon, and is a prehistoric monument that consists of rings of standing stones. These stones are arranged in an outer ring that looks like a circle, and an inner ring that looks like a horseshoe, with several fallen stones at the bottom of the horseshoe. These stones are each around thirteen feet high and seven feet wide and weigh around twenty-five tons.*

Archaeologists believe Stonehenge was constructed in three phases, using more than thirty million hours of manpower. However, we are still discovering exactly how these stones were moved and arranged—and why. Constructed to align with significant astronomical events, such as the sun rising and setting on the summer and winter solstices and various lunar phases and constellation patterns, Stonehenge could have also served as a burial ground and memorial to the dead, as archaeologists have found deposits containing human bone fragments that date to 3000 BC.

Since 1882, Stonehenge has been protected by the British government as an ancient monument and was recognized as a UNESCO World Heritage Site in 1986. These protections prohibit unauthorized excavation.

"Here you go. Table service." Blane held my coffee like a magician about to pull a rabbit out of a top hat. "I let it cool a little, but it still might be hot, be careful."

I closed my book, using my pencil as a placeholder. "Thanks! I'll tell you how I like it." I cleared my books to make room for the coffee.

"Is that Dr. Hasserin's book?" Blane asked, pointing at the cover.

"Yes. I'm sure you got the email about his passing."

"Certainly did. I was supposed to be in that class."

"Me too! I was really looking forward to it."

"Brilliant guy. Expert on Stonehenge, a real good scholar," Blane added. "Odd, he was really young to die, if you ask me.

But no one official or important has asked the great Blane Henley for his opinion." He chuckled. Blane always seemed to be saying something funny or laughing at himself. I liked that he didn't take himself too seriously. "A real shame," he went on. "I would really have liked to meet him."

"I would have too. I'm not official or important, but I'd like to hear your opinions, Blane." I grinned and looked up at him. "And, I think Dr. Hasserin was way too young too. Maybe there's something else we are missing."

"What are you implying?"

"I'll tell you later," I said as I looked around the café. "I don't think here's a good place to talk about it." The line for coffee had gotten longer, as more and more students came to Café Naiviv for a study break and discounted pastries.

"I see, a mystery! Well that certainly leaves me hanging—and it certainly guarantees you'll have to see me later." He grinned. "Your coffee should be okay now. Try it."

I brought the coffee to my mouth, blowing on it to cool it down. I noticed the swirl of chocolate sauce on the top. It was in the shape of a *C*.

"I like it already. It's got my initial on it!" I took a sip.

"Yeah, I like to customize my creations—and customize them a latte!"

I laughed, spitting out a bit of coffee in the process.

"That was terrible. Absolutely terrible." I kept laughing. "But I really like this coffee creation. Five stars, will recommend."

Blane pulled a napkin from his apron pocket and handed it to me. "Might find this useful."

"Hey, Blane, gonna need your help back here with these mugs!" a voice from behind the coffee bar called to Blane.

"Coming, Allison. Enjoy your book, Carly. And your coffee." Blane smiled. "And let me know if you ever want to meet up in the Archaeology Research Room and talk Stonehenge."

IV

Stuart, Carlyle. You're up."

"Go get 'em—you look great, and you'll be great!" Blane patted my back as I uncrossed my legs and got up. "Great shoes too!"

I smiled as I glanced at my shoes. I was wearing Gran's black leather ankle-length boots—the ones with big silver studs on the heel. "Thanks!"

I clutched my pendant. *Be brave.* I walked to the front of the room with my laptop. Dr. Kells had never replied to my email about office hours, so I ended up completing the project in the best way I could. In my research, I'd noticed Gran had written every book. Elkay wasn't even mentioned. Was Rockfire's collection complete? Was it possible Elkay had not gone the publishing route?

As I walked up to the stage, I took a deep breath. This was my first college presentation. Even though I was talking to my peers, an audience of a hundred was intimidating. As I set up my laptop, I imagined myself years from now, presenting to an international audience at a major archaeological conference. Maybe some of my classmates would be in that audience, with successful careers of their own. I turned to the screen to make sure my first slide was visible. I took another deep breath, picked up the clicker, and started.

"I'm Carly Stuart. Don't worry, I won't be presenting on Indiana Jones, like one of our other presenters did—or tried to do, at least." I glanced at Blane; he smirked back at me. "I will be presenting on the archaeologist who helped me understand what grace, courage, faith, and being a leader truly mean."

I clicked from my title slide to the next slide.

"Dr. Lyle Ainsley was an incredible woman, one of the world's most renowned archaeologists and a trailblazer. This is what drew me to her. She was incredibly brave, bold, and absolutely fearless, in a field where many women were subtly asked to stay out of the dig, because 'it was too dangerous for a lady.'" I made air quotes around the words. "I think it's important that as scholars and explorers, we let each person decide how to deal with adventure—without closing the door in their face from the beginning. Instead, we should give them the support they need as they face adventure." I added, "And, sometimes a woman's intuition and wits are exactly what you want with you in the dig—especially when facing adventure."

Dr. Kells and many of my female peers were smiling and nodding. Blane gave me a thumbs-up and grinned. A wave of confidence rushed through me.

"Sure, you had a handful of famous female archaeologists, but they were in the minority. Dr. Ainsley had many great accomplishments, not only as a scholar and archaeologist, but also as a mentor. She created access to opportunities for younger women. She didn't settle if she and her partner were the only women at the dig. She tirelessly pushed for other women to be involved. She felt it was important for them to see themselves at the dig, and learn they belonged there as much as anyone else. She was a champion of archaeological education for women."

I pointed the laser from the clicker at a picture of Gran with a group of thirty women. The picture showed the group lined up in rows on the stage of a lecture hall, each holding a little shovel.

"She created 'I Dig It,' a week-long intensive bootcamp for women interested in archaeology. Every participant got a shovel as a reminder that she belonged at the dig. In addition to championing this education, Dr. Ainsley also had a leading role in most of the prominent archaeological digs of the twentieth century. I've listed a few of these on the next slide."

I clicked and saw several of my classmates nod when they saw familiar—and famous—digs.

"She also published hundreds of books, book chapters, and articles, and even appeared numerous times on The History Channel."

I had decided not to share that Dr. Ainsley was my grandmother. I didn't want my classmates thinking I was another famous kid, that I had chosen Dr. Ainsley only since she was my grandmother, or that I was stuck-up and full of myself. I didn't even tell Blane when we were in the Archaeology Research Room.

Presenting wasn't as bad as I thought it would be. I was sharing all Gran's stories—my favorite stories—with my classmates. These were the stories I had grown up hearing and those that had inspired me to get to where I was today. Aside from brushing up on Gran's publications, I hadn't done too much additional research on Gran—I relied mostly on my knowledge of her stories. I might not have been as theatrical as Blane, but I told of Gran's adventures, accomplishments, and significant findings with passion and purpose.

I watched Dr. Kells the whole time, trying to see her reactions. She smiled—a smile that said, *I remember that one*, and nodded as I shared the stories. Was my theory right, about Elkay, LK, and Dr. Kells being the same person?

"That's what Dr. Ainsley did. She and her partner paved the way for younger women to realize they, too, could pick up a shovel, go on a dig, and walk some steps—or a few miles—in their own boots. That's Dr. Ainsley and her partner right there," I said as I clicked to the last slide—the picture of the Henge Piece and Gran and Elkay, wearing their olive-green jumpsuits, gold-rimmed aviator sunglasses, and Atlas heels. "They both inspired me to be brave enough to get to where I am today, to read everything I could about archaeology, to love the field . . . and to devote my life to the pursuit of unearthing our past."

Blane beamed at me and gave me two thumbs up.

"Thank you, Ms. Stuart, that was wonderful," Dr. Kells said. "Unfortunately, as we're out of time, we won't do Q&A. If you did not go today, you'll go next week. Looking forward to more phenomenal presentations!"

Dr. Kells dismissed the class and walked up to me as I packed up.

"Ms. Stuart, do you have a moment? I realized I never replied to your email, but now is as good a time as ever for office hours, if you can make it work."

"Sure." I followed her out of our classroom. Any excuse to be late to—or get out of—chemistry class, I'd take.

We walked down the hallway to the other side of the department building, then down the hallway with the Gothic windows, faculty offices, portraits, and artifact display cases. She unlocked her door and flicked on the light. "Come on in. Make yourself at home."

Dr. Kells' office was everything you'd think a tenured, world-renowned archaeologist's office would be. It was filled with bookcases, making it feel cozy. Each bookcase had replicas of ancient archaeological sites, such as the Tower of Babel, the Great Pyramids, the Colosseum, and the Luxor Obelisks. Books, boxes, and folders were stacked haphazardly on one side of her desk; on the other, she had a little replica of Stonehenge. Each piece was 3D-printed in different colors. A well-loved sofa and a coffee table with a red rug underneath it were in the center, opposite her desk and chair. Sunlight streamed in through one of the windows, illuminating her Stonehenge replica and filling her room with natural light. In the light, the red rug had a warm and inviting glow.

"Sit, Ms. Stuart," she said as she rearranged the pillows from the sofa. "I know you probably only have a few moments, but your presentation was excellent. Love your shoes, by the way. I've seen only one other pair like them."

She moved a few books off the coffee table and sat in her

chair, taking her laptop out of her satchel and placing it on her desk. Her gold bracelet glimmered in the sunlight as she picked up a few of her Stonehenge pieces and played with them. "You clearly did your research and shared a lot of great stories. Well done."

I sat on the sofa. "Thank you so much."

"Ms. Stuart—"

"Dr. Kells, you can call me Carly."

"Carly, where did you get that picture? You know, the one at the end of your presentation, with Dr. Ainsley at the party?" She arranged her bun, patting it with her hand to make sure her hair was still in place.

As I stammered, Dr. Kells must have realized I didn't really know how to answer her question. Up until now, I was sure she was Gran's partner. But sitting in her office, surrounded by her replicas, bookcases, and books and papers, I was overcome with nervousness. *Could I be totally wrong?* The last thing I wanted to do was embarrass myself in front of Dr. Kells.

"You do know Lyle and I were partners, right?" She grabbed a few books off her desk. "I miss her every day, so much." Dr. Kells pressed her lips together as she teared up. "Sorry." She reached for a tissue from a box on her desk. "The last three years have been tough." She dabbed her eyes with the tissue, then crunched it into a little ball in her fist. She handed me the books. "Here."

I took the books from her, a huge sigh of relief flooding over me. There, on the covers, were Gran's and Dr. Kells' names. Why were none of these books at Rockfire? I opened one and saw Gran's and Dr. Kells' bios, which listed some of the digs they had been part of. I was sure that one of them, the Amesbury Dig, was the dig at which they found the Henge Piece.

There were so many questions I wanted to ask Dr. Kells. *Why didn't you come to Gran's funeral? What do you know about the Henge Piece? How did your partnership with Gran get started? Did you decide not to go the publishing route, and Gran did?* I wanted to show Dr. Kells my part of the Henge

Piece. *Could I trust her?*

Instead of saying anything, I stared at Dr. Kells as I thought about all the times Gran had mentioned "Elkay" in her stories. If Dr. Kells and Gran were partners, and Dr. Kells was the one in the picture with Gran, she definitely would know more about the Henge Piece. There was no indication I couldn't trust LK, but there was no indication I could. I would have to start asking her questions.

"Carly," Dr. Kells finally said. "Is everything all right?"

I snapped out of my gaze, blinking as I blurted out, "No way."

"No way, what?"

"I don't believe it. You're LK."

"Of course, I'm LK." She grinned. "What is so shocking about that?"

"I'm surprised. It's a good thing. Dr. Kells, tell me about Dr. Ainsley."

"Dr. Ainsley—Lyle . . . Well, your presentation got her character to a T. She was kind, fiercely smart, driven, and funny. She wanted women to succeed, and she created the pathways for them to do so. She had a magnetic personality; her passion poured out of her. She and I traveled the world together. She was my role model and partner—and best friend. I trusted her with my life—and there were certainly some situations, where had it not been for her woman's intuition and wit, I probably wouldn't be here. I miss her every day."

I smiled. I was proud to be Dr. Lyle Ainsley's granddaughter. "Tell me more about your partnership with Dr. Ainsley."

Dr. Kells smiled. "Well, like any other partnership, we had our ups and downs." Her smile turned into a wistful gaze. "But we figured out a way to make it work. Partnership means two people coming together as a team with shared goals. It means you've got to give space for each person to pursue their dreams too." She paused. "Lyle loved writing and publishing. I loved planning and teaching. We gave each other space and support, no matter what adventure we were on."

I smiled, realizing why I'd never seen Dr. Kells' name on publications. "Like ride-or-die friends?"

Dr. Kells nodded, grinning.

I continued. "If Lyle meant so much to you, why didn't you go to her funeral?"

"What? I did go, of course I went. I wore sunglasses and a hat the whole time so no one would see how red my eyes were. Lyle was my everything. How could I not go?"

It clicked. Dr. Kells was the one at the funeral who was wearing the gold aviators and straw hat.

"I need to show you something." I grabbed my necklace and pulled out the pendant from under my sweater.

Dr. Kells gasped. "My goodness, never mind the picture, where did you get that pendant? Do you know what it means?"

"I found it in a shoebox, with a Post-it with my name on it. It used to belong to my grandmother." I pointed at my black leather boots. "So did these."

Dr. Kells looked at me, stunned. She tilted her head to one side and then the other. Then, she rolled her chair forward and looked at my face. An instant later, she brought her hand to her mouth and gasped. "Oh my goodness. I don't believe it. Carlyle Stuart. Stuart. Stuart, duh, that's your mom's married name. Oh my gosh! Carly. You're Lyle's granddaughter!"

I nodded, smiling.

A broad grin spread across Dr. Kells' face as her eyes twinkled with delight and tears. "Oh my goodness, well I'll be darned. I remember you now, from Lyle's funeral. You sat by her grave the whole time. Wow, you've grown up in three years. You have Lyle's beautiful green eyes. I see the resemblance so clearly now! How could I have missed it before? Oh, Carly. It's great to meet you. She used to talk a lot about you. She was so proud of you. I've heard all the stories about your accomplishments in school. And here you are now, a brilliant young scholar, at Nassauton, in my class, in my office."

Dr. Kells clasped her hands together in astonishment and

exuberance. I grinned. I missed Gran even more.

"And those boots. I was with Lyle when she bought those. We were out west, and she found them in a shop in the town square and picked them up on the spot. Next thing I know, she was trying to pay for them, and the shop owner was so enamored by the fact that she was a female archaeologist that he gave them to her for free. So, she sent him a postcard from the town near our next dig site. He wrote her back and said he'd pinned it up in his store. She had quite a fan club."

I chuckled. I always pictured Gran at fancy galas, not making friends in shoe stores in town squares.

"Carly . . ." Dr. Kells' tone turned from wonder and excitement to caution as she pointed at my Henge Piece. "That pendant has a very interesting story. You must not let anyone know you have it. No one. Not your roommates, your friends, no one. You really shouldn't be wearing it like that, either. It's priceless."

Dr. Kells got up from her chair. She stuck her head into the hallway, looking in both directions before closing her door.

"I think its safest around my neck. I don't have a safe in my room."

Dr. Kells paused. "I should probably keep it here."

"I think it's safest around my neck," I repeated, staying firm. Gran had told me to keep it safe. I wasn't going to let her down.

"If others find out you have it, your life will be in grave danger."

"What? What danger?" The hairs on the back of my neck stood up as fear pulsed through my body.

"Do you know what your pendant means?"

I shook my head. I wasn't sure I wanted to know. This was serious. Dr. Kells' warning gave Gran's poem, and my mom's apprehension, more weight and urgency. I had finished the first presentation of my freshman year, and even though I wanted good grades—and maybe a little adventure—I didn't want danger.

"Your pendant," said Dr. Kells, "is part of the Henge Piece.

Lyle and I found it three years ago, on a dig not too far from Stonehenge. It was our last dig before she passed away. We were called in to excavate a Roman village. There were many British Isles experts and PhD students there. Given your interest in archaeology, I'm sure you've heard of them: Dr. Allister Leith—he's a good friend and was a good friend of Lyle's—and Dr. Sidney Hasserin. Yes, he's my colleague who recently passed away. But back then, he wasn't a professor—he was a PhD candidate, on track to becoming one of the world's most promising archaeologists. I met him at that dig."

I took out my journal and jotted down notes as Dr. Kells talked. Gran had never told me this story. I couldn't believe what I was hearing. In listening to Dr. Kells, I felt like an investigative reporter, or a historian, recording the story as one of the star witnesses told it. Because Gran had left the Henge Piece for me, I felt connected to this artifact. I couldn't help but think that its story—and mine—were about to intertwine in ways that would forever bind us together.

I glanced up from my journal and looked at Dr. Kells. "I had no idea about the dig—or that you knew Dr. Hasserin that well! I was supposed to be in his seminar. I really wanted to learn from him."

"I'm still in shock. I was his mentor. Oh, that reminds me, I still need to pick up my books from his house. And check the job board for applicants."

Dr. Kells paused and wrote a note to herself. I twirled my loose curl as I thought about Dr. Kells' and Gran's last adventure.

"It's hard to fill a teaching job this late in the year. And Sid—Sid is irreplaceable. From the moment we met him, I knew he would be a great professor. I asked him to call me when he was ready to apply for jobs. I wanted him on faculty here."

I smiled. "He leaves a great legacy—like Gran."

"Yes. And speaking of Lyle, back to the dig. She tripped and fell as she was moving the Henge Piece. She'd taken it out of the box we found it in, and she fell. She says she was pushed, but I don't remember anyone being there. A few students said it could have been the ghosts of the village residents, guarding what was theirs. I mean, ghosts don't exist, so I still think she tripped. I was a few stations away, talking to Allister. Three or four people rushed over to her. She had passed out, had a concussion, and needed medical attention. The doctors said she had ruptured a brain aneurysm—and was lucky to be alive. She declined quickly after her fall. I think the head trauma did more damage than we knew. She never recovered. Barely six months later, she passed away."

Dr. Kells paused. I used the opportunity to furiously scribble down my notes.

"Soon after we discovered the Henge Piece, we realized it aligned with Stonehenge—and what's more, we learned evil people desperately wanted it. We never could figure out exactly who those people were, and why they wanted it, but I am sure they will stop at nothing to find it."

I was stunned by what I heard. I knew Gran's mysterious poem had mentioned evil ones and warring knights, but I didn't realize her warning was real. Dr. Kells confirmed Gran's warning.

"Here, give it to me, let me show you."

I took off my necklace as Dr. Kells opened one of her desk drawers. She took out a box and removed a few index cards, then pulled out a small Tupperware container from inside the box. "Gloves," she said. "I need gloves." She rummaged through the drawer and pulled out a pair of latex gloves from another box. Then, she popped the lid off the Tupperware and carefully unwrapped the microfiber towels off the object inside.

I gasped. *There's the missing second part of the Henge Piece.* Its gold circle glistened in the light of Dr. Kells' office.

I handed Dr. Kells my necklace. "Thank you," she said. "Lyle must have taken really good care of this," she added as she examined the horseshoe with the dagger. "Or maybe she kept it in that shoebox the whole time."

She carefully positioned the two pieces together. My

pendant fit right on top of hers, the hilt and tip of the dagger snapping my piece and hers together.

"See?" she said, holding up the pieces and pointing at her replica on her desk. "Stonehenge."

I looked at our pendants. They formed one outer circle, with little gold nubs on it, and one inner horseshoe. The gold dagger extended across the bottom of the horseshoe, its tip pointing to some of the gold nubs on the outer circle. I walked up to the replica, took the complete pendant from Dr. Kells, and held it above the replica. Now I saw how the pendant aligned with Stonehenge, like Gran said. It was as though whoever made the pendant knew exactly how Stonehenge was laid out. *Is the dagger's positioning significant?* The sunlight streamed through the Gothic windows and danced around the dagger, as if shooting sparks out of the tip.

"But there's still a piece missing," I said, pointing at the gap in the dagger's hilt.

"Yes. It's missing—Carly," said Dr. Kells, looking at her watch, "do you have a class now?"

"Chemistry."

"You are probably going to miss it. I hope that's okay with you. I'll email your professor."

I nodded, happily providing my chemistry professor's name. There was no way I was trading office hours with Dr. Kells for our review of atomic trends. She turned to her desk, opened her laptop, and sent the email. I took out my journal and pencil from my satchel.

"It's missing a ruby," Dr. Kells said. "There was a ruby at the hilt of the dagger, which was on the same line as the Heel Stone. The dagger points at the fallen stones in Stonehenge's outer circle. We didn't think the piece was of Roman origin. It might have belonged to English royalty since commoners would probably not have been able to afford a ruby like that. We also couldn't quite tell the age of the Henge Piece. We figured it was at least hundreds of years old, based on where Lyle found it, but as you can see, the gold gleams like it was made yesterday."

"Was the ruby there when you found it?"

"Yes. When Lyle fell, the Henge Piece broke. We were able to recover two pieces, but the ruby was gone. The whole team looked for it, but no one found it. Lyle was devastated. This was one of her first mishaps—maybe the first time she'd ever broken an artifact. I told her it wasn't her fault."

"Wow. And you never found the ruby?"

"No. Someone probably stole it and pawned it off. So, there's probably some very lucky thrifter in England who has no idea that their hunk of costume jewelry is really a priceless gem. I mean, it's probably as big as a celebrity's engagement ring, definitely not on the small side. You can't miss it."

"What would happen if the ruby were found?"

"We'd reunite it with the rest of the Henge Piece." She pointed at the gap in the dagger's hilt.

"And then what would we do with the complete Henge Piece?"

"We'd take it to Stonehenge. The Henge Piece has got to be more than a decorative tribute to the monument."

"How do you know that?"

"Well—Sid Hasserin," she answered simply. "First, we couldn't even find the artifact's real name. We started calling it the Henge Piece, and it stuck."

I nodded as I thought about how I'd used keywords to search for the Henge Piece. That would explain why there was no record of the Henge Piece in the library catalogue.

"Second, Sid was certain it couldn't be a coincidence the Henge Piece mapped perfectly to the pattern of stones—or that the ruby aligned with the Altar Stone and the Heel Stone. He said this alignment must mean the Henge Piece was significant to Stonehenge. But he couldn't figure out why. We knew it was important. Our hunch was confirmed when the notes started."

"Notes?"

She reached into one of her desk drawers, took out a few folders, and pulled out a box. "Yes, notes. Look." The box contained a stack of papers. I pulled the first one out and immediately noticed two crosses at the top of the poem.

††

Drs. Ainsley and Kells:
Return what you have taken
For it is not yours to own
Meet at Stonehenge's center
So we can reveal what's etched in stone

Bring the Henge Piece with you
The rubied dagger must rest where it belongs
You cannot write your own story
To right all of history's wrongs

History is the tragic story
Of mankind and his severest sins
Bring the Henge Piece with you
And the world will have its wins

I read the poem slowly, then reread it stanza by stanza. "We? Etched in stone? Is there a message written on a stone? Who is the 'we'?"

"Not sure about any message or if 'etched in stone' referred to an actual stone at Stonehenge, or to the ruby—or both," Dr. Kells said. She pointed at the note. "That was the first poem we received. We later learned they called themselves knights, but who knows what that meant."

"Do you think the Henge Piece has historical significance?"

"Yes. We thought historians on the dig saw the artifact and wanted it for themselves."

"When did the notes start?"

"Right after one of our parties—the picture in your presentation. That was one of the last parties we had. We invited a whole bunch of our friends."

"So, whoever sent the notes could have been at the party."

"Yes, or was at the dig."

"And whoever sent the notes also maybe knew the Henge Piece's purpose?"

"Maybe—or maybe they were making it up based on what they'd heard from us. Maybe they had done their own research on it. It was all very mysterious—and terrifying."

"That's intense!" With each new fact I learned, I was getting more and more drawn into the mystery of the Henge Piece.

I picked up a second paper that had the same two crosses at the top.

"What are the crosses?"

"They're not crosses; they're daggers." She pointed at the dagger on the Henge Piece.

"How'd you make that connection?"

Dr. Kells smiled. "Read the note."

††

Drs. Ainsley and Kells:
The Knights of the Dagger need
The Henge Piece back straightaway
You must give up what's not yours
Or you won't see the light of day

You've stepped into an adventure
That goes back throughout the years
We need the Henge Piece now—or else
There will be more death and tears

The two daggers are sharp and ready
Their blades are forged in steel
Bloodshed will be upon us
The world must purge so it can heal

This note had a much more sinister tone—and death threats! *Who, throughout the years, had been looking for the Henge Piece?* Reading the third stanza gave me chills. Whoever the Knights of the Dagger were, they were out for blood!

I looked at Dr. Kells as I thought about the connection from the "we" in the first note to the Knights of the Dagger in the second note. "What did the Knights of the Dagger want to do with the Henge Piece?"

She pointed at the box. "Read another note."

††

Drs. Ainsley and Kells:
This is a matter of life and death
And the Henge Piece holds the key
Time is running out
You are both blind and you can't see

We need a new world order
Before it becomes too late
We need the Henge Piece now!
Or else mankind will meet his fate!

The dagger points to the fallen,
You must see what's etched in stone
The world must be cleansed so it can heal
For past sins we must all atone

The day of atonement is not far
The fallen ones will rise again
For they will drink of the sacred cup
It's not a matter of if, but when

I reread the note. My heart was pounding as I mouthed the words "new world order" and "mankind will meet his fate." What was "etched in stone"? Did the dagger refer to the dagger of the Henge Piece? Or a dagger that had been used to write something into the stones at Stonehenge? I looked at Dr. Kells in fear.

"That note in particular terrified us," she said. "We still had no idea who was sending the notes or from where. We didn't know who the Knights of the Dagger were. We called the police. They couldn't trace the letters—they didn't have a return address or anything. They were typed, too, so we couldn't analyze the handwriting. No research came up on the Knights of the Dagger and their threats, but clearly they wanted the Henge Piece."

"So, what did you do?"

"Once we realized that whoever was sending these notes thought we had the complete Henge Piece, we ran a press release that made a big deal about how we were missing the ruby and had turned in what we had to an anonymous museum for storage and safekeeping—"

"So you shifted attention from you to the museum, which got the Knights of the Dagger off your backs. That was smart! But wasn't it risky too? What if it didn't work?"

"Yes, but we were willing to take that risk. Would you believe, the notes stopped. Whoever wanted the Henge Piece needed the complete Henge Piece—including the ruby." Dr. Kells paused. "You're very quick-witted."

I smiled as a sense of pride rushed over me. Gran's partner

had called me quick-witted! “Thank you. Guess I get it from Gran. So, what happened next?”

“With no more notes or evidence, the case was closed. Whoever wanted the Henge Piece probably was still out there, but since they stopped sending the notes, and since the police closed the case, they weren’t my concern. I needed to move on and focus on growing the department here. The dean was pressuring me to create new programs, bring in more students, and hire more faculty. And after Lyle passed, I wasn’t in the right emotional mindset to revisit the Henge Piece mystery.” Dr. Kells paused and arranged her bun as she gazed at her office walls. “These past three years have sure been a wild ride. Almost makes me want to get out of academia and retire somewhere with a lot of good food and great culture.”

As I listened to Dr. Kells, I couldn’t help but think that despite being consumed by her Nassauton work, she still had her spirit of adventure. Was there a part of her that wanted to know why the Knights of the Dagger had sent the notes? Did the fact that I’d shown up in her office with my pendant change her thoughts about moving on from the Henge Piece mystery? The Knights of the Dagger were still a threat, because according to Dr. Kells, they had sent similar notes to Dr. Hasserin after the conference. What if they were involved in his murder?

“Doesn’t it bother you that the Knights of the Dagger are still out there?”

She looked at me quizzically, as if she didn’t expect my question. Her mouth opened slightly like she was about to say something. She closed her mouth, then opened it again.

“It does. I was thinking about that after our conference. But I’m too busy to do anything about it, especially with finding someone to replace Sid.”

I stared at her. I knew she was thinking about the conference, Dr. Hasserin’s discovery and notes he’d received, and her speculation that he’d been murdered.

“What conference?”

“Oh, a conference the department attended over the summer. But anyway . . .” Her voice trailed off as she changed the subject. “I think we’ve covered enough topics today. Let’s put the Henge Piece back. I’ll hang on to both pieces for safekeeping.”

“I want to keep my pendant with me. It reminds me of Gran.”

Dr. Kells looked at me. “But it is a priceless artifact, and you’re endangering yourself by wearing it.”

“Only if someone sees it—and knows what it is.”

“I’d prefer if you—”

“I promise I’ll keep it safe—and tucked under my shirt at all times. It’s gold. I’m not going to damage it. I promise.”

Dr. Kells paused and looked at her piece. Finally, she mused, “Maybe it is better to keep the two pieces separated. If Lyle trusts you to keep it safe, I should too. I’ll let you keep your pendant, but on the condition that you must hide it. If the Knights of the Dagger catch the slightest whiff that there are new leads on the Henge Piece, there’s no telling what they could do. Do you promise?”

I blurted out, “I promise.” I knew that agreeing to what Dr. Kells suggested was the only way to keep my pendant.

“I’ll give you a Tupperware and a towel.” Dr. Kells unsnapped the two pieces and grabbed an empty Tupperware container from a stack by her feet. She handed me a microfiber towel from a pile on her desk. “The Tupperware is airtight, and microfiber helps protect the artifact.”

I grabbed my pendant, wrapped it in the towel, and placed it in the Tupperware.

“One more thing, Dr. Kells. I need to show you something that I think you’ll find intriguing. When are your next office hours?”

“How’s tomorrow at ten?”

“I’ll be here,” I said as I slid the Tupperware into my satchel.

††

I chewed the last few pieces of my falafel. It was a surprisingly delicious dinner. I'd been lost in thought for the past half hour, my brain racing with theories and questions. I should have asked Dr. Kells if I could take pictures of the Knights of the Dagger's notes. I tried to remember some of the words. *Etched in stone. The new world order. Atonement.* Where was the ruby? What was the significance of the Henge Piece aligning with Stonehenge? Who were the Knights of the Dagger? Why did they want the Henge Piece? And what about Dr. Hasserin and his own Stonehenge secrets? I couldn't believe I had a piece of a priceless artifact, which was also part of the Knights of the Dagger mystery. My quest was getting more exhilarating.

I was so lost in thought; I didn't even notice dinner was over.

"We gotta clean up for the night," said the dining hall staff as he tapped on my table.

"I'm sorry." I gathered my utensils and plate and pushed my chair back. Its wooden legs screeched on the stone floor. I swung my satchel over my shoulder. "Didn't mean to hold you all up."

As I took my tray up to the conveyer belt, I noticed I was the only one in the dining hall. The empty tables went back for rows and rows. The setting sunlight streamed in through the windows, casting long shadows of the tables and chairs on the floor. The walls were wood paneling, beautifully detailed with ornate designs. I marveled at their intricacy. How many generations of scholars had eaten here throughout Nassauton's history?

I put my tray on the belt and headed out of the dining hall, straight for the Archaeology Research Room. I'd taken Blane up on his offer to discuss Stonehenge. Getting lost in thought over dinner had made me more than twenty minutes late.

En route to Rockfire, I called my mom. It had been a while since we spoke. Her work had picked up, and I was engrossed in the semester and the Henge Piece mystery. I decided not to tell my mom that I'd met Gran's partner—or that I'd learned more about the Henge Piece. I focused our conversation on my classes and how well my presentation went, without getting into any details. While I was going through the proper channels at Nassauton, like my mom had asked, I felt if she realized how deep the mystery was, she'd get overprotective and make me give it up—especially if the Knights of the Dagger were still at large and were behind Dr. Hasserin's death. As I entered Rockfire, I told her I had to go do my homework.

"Love you," she said. "Keep up the great work in your classes!"

"Will do, Mom! Love you too."

I hung up the call and headed down to the Archaeology Research Room. The best way to handle my mom was to tell her what would keep her calm and out of my business.

"Hi Blane!" I waved as I set my satchel down on the table across from his workspace. He had stacks of books next to his laptop and his headphones on. He was drumming along with his music, tapping his fingers by his laptop, or flicking them like mini drumsticks. I thought it was cute. As soon as he saw me, he immediately stopped drumming and took off his headphones.

"Hey Carly, what happened to you? I thought you were never gonna show up."

"Sorry, dinner ran late," I said. I unpacked Dr. Hasserin's book, a pencil, my journal, and my laptop.

"No worries, but could I get your number so next time, we can text if you're running late? I'll text you mine."

I grinned, feeling my face blush as I gave it to him. I wasn't used to guys—let alone smart and cute archaeology nerds—asking for my number.

"Next time?" I asked, looking at Blane as I pulled my chair out and sat down.

"Yeah. I want to go to Archaeology Talks next Saturday night, and I was wondering if you wanted to come with me and maybe we could, you know, get dinner afterward?"

Blane's hazel eyes looked everywhere but at me, doing little to hide his nervousness. I found it endearing. It gave me a vibe that he wasn't a smug player out to break my heart. More so than giving me a vibe, the fact that he'd asked me out to dinner was good enough evidence that he liked me.

I blushed even more. "Blane, are you—"

He stared at the table, then looked in my eyes. "It's only a talk and dinner. It will be fun!"

"Of course. Let me check my planner." I pulled my planner out of my satchel and flipped to Saturday night. "I'd love to go with you. What time is it?"

"Five thirty at the Commons. I'll save you a seat." Blane grinned. "Guess it's a date."

I looked at Blane, grinning as I tucked a loose curl behind my ear. "It's a date." I opened my laptop and my journal. "So, what can you tell me about Stonehenge?"

"Oh, lots. For one, it's the center of so many legends, from King Arthur to Druidic lore, to the Nazis. Hitler thought the Holy Grail might have been buried there—remember our friend Indy? Yeah, *The Last Crusade* was inspired by Hitler's actual quest for the Grail. Hitler was also so intrigued by Stonehenge that he built a replica in Poland, right by the Czech border. Muchołapka, or Hitler's Stonehenge." Blane got up and started pacing. "The real Stonehenge, at one point, used to be an ancient burial site. Hitler's Stonehenge . . . well, let's say people have speculated it could be anything from a missile launching to a time-machine testing site. Hitler was obsessed with time travel and science fiction experiments. Who knows? But the original Stonehenge, I mean I'm sure you know the summer and winter solstice festivals?"

"Yeah, the festivals celebrating the longest day and night of the year."

"Yep, exactly. I went to the summer one once. Way back when I was a kid, my mom and dad took us to England. My mom was working on a painting of the summer solstice for her collection and wanted to see it in person. We booked a bus from London. It was a short daytrip or something. Big mistake, zero stars, do not recommend."

I scrunched my face in disappointment that Blane didn't recommend an item on my bucket list.

"Why?"

"There were way too many people. Cool thing to do once, I guess, but you gotta understand that everyone, from everywhere, shows up for the solstice. Dancing, drunkenness, debauchery. I almost got lost; it was pretty scary."

"But you were a kid. Maybe it will be different if you go back now that you're older."

"Maybe. And maybe if I didn't go with my family. Maybe with friends or something."

"What about the legends?" I picked up my pencil, ready to write down whatever Blane said.

"Well, a lot of legends surround Stonehenge since we don't really know its purpose. We do know it was used for burials, but of whom? And why? Did Druids build it? Did aliens? Are Druids aliens? Is the Holy Grail buried there? What about how fourteen lines of Earth's energy grid meet at Stonehenge, making it one of the, if not *the* most powerful place on the planet? We do know it has a lot of secrets, most of which are still left to be discovered. So, we find ourselves captivated by the secrets of Stonehenge, always asking ourselves what it can teach us about our past, so we can perhaps understand what lies ahead for us in our future. Thank you for coming to my TED talk."

I laughed and applauded as Blane took a little bow.

"Bravo, bravo, you are funny. And you are quite the expert! Summer solstice at Stonehenge has always been on my bucket list. Right up there with New Year's Eve in Times Square, seeing a Broadway show, and going to Easter Island. I guess I have a thing for bucket list items in famous places."

"And for crowds, and for extremely isolated places." Blane laughed as he sat back down. "Seriously, so many people show up. I think you're right though. If I were to go now, it would be a different experience. It was a little too scary for a kid."

"Well, maybe one day you will go!"

"Maybe! Oh, and there's one more thing that always stuck out to me about Stonehenge. How much do you know about King Arthur?"

I put my pencil down. "A fair bit. I know he was a British king who fought the Saxon invaders in the fifth and sixth centuries. That's why I was so excited for Dr. Hasserin's seminar. I know about the Knights of the Round Table and how Arthur pulled Excalibur out of the stone."

"Right! But there is so much more to Arthur—especially in relation to Stonehenge." Blane leaned across the table.

I sat up and leaned in closer to him.

"Well, as legend goes, Merlin—he was Arthur's magician—used magic to transport Stonehenge from Ireland to England. It wasn't even called Stonehenge then. It was called 'The Giant's Dance,' and the king at the time wanted a memorial for all his men who'd been killed in a gruesome massacre. Arthur had always been fascinated by the concept of Stonehenge as a place to honor the dead—and as a giant's playground. He even modeled his Round Table after it. Bet you didn't know that!"

I shook my head. I loved how much Blane knew and how he wove it all together into a thrilling story.

"This is fascinating! How do you know all this?" I brought my elbows to the table, resting my face on my hands as I listened.

"Have you ever seen *A Kid in King Arthur's Court*? After I watched that movie, I begged my dad to take me to the library. I checked out all the books on Arthur. All I wanted was to be a knight—to be part of the Knights of the Round Table! Then, for my eighth birthday, my mom bought me a book on Arthur. I'll never forget it because it had this fascinating picture of Arthur and Guinevere. She was his queen, and she also caused the destruction of Camelot—but that's a story for another time, if you want to hear it."

I nodded, my eyes gleaming with wonder. "Of course, I would love to," I said excitedly. "What was the picture?"

"It was like a stained-glass window of Arthur, his knights, and Guinevere. King Arthur was wearing a necklace with an intriguing pendant, and Guinevere was wearing a necklace with the same pendant. It stuck out to me. Eight-year-old Blane thought to himself: *Why would a dude wear a necklace?* But I guess when you're King Arthur, you can do whatever you want."

I was very curious now, especially to learn more about the necklaces. "What did the pendants look like?"

"They were so cool! They had these gold circles and a dagger with a ruby in the hilt. The ruby was glistening, like it had a halo or something!"

Whoa. I thought of Dr. Kells' and my conversation and the Henge Piece. "Did the book have any caption for the picture?"

"I'm not sure. It's been a decade." Blane laughed. "I'm not even sure where that book is anymore—probably at home in one of my boxes. My mom keeps everything from when I was a kid."

"Do you think we can ask her to find the book?"

"You're really developing quite an interest in Stonehenge, aren't you!" Blane teased. "Sure! I can text her."

††

Later that night, I couldn't sleep. I sat in my bed, gripping my journal and Henge Piece and staring at the dagger as I read over my notes. *Could the Henge Piece and King Arthur's and Queen Guinevere's necklaces be the same thing?*

I had to know more about the picture in Blane's book. And I still had to solve Gran's mysterious poem. I'd decided to show the poem to Dr. Kells tomorrow. I felt I could trust her, since she was Gran's partner. The only way to know was to show her the poem and see what she said about it.

After reading the Knights of the Dagger notes and learning about King Arthur and Queen Guinevere's necklaces, I believed there were deeper layers to the Henge Piece mystery. I also started suspecting that Dr. Hasserin *was* murdered for his Stonehenge discovery. *Could Dr. Hasserin's death and the Henge Piece be related? Did the Knights of the Dagger murder Dr. Hasserin? Am I wearing the key to unlocking one of Stonehenge's secrets that King Arthur kept buried for years? Did Dr. Hasserin discover this secret?*

With these questions swirling in my head, waves of fear began to hit me. My head throbbed, and my pulse raced. *If Dr. Hasserin was murdered, would whoever killed him . . . kill me?*

I took my pendant out of the Tupperware container. I didn't trust it in there. What if something happened to it? What if Lara walked into my room and found it? The safest place for it would be on me, under my shirt. Gran had said: *Wear it, hide it, keep it safe, and in your sight.* Not "hide it in a Tupperware." I was going to trust Gran on this one, not Dr. Kells.

I looped the necklace around my neck. I clutched my pendant, feeling it on top of my beating heart. As my fear intensified, the pendant didn't provide any solace, despite its connection to Gran. All I heard was my heart beating, faster, and faster, and faster.

V

At 9:59 the next morning, I knocked on Dr. Kells' door. She opened it and ushered me in, closing the door after me. I sat on her sofa and pulled the Henge Piece box, my journal, and a pencil out of my satchel. I noticed she had been playing with her Stonehenge replica.

"What are you working on?"

"Oh, nothing. Holding the pieces calms me down. It's a meditative thing." She chuckled.

"Dr. Kells, I need to show you something." I put my journal on the coffee table and reached for the Henge Piece box.

"Please, I think it's okay for you to call me Lydia." She looked me in the eyes with a kind smile.

I was caught off guard. It was very unusual, if not unheard of, for professors to give students permission to call them by their first name—especially a professor as tenured and seasoned as Dr. Lydia Kells. Dr. Kells giving me this permission was a reassuring and special sign. As Dr. Lyle Ainsley's granddaughter, I felt like Dr. Kells was welcoming me as her new partner in solving the Henge Piece mystery—and the murder of Dr. Hasserin.

"Okay, Lydia." I grinned. I handed Lydia the box. She opened it and read the poem, her look of surprise changing to a deep pensiveness as she read the stanzas. She nodded as she mouthed the words to herself.

After a few moments, Lydia looked at me, then reread the poem slowly. She picked up a piece of her replica and gazed at it as she turned it around in her hands. Finally, she said, "It seems like Lyle wrote a poem for you, modeled on the Knights of the Dagger notes. Was there anything else in the box?"

"Only the Henge Piece pendant."

Lydia nodded. "Hmm, you've found one missing piece—that's my part of the Henge Piece. You know the ruby is the other missing piece. *Stand at Stonehenge in the sunshine* must have something to do with how the Henge Piece aligns with Stonehenge and the Heel Stone; maybe Lyle means the summer solstice here. Now, the Riddle of the Ages—that one is easy." Lydia smiled.

"It is?"

"Sure it is. The Riddle of the Ages is this: What is constantly running but never gets tired? What is constantly flying but never has wings? What do you always want more of, but money can never buy?"

I repeated the riddle. I was stumped. "What?"

"Time," said Lydia. "Think about it. It's time."

I grinned. I had found my guide.

Hardly a second later, there was a loud knock on the door. We both jumped at the unexpected sound.

"Come in," said Lydia, clearly surprised by the knock.

A man stepped into Lydia's office. He was wearing khaki pants, a white button-down shirt, a navy-blue tie, and a black blazer. He had a pale-blue pocket square with white polka dots on it. On his blazer lapel, I noticed an old brooch that looked like it was made of pearl.

"Here, Lydia, I printed these CVs for applications for Sid's job. You might want to check them out."

I recognized the voice. It was Daniel, the man I'd overheard in the office in the hallway, when Lydia brought up the murder speculation. He placed a folder on Lydia's desk, knocking over a piece of her replica in the process.

"Thanks, Daniel. I'll look. I'm with a student right now."

"But these are important."

"So is my student. I said I'll look."

"Okay, suit yourself. I'm only trying to help you fill the role."

Daniel walked out the door and shut it, leaving Lydia and me alone again. Lydia swiveled to her desk and picked up the piece, placing it back in its position. "I wish he wasn't so disrespectful sometimes. I'm clearly with a student, and he had no right to knock over this poor little piece."

"It's fine. It's only a small interruption. He's probably also feeling the pressure to fill Dr. Hasserin's role. We were talking about the Riddle of the Ages, and you know the answer."

"Guess that makes me your guide." Lydia grinned, moving a stack of papers to reveal a framed picture of her and Gran. "Lyle and I had a secret phrase we'd use if we ever needed help. You know, if we were at a cocktail party and there was a clingy person, or if we need to subtly ask the other for assistance. It was: 'It's about time for the Riddle of the Ages!' It worked out very well."

"That's so cool," I said. "A secret phrase to help you in times of trouble."

Lydia nodded. "Yep," she said, looking at her picture. "So of course, Lyle," said Lydia, talking to the picture, "it would be my honor to be your granddaughter's guide."

"So, how is the search going for Dr. Hasserin's job?" I asked, changing the subject.

"Not well. We can't find qualified candidates. Each of them is missing something—a course here or there, number of years of experience, they're not interested in teaching freshmen, they only want to focus on research . . . You name it. It's always something."

"Did the university ever tell the faculty how Dr. Hasserin passed away?" I knew I was asking a leading—and logical—question. I figured how Lydia responded would indicate how much she trusted me.

"No, no, they did not."

"Don't you find that strange? I mean the email said he was thirty-six."

"I do, I really do. It makes me wonder—"

"If his death wasn't an accident?" I blurted out, hesitating to call it a murder. "I'm sorry, I shouldn't have said that. But, thirty-six is too young to die naturally. It's really suspicious."

"Carly, it's okay. If I'm being honest with you—and I feel I can be—I think Sid was murdered." Lydia looked at me and sighed. "Thank you for hearing that and not immediately thinking I'm crazy."

"I don't think you're crazy. I want to hear more."

Bringing a few pieces from her replica with her, Lydia got up from her desk and sat next to me on the sofa. She crossed one leg over the other, adjusting her skirt and riding boots in the process. She turned toward me and rested her hands on her knees, giving me her full attention.

"It started when we went to this conference a few weeks before the beginning of term. Sid said he discovered something important about Stonehenge. We were at one of the networking parties. Maybe he'd had one too many drinks. I'm not sure what exactly he said. I wasn't around him during the party. I'm certain he didn't say what he'd discovered, since he wanted to drop teasers for his forthcoming book. He hinted that what he discussed in his book would change the world." Lydia rolled a few pieces around in her palm.

"And the world never had a chance to learn what it was—especially with Dr. Hasserin getting murdered before he could publish his book," I added, twirling my loose curl. "Do you have any idea what his discovery could be?"

"No, but if I can tell you something—sharing something in confidence, Lyle's partner to Lyle's granddaughter—" She pointed to the pieces in her palm.

"Yes, of course," I said, leaning in and picking up my journal and pencil.

"I think he discovered how the Henge Piece could be used to find something at Stonehenge."

I sat upright as I looked at Lydia and felt the weight of my pendant under my shirt. She couldn't even tell I was wearing my half of the Henge Piece. I scribbled *Henge Piece discovery* in my journal.

"See, a week or so after the conference, when we got back here, he started receiving notes. These notes were the same as the ones Lyle and I received—the same double dagger marks and poetic style."

"Wow." I paused as my thoughts trailed off. "So, whoever sent the notes had to have been at the conference."

"Yes—or had gleaned what Sid shared."

"I wish we could figure out who was at the conference."

"Well, it was our whole department—maybe twenty of us. It was our tradition for the whole department to go. But as for who else was there, and who else was at the cocktail party, there's really no telling. Probably impossible to go back and find that out. It's one of the biggest conferences in the field. Thousands of archaeologists from all over the world attend."

I sighed. We needed another way to learn what Dr. Hasserin had discovered. I looked at my notes. "Do you have any of the notes Dr. Hasserin received?"

"No. He never showed them to me, only told me."

"Can we find them? Maybe they're in his office?"

Lydia gripped one of her Stonehenge pieces. Her gaze shifted from the ceiling to her desk, to her bookcases. As she stared at her bookcases, her face lit up.

"Or maybe they're at his house! I still need to pick up my books. I can check his desk when I go and see if there are more notes!" Lydia walked to her desk and flipped open her planner. "I can go on Thursday night."

"Awesome," I said. "I'll go with you!"

"I love your enthusiasm, but it's probably safer at this point if you don't." Lydia looked at me. She could tell I was disappointed. "But there is something you can do. Why don't you take pictures of the notes the Knights of the Dagger sent Lyle and me, and you can start deciphering what they might mean?"

I smiled. "Sure thing!"

††

"So, what are you and Jesse up to this weekend?"

Lara and I were walking to our dining hall. I'd been working on a chemistry lab report, and she'd been reading for one of her classes. We decided to take a break and grab dinner before the dining hall closed. If freshmen missed the dining hall hours, the only option available for on-campus dining was at our campus center. Their salads and sandwiches weren't too bad, but they didn't have a hot bar like our dining hall did.

"We're going to a little painting studio in town! He booked us a date there," Lara gushed. "I noticed it running errands one day and mentioned it to him. Next thing I know, he's taking me there! Isn't that so sweet?"

"That's adorable! I'm so glad things are going well with him."

"Oh yes, I'm so in love with him!" Lara showed me the picture of the two of them that she had set as her phone background.

I smiled. I didn't understand how Lara could say she was so in love with him when they'd been dating for a handful of weeks. But I was glad she and Jesse were having fun. We passed the quad with the volleyball court and entered the breezeway. The stone gargoyles on the Gothic columns seemed to stare at us as we walked.

"And what's going on with you and Blake? I know you study a lot with him in that room. Spill the tea!"

I laughed. I found it amusing how she was so obsessed with herself and Jesse but couldn't even remember Blane's name. "Blane is doing well. We're study buddies."

"Just study buddies?"

"Yeah—but he did ask me to go to Archaeology Talks with him, and grab dinner afterward."

"He did?" Lara stopped in the middle of the breezeway. "So, he asked you out!"

"Yeah." I grinned. "I'm super nervous though."

"Why? Two archaeology nerds, going to a talk and then to dinner. That will be perfect."

"I don't know what to wear or how to do my makeup. I'm nervous! I really haven't been on a date before."

"You didn't date in high school?"

"Not really. Well, there was one guy from church, but that was a few dates, and it was bowling. Nothing too crazy."

"You'll be fine. Be yourself! And I can help you with your outfit. I'd love to."

"You can?"

"Of course! It will be fun. I like these kinds of things."

I smiled. "Thank you. I really like him. Saturday will be a big day for me."

We opened the dining hall door and caught the last few minutes of dinner.

VI

Saturday evening's Archaeology Talks was a welcome break from my homework. At the end of the week, my work had piled up out of nowhere. I hadn't heard from Lydia about retrieving her books from Dr. Hasserin's house. I figured that between reviewing resumes for his position and preparing for her own courses, she had been swamped. As I tried to finish my homework, all I could think of was Blane, our date, and the talk: "Does this Float Your Boat?: Examining the Evidence for Noah's Flood." I got butterflies in my stomach every time I tried to pull together an outfit.

"You look amazing," Lara said as she put the finishing touches on my makeup. She'd spent the past thirty minutes testing different shades of blush, eye shadow, and lip gloss on my skin and coordinating these shades with my outfit. "Here, see for yourself." She ushered me to the mirror in the corner of her room. Lara's mirror was actually three door-size mirrors, nailed next to each other on the wall. "I need mirrors," she joked. "How else am I supposed to see myself?"

I stepped in front of her mirrors. I gasped as I saw the person looking back at me. She was a far cry from an archaeology nerd whose go-to outfit was a vintage Indiana Jones T-shirt, shorts, and moccasins. Lara had chosen a soft gray eyeshadow, which made my green eyes appear blueish green. She'd applied eyeliner and chosen a rose-colored lip gloss to complement my maroon sweater and light-pink shirt. She even gave me some of her lotion.

"It will make your hands super soft, and guys love soft skin," she said as she squirted a big dollop into my palm.

"Wow. I look like a whole different person." I smiled. "I love my new look."

"You look like you're ready for your first date with your crush." Lara grinned. "Have fun tonight. You deserve it."

I clutched my pendant through my shirt. "Be brave," I whispered to myself, closing my eyes and inhaling and exhaling.

"And remember to be yourself!"

††

At 5:20 p.m., I walked into the Commons. The Commons was a four hundred-seat theater in Nassauton's campus center, spread out over an orchestra level and a balcony. I scanned the theater for Blane, walking down the center aisle to see if I could find him. I recognized a few students from Archaeology 101, and some other people from my dorm. I imagined that given its subject, this talk drew archaeology, history, science, and religion majors. There seemed to be a mix of under- and upperclassmen, steadily filling up the space as they found their friends and settled into their seats.

After a few moments, I saw Blane sitting two rows back from the front, saving the seat next to him with his jacket. He was wearing a loose-fitting polo shirt, jeans, and Top-Siders—a big step up from his usual T-shirt, shorts, and sneakers.

"Hey Blane! You're all dressed up. You look nice." I smiled as I sat down, crossing one leg over the other and placing my satchel on my lap. "Thanks for getting us great seats!"

"Well hello Carly! No problem, and I will say the same for you. You look very pretty." Blane gazed at my face and the rest of my outfit.

I blushed and nervously tucked my loose curl behind my ear.

"I like your sweater, and you always have the best shoes!

Look at your heels! Is that Atlas?"

I nodded. "Yep, holding up the weight of the world."

"That is so cool. What a neat design!"

"Thank you. These used to be my grandmother's. She had quite the collection of shoes, from all around the world."

"How neat. Your grandmother sounds pretty cool—at least her shoes are pretty cool!"

I laughed. "She was pretty cool."

"I'm so excited for this lecture. Thank you for coming with me. Dr. Wryght is an incredible archaeologist. He has even worked with Robert Ballard's team. He's been on many famous international digs. This will be great!"

"I'm excited too!"

"Oh, I almost forgot. Remember that kid's book on King Arthur?"

I nodded.

"I asked my mom if we still had it. Sure enough, it was in one of my boxes. God bless that woman; she never throws anything away."

"It was?"

"Yep, and she texted me the picture I was talking about. Here!" Blane handed me his phone.

I looked at the screen, zooming in on the picture. Around King Arthur's and Queen Guinevere's necks were pendants. They looked exactly like the Henge Piece. I read the caption below the picture.

> *Stonehenge was very important to King Arthur. He had a pendant made so he could always keep it close to his heart. To show his undying love for Guinevere, he had the same pendant made for her. It was his way of being connected to Guinevere no matter what*

happened at Camelot, no matter in this life, or the next. In fact, legend has it King Arthur buried a very important treasure at Stonehenge.

What could be buried at Stonehenge? I tried to slow down the torrent of questions that flooded my mind. *What are the odds that, centuries later, King Arthur's treasure is still buried at Stonehenge? Did Dr. Hasserin discover this treasure?* The mystery of the Henge Piece—now Henge Pieces—had gotten much, much deeper.

I looked at Blane.

"Did the rest of the book say anything about the treasure, or only the necklaces and Arthur and Guinevere's romance?"

"I'm not too sure. I think it focused mostly on King Arthur, his knights, and their battles."

Now I'd gotten enough evidence to link the Henge Piece to King Arthur. I'd gotten more evidence that linked the Henge Piece to Stonehenge. I'd also learned King Arthur and Queen Guinevere both had Henge Pieces. So, if Gran and Lydia had found one of them, where was the other one? *How do the two Henge Pieces work? Could the Knights of the Dagger have the second one—and that's why they wanted Gran and Lydia's?* As I waited for Archaeology Talks to start, I slid my journal out of my satchel and jotted down my questions.

"Good evening, everyone. My name is Dr. Daniel Pritzmord, the dean of the Archaeology Department. I'm proud to share that under my watch, I grew the department through more research opportunities and support for faculty and experiential learning initiatives for students. I've kept Archaeology Talks going strong by bringing in diverse and engaging speakers."

The house lights dimmed, leaving only the stage lights. Dr. Pritzmord held his microphone up to his mouth. He glanced behind him to make sure the projector was on.

"Archaeology Talks introduces students to the world's best

archaeologists, who share their experiences directly from the field. This is our first talk of the year, and we have a full house tonight! I have the distinct pleasure of introducing tonight's speaker."

Dr. Pritzmord wore khaki pants, a white button-down shirt, a navy-blue tie, and a black blazer. He had a pale-blue pocket square with white polka dots on it. On his blazer lapel, I noticed his pearl-colored brooch. I recognized his clothing, and as he spoke, I recognized his voice too. He was the same Daniel I'd overheard in the hallway when Lydia brought up the murder speculation. More recently, he had brought the CVs to Lydia's office when I was talking to her.

He sure had his own style. I thought it made him look distinguished. I imagined him as a celebrated guest at one of Gran's parties. I valued the quality of Nassauton's professors and was grateful to have opportunities like Archaeology Talks.

"Dr. Edward Wryght is a world-renowned underwater archaeologist, most notably having worked with Robert Ballard on the evidence for Noah's Flood—and the real location of Noah's Ark. Some say, as I'm sure you are aware, it was found on Mount Ararat. Others say those scans are fakes—expertly and very, very, very convincingly created fakes. With Dr. Wryght leading us tonight, I think you're in for a real treat. Please join me in welcoming Dr. Edward Wryght!" Dr. Pritzmord clapped, leading the whole theater in applause.

Dr. Wryght walked on stage, shaking Dr. Pritzmord's hand before he grabbed the microphone.

"Good evening! Can everyone hear me?" Dr. Wryght tapped the microphone, then pushed his glasses up his nose bridge. He was wearing a loose-fitting T-shirt, jeans, and a corduroy blazer.

Dr. Wryght paced the stage as he talked. "Go back in time with me to an age, thousands of years ago, when ice caps covered the world. Glaciers were everywhere—and I mean everywhere. Over time, that ice started to melt, causing water to rush into the world's oceans. Take, for example, the Black Sea region. It is one of the saltiest places in the world. Was it always this way?"

Dr. Wryght stopped pacing, clicked to a slide of the Black Sea, and pointed his laser light around it. "This area here was all farmland that surrounded a once-freshwater lake, which was flooded by water rising from the Mediterranean Sea."

He pushed his glasses up again and clicked to the next slide. It showed water and arrows indicating the rising water and its movement.

"So how is this area now salty water when it was once freshwater? The answer lies in the mystery of the Great Flood. This water swept away everything in its path. The Great Flood, the likes of which no one had seen before, and the likes of which we haven't seen again, was an extremely disruptive event to local agriculture, vegetation, and life. Our world really wasn't designed to experience the massive shock of water released all at once. So, this shock disrupted the shoreline, displacing shells and rocks in the process."

Dr. Wryght clicked to a picture of him and Robert Ballard in sunglasses and wide-brimmed straw hats. The whole theater ooohed and ahhhed, delighted to see Dr. Wryght with such a famous person. As I glanced at Blane, I saw all the students in the theater smiling. I thought it was neat how scientists, historians, religion majors, and archaeologists were united by the history of Noah's Ark. Blane caught me looking at him and winked at me. Embarrassed, I blushed and looked up at the slide. Dr. Wryght had three charts displayed: *Old Testament Longevity Chart*, *Corrected Carbon 14/Carbon 12 Reduction with Age*, and *Age Predictions from Standard and Corrected Theories*.

"Radiocarbon dating helps us understand when Noah's Flood occurred." He paused as he looked out at the audience. "Radiocarbon dating relies on the ratio of Carbon 14/Carbon 12. The ratio is assumed to be constant over time. But volcanic eruptions, nuclear testing, and, for example, great floods, can disrupt this ratio. So, the math behind how we date the flood is fascinating—and corroborates the biblical timeline."

The audience murmured. I was enthralled by what Dr. Wryght had shared about the science matching up to the biblical timeline. From his explanations, I could see how the science and religion complemented each other. I thought of my dad, who also believed that science and faith were two sides of the same coin. *I wish I could text him what I'm learning. What would he have to say?*

"So, if you're interested in radiocarbon dating and the math behind it, check out Dr. John Carmen's research. He goes well into the weeds on how the numbers work out, showing us fascinating, highly accurate evidence that supports Noah's Flood occurring when the Bible said it did."

Noah's Ark was one of the first stories we memorized for confirmation class. As a high-schooler, I had so many questions on how a flood could have drowned the whole world and how Noah could have taken all the animals with him. But my teacher made it clear we didn't have time to ponder questions. We had to memorize the story, complete the course, and accept what the Bible said since that's what the Bible said.

Now, as Dr. Wryght presented the evidence, I believed the story of Noah's Ark was true. Because he presented evidence so clearly, I believed I could go on a dig and discover Noah's Ark.

"In conclusion," Dr. Wryght said, "the evidence points to the flood occurring, and occurring when the Bible said it did. So, when we think about Noah's Flood, did it happen? The evidence points to yes. The remaining question, then, is where is Noah's Ark? Is Rondo Weeyatt, another leading archaeologist to study it, correct? Does the evidence point to the Durupinar site, where a boat-like shape has been observed by archaeologists, scientists, historians—and pedestrians—alike? When and where will we find it? Maybe that's a question you will help answer as you embark on your own archaeological careers."

The audience erupted in applause as Dr. Wryght clicked to his final slide and asked if anyone had questions.

††

"Well, here we are! Are you surprised?"

Blane and I were standing outside Winnie B.'s. I'd asked Blane where we were going for dinner, and he wouldn't say. He only said he thought I'd like it, given how I liked studying the past. When he said he made us reservations at one of the oldest restaurants in town, I knew it was Winnie B.'s.

"I've been wanting to go here ever since the year started! This place is legendary." I beamed. "Thank you." I was trying to stay calm and not let my nervousness get to me.

Blane grinned. "I was hoping you'd like it."

We'd walked there after the lecture, ambling in the crisp September evening air, from the Commons to the restaurant. Winnie B.'s was a block off the main street that separated Nassauton's campus from the town. It was only a ten-minute walk from the Commons. Those ten minutes walking with Blane in the autumn air, stepping over the fallen leaves, were some of the most perfect minutes I'd experienced at Nassauton. The leaves were starting to turn all sorts of colors as summer slid into fall. The trees were mostly bare silhouettes in the evening sky.

"I don't like it, I love it. I'm very excited!"

"Well, shall we?" Blane opened the door and ushered me in. "Ladies first."

The entrance of Winnie B.'s was a big, oak door surrounded by a stone arch. On either side of the arch, detailed into the stonework, was a gargoyle. One had a mortarboard on its head; the other had a football helmet.

Nassauton lore was that depending on whichever the student noticed first—the scholarly one or the sports one—the student would become known for their accomplishments as a scholar or an athlete during their tenure in college. If the student noticed both at the same time, they'd have to make a difficult decision between the two before they finished their second year.

I'd noticed the gargoyle with the mortarboard on its head.

"Welcome to Winnie B.'s! Do you have a reservation?"

"Yes, Henley, for two, please."

"Thank you, right this way." The host grabbed two menus. "Follow me please."

Right after the entrance, a small flight of stairs and a hallway led to the main dining room. Letter jackets, set against white canvas boards and encased in big, wooden frames lined the stairs and the hallway. These jackets, and the rest of the memorabilia, showcased the achievements of our college's football players—transporting diners to a time when going to college football games was the only thing to do on Friday nights.

In the main dining room, which was full of booths and tables, more pictures lined the walls. These pictures showed some of our college's very first women and captured snapshots of them walking around lecture halls or socializing at iconic campus locations. Our college was one of the first to admit women. Looking at their pictures made me proud to walk in their footsteps.

"What did you think of Dr. Wryght's talk?"

Blane and I had settled in our booth.

"I really, really enjoyed it."

"Why?" Blane asked me. "Tell me more."

"Well, I don't know where to start." My eyes darted from the tabletop to the wall in nervousness. "It's probably a long story."

"Start at the beginning," Blane said. "I'm looking at my only plans for tonight."

I blushed, and blushed hard. Blane's charming nature and the vibe of the whole evening was giving me the biggest butterflies in my stomach. I knew I was starting to fall for him.

"I guess I'll start by saying these stories fascinate me. I was raised in the church. You know, went to Sunday School. Read all the stories: the Garden of Eden, the Fall, Noah's Ark, the Flood, Moses and the Exodus, Abraham sacrificing Isaac, all that. Grew up believing these stories were true."

"So did I," said Blane. "That's another one of the things that got me started on archaeology—the Flood."

I smiled. "So that's why you were so excited for Dr. Wryght's talk?"

Blane nodded. "Yeah, I've followed his work for a while. I love the whole science-and-faith-are-aligned theme. It makes total sense to me. I don't see how people can argue that they're divided. And the stories—the stories in the Bible give us insights into the science behind the Scripture."

"What do you mean, Blane?"

"Well, the stories teach us lessons in ways equations can't. They make us ask questions, see things differently, see things that we might not have seen if we look only at the numbers."

I grinned. Blane was making a great point. "The stories also leave room for interpretation, don't they? They're all so intriguing."

"Yeah, and that's part of their timeless appeal."

I nodded. "They made us memorize all of them in confirmation class. I stood in front of my whole church and mumbled, 'I believe in God the Father Almighty, the Maker of Heaven and Earth,' and so on. I believed what I was saying, even though I didn't really understand it. I had a lot of questions."

I sipped some water. "But I said the words. I believed them. At least I thought I did."

"It's totally okay to have questions! Questions are a part of faith, not separate from it. But what happened? Did someone tell you otherwise?"

"Not really. Well, afterward—after my confirmation, my mom and dad and I celebrated by going out to lunch with my grandmother. It was great."

"Sure sounds great. I was confirmed too. Let me tell you, I was terrified when I had to stand in front of the church and state my beliefs, I stuttered so badly, I didn't think I'd be able to make it through."

"You had a stutter?"

"Oh yes. So bad I went to speech classes for it."

"I'd never be able to tell."

"Because I had a great speech coach! Anyway, back to your story."

Blane didn't take his eyes off me the whole time I was sharing. I felt like he was listening with his whole body, instead of only with his ears.

"Well, later that day, my parents said they had something to tell me. They said they didn't want to tell me this before, because they wanted me to 'have my moment' in church. I was sitting on the couch in front of our TV. They both sat next to me, and hugged me, and Mom started crying. Finally, my dad said, 'Carlyle, I have terminal cancer.' Then he told me about how he and Mom had known for a few months, but didn't want to tell me, how they were trying to treat it, and how nothing had been working. He told me his doctors had caught it too late, and there was little that could be done."

"Oh Carly," Blane said. "I'm so sorry. That is unimaginably awful."

I stared at my water glass, studying the ice cubes inside. I hated talking about my dad's experience. But, I felt it was important for Blane to know, since coping with my dad's death had influenced how I saw and interpreted my world. Learning of my dad's cancer and watching him pass away on the heels of Gran's death were major turning points in my life. They were the first times in my life I'd questioned everything I thought was true.

I stared at the tabletop, looking at my napkin, then my glass, then back to the tabletop. Finally, I looked at Blane.

"My dad told me how, although he was lucky and was one of a handful of patients admitted into a Phase I trial for a new immunotherapy drug, the dosage didn't work. The administrators told him his body was too weak to handle a higher concentration. They released him from the study. I'd remembered that day. He'd come home with a huge bandage on his arm and pamphlets and papers that said *Eternae*, with paragraphs of small-print text. When I asked him what it was, he said it was nothing. Three and a half months later, Mom and I buried him. We had just buried Gran too. I wasn't even halfway through high school."

I paused, taking a big gulp of water. I was nervous to begin with, and talking about Gran and Dad brought up more anxiety. Holding the water glass and concentrating on it helped me focus.

"Mom didn't remarry, and I stopped believing in God. Part of me—actually, I'd say more than part of me, all of me—wants to believe He exists, but how can He exist when my dad doesn't anymore? I want those words I said to be true. But after all that's happened with Gran and Dad, I don't know. I have too many doubts—and way too many unanswered questions." I paused again, staring at the wall of our booth. "I don't know. I want to be able to take a leap of faith, like Indy, like my Gran . . . but I don't know. I don't know at this point."

"Good ol' Indy and his leap of faith," said Blane, as he smiled compassionately. "Thank you for being brave enough to share all that."

"So, I guess that's a long answer to your question, but I liked Dr. Wryght's talk, because he gave us evidence that suggests these stories are true. He challenged us to find Noah's Ark—using the facts. He presented the evidence that made me think—no, I guess I'd say, *know*—that these stories are true."

"And it is powerful evidence, rooted in history and science. He's not making it up."

"Right. When I hear it, my mind goes to a place where if these stories are true, then maybe the whole rest of the stories are true as well. Places like the afterlife, Heaven—you know, that maybe if Gran and Dad don't exist in this world, they exist in another. That maybe I'll see them again, someday."

My voice trailed off as I caught myself. I hadn't intended to share this much with Blane on our first date, but something about the way he listened and looked at me made me feel safe, heard—and not judged for having questions and doubts.

"I'm sorry, I know I've been talking a lot about heavy things."

"Talk. I'm here to listen." Blane reached across our table for my hand. "May I?"

I smiled as I gave him my hand. As soon as he held it, I felt calm—like he was holding me and would never let me go.

"You have such smooth skin."

I smiled, thinking of Lara's lotion. I could feel my face about to blush, so I picked up my glass of water and took another sip.

"Thank you. And sorry, I really mean it, I'm hogging up the airtime. What did you think of Dr. Wryght's talk?"

"No, no it's fine. I asked. You shared. That's how communication works." Blane smiled as he squeezed then released my hand and picked up his menu. "And speaking of sharing and communication, would you like to share an appetizer or something?"

I grabbed my menu. I loved how even Winnie B.'s menu had little vignettes of yesteryear sketched onto its pages. The vignettes showed scenes from football games, friends at dinners, and cheerleaders and pom-poms. I looked at the appetizers.

"What sticks out to you?" Blane asked.

"Oh anything, I'll eat anything. I'm not picky, but I'm lactose intolerant."

"How about their bread, olive oil, and hummus? That sounds like a great starter, and it looks like their bread is homemade. And we could get a pizza for the entrée or something?"

"Works for me—but no cheese."

"No problem. No cheese it is! Looks like they have a Fall Harvest Pizza. It's got pecans, pears, spinach base, and a drizzle of honey. Does that work for you?"

"That sounds delicious."

We gave our order to the server and continued our conversation about Dr. Wryght's talk.

"I really liked the talk," said Blane. "I'd never really thought about the impact of catastrophic events, like a big flood, on the carbon count of the world. Makes you realize how delicately and precisely balanced our tiny little marble that we call home is."

I smiled. I appreciated how poetic Blane was with his descriptions.

Our bread arrived, hot and crispy on the outside and warm and chewy on the inside.

"Blane, tell me something about you that no one else would guess."

"Well, I have lived on every continent in the world—even Antarctica."

"No kidding! Tell me about that."

"Yep. My dad is an architect and designs sustainable buildings. My mom is an artist who paints scenes from nature to create awareness of climate change. So, their work is very place-based. It took them everywhere. We moved to a different continent every two years."

"That's super cool. Which one was your favorite?"

"That's a tough question. I liked them all, and for different reasons!"

By the time our pizza arrived, I felt like I'd seen a softer side of Blane—a side that he tried to keep hidden behind the goofy, theatrical student he wanted others to see.

We both eyed the pears and honey on the pizza. "Dig in!" said Blane. "This looks delicious!" He reached for a slice.

"Don't have to tell me twice," I said. Blane's and my hand reached for the same slice, and we both giggled when we realized it.

"Take it, it's yours," Blane said, chuckling.

"That's funny," I said. "We went for the same slice."

"Well duh, it had the most honey on it—and I sure do love some sweetness in my life."

I laughed, grinning as I picked up the slice. Blane took the one next to it.

"To sweetness!"

"To sweetness!" I replied as we toasted with our slices.

As I chewed, I thought about how much fun I'd been having. I'd really enjoyed Archaeology Talks, Winnie B.'s, the conversation—even though I'd ended up sharing some pretty personal memories—and the company. Blane took the deep conversations in his stride, being patient with me and listening to me. I felt I could trust him with anything.

Beyond being a great study buddy, Blane, as I was realizing, was also an incredible person to talk to. I loved how goofy and genuine he was—it showed me he didn't take himself too seriously, but just seriously enough. He was interested in archaeology and academia, and we both liked the past—but for different reasons. We complemented each other in other ways, too. While I saw faith as something I couldn't connect with unless I saw or touched the evidence, he saw faith as a mechanism that extended the evidence and took the person the extra step to accomplish their goal.

"Like in *Indiana Jones*, when Indy has all the evidence he needs. All things point to the Grail being there," Blane said. "But in that moment, Indy can't see his next steps. When he gets to the edge of the ravine, he realizes there is no bridge to get him across. And without the bridge, there is no way Indy can get the Grail."

Blane had a good way with words. I thought it was cool—and adorably nerdy—how he was using the Leap of Faith scene to help convey his point.

"Indy is stuck, but then . . . he decides to take that leap of faith. He decides to walk, even though he can't see the path ahead. That one extra step—that's the step that leads Indy to get to the Grail. That's the step where something happened in Indy's head and maybe even his heart, where he built from the evidence—and extended it. The evidence, with his faith, helped him know to take that step—even though he couldn't see it. That's faith. How many others do you think would get to that point and turn back, because they didn't see that step—even though it was there?"

"I'm sure many."

"Yeah, exactly. Faith takes us that much further, and taking that new step, that jump, that leap—sometimes that's all we need to be completely transformed. Even though we can't see the next step, or have doubts, or questions, we take that leap anyway—because deep down . . . well, deep down we know that's the step we must take to accomplish our goal. The trust we have that it will work out—and work out for the better—is stronger than our doubt that it won't. And all the doubts we have—those make our trust stronger, because they force us to ask the tough questions."

I smiled. I loved listening to how Blane viewed faith and put it in the perspective of doubts and questions. He made it seem like doubts and questions were essential to faith, because they could lead to deeper and richer faith.

I nodded. "Thank you for sharing that. I appreciate it. It sounds like you've spent a lot of time working that out."

"Yeah," said Blane. "I have. I have a lot of questions I'd like to ask God. I've been through some pretty tough things in my life too." He stared at the wall. "I'm just not as good at talking about them as you are. Hopefully one day I will be."

I reached across our table for his hand. "May I?"

He gave me his hand. "You may," he said, winking.

"Hey, I need to ask you something." Even saying that caused me to be nervous, since Lydia had explicitly told me not to show my pendant to anyone—not to mention my mom had told me to destroy it. But deep down, I felt I could trust Blane. I'd shared my story and struggles with him. I knew I was ready to take my leap of faith. "Remember Stonehenge and your book with the picture of King Arthur's and Queen Guinevere's pendants?"

"Yep, of course I do, why?"

I reached under my sweater and pulled out my pendant. "Look familiar?"

"Whoa!" Blane's eyes widened as he leaned across the table. "It's like King Arthur's necklace! How did you get that?"

"Or it could be Queen Guinevere's—how would you know the difference?" I teased.

I told Blane everything. I told Blane that Gran was Dr. Ainsley and Lydia was her partner. I told him about Lydia and Dr. Pritzmord's conversation I'd overheard, about Dr. Hasserin's discovery, and Lydia's murder speculation. I told him about the mysterious poem in the Henge Piece box, the dig Gran and Lydia had gone on, the missing ruby, and the mysterious notes Gran and Lydia had received.

"I have so many questions. I keep a list of them in my journal. I don't know what Dr. Hasserin discovered, and I have no idea where the ruby is. Maybe he found the missing ruby. Maybe he discovered something King Arthur buried at Stonehenge. Whatever Dr. Hasserin found, I'm pretty sure my pendant is related to it."

"That's incredible! If it weren't for you telling me this, in person, right here, holding half the Henge Piece, I wouldn't believe a word of what you're saying. You're barely a month into college and you're already tackling a murder related to a groundbreaking discovery—and with a world-famous archaeologist on your team. Not to mention an artifact that is literally thousands of years old. Aren't you scared?"

I smiled. I'd been so busy jotting down the details in my journal that I'd lost sight of the bigger picture of how my Henge Piece adventure was developing. Hearing Blane say it like that gave me a deep sense of purpose and pride. I was following in Gran's footsteps, one step at a time. I was also filled with an overwhelming sense of doubt, as more questions crept into my mind as I thought about the magnitude of my quest. Did Lydia really view me as her teammate? Or did she view herself as my guide? What if I failed or tripped up and ended up embarrassing myself in front of her? What if, after sharing all this with Blane, nothing came out of my work?

I took a deep breath. "I can't say I don't have my doubts. But, no," I replied. "I'm not scared. I've been preparing for this adventure my whole life."

"You're incredible, Carly." Blane gazed right into my eyes. "Most archaeologists don't get a lead like that till later in their careers, after they've done their PhD. Yet here you are. You're incredible."

He reached for my hand and squeezed it.

"Would you like dessert or anything?"

"I'm good. You?"

"Oh no, that pizza was plenty. I'll get the check. Would you be down for walking around campus before I walk you to your dorm?"

I grinned. "Which is also your dorm."

"Yep, funny how that all works out."

"And yes, I'm in for a walk."

Holding Blane's hand made me feel calm and grounded. I had found something—or someone—worth holding on to. Every now and then, as we walked, Blane would swing my arm and his in excitement as he pointed out fun facts about our campus.

"What, are you my unofficial tour guide for tonight?" I joked.

"Nassauton College has such a rich history," said Blane. "It's architecturally stunning, and so much has happened here over the years—from Revolutionary War battles to college traditions."

Blane was right. Nassauton did have it all. At night, the lights around campus illuminated the gargoyles, making them look slightly menacing in the shadows. There were a few stars scattered in the sky, like a handful of diamonds had been thrown against a midnight black velvet blanket. When we got back to our building, Blane hugged me goodnight. I welcomed the hug, finding I had to stand on my tiptoes to reach up and fit into Blane's arms.

"Hopefully we can do this again—maybe next week? It sure gets us out of the Archaeology Research Room." Blane smiled.

"I'd love that. Tonight, from Archaeology Talks to our walk, was wonderful. I really enjoyed it."

"Happy to hear it. Goodnight, Carly."

"Goodnight, Blane."

I touched my pendant through my shirt and grinned as I walked to my dorm room. I was excited to see where the next leap of faith with Blane would lead me.

VII

Between my workload and Lydia's schedule and pressure from Dr. Pritzmord to review applicants, it wasn't until the following Friday that we had a chance to meet for office hours. I was desperate to know what updates Lydia had.

I bounced into her office after lunch and closed the door. "Hi Lydia, happy Friday!"

"Well, you're certainly in a great mood, Carly. I hope your day is going well!"

"Thank you. I'm happy to be done with a long week. I had a few papers, prompts for my precepts, and a big chemistry lab report due." I sat on her sofa.

"Me too," said Lydia. She sighed, pointing at the stack of papers on her desk. "No research papers—or lab reports—this weekend, but I have a lot of grading. But, I did get to Sid's house." Lydia picked up a few pieces of her Stonehenge replica and rolled them around in her hands.

"And?" I asked, sitting up and taking my journal out.

"Fortunately, his spare key was still there, under his doormat. But, unfortunately—and very mysteriously—my books weren't."

I scribbled in my journal as I asked my questions. "What? How do you know? What books did you lend him, anyway?"

"I'd lent him some on Ancient Rome, Early Christians, and the Holy Grail. He needed a citation for one of his talks for that conference over the summer. The library didn't have the books. I had them as part of my collection."

"How do you know they weren't in his house?" I was surprised. "Did you look everywhere? How can books go missing from a dead man's house?"

"I did. I looked all around his office, dining room, and kitchen. There was no sign of them." Lydia shook her head. "He was very careful with his own books—let alone books he'd borrowed. He wouldn't have lost them. There was nothing. They were gone. Something isn't adding up here."

"Maybe he moved them to his car to bring them to campus?" I picked up a Stonehenge piece from Lydia's desk and looked at it. The print quality was incredible: I could barely see the 3D-print lines on the piece.

"Nope, Sid didn't drive—he walked or biked here. Plus, the day before we were notified about his death, I saw him walking around campus with his monogrammed journal. We chit-chatted. He laughed and mentioned he had my books on his desk. He said they were right there, and every evening he made a note to bring them with him, but every morning he forgot. So why would they be anywhere other than where he'd last put them?"

I added a note in my journal and reviewed what I had written. Looking up at Lydia, I asked her, "So, do you think they were stolen?"

"That's what I'm starting to wonder. I bet whoever murdered Sid took the books too."

"When you went to his house, was anything broken? Like windows or places where someone could have forced their way in?"

"No, no break-in, no broken windows, and no signs of trouble. Everything was in pretty good shape."

"Hmm, isn't that a little odd?"

"Very," said Lydia as she pulled her desk chair closer to the coffee table, "I think whoever overheard Sid at the conference murdered him and took my books. I think that person didn't want him to go publish his book—maybe they wanted the glory for themselves. With my missing books, the conference, and the double dagger notes, we have enough reasonable evidence to believe Sid was murdered—and murdered by the Knights of the Dagger, especially considering what I found on Sid's desk."

I stopped taking notes in my journal and focused all my attention on Lydia. She took her phone out and showed me a picture:

††

And so the scholar meets his fate
He thought he could get the Grail
But alas—here he lies
The Knights of the Dagger will prevail

Throwing speculations around was one thing. Laying out the evidence was quite another. I wrote the poem down. I flipped through my journal pages, looking at my questions and notes. I closed my eyes as I thought about my conversations with Blane—how he'd told me Hitler thought the Grail was buried at Stonehenge. I thought about how Lydia said the Henge Piece's ruby aligned with the Heel Stone and the Henge Piece itself mapped to Stonehenge. I thought about the research I'd done and Dr. Hasserin's book I'd read. I thought about the books on Ancient Rome and the Grail that Lydia had let Dr. Hasserin borrow, and the Knights of the Dagger and their threats. My head was spinning as I started connecting the dots.

"How did the Knights of the Dagger know Dr. Hasserin was looking for the Grail?"

"I don't know," said Lydia. "But I think they did know he figured out that *etched in stone* referred to the missing ruby of the Henge Piece. On Sid's desk were Post-it notes that had doodles of the Henge Piece—with the ruby in it. One of the doodles also had a phrase: *Etched in stone.*"

She opened her journal and showed me three Post-it notes. "I took them with me. I figured they might help us learn about the Henge Piece. I bet Sid discovered how the Henge Piece works in pointing to something at Stonehenge."

I grinned at Lydia's detective spirit—something I didn't expect given her age.

"So, Dr. Hasserin never gave up researching the Henge Piece? Wasn't the dig three years ago?" I pulled my phone out to take a picture of the notes.

"Yes, it was. I don't know, Carly. He never brought it up with me after our case was closed, but who knows what he was studying in his free time. Sometimes it's hard for younger scholars to let go of their research ideas. Don't know if it's idealism, or wanting to find that one discovery for which they'll be remembered, but whatever it is, Sid must have never let it go."

I skimmed through my notes. As I'd been thinking about Lydia's missing books and the Henge Piece doodles, I kept coming back to Blane's book with the picture of King Arthur and Queen Guinevere. That picture suggested the connection from the Henge Piece to buried treasure at Stonehenge. "I think I have something that can help us."

I told Lydia about the picture.

"Well, that is certainly interesting. It's a children's book, which means we don't know if it's historically accurate. It's not archaeological evidence, but it's a source nonetheless. We can't discount it for now. I wonder if . . ." Lydia paused, thinking. "I wonder if Sid discovered that the second Henge Piece is buried at Stonehenge?"

"Or," I added, "did he discover the Grail was—and is still—buried at Stonehenge? I think he also discovered how the Henge Piece can be used to find the Grail's exact location."

Lydia's jaw dropped. "What? But he didn't have the ruby. How could he know how the Henge Piece works without the ruby? Not to mention the Grail doesn't exist in the first place, but that's a whole separate conversation."

"I didn't say he had it. I think he was able to determine how the Henge Piece worked and where the Grail is, from his research—without having the ruby or the Henge Piece."

"But how can that be true? The Grail isn't real." Lydia started pacing around her office.

I looked up at her, unsure of what she was going to say next.

"How can you locate an object that doesn't exist? There is no legitimate, archaeological evidence for the Grail—only an excess of lore, legends, secret documents, and hearsay. All these are conspiracy theories, which have led men down atrociously evil paths. Crusades. Murders. Bloodshed. Even if the Grail does exist, show me the evidence Christ actually performed miracles, He actually was part human and part divine, and the Grail is actually real. It simply doesn't exist." She paused by her window.

I stared at the rug under the coffee table. Its reddish colors no longer seemed warm and inviting, but full of anger. I sighed, tracing the rug's pattern with my eyes as I thought about what I'd heard. I couldn't believe Lydia felt this way about an artifact that had likely led to Dr. Hasserin's death. I felt she was closing a door to a case before we ever got a fair chance at solving it—because she didn't have evidence for Christ being divine and wouldn't take a leap of faith. In listening to Lydia, I realized even with all my own doubts, anger, and resentment toward God, I'd never stopped believing Christ was divine. Maybe this was why I'd never stopped asking questions—and seeking their answers. I sighed again, unsure of what to say.

"But that's exactly my point. You don't know the Grail *doesn't* exist. Maybe Dr. Hasserin proved it does! Maybe that's why his discovery was so groundbreaking. Maybe that's why he was killed. Finding the Grail has kept every archaeologist up at night for the past two thousand years—aren't you in the least bit curious as to whether it is real?"

"Hasn't kept me up," Lydia replied flatly. "It used to when I was younger. But at some point, I stopped thinking like a child and became an adult. I accepted that if there is no solid, irrefutable evidence for something, maybe there's a reason—that it doesn't exist in the first place. I stopped chasing the dream, because I realized it was just that—a dream, and a dream that wasn't grounded in reality."

She continued pacing, walking to the other end of her office. "The Grail, the cup that Christ supposedly used at the Last Supper, the cup that Joseph of Arimathea supposedly used to catch Christ's blood when He was crucified—that's where all these legends of eternal life come from. That if you drink from the Grail, you 'magically' get Christ's blood and get eternal life. *Magically? Eternal life?* I mean, listen to that. No one has ever found the Grail. That should at least indicate something. There is no evidence. The source story is a religious text. It isn't a science textbook, a historical account, a city record. And now, the source stories are fan fiction novels."

She paused by one of her bookcases, running her hand along the book spines. "I don't even know what new theory has taken hold of people nowadays. It used to be that one author who sensationalized the Grail, and everybody swarmed the Rosslyn Chapel and thought they were going to learn the secrets of Mary Magdalene's bloodline, fertility, children, and all that. Every day some 'scholar' is spreading some new opinion based on their Wikipedia research and the one YouTube video they watched. Maybe even a Reddit discussion or two if they really wanted to go for the peer review." She laughed. "Peer review—review by whom? Other Reddit users? Who have exactly what credentials? How have they verified their data? They haven't!" She reached for a book. "*This* is peer-reviewed, Carly," she said as she flipped through the pages. "These chapters don't make it in here if they're not subjected to rigorous review."

Lydia put the book back and walked to the sofa. She sat down next to me. "As far as the Grail is concerned, everything is a tantalizing speculation. These speculations fuel the minds of evil, wicked, sick people, who use them as 'evidence' to 'legitimize' their work. They believe the Grail is historical and is the key to purifying the human race. And what comes out of it? Killings. Murders. Holocausts. The Nazi Party was full of secret societies. They keep killing in pursuit of the Grail. So, it sure has led a whole bunch of people to pervert religion and do some pretty horrific things to their fellow humans."

She took a breath. "That was a lot. That all came out at once, sorry."

Chills ran down from my neck to my back as I listened to her. "That's super disturbing." I could tell I'd somehow hit a nerve in Lydia by bringing up the Grail. She hadn't stopped talking, barely catching a breath. I jotted down her comment about secret societies, wondering if the Knights of the Dagger could be one of them. "How did you learn all this? I didn't think your research covered the Grail."

"Sid. Sid was my mentee, remember? He taught me a whole lot about King Arthur and the Grail, from his research. But it's all legends and lore—fan fiction that has driven men to murder, and nothing—nothing!—has come out of it. The Grail is only a concept, an abstraction, and one that has done a whole lot more harm than good. I wouldn't be surprised if there are descendants of the Nazi Party who, to this day, will stop at nothing to possess the Grail."

"So don't we have a moral obligation to humanity to stop them?"

"That's quite a big statement, Carly—'moral obligation.' Who tells us we have any moral obligation? And to whom? Or is it us, motivated by our own self-interests, trying to find a place in history by putting our name on something bigger than ourselves—and saying we are doing this in the name of morality? Where is the archaeological evidence? The truth is that we don't have any. In the absence of evidence, there is no truth. There's a whole lot of lore on it, a lot of emotion, but not a whole lot of evidence." She got up and sat at her desk.

Lydia was a woman of evidence, indeed. I scribbled down

some notes in my journal. I was captivated by our conversation and frustrated that Lydia thought the Grail wasn't real. Finding the Grail was every archaeologist's dream. If my own adventures as a young explorer took me on a quest half as exciting as the Grail, I'd be ecstatic.

"Everyone knows how you feel about evidence versus emotion."

Lydia smirked. "At least someone pays attention in that first class." She looked at her Stonehenge replica. "I'm sorry, but if the best you can come up with is an emotional outpouring that Sid was murdered because of a nonexistent object, then I need to do some more thinking on my own. Maybe focus on applicants for Sid's role—and take a different approach to discovering why Sid was murdered."

I think I need to do some more thinking on my own. Her words cut me like the Henge Piece's dagger. My lower lip trembled as tears formed in my eyes. I was devastated. She was saying we were no longer partners on the case.

I was too frustrated to do anything other than sigh. We'd started office hours with Lydia being convinced Dr. Hasserin was murdered. But now, it seemed like she and I hit a block—a block that had everything to do with her personal thoughts on the Grail. Lydia's weakness was her reluctance to pursue anything unless she had enough evidence.

I sighed. "I need evidence too. Sometimes our emotions lead us places we shouldn't go. But sometimes—sometimes our emotions are the first steps to taking the leap of faith to find more evidence," I said flatly. "I've got a lot of thinking to do, too, Dr. Kells." I purposefully didn't call her Lydia. "I hope you find who murdered Dr. Hasserin, and why. Maybe you have a moral obligation to do that since he was your colleague and mentee. And I . . . well, if the Grail is buried at Stonehenge, I believe I have a moral obligation to find it."

VIII

Fall was in full swing at Nassauton, leaving the tree branches bare and the ground full of leaves. Fall was my favorite season, since the colors were some of the most beautiful ones I had ever seen. I loved walking outside as the leaves crunched under my shoes and smelling the scent of freshly fallen leaves. Even more than the smell, I loved gathering all the leaves and jumping in the pile. Making leaf piles was something my dad and I did after our hikes. We'd come back from the park, order hot Thai food or make warm soup, and then we'd make leaf piles in our front yard. I loved doing that because I saw a more whimsical and less serious side of my dad that he rarely showed to anyone.

I was hitting my stride with my schoolwork. I had a good routine and loved hanging out in the Archaeology Department. I'd befriended Joyce, the administrator who'd filed my paperwork before I started my semester. I enjoyed our discussions on Nassauton's artifact collection and loved learning about her previous career as an assistant curator. She was also the first one to tell me that the department had filled Dr. Hasserin's role. Like Dr. Hasserin, Dr. Kenneth Wengaro was a British Isles expert. The hiring announcement quoted our provost, who described Dr. Wengaro as "far superior to others in his field."

Dr. Wengaro had jumped right into the seminar—and moved right into Dr. Hasserin's old office. One morning, as I was talking to Joyce about her experience curating a collection of eighteenth-century furniture for a high-end auction house, Dr. Pritzmord walked in.

"Has Kenneth completed his onboarding?"

Joyce nodded. "Yes sir. He's all good."

"Great. Never heard of him before, but from all his application materials, he seems very impressive." Dr. Pritzmord chuckled. "But number of publications doesn't translate to ability to get set up in our learning management systems and dive into catching up on a month's worth of missed classes."

"Don't worry. I helped him. He's good to go."

"Thank you, Joyce." Dr. Pritzmord smiled. "I'll let the provost know. With October beginning, he's been anxious for that class to get started."

I smiled. I was excited to finally start Grail Times. Maybe that class would yield answers in the Henge Piece mystery, especially since Lydia and I hadn't met at all to discuss Dr. Hasserin or the Henge Piece. I'd left our last meeting frustrated and unable to understand why Lydia's interest tanked when I suggested the Grail was buried at Stonehenge. Her whole tone had changed, and she left me feeling like she didn't want to help me pursue the Grail.

I thought she was motivated to solve the Henge Piece's mystery and Dr. Hasserin's murder—and maybe she still was. But she had made it clear she didn't want to have anything to do with a Grail quest. Did she not want her name—and her reputation as a leading female archaeologist—associated with a fan-fictionized relic? I understood she needed evidence and was reluctant to take too much of a leap of faith, but I also believed we'd had several plausible next steps.

I still had my half of the Henge Piece. And I still believed it would lead to where King Arthur had buried the Grail at Stonehenge. I felt it was my moral obligation to do something to prevent "evil ones," to use Gran's words, from obtaining the Grail. I'd spent a lot of time in the Archaeology Research Room searching for any leads on the Knights of the Dagger. My searches didn't yield anything, but I was determined not to give up.

On the day of our first Grail Times seminar, Blane and I grabbed coffee in Café Naiviv and headed to our classroom. It was a small seminar room tucked on top of an archway in one of our buildings. It had three windows at the back and the blackboard at the front. The windows were on the south side of the building and overlooked one of the upperclassmen quads.

We sat around an oval table. It was unmovable and felt like solid oak. Its thick top and sturdy legs filled up most of our seminar room. It had about fifteen seats, all of which were occupied. In addition to Blane, there were a few people in my seminar from Archaeology 101. I also recognized one student who lived across the hall from me. The rest of the students I had never seen before.

I looked around our seminar room. The woodwork on the walls and the thin, well-worn green carpet on the floor gave our room a cozy feeling. Hundreds of Nassauton students before me had spent countless hours in this room, diligently studying. Sitting in my seat, I felt part of a community of scholars whose research spanned decades and subjects. I knew I belonged at Nassauton.

The analog clock by the blackboard seemed to barely move as Dr. Wengaro droned on and on about his life. Within the first half hour, my excitement for the seminar had turned to boredom as Dr. Wengaro rattled off his accomplishments. Now, at almost an hour in, he hadn't even bothered to ask us why we were taking the class. Although Dr. Wengaro's accomplishments were remarkable, especially given his age, I hadn't signed up to hear a CV read aloud to me. Had Nassauton made the right decision in hiring Dr. Wengaro?

Dr. Wengaro was probably around his mid- to late thirties—I'd guess around Dr. Hasserin's age. He was wiry and had long, curly brownish hair that he'd pulled back into a ponytail. He looked more like a drummer from a classic rock band, and less like a professor. He told us he'd applied for this job because of the well-known fact that Nassauton had the best rare books collection in the country. He had a special interest in rare books, particularly those related to ancient burial sites. He was elated that through his faculty position, he'd have access to our collection.

Then, he told us his career story as he explained every publication on his CV and how it advanced the field. If there ever was a shining example of humility, it was not Dr. Wengaro. He had been on numerous digs around Europe—and he made sure we knew how prestigious they were. He dropped names of famous archaeologists with whom he'd collaborated, given talks, or simply rubbed elbows at cocktail parties. He was interested in British, Irish, and French burial sites, sacred grounds, and elixirs used in ancient surgeries. He'd done his PhD on the Hill of Tara, one of Ireland's most famous ancient burial sites.

I started doodling on the syllabus, drawing Henge Pieces and rubies in the margins as I imagined what the missing ruby looked like. Lydia said she didn't remember how big it was—"Probably as big as a celebrity's engagement ring, definitely not on the small side," she'd joked. I erased one ruby drawing, then redrew it, making the ruby bigger. I wrote *etched in stone* near the Henge Piece, playing with cursive and print letters. I doodled dagger marks, trying to copy what I remembered of the dagger marks on Lydia's letters.

Blane looked over at my syllabus and whispered that it looked like his math notebooks. "You're a doodler too," he laughed. "Don't worry, you're not missing anything. Wengaro is still talking about himself."

I ran out of space in the margins. I turned the page and looked for a good spot to keep drawing. Dr. Wengaro had his PhD title and Committee Chair's name printed at the top of the page. Immediately, I noticed the name. It was none other than

Dr. Allister Leith, the British archaeologist who had supervised Dr. Hasserin, was friends with Gran and Lydia, and was on the Henge Piece dig. *Whoa. Dr. Leith had supervised Dr. Wengaro and Dr. Hasserin?* I circled Dr. Leith's name. This was certainly a lead worth looking into.

As Dr. Wengaro wrapped up our class and gave us our assignments, I couldn't help but think something was very odd about him. He was aloof and seemed to care little for his students and our questions. He made it clear that his research was his priority. If we wanted to attend office hours, we had only a few windows to schedule them, and we had to send him an email at least a day in advance.

I was upset and discouraged. Dr. Wengaro's seminar was a far cry from how I'd imagined Grail Times would be. I was sure that if Dr. Hasserin were teaching the seminar, things would be different. These frustrations fueled my desire to find out who murdered Dr. Hasserin—and to find the Grail.

As Dr. Wengaro dismissed our class, I packed up my syllabus and laptop into my satchel.

"Well, that was a bit of a letdown, but at least I have my Henge Piece and ruby doodles—and some very beautiful, scripted lines of *etched in stone*." I laughed as Blane and I tucked our chairs in under the table. "Wanna go to the Research Room and start our midterm for Archaeology 101?"

"Sure do," Blane said as we joined the other students filing out of the seminar room. We held hands as we walked into the hallway and down the stairs. "Let's at least get ahead on it so we're not scrambling at the last minute."

"Agreed."

Blane pushed the door open. "Ladies first." He smiled. "Dr. Wengaro might have killed any fun we would have had in Grail Times, but chivalry sure isn't dead."

I laughed. Blane's humor was very funny to me. "Thank you," I said as we walked out the door and under the archway.

"So, what do you think his deal is?" asked Blane. The leaves on the walkway crunched under our feet as the fall breeze blew them into and out of our path.

"I'm not sure. He seems very smart—and very stuck-up. Kind of weird, like there's something off about him. Oh, and get this—guess who chaired his PhD Committee?"

"Dr. Leith."

"You noticed that too?" I smiled. I liked how Blane's mind and mine worked the same way.

"Sure did. Something, something great minds think alike, right?" Blane looked at me and winked. "Dr. Leith is a celebrity to archaeology nerds like us. I notice these things."

"But did you know Dr. Leith also supervised Dr. Hasserin—and he was on the Henge Piece dig with Gran and Lydia?"

"Nope! How interesting. Look at you, connecting the dots like that. Smart girl."

Blane squeezed my hand, making me grin. It made me happy Blane thought I was smart. I valued his intelligence too. He always made it a point to keep himself well-informed, and if he didn't have an answer, he would find it.

"Well, this smart girl is certainly in a smart guy's company!" I returned the compliment to Blane, who flashed a big, goofy grin.

"I read and I know things—I guess."

"I think that's awesome," I said. "I guess it's not all that strange that they'd have the same PhD supervisors. They had overlapping research areas, and Dr. Leith is the best of the best. Do you think they knew each other?"

"That's a great question. They seem around the same age. Maybe they did their PhDs at the same time? Why, what's turning in that big brain of yours?"

I beamed. I loved when Blane said I had a big brain.

"I'm thinking if Dr. Wengaro knew Dr. Hasserin, maybe he can tell us a little bit about him."

††

Blane and I had made good progress on our midterm project. We had to compare the methodologies of four archaeologists. They couldn't be from the same time period. The point of our comparative project, in Dr. Kells' words, was to "examine the methodologies for unearthing the evidence, noticing what methods stay the same, across the ages, and what methodologies change."

"Hand me that book on Ballard, would you please?"

I handed Blane the navy-blue hardcover book next to my laptop. Blane and I had chosen Dr. Sidney Hasserin, Robert Ballard, and Kathleen Mary Kenyon, a trailblazer archaeologist who had led several excavations of Jericho and one of the most influential archaeologists of the twentieth century. For our fourth archaeologist, we'd chosen the Bedouin shepherds who had accidently found the Dead Sea Scrolls.

Lydia was known for not giving exams, which was something I loved about her teaching philosophy. "What do they really test?" she'd asked when she explained the project. "They test how fast you can write everything you know on blank pieces of paper and then make up some theory based on how well you think you understood everything. I'm more interested in how we practice working together to research and present our work. Excavating a site is not as clean as filling a bubble in on a multiple-choice test. Unearthing the past requires reflecting on what you know to be true—what the evidence says—rolling up your sleeves, grabbing your partner, and getting messy as you dig up the dirt, literally—and figuratively, of course."

I'd loved what Lydia had said about unearthing the past. That was how I thought too: I liked to introspect and take notes in my journal. After that, I liked to discuss my thoughts with someone I trusted before planning my next steps. In high school, I'd hated multiple-choice tests, because to me, they didn't seem to test anything, other than my ability to differentiate between two very similar answers—and inevitably pick the wrong one.

Our midterm project was due the first week in November, which was a week before Midterm Week. Lydia explained she'd be at several conferences during Midterm Week and over Thanksgiving break, so she preferred to get everything out of the way earlier.

And so did I. It would be one fewer midterm to take. I was thrilled with the four archaeologists Blane and I had chosen. It felt important to honor Dr. Hasserin's memory in some way. I could think of no better way than a project for my favorite class. The archaeologists represented a range of perspectives and discoveries, and the more I read about the Dead Sea Scrolls, the more fascinated I became by them. I marveled at how old they were. They contained the second-oldest surviving manuscripts of books in the Bible—and over 225 copies of these books! It was astonishing that scribes could create all those copies. I imagined the scribes writing by sunlight, then by candlelight, each waking hour from dawn to dusk as they toiled to put the stories on paper.

As Blane and I were researching, it started raining. Since there wasn't too much to do around campus on a rainy afternoon, we decided to stay in the Archaeology Research Room and make more progress on our project. I'd piled up a few more books and was looking forward to uninterrupted time reading them.

One of the coolest things I discovered about the Dead Sea Scrolls was that they were evidence for the existence of different versions of books such as Exodus, Samuel, the Psalms, and Daniel. These were some of the most important books in the Old Testament, since they helped religious scholars and archaeologists understand ancient Jewish history and the Bible's origins. They also helped scholars understand the spread of early Christianity. The more I learned about the Dead Sea Scrolls, the more I realized they were historical evidence for the stories I'd grown up memorizing.

"That's so crazy." I looked up from my book. "Did you know

that several people have tried to make forgeries of the Dead Sea Scrolls?"

"No, but I'm not surprised. I mean, think of all the fame that person would get—fact or forgery, that dude would still be notorious!" Blane grinned.

"Yeah, but archaeology is more about celebrating the authenticity of the source, rather than reveling in the fame associated with finding it, right?"

"It should be—but so many people want the fame for themselves. I mean, think of this Dr. Wengaro guy. He spent the whole first class talking about himself."

I nodded. "Yeah. You're absolutely right."

By the time evening rolled around, Blane and I had finished half our project. We decided we'd spend another thirty minutes working on it, then we'd grab dinner and call it a night.

I opened my last book by Dr. Hasserin. As I flipped through the first few pages, I realized it was a collection of journal articles he'd compiled and published. I scanned the table of contents, and my jaw dropped.

One of the journal articles, dated three years ago, was titled: "Can't Keep a Dead Man Down: Uncovering the Secrets of the Hill of Tara" by Sidney Hasserin and Kenneth Wengaro.

Oh my gosh, I thought. *Dr. Hasserin and Dr. Wengaro had co-authored a paper!* I couldn't believe what I'd discovered.

I flipped to the journal article. "I don't believe it!"

"What's that?" Blane asked without looking up from his laptop.

"Remember how we were wondering if Dr. Hasserin and Dr. Wengaro knew each other?"

"Yep, why, what's up?"

"They're co-authors on this Hill of Tara paper."

"No way! Show me!" Blane looked up from his laptop.

I scooted my chair over to Blane and leaned closer to him, sliding the book under his face. He took it from me, opened it, and skimmed the first few paragraphs of the abstract.

"Well, no way!" Blane was as surprised as I was. I huddled in closer as he flipped the page. We continued reading.

This ongoing research was supported by funding from the Royal Archaeological Institute. Sidney Hasserin and Kenneth Wengaro, graduate students working together under the supervision of Dr. Allister Leith, are grateful for this support to further efforts to unearth the past. In this paper, they examine the Hill of Tara, an incredibly sacred burial site that is also connected with everything from Irish Legends to Christianity—as a suspected location of the Ark of the Covenant. Their forthcoming paper, also funded by the Royal Archaeological Institute, will focus on the Holy Grail, providing conclusive, historical evidence for its existence by examining Grail locations throughout Europe and the UK.

More than co-author the paper, Dr. Hasserin and Dr. Wengaro had done research together—and under Dr. Leith. I looked up from the book and gazed around the shelves. My mind was racing as I tried to make sense of my thoughts.

"Blane?" I asked, turning my head to him and pointing at the book.

"Yes?"

"They did research together. They went on a dig together. They weren't only co-authors, they were partners. They were about to write on historical evidence for the Grail."

"Oh my, there's that brain of yours," said Blane, handing me the book as he got up and started pacing. "So, what are you thinking?"

"Well, I gotta ask the obvious question." I got up and started pacing with Blane as I gripped the book with my hands. "Knowing what we know now about their relationship, don't you think it's a bit too much of a coincidence that Dr. Hasserin died after hinting at a major Stonehenge-related discovery, then Dr. Wengaro shows up here at Nassauton and replaces him?"

As I asked that question, chills ran up my spine. Blane looked at me, nodding along. I could tell we had the same idea.

After a few moments, he said, "I think you need to email Dr. Kells."

††

Ever since Dr. Kells' and my disagreement, I chose to sit farther back in class. Blane sat with me, too, to support me. Even though I still enjoyed the course, I didn't feel comfortable sitting in the front. But today, Blane needed to skip class to finish his economics problem set. I'd decided to sit a little closer to the stage. I was determined to catch Dr. Kells as she was packing up.

"Hi Dr. Kells." I walked up to the podium. I didn't feel comfortable calling her Lydia. She barely glanced up as she packed her laptop in her satchel.

"Hi Ms. Stuart. Can I help you?"

The professor of the next class put his Styrofoam coffee cup on the table near the podium. He dumped his briefcase next to it and started setting up his laptop.

"Did you get my email?"

"Yes. I've been very busy these past few days. I need to prepare for my conferences. I've been underwater with writing and reviewing journal papers—the real, evidence-based studies." Her tone was flat and emotionless, except for how she emphasized "real, evidence-based studies," as if everything else was fan fiction and the archaeologists she was reviewing were the only serious ones in the field. As she replied, it dawned on me that she probably had abandoned our research because she thought I was going down the fan fiction route. I felt deflated that she thought I wasn't a serious, scholarly archaeologist.

"I need to talk to you. It's about Dr. Hasserin."

"Ms. Stuart, I'm afraid I don't have time." She snapped her satchel shut.

I wasn't taking no for an answer. "Dr. Kells, Dr. Hasserin and Dr. Wengaro were partners. Dr. Leith was their PhD supervisor."

She looked up at me. "That's interesting, but so what? What does that have to do with anything? What does that prove? That they worked together?"

"Don't you think it's too much of a coincidence that Dr. Hasserin got those notes, then died after hinting at a major, Stonehenge-related discovery, then Dr. Wengaro—his partner, his co-author, his friend—shows up here at Nassauton and replaces him?"

"It could be coincidental; it could not. Where is your evidence these events are related?"

Dr. Kells was right. I didn't have any evidence. I had a suspicion. She slung her satchel on her shoulder and stepped away from the podium, heading toward the stairs on the side of the stage. I followed her as she walked out the door and into the hallway.

"Dr. Kells—Lydia—please. I don't know what happened when I brought up the Grail, but it seemed like that changed everything. Before the Grail, you seemed to want to find who murdered Dr. Hasserin. He was your colleague, your mentee, and your friend. What happened? What happened when I brought up the Grail?"

Lydia sighed—a sigh of sorrow and heartbreak. "Oh Carly. Here, let's step in here for a moment." She pointed to an empty classroom. "Close the door."

She put her satchel down on a desk and looked at me with tears in her eyes.

"I'm sorry. It's been so much." She dabbed her eyes with her shirtsleeve, and her bracelets and Ailm charm clanged together. "Thinking of the notes, Lyle, the double daggers, it's bringing back too many memories of Lyle. We used to have so much fun. We were young. We were chasing the artifacts. Chasing our dreams. We chased the Grail too—those were some of our favorite adventures. We went all around the world."

Now I realized why Gran never wanted to talk about the Grail—and why Lydia had reacted the way she did when I brought up the Grail. Watching her cry, I felt her pain of losing her partner and best friend. "Oh Lydia," I said. "I'm sorry. I never knew. Gran never told me the Grail stories."

"We never found it. The Grail is not real. There is no evidence for it. We're scholars—serious archaeologists—not characters in a fan fiction book. The Grail is only an abstract—"

I interrupted her. "No. Look." I pulled Dr. Hasserin's book out of my satchel and showed her "Can't Keep a Dead Man Down: Uncovering the Secrets of the Hill of Tara." As soon as she read the sentence about their research on the Grail, and the conclusive, historical evidence for it, she looked straight at me, the inklings of renewed vigor in her gaze. She clutched the book and skimmed the abstract.

"The Royal Archaeological Institute provided funding for their Grail research? They must have presented evidence in their proposal. The RAI doesn't fund projects unless there is clear historical proof for the validity of those projects. The RAI's high standards are what makes them one of the best institutes in the world. That's very interesting."

I could feel a small, hopeful smile forming.

"We need to find their Grail paper. Is it in this book?" Lydia flipped to the table of contents and started skimming it.

"No, I already checked."

"Hmm. We can look it up in Rockfire's systems. Come on, let's head to my office."

††

In the time it took Lydia and me to walk to her office, I'd texted Blane to stop working on his problem set and meet us there, as this was important. He had gotten there ahead of us and greeted us as we approached the door.

"Hello, Mr. Henley," said Lydia as she unlocked her door. "I'm with a student now, but I can see you in fifteen minutes or so."

"Hi Dr. Kells, it's okay. I'm here to support Carly." He smiled at me, wrapping his arm around my shoulder. "She's cracking one of the most important cases our world has ever tried to solve."

I grinned. I was a little caught off guard that Blane was displaying affection for me in front of Lydia, but as we followed Lydia in, I realized I really didn't mind. It felt like Lydia and I were back on track as teammates.

"Good to see you two working together," said Lydia, picking up on Blane's signals. "You're two of the strongest students in the class." She smiled.

Blane and I grinned at each other as we sat down on the sofa. My leg and Blane's were touching. I could feel myself getting nervous with excitement—not only for where the next fifteen minutes would take us with the Grail and Dr. Hasserin, but also because being this close to Blane gave me butterflies.

Lydia opened her laptop and pulled up the library website. After typing in a few keywords and Dr. Hasserin's and Dr. Wengaro's names, she swiveled her chair around and looked at Blane and me.

"I'm afraid I have some bad news. This paper was never written."

"What? How can that be? They said they were working on it."

"I'm not sure, Carly. I know this search engine contains a record of every paper published by a given author—and nothing is coming up for Dr. Hasserin and Dr. Wengaro as co-authors on this topic."

I covered my mouth with my hand, staring at Lydia's Stonehenge replica. "That's so strange," I finally said. "Why would they never publish a paper that had concrete evidence on the Grail?"

"And a paper for which they had secured the funding!" added Lydia. "Maybe the funding was rescinded? But there would have had to have been a good reason for that."

"Maybe they never finished the paper," Blane chimed in, leaning forward off the sofa.

Lydia picked up a few pieces from her replica. "Who knows. I don't suppose I should go up to Kenneth and ask him. That would be a little out of the blue."

"Yeah, and . . ." I paused. "If Dr. Wengaro had anything to do with Dr. Hasserin's death, we don't want him to know we're on to him—until we have better evidence and can trap him into a confession."

"Carly's right," said Blane.

Lydia was shaking her head in disbelief. "This is so strange. I had no idea Sid and Kenneth were partners. Or that Allister was Kenneth's Committee Chair too."

"Didn't you look at Dr. Wengaro's application?" I asked.

"No, the provost had taken over the process by then. Daniel was concerned with the timing and my workload with preparing for my conferences. He wanted me to focus on representing the university well as conference chair." Lydia put her Stonehenge pieces on her desk, opened the book I'd given her, and started skimming a few pages. Without looking up, she continued. "And seeing how slowly the search was going, the provost even removed Daniel from the process and handled it himself. He's the one who found Kenneth. We're lucky Kenneth accepted."

Blane and I shook our heads. Nassauton had certainly scrambled to replace Dr. Hasserin.

"Oh Sid," Lydia exclaimed as she threw her hands up in the

air. "Why is all this happening? Does the Henge Piece point to the Grail's burial spot at Stonehenge?" She moved her hands to the back of her head and arranged her bun.

"We're all wondering the same things," said Blane. "To get to the evidence, we need to start with the questions."

I grinned when I heard Blane say that. He sure knew how to speak Lydia's language. I took out my journal and pencil as Lydia put the book down on the coffee table. Blane leaned forward and picked up the book.

"All right," I said as I flipped to the next blank page in my journal. I saw my notes and thought about my questions on my pendant, my poem, the Henge Piece dig, Sid's discovery and death, the missing ruby, and the Nazis and the Grail.

Lydia picked up a Stonehenge piece from her desk. She scooted to the coffee table and rolled the piece around in her palm. The sunlight from the window caught her Ailm charm, scattering some of the light around the office.

"Well, it seems that our first set of questions are around Dr. Kenneth Wengaro. We need to learn more about him—without involving him. What is his background, his story, his passion? Where is he from?" Lydia paused. "I'd like to get ahold of Allister. He is *the* expert on the British Isles. He's done groundbreaking work on burial sites and relics in Scotland. He's led countless digs in Ireland, Wales, and England. He's one of the few archaeologists who seeks the truth—the evidence—and understands that in the absence of evidence, all you have is imaginative speculation."

I jotted down Dr. Leith's name, listening as Lydia continued. I loved that she was taking our work seriously now. It felt good that we were back on track and working together again. Blane was still reading Dr. Hasserin's book. I glanced at my notes, circling what I'd written and drawing a line from my words to Dr. Hasserin's name. As I did, a thought came into my mind. I flipped back a few pages in my journal.

"You mentioned the Henge Piece dig is where you and Gran

met Dr. Hasserin—and he was finishing his PhD, right?"

"Right," said Lydia.

"So, he had to have been there with Dr. Leith."

"Right."

"When was the dig again?" asked Blane.

"Three years ago," Lydia and I said at the same time. Lydia added, "In the summer. I remember since there's no way I would have had the time to go during the school year."

"Look at the date of this paper."

Blane placed the book on the coffee table. Lydia and I leaned in and looked at the date.

"It was published in August of that same summer," I said. "So they published 'Can't Keep a Dead Man Down' right after the dig, which means they were probably working on it that summer, which means—"

"Do you think Dr. Wengaro was at the dig with Dr. Hasserin?" Blane blurted out. "Sorry, I interrupted you."

"No worries, and something something great minds, great minds. That's exactly what I was going to say."

"I bet they were at the dig together," said Blane. "And I'll also say, Carly, you're amazing, something something great minds—and big brains." He winked and held up his hand to high-five me.

I looked at Blane, grinning as I returned the high-five. I loved when he winked at me. "Thank you. Also, how is it that you can read and listen at the same time? You were completely engrossed in Dr. Hasserin's book."

"I can multitask—it's my superpower." Blane grinned and started chuckling as he added, "It's probably my only superpower, but at least it's a good one."

"It is a good one. I wonder what type of superpower we would need to find out whether Dr. Wengaro was at the dig?"

"Easy," said Lydia. "It's called a telephone."

Lydia opened one of her desk drawers and took out a notebook with Post-its stuffed on every page. "Allister's number is in here, somewhere."

After a few minutes of flipping pages and muttering about how she wished she had a better system for saving contact information, she looked up, triumphant in her quest to find Dr. Leith's number. She moved a few stacks of papers, binders, and manila folders out of the way to reveal her office phone.

"Hope he picks up," she said as she dialed.

The phone rang to voice mail.

"We'll try again later," Lydia said. "England is five hours ahead of us."

"When's later?" I asked.

She reached for her planner. "Darn it, I'm swamped this week. I really need to not sign up to chair all these conferences. How's next Monday at one o'clock?"

IX

After dinner, Lara and I hung out in our common room. I was catching up on my email, and Lara was watching TV as she painted her nails.

"How's Jesse?" I teased. "Haven't heard you talk about him lately!"

"Who? Oh Jesse. No, yeah that fizzled out. I lost interest, I guess. But I met this new guy. Mark is in my English class. He's really hot—and he's on the varsity water polo team, even though he's a sophomore."

"Ooh, that's awesome!"

"How's your archaeologist man?"

I blushed. "He's not my man!" I said, giggling, trying to hide my face with my hands so Lara wouldn't see how red it had become. "We're hanging out. We're study buddies. He thinks I'm smart, that's all."

"Uhh, you've been hanging out—a lot!" Lara looked at her manicured fingers. "Study buddies? Since when are study buddies practically inseparable? And look at you, you can't even think about him without turning red, blushing, and getting nervous. It's cute. I think someone is crushing—and crushing hard!"

As usual, Lara was spot on with her assessment of boys—and how I felt about Blane.

"Okay, so I like him," I admitted. "And he does hold my hand. But he hasn't asked me *out* out, like to be his girlfriend out.

We had that one dinner at Winnie B.'s, and we're working on our midterm together, and I don't even know if he likes me, like you know, *likes me*, too."

"Carly, you've been studying together, working together, and he's showing you some PDA. And he thinks you're the brainiest brainiac at Nassauton. He likes you back. Guys don't hang out with girls that they're not interested in. He'll make a move, soon. I feel it."

I smiled. I hoped Lara was right.

††

It poured the whole rest of the week. The smell of damp leaves and wet soil lingered in the air. By the time Friday rolled around, Blane and I needed a break from campus. We, like everyone else, had the same idea for a rainy Friday night in our small town. We decided to see the new release at the Gardenia Theatre and head to dinner afterward.

The theater was on our town's main street, not too far from campus. Blane met me at my dorm room with an umbrella, and we walked to the theater together. My jeans were safely tucked into my rain boots, whose insulated lining I was thankful for in the cold and rainy weather. I'd worn one of my favorite raincoats and had taken extra care to zip it up so my Henge Piece pendant wouldn't get wet under my shirt. Blane linked arms with me as I huddled under his umbrella. Even though it was raining, I didn't mind the walk. I especially didn't mind the walk when my arm was linked with Blane's.

Luckily, we managed to find two seats together in the back row. "Want popcorn or anything?"

"I'm good, thank you!"

Blane grinned. "Only trying to do the gentlemanly thing."

"I know." I smiled. "But I don't want to ruin dinner afterward."

"Speaking of, where do you want to go?"

"How about the new brick-oven pizza place across from Winnie B.'s?"

"Sounds great to me."

The lights dimmed as the pre-movie commercials started. When Blane put his arm around my shoulder, I didn't object.

††

By the time the movie ended, the rain had stopped. We walked to the new pizza place, Pi's, carefully side-stepping the puddles on the sidewalk. Pi's was one of the only restaurants in town to be in a basement, which gave it a snug ambiance in the cooler, damp weather. Blane opened the door and gestured me in. We walked down the stairs to the restaurant. Pi's was packed, but within fifteen minutes, we got two stools at the end of the bar.

"This is so cool," Blane said as he looked at the big chalkboard menu behind the bar. Under the heading MAKE YOUR OWN PI, half the board had items ranging from avocado to eggs, beets to bacon. "Do you want to make our own pizza?"

"Let's do it! What toppings do you want?"

"How about mozzarella, tomatoes, grilled chicken, basil, and arugula, with a drizzle of olive oil?"

"Sounds delicious, but let's make sure they have dairy-free mozzarella!" I twirled my loose curl and looked around the bar. "If not, we could do without it." More and more people were packing around the bar, eager to order their drinks and food. We had gotten there at the best time.

"Carly, I have another question I'd like to ask you." Blane turned and looked me right in the eyes, swiveling his barstool toward me. His hazel eyes had streaks of gold, and his pupils were the biggest I'd ever seen them.

"Yes?"

"I don't really know how else to say this, so I'll start talking and see what comes out." He put his hand on my knee. Instantly, I felt a rush of emotion like I'd never felt before. It was as though the warmest wave of energy had cascaded over me, starting at his hand and radiating through my body. "We've been hanging out a lot since the beginning of the year. We work well together—*really* well—and we're a really good team. I really like you. I was wondering . . . how about we officially become boyfriend and girlfriend?"

I grinned. I could feel my cheeks burning as my face turned bright red—redder than the tomato sauce that would be covering our pizza. I put my hand on top of his.

"I'd love that," I replied.

Blane winked at me. "Good, I was hoping you'd be down for that." He put his arm around my shoulder and kissed my forehead. I grinned and grabbed his hand as we waited for our pizza.

††

Monday morning came in no time at all. After I finished lunch, I went to Lydia's office. She was there, on the phone, but motioned for me to come in and close the door behind me. Blane wanted to come, but he hadn't finished his economics problem set and it was due that evening.

I sank into the sofa. As I waited for Lydia to finish her call, I looked at the sunlight streaming in through her windows. The windows were beautifully designed, with attention given to the smallest detail of the sill and the glass panes. How many generations of scholars and researchers had sat in Lydia's office before me?

"Sorry about that," Lydia said. "We're coordinating last-minute logistics and travel for the conferences. I really need to learn to say no to being chair, but I'm excited for this conference. One of the sessions I'm moderating has emerging archaeologists presenting their research on Ancient Greece. It's going to be a busy week." She looked at my feet. "Another pair of Lyle's shoes?"

I nodded. I was wearing my moccasins. "Oh, that's very cool, I'm sure you're excited."

"Yes, we owe it to the younger generation to train them, teach them, pass the torch to them, then move out of the way. Or else the field suffers, stagnating from artifacts of the past taking up space. Literally—old artifacts." She laughed as she pointed at herself. "The field needs new life. That's what keeps it interesting. Well, shall we?"

I grabbed my journal and pencil and walked to Lydia's desk. She dialed Dr. Leith's number and put the phone on speaker.

After a few rings, a man's voice picked up. "Hullo?"

"Allister?"

"Yes. Who is this?"

"Allister, it's Lydia."

"Lydia? Lydia who?"

"Lydia Kells."

"Oh, my goodness, Lydia, how do you do? Been a long time—too long."

"I'm okay. It has been a while. I'm sorry, I should have called sooner. The semester has been busy and I'm chairing all these conferences—"

"There's your problem there." Allister chuckled. "Conference chair? I gave up those requests years ago, got hours of my life back."

"Well, you know I've never been as quick on the uptake as you. You're miles ahead of me in offloading administrative requests to your former students."

I heard Dr. Leith laughing. I could tell they had a good working relationship and respected each other.

"Do you have a few minutes to chat?"

"I'm in middle of dinner with Beth. Can we talk tomorrow?"

"It's important. I think we might have a murder on our hands."

I was surprised Lydia blurted that out. Technically we still didn't know if it was a murder.

"A murder? Give me a moment. Let me excuse myself." There was a pause on the other end of the line. "Right, Lydia, here I am. What's going on?"

"Remember Sidney Hasserin?" Lydia's voice trailed off.

"Yes, of course. Brilliant guy. Wait, did he murder someone?"

"No, no, Sid died—we think he was murdered."

Dr. Leith gasped audibly. "What? How? Sid? Are you sure you have the right—"

"Yes."

"Sid was so young! Oh I'm absolutely gutted."

"I know, believe me, I know."

"When?"

"A few months ago."

"A few months ago? Why didn't you call me then?"

"Because we didn't realize there was more to his death. But now we have some interesting speculations, maybe not evidence yet, but speculations. And questions."

As Lydia caught Allister up, his surprised exclamations punctuated her monologue. I started taking notes in my journal.

"So, what do you think happened?" Dr. Leith finally asked.

"I think someone murdered him because they knew what he discovered—and didn't want him to share it. He might have even discovered the Grail."

"Unbelievable! Who would do such a thing?"

"I think the Knights of the Dagger—the same ones from Lyle's and my notes. We need proof it's the Grail, and if our theory is true, then we're in the middle of a case as old as history itself."

"You're kidding."

"Nope—and one more thing. I'd like to introduce you to my new partner." Lydia motioned for me to say hi. A rush of pride came over me, and I blushed as I looked up from my journal. "Allister, meet Carlyle Stuart."

As soon as Lydia introduced me to Dr. Leith, I got very nervous. *The Dr. Allister Leith!* I clutched my pendant through my T-shirt. *Be brave.*

"Hi Dr. Leith, it's a pleasure to talk to you."

"Carly is Lyle's—Lyle Ainsley's—granddaughter. She's a freshman here, taking my class. It's barely been two months, but Carly is filling Lyle's shoes and following in her footsteps as a brilliant archaeologist."

I beamed, swelling even more with pride. There was nothing more I wanted to do than to fill Gran's shoes. Lydia had said I was—and to none other than the world's expert on the Grail.

"Hi Carly, pleasure to meet you. I know it's been a few years, but I was so sorry to have heard Lyle passed away. She was a dear friend—she'd call me up and we could talk about anything. Sharp as a tack, real difficult to see her cope after her brain injury. Lyle was truly something else—an inspiration to us all. Anyway, tell me Lydia's class is not one of the greatest adventures you've been on." Dr. Leith's tone conveyed his great admiration for Lydia.

"It is." I smiled, looking at Lydia.

"Allister, Carly has Lyle's half of the Henge Piece."

Dr. Leith's tone went from admiration to caution. "What? She does? Oh Carly, you should be very careful! They could be after you too!"

"She knows. I told her. We have a question for you, about one of your former students. Remember Kenneth Wengaro?"

"Oh yes, very hard worker. Kind of obsessive about his research. Poured his heart and soul into his work. He finished his PhD three years ago or so. Never heard from him after he defended. I have no clue what he's up to now. But funny you should ask. He was Sid's friend."

"Sid's friend?"

Lydia and I looked at each other in surprise. Dr. Leith had confirmed my theory about Dr. Hasserin and Dr. Wengaro.

"Yes, they were my students at the same time—co-published a lot of research on the Grail, if I'm recalling correctly. They were both fascinated by it. They both desperately wanted to find it—and passionately pursued the evidence for its existence. They believed they could find it."

I had been twirling my curl with my pencil as I listened. As soon as Dr. Leith mentioned the Grail, I stopped and started jotting down notes.

"Allister, what evidence? The Grail doesn't exist. You and I both know how I feel about that."

"Lydia, it's not about what you feel, it's about the evidence—"

"There is none. There is no evidence."

"That's simply not true. Sid and Kenneth were working on that paper—they had a lot of evidence."

My ears perked up. *This must be the paper on the Grail that was never published.*

Dr. Leith continued. "There is some evidence that points to the Grail's existence. Sid and Kenneth were researching its history. They came up with some fascinating evidence. And we are learning more ever—"

"Did they ever share that evidence with you?" I asked, interrupting Dr. Leith.

"No—"

"Because they never published the paper. They never completed it," added Lydia.

"How do you know?"

"Because Carly and I can't find it. The Grail has provided an excuse for certain humans to do horrific things to their fellow humans. Allister, sometimes I think you are chasing this dream, too, but that is how I feel."

"And you're entitled to feel any way you want, but at least consider the evidence. What was the question you wanted to ask me about Kenneth? We got sidetracked by the Grail."

I jumped into the conversation. "Dr. Leith, was Kenneth with you and Sid at the Amesbury dig?"

"Absolutely. He and Sid went everywhere together. They worked together and went to the pub together. They were constantly chatting about something or sketching their next research proposal. Both so young, so enthusiastic, so full of energy." Dr. Leith chuckled. "They were inseparable. It got annoying sometimes, but it sure made it easy to find them when you needed them. If you saw one, the other wasn't too far away. In fact, Lydia, remember when Lyle tripped and fell? Remember who was the first to run and help her?"

"No."

"Kenneth. And he immediately called for Sid. I was so proud of them that day, my two PhD candidates, dropping everything and helping Lyle. They did the right thing."

"Dr. Wengaro was the first to find Lyle?" I held my pencil at the ready, prepared to write down Dr. Leith's response.

"Yes."

Not missing a beat as I scribbled, I asked another question. "Dr. Leith, was Kenneth close enough that he saw the Henge Piece break?"

"Oh, now that I couldn't say. Why?"

"Because maybe he saw the missing ruby?"

"I really couldn't tell you. He's never mentioned it to me. As far as I know, that ruby is lost to time. Could be anywhere by now."

"Hmm," said Lydia as she jotted down her own notes. "The ruby might be lost to time, but you'll never believe that we recently hired Kenneth to take Sid's place on staff here."

"Kenneth surfaced? Well! I'm happy to hear it. Brilliant hire! You've got one of the best minds in the field at Nassauton."

"I hope so. His CV is certainly impressive."

There was a pause on the other end of the line. "I have to go. Beth is calling me—dinner's getting cold. Great chatting with you. Hopefully we will talk again soon. And Carly, great to meet you!"

After Lydia and I hung up, we reviewed our notes.

"Well, these are all interesting developments, which give us a lot to work with—a lot more than, admittedly, I thought we'd have."

I nodded excitedly.

"But as much as I want to focus on this now, I do have to prepare for my meeting with Daniel. How about we both do some thinking, and you can text me if you need to?" She scribbled her number on a blank page and tore it out of her journal.

"That sounds great, Lydia. I can get to Rockfire tonight and tomorrow—and hopefully I'll find something." I grabbed my satchel from the sofa.

"I look forward to tackling this case with you."

I grinned. "I'm excited too!"

I opened Dr. Kells' office door—and immediately jumped back upon seeing a man right outside it.

"Dr. Wengaro, you scared me!"

"Are you okay, Carly?" asked Lydia.

"Yes. Sorry, I got startled. Dr. Wengaro was about to knock on your door." I stepped back as Dr. Wengaro took a few steps into Dr. Kells' office. He was wearing a tweed blazer with hunter-green stripes and brown suede elbow patches. His ponytail was messily swept behind his left shoulder. His face was flushed as he gazed around Lydia's office, from her sofa to her desk, to her Stonehenge replica, to her books.

"Hi Lydia, I had a question for you about my seminar. Nice Stonehenge replica, by the way. And is that a model of the Tower of Babel?" Dr. Wengaro looked at a ziggurat on the top of one of Lydia's bookshelves. "Lots of replicas around your office. Cool."

Lydia arranged her bun, making sure no hair was out of place, and got out of her chair. She walked to the door.

"Kenneth, hi, yes, thank you. Yes, it is. What's your question? I gave you the rubric for the midterm paper. Everything else should have been covered in your orientation. Was it not?"

I felt my pulse race. Had Dr. Wengaro heard any of our conversation with Dr. Leith? The door had been closed, after all. I stared at the floor, as if by doing so, I'd be less anxious.

"No, it's not about the rubric. Do I have to cover all the material Sidney covered? What's your advice for restructuring the lessons given the timing?"

"I don't know. I'm sorry, now is not a good time. I have to prepare for a meeting. But you're the professor. You have full authority to decide how you want to handle the pacing. Maybe let students work in teams and do their own project. That way you don't have to go as linearly through the syllabus, and students can research different topics at the same time?"

"Thank you. That's an interesting idea. I'll think about it. Have a good day."

I followed Dr. Wengaro out of Dr. Kells' office. He held the door for me as we exited. We headed in the same direction, his pace a little faster than mine. We'd walked a few steps when his phone rang. My heart raced as I overheard the few sentences he said before he changed direction and headed a different way. "Look, I've told you a million times, the books on his desk didn't yield anything . . . Yes. But I don't have the other pieces. I'm sure she knows where they are—or has them herself."

I stopped dead in the middle of the walkway. Anxiety washed over me. I ran back to Lydia's office. She was packing up her satchel and heading out the door.

"Carly? Is everything okay? I'm about to leave for my meeting."

"I overheard Dr. Wengaro on the phone. He said something about the 'books on his desk' not yielding anything and that he was sure 'she' had the other pieces. He has got to be talking about the books on Dr. Hasserin's desk and the Henge Piece. Please be careful—he's on to you!"

"Lydia, you coming to our meeting?" Dr. Pritzmord ducked his head into Lydia's office. "Hi there Carly. How's it going?"

"Yep, was on my way." Lydia pointed at her satchel.

"Good, Dr. Pritzmord, thanks." *How does Dr. Pritzmord know my name?* It was a small department, but I didn't think the dean would know freshmen by name.

"See you in a minute, then." Dr. Pritzmord left Lydia's office and walked down the hallway.

"How do you know any of that is about Dr. Hasserin or me?" Lydia asked.

"I don't know. But, who else would have 'books on his desk' and 'the other pieces'?"

Dr. Kells took her journal out and wrote down what I'd told her. I wrote what I'd overheard too.

"You need to be extra careful from now on," I said as Lydia stepped out of her office and locked her door.

"We both have to be, Carly. We both have to be."

††

After dinner, Blane and I headed to the Research Room to work on our midterm project. He grabbed my hand as we walked across campus.

"You are truly something else. You amaze me. You're tackling these tough mysteries and working with a world-renowned professor."

I squeezed Blane's hand. I loved when he complimented my work ethic. I valued that he wasn't threatened by my collaboration with Lydia. I also considered him my teammate too. "Thank you, I'm lucky because I also have an awesome boyfriend who supports me, tackling these adventures with me."

Blane winked at me. I grinned. We neared one of Nassauton's prettiest buildings, Greenlor Hall. Greenlor was one building over from Rockfire. Constructed out of brownstone in the late 1800s, it was shaped like a rotunda, attached to a building with an open-air courtyard in the middle.

During the day, students lounged in the courtyard, sitting at tables or benches. But the best part about Greenlor was its stained-glass windows. On clear days, the sunlight streaming through the windows caught the stained-glass patterns and lit up the building's lobby with patches of rich reds and blues. In the evenings, when most students were hunkered down studying and hardly any were outside, the lights from the hallways inside shined through the stained-glass windows, backlighting them with a romantic glow in the darkness of the night sky.

"It's so beautiful at night," I said as we walked through the courtyard. "It's like the light is pouring through the windows, from the inside out."

As we approached the other side of the courtyard, Blane paused mid-stride, wrapped his arm around my waist, and kissed me on my lips.

Everything around me stopped. I surrendered my senses to returning his kiss. Nothing else mattered. My mind went blank as a surge of emotion pulsed from my head to my toes. All my anxiety over the Henge Piece, Dr. Hasserin, and Dr. Wengaro—and the danger that certainly was ahead of us—disappeared.

I didn't know how many minutes passed, but, standing in the courtyard in Blane's embrace, I had completely lost track of time.

Of all my adventures at Nassauton, Blane's and mine was one of the most unexpected. It was also turning out to be one of my favorites.

X

Over the next three weeks, our quest for the Grail and focus on Dr. Hasserin took a backseat to my workload. Balancing the case and schoolwork, and trying to spend quality time with Blane, was becoming difficult. I didn't even have time to call my mom and catch up. I tried to text her a few school-related updates every day, but sometimes it would be days before I replied to her. She seemed to be doing well with her work too.

I knew if I kept directing her focus to what I was learning at Nassauton, she was less likely to ask about the Henge Piece mystery. It wasn't that I was lying to her, but I certainly wasn't going to clue her in to the whole truth. She didn't need to know the whole truth. What she didn't know couldn't hurt her, and by keeping her in the dark, I could pursue the case more. And if I did everything my way, she'd never find out until afterward—when she'd have no choice but to be proud of me for getting the Grail.

The workload had increased out of nowhere. Even though I was upset about not prioritizing our case, I was proud that with our discipline, Blane and I had finished our midterm project ahead of schedule. Lydia told us she would invite some of her colleagues to listen to and provide feedback on our midterms, so it felt like we were at a conference, giving a real lecture to a formal audience. Blane and I were excited, and I wanted to do a good job—not only for the sake of the project, but also to get the most out of the experience of presenting in a "real-world" setting.

No matter how much work we had, Blane and I prioritized date night every week. This helped break up the endless cycle of assignments and papers. We'd explore a new restaurant, see a show or movie, or attend a concert or arch sing. Some of my favorite dates were when we went to The Full Scoop, a little cupcake and artisan ice cream shop, with delicious sorbet and vegan ice cream, and the most amazing mini cupcakes.

Nassauton had no shortage of student-run a cappella groups, each with their own style and genre—and preferred archway for arch sings. Students would pack in the archway and listen as their friends showed off their skills singing, beatboxing, and hitting close harmonies and high notes. Each arch sing always ended with the group and the audience singing our school song. I felt a buzz as the notes resonated in the archways in rich, round tones.

Sometimes Lara, who had long since ditched Mark, would join us with her new boyfriend, Paul. She had met Paul, who lived off campus, at a party and was never around our room that much anymore. I missed our girl time, since I felt like I'd lost a friend with whom I could share anything—especially my relationship and fashion questions. Without Lara's advice, I decided my default answer to any question I had about Blane, or makeup, or outfits, was to be myself and see how it went. This was one of the things that made me the most nervous. *What if Blane thinks I'm boring, or he really doesn't like me after he realizes how much of an archaeological nerd I am?*

Our double dates were the only times I'd see Lara. The four of us took advantage of the crisp fall weather, spending as much time outside as we could before it got too cold. The leaves changing colors from greens to reds, golds, browns, and oranges reminded us the earth was constantly cycling through seasons.

One of the highlights of the season was Homecoming, which was a big event for the whole town. Everyone got into the football spirit, hosting tailgates and meetups around the stadium. Winnie B.'s had a tent, serving everything from soup to sliders to appetizers and apple pie. Nassauton's marching band paraded through campus forty-five minutes before kickoff, playing all of our college songs as they marched to the football field.

If we beat our rival football team, we would celebrate in two ways. The first tradition was that all the freshmen would rent out Winnie B.'s on Homecoming night and set it up like a casino, with raffles and carnival games. The prizes were gift cards to restaurants, school store credit, free meals, tickets to shows, and more.

The second tradition was that the following weekend, we'd have a bonfire, complete with s'mores and hot apple cider. The seniors and juniors would line up behind tables and serve all the freshmen and sophomores. It was a great bonding experience for the whole college.

"You ready, Carly? Here comes the band!"

"Here we go!" I was wearing jeans and a letter sweater in our school colors and had done my hair in braids with ribbons. The big, silver studs on Gran's black leather ankle boots added a bit of edginess to my otherwise preppy outfit.

"Love your shoes, gorgeous—you look like a rockstar!" Blane kissed me.

I blushed as I kissed him back. "Look who is talking, handsome!" I grabbed his hand as we ran out the door to meet the band and parade with them down to the football field.

When we got there, I was swept up in the excitement of students, faculty, families, and alumni cheering from the stadium. Even though I didn't understand football, I could follow the basics of the game. Our high school football games were nothing like this. This was the college football experience that everybody talked about.

After the game, Lara, Paul, Blane, and I—along with our entire freshmen class—went to Winnie B.'s to celebrate our win. It felt good to get out of the Research Room for the evening. The music was blaring, and appetizer stations had been set up across the whole dining room. Once we got our tickets, Blane held my hand tightly as he led us past the buffet tables to the games. We headed to the roulette wheel and gave the operator two tickets.

"You first!" I kissed Blane as he stepped up to the wheel. He spun it, and it landed on 20% OFF WINNIE B.'S. "Sweet!" he said. "I know where we're going for date night next weekend!"

I high-fived Blane as he kissed me.

It was my turn to spin the wheel.

"WILD CARD!" The operator applauded and said, "You get to pull one of these envelopes out of the box!"

"Wooo, Carly, look at you!"

I reached into the box and pulled out the first envelope my fingers touched.

"Go on, open it!" the operator cheered.

I pulled out two coupons, redeemable for two front-row seats to a Broadway show.

"OH MY GOSH! My bucket list!" I screamed in elation as I repeated Blane's words back to him. "I know where we're going for date night next weekend!"

Blane hugged me as I kissed him. "That is so amazing!" He released the hug, leaving his arm around my shoulder.

I couldn't believe it. I'd always wanted to see a Broadway show from the front row, but the tickets were way too expensive.

"But we'll miss the bonfire if we go next weekend," Blane said. "Let's save the coupons—they don't expire for a while!"

I nodded. Blane had a great point. "Good thinking! We'll do Winnie B.'s and the bonfire next weekend." I smiled, uncurling Blane's arm and grabbing his hand. "For now, let's keep working our luck at the other tables. The night is ours!"

††

The bonfire roared as its fire warmed up the chilly night. It was in a big pit in the middle of one of our quads, which had long tables for the s'mores, and hot apple cider set up along its sides.

The gargoyles on the buildings peered down on the table and the bonfire. They seemed to celebrate our football team's win with us. For one evening, our whole campus took a break from studying and celebrated our football team. Blane and I had another reason to celebrate. We were especially proud of our A+ on our midterm project for Lydia. Even Dr. Pritzmord said we had pieced together the past like seasoned partners in the field.

For the s'mores, Nassauton bought the chocolate from a family-owned shop, which had been handmaking their chocolate in town for over two hundred years. The last time I had a s'more was with my dad a few months before he passed away. We had spent the day hiking and had come home for dinner and s'mores. We made them over the firepit in our backyard. Mom, Dad, and I sat around the pit on a cool summer's night, our faces glowing in the fire as it roared up into the pitch-black night sky, its darkness punctuated by little diamonds in the distance.

††

"Those stars have been sparkling for thousands of years," my dad said. "And yet, they are still sparkling today, on this night, for us."

"How is that possible, Dad? What makes them shine like that?"

The sparks from the fire leaped up into the night with such energy, as if to show gravity it was powerless against them. My dad had brought a blanket for me. He got out of his chair and wrapped it around my shoulders. As he sat down, he replied to my question.

"Well, the stars are complex celestial bodies. They have been here since the creation of the universe; they've seen history before we realize it's even been written. They store the secrets of space. And every now and then, they let us listen in for a secret or two. Sometimes, they flat out disappear, taking their secrets with them. But as much as we know about the stars, we don't know all that much. We have a lot—a whole lot—of evidence, but we don't have all the answers. We have little puzzle pieces, but we can't see how each piece fits together to make the whole puzzle. The evidence is a foundation, which supports our quest for answers. Quest and questions—both have the same root prefix."

"A quest." I grinned as I looked up at the stars. The stars, and the vastness of the night sky, had always amazed me. Whenever I looked at the stars, I always felt that I was on the underside of a black velvet blanket, seeing pinpricks of light shining through from the other side. I wondered what the other side looked like—and how bright it would be.

I'd always felt connected to the stars, especially because of the birthmark on my back. As a child, I tried to hide it every chance I could. But since the day my dad referred to it as my "star map"—since it looked like a constellation of stars in the shape of an infinity sign—I considered it one of my most unique traits. It connected me to the stars.

"An adventure," I said without lowering my gaze.

"That's right. No matter where our journeys on this side of Heaven take us, we will never know it all. So, we keep seeking—keep questioning—because questions get us closer to the truth."

I liked how my dad acknowledged evidence as foundational to our quest. As a physical chemist, my dad used mathematical computations, examined how chemical reactions worked, and analyzed what their properties revealed. In studying how matter behaved at the molecular and atomic level, he gained a unique ability to bridge the divide between science and faith. To him, the laws of science and the laws of God were one and the same—and they were evidence for the Creator.

My dad grabbed two graham crackers and two marshmallows and placed them on a paper plate. He broke off two pieces of chocolate from the bar on the table next to him.

"How many marshmallows do you want?"

"Three."

The secret to the perfect s'more was the ratio. Two graham

crackers, two pieces of chocolate, and three marshmallows. Most people went with one or two, but with three, you could slide off the burnt bits and have the perfect amount of marshmallow left.

"You got it, sweetheart," he said, grabbing one more.

My dad slid the marshmallows onto his stick and stuck it over the firepit.

"How do questions get us closer to the truth?"

"The day we stop asking questions is the day we think we know it all. When we think we know it all, we convince ourselves that we are right. We convince ourselves we see—and know—the whole puzzle, when we only have a few pieces. Our arrogance, rather than our questions, becomes our truth."

"I don't get it, Dad." I looked at the fire. The wood burned, leaving white ashes at the bottom of the firepit.

"Well, like my cancer. What piece of what puzzle is that? I can't tell you what it is or why I got it—only that it was the piece I received. I did everything you were supposed to do in trying to be healthy. And cancer still came for me."

He pulled the stick out of the fire and inspected the marshmallows. "Almost there; we need a few more minutes."

He stuck the stick back in the fire, rotating it to evenly distribute the heat. "We are constantly subjected to forces beyond what we can see or rationalize. It's like what we discussed on our hike. If we can't see it, does that mean we can't measure it? Does it mean it doesn't exist?"

"How *do* we measure what we can't see, Dad?"

"Well, we would need a different tool, that's for sure. But if we don't know what we're looking for, how can I know what tool to use? That's something the *Eternae* folks kept telling me. They wanted to use every available tool to measure my cancer. They said they'd never seen one with such distinctive biomarkers as mine. It metastasized so fast into cells I didn't even know were in my body. The cancer found these cells before I even knew they existed—and these cells were part of me all along."

My dad pulled the stick out again. He inspected the marshmallows. "Perfect." He nodded as he placed the stick in between his knees. He picked up the graham crackers and chocolate to assemble the s'more, with the precision of a scientist assembling her or his lab equipment. Once a physical chemist, always a physical chemist, they said—and they were right. The sparks flew up from the fire into the sky, disappearing long before they came close to the stars.

He continued. "It's like the stars. We see them every night, and we want to use every tool we have to understand them. In understanding the stars, we learn more about ourselves. Our purpose, our origin. We see we have a history that is bigger than us—and a future that is always unfolding. We embark on a path of self-discovery that forces us to put the stars' stories and our stories side by side. There's a universally inspiring, humbling beauty in that."

I gazed at the fire, then at my dad. I loved picturing my story and the story of the stars side by side. It made me feel like I could reach over and touch the stars.

"We can't help but wonder how the stars came into existence, hung so perfectly and purposefully as constellations in the cosmos. How did I come into existence? How did our world come into existence? Why? What was it like at the beginning? Is there something more out there—a deeper truth about our origin and about us?" my dad said. "The more questions we ask, the more patterns we notice, the more we realize we don't know it all. So, we start asking more questions."

We both looked up at the stars.

"So, the stars remind us to ask questions, because the truth exists, even if we can't measure, understand, or explain it, even if it's in the distance, far, far away from us?"

"Yes, Carlyle. And one day, we'll not only see the stars, but we'll also be among them—forever."

My dad handed me a perfectly toasted s'more.

††

"Hey Carly, what secrets are the stars telling you?"

Blane took his coat off and wrapped it around my shoulders. He stood behind me and pulled me in for a hug. "I was gonna suggest we get in line for s'mores, but you were so intently looking at the stars, I knew something was going through that big brain of yours."

"Those stars have been sparkling for thousands of years," I said. "And yet, they are still sparkling today, on this night, for us."

I smiled at the memory of my dad's and my conversation. *The truth exists, even if we can't measure, understand, or explain it.* I wondered how the Henge Piece, and its alignment with Stonehenge and the missing ruby, could help us find what we couldn't see. What secrets of Stonehenge did the dagger point to?

I squeezed Blane's hand. "To the s'mores?"

††

Lydia and I were behind on the Henge Piece mystery and Dr. Hasserin's case. With no evidence and no Grail paper, we didn't have a case—only theories. Dr. Wengaro hadn't done anything suspicious, and Lydia and I hadn't had time to meet. With our workload, there was little we could do about it. Midterms had to take priority. If my grades dropped, I'd be on academic probation.

One of my hardest midterms was for Grail Times. Dr. Wengaro expected us to memorize every Arthurian legend—every plot, character, battle, and detail—that we'd learned. I loved studying King Arthur and his court and wondered what it would have been like to be there, in knight regalia as part of the Round Table, or a courtly robe as a beautiful maiden. But I was overwhelmed by the amount of information. Dr. Wengaro hadn't taken Lydia's advice to let us do our own research projects. Instead, he'd lectured us and posted slides to our course page. I didn't learn that way and was struggling to keep all the legends straight.

British legends. Welsh legends. German. French. The Lancelot–Grail cycles. Excalibur and how Arthur became king. The Knights of the Round Table. Sir Gawain—one of the greatest knights and closest companions of Arthur. Sir Kay—one of the knights with superhuman abilities. He could go nine days and nights without breathing or sleeping and could radiate heat from his hands. Sir Percival—the original hero in the Grail quests. Sir Galahad—the only knight who was pure enough to get the Grail.

Each knight had their own series of quests—quests through which they proved themselves to be a knight of the Round Table. We had to know all of them. Geoffrey of Monmouth's twelfth-century *Historia Regum Britanniae*. Sir Thomas Malory's fifteenth-century *Le Morte d'Arthur*. And then there were all the fairies, enchantresses, and women involved in the Arthurian Court. Guinevere. Morgan le Fay. The Lady of the Lake. Elaine. Isolde. And on and on and on! I was terrified I'd blank and forget a detail on the midterm.

To help me study, I'd bought a deck of cards with the knights, fairies, enchantresses, and women of King Arthur's Court. It was much easier to look at the person's picture on the face of the card, then link the details on the back to that picture. Sir Kay had light around his palms to indicate his superpower of heat. That helped me remember his superhuman ability, which was described in detail on the back.

Sir Gawain was drawn riding Gringolet, his trusted warhorse, and had several swords, to highlight his swordsmanship and prowess as a warrior. Morgan le Fay's card had a beautiful woman with piercing green eyes and long, flowing black hair in what looked like a laboratory. She was wearing a gold, silver, and aquamarine necklace. Her right hand rested on a table that had a book and a mortar and pestle, and featured a gold, silver, and aquamarine ring. I loved how the illustrator had drawn each person's traits into the picture. The deck had helped me learn the characters in King Arthur's court. *What would it be like to meet each of them?* I wondered.

By the time midterms finished, I barely had any energy for Semi-Formals. Still, I didn't want to let Blane, Paul, and Lara down, because we planned to go together.

"What are you wearing?" Lara asked as we got ready in our dorm room.

"A black cocktail dress and my Atlas heels. And I'm going to curl my hair!"

I was delighted Lara and I could have some girl time as we got ready.

"You'll look beautiful! Should I wear the sparkling red bandage dress or long purple gown?" Lara held up two dresses and carefully studied them under the light of our common room.

"Red!" I smiled. Lara approved of my outfit—and she was asking me for fashion advice.

"Red it is." She disappeared into her room.

By the time she emerged, I'd placed my Henge Piece pendant in its Tupperware, hiding it in my sock drawer, and finished curling my hair. Lara looked incredible. She'd accentuated her blue eyes with black mascara and smoky eyeshadow. She'd braided her hair. She complemented her dress with a black velvet choker with a big, brilliant ruby in it.

"You look amazing! I love your necklace."

Lara's ruby reminded me of the Henge Piece's missing ruby. I sighed. Midterms, and my workload, had defeated me. I had started the semester prepared for anything. Now, I doubted how much I could handle. I had to keep my grades high, but that came at the expense of our case. I was eager to use Thanksgiving break as uninterrupted time to explore our theories. I'd checked out a bunch of Dr. Hasserin's books and needed to figure out if Dr.

Hasserin had discovered whether the Grail was at Stonehenge. Without that answer, we couldn't move forward.

"Aww, thank you! I'm so excited. I hope Paul likes my outfit."

"I'm sure he will!"

"And you look so pretty yourself. I love how you curled your hair in all those little curls. And your makeup is perfect. You must have had a great teacher." She chuckled.

I smiled. I was getting better at wearing makeup and dressing up.

"Blane's gonna love your look. You've come such a long way since we got you ready for your first date. Remember how nervous you were?"

I grinned. My first date with Blane seemed like ages ago.

"Knock knock."

I heard Blane's voice in the hallway as he and Paul knocked. Lara and I grabbed our keys and opened our door. We stepped out into the hallway to greet our boyfriends. Blane gave me a big hug and kiss.

"You look amazing." He smiled.

"Speaking of amazing, you make that suit look like a million dollars." I teetered back so I could get a full look at Blane's suit and tie. My Atlas heels clacked on our hallway floor.

"Love those heels," Blane said as he linked my arm and his. "Well, shall we?"

"We shall!" Lara and Paul grinned in the middle of the hallway as they waited for me to close our dorm room door.

I locked it, then placed the key in my purse.

"See, our key is safe right here. No way we will be locked out."

Lara giggled. "Our key is safe with you!" She linked arms with Paul.

The four of us headed down the hallway and out of our building to dance the night away.

XI

As soon as I came home for Thanksgiving break, I'd set up shop in my childhood room, placing Dr. Hasserin's books on my desk. I felt like I'd gone back in time. All my high school posters and pictures—pictures of my sports teams, of Gran and me, of my mom, dad, and me—were on my walls.

I spent the first week reading, as my mom worked. I'd finished two books and had one more to go. In the evenings, Mom and I would chit-chat over dinner. I told her about my classes, dates with Blane, and Dr. Wengaro—leaving out details about the Henge Piece mystery and Dr. Hasserin's murder.

The day before Thanksgiving was a slow day at work for Mom. She ended early so we could cook dinner. We'd made baked chicken casserole with herbs. Mom had brought out special honey to drizzle on top. I finished chewing a bite of the chicken. The honey had a hint of lavender in it and complemented the herbs in the casserole. I looked at the jar, noticing it said PRODUCT OF FRANCE on the label.

"Where'd you get this honey? It's delicious." I cut another slice of chicken and put it on my plate.

"Oh! J. Carmichael got it for me. He was in France a few weeks ago and sent it as a surprise."

"J. Carmichael! Now that's a name I haven't heard since Gran's funeral. How is he?"

"He's good, working, traveling. He's here in town every now and then. He's very busy with work."

"What does he do again?"

"I couldn't tell you the details. I know he's in the drug testing and regulatory field. He speaks five languages, and he's always talking about new drug developments and regulations. He has stories of researchers who want him to approve their drugs or plants with medicinal properties they discover. He travels around the world to these labs, auditing them, making sure their procedures and processes are compliant, making sure the medicines aren't tested on animals and are safe for humans."

"That is so cool! I had no idea. He used to visit Gran. He was one of her closest friends."

"Yep. He's become one of my closest friends these last few years too. He always makes it a point to check in on me when he's in town. I'd have invited him for Thanksgiving, but I think he's in Switzerland. He'll be happy to hear you liked the honey."

"Switzerland?" I asked. "That must be nice. Spend your holidays wherever you want, jetting off on a moment's notice to your next adventure."

"Well, traveling all the time can be lonely," Mom said. "He doesn't really have family. He has a sister who lives a few towns over. She's busy raising her kids. When he's in the area, he stops by and dotes on his nieces and nephews. He travels too much to really settle down. But he's happy like that."

After we cleaned up after dinner, I made some lemon tea and stationed myself on the couch as Mom sat at her desk and answered a few emails.

"Read your book, let's let dinner settle, then we'll sneak in a TV show or two, and dessert!"

I smiled. I loved that my mom had a child-like side to her—a side that delighted in TV shows and dessert. I was determined to finish the last of Dr. Hasserin's books. Published a year ago, *Getting the Grail: Legends, Lore, and Literature* examined King Arthur's Grail quest and presented places Arthur visited that were also associated with Grail history. While the other books had discussed Stonehenge and Arthur, they didn't have any new or relevant evidence for our case.

I was frustrated since I didn't want to return to campus after break and have nothing to share with Lydia. I desperately hoped this book would have something. Wrapping my blanket around me, and keeping my tea at arm's length away, I perched on the couch and started reading.

> *Due to its sacred association, the Holy Grail was thought to have many miraculous properties, including giving whoever drank from it immense power and eternal life. King Arthur and his knights searched everywhere for it, battling evil foes across Arthur's kingdom—and beyond. But, as the legend goes, King Arthur was never able to find the Grail, since he had an impure heart. For the Grail was bound, throughout the ages, to be discovered by only those with a pure heart, namely Sir Galahad. The questions on every scholar's mind, when we take the legends and compare them to the historical evidence, are: What is fiction and what is fact? Did Arthur or his knights find the Grail? If so, where did they bury it?*
>
> *This book analyzes the literature, legend, and historical and archaeological evidence, presenting firsthand accounts and narratives from eyewitnesses who testify to seeing Arthur in, miraculous acts of healing at, or secret societies descending on these places. In doing so, this book separates fiction from fact,*

presenting the reader with the historical evidence to conclude that King Arthur did indeed find the Grail. This chapter also presents evidence for where Arthur buried the Grail, and more importantly, where the Grail could be located now.

Bingo! I pumped my fist in the air. This book would have some answers! I opened my journal and wrote down the title. I finally felt like I was about to make progress.

I kept reading, enthralled by how Dr. Hasserin presented the historical, archaeological, and scientific evidence. His style reminded me of Dr. Wryght's. I followed along each line with my pencil, careful not to let the lead smudge the page.

There are many places King Arthur and his knights are thought to have visited in their Grail quest. These places are all around the British Isles—modern-day England, Scotland, Wales, Ireland, and Northern Ireland. Several places associated with the Grail are Camelot—Arthur's castle and court; the Kelly Rounds, near Celliwig, Cornwall; Pen Rhionydd, Arthur's Northern court in what is now Northern England/Southern Scotland; Isle of Arran, an island off the west coast of Scotland; Arthur's Seat, in Edinburgh, Scotland—barely a stone's throw from the Rosslyn Chapel; the Chalice Well at Glastonbury Abbey; the convent in Amesbury, where Guinevere was banished after her trial; and Stonehenge, England, the final resting place of Uther

Pendragon, King Arthur's father. Each of the chapters in this book examines the evidence for what places Arthur actually visited, what he was doing there, and where he could have buried the Grail.

I raced through the book, absentmindedly sipping my tea as I focused on the evidence from eyewitnesses at each location. In the Amesbury section, I'd learned Camelot was supposed to be the ideal kingdom. King Arthur tried very hard to ensure law and order prevailed.

He established a strict code of chivalry and rules that his knights had to follow. These rules promoted gentlemanly and moral behavior. The penalty for breaking them was death. Sir Lancelot's and Queen Guinevere's affair disrupted the law and order Arthur had worked so hard to create. He couldn't let Lancelot go unpunished—even though he was one of his most gallant knights—and his heart was broken because Guinevere was his wife.

The affair rocked Camelot to its core. It put a deep rift in the Knights of the Round Table, causing several factions to form. Some knights supported Arthur and some knights, such as the Knights of Vanora, took an oath to protect Guinevere, adopting her sign—the white wave.

After reading that, I flipped back in my journal to my notes on Gran's mysterious Henge Piece poem. *Warring knights seek this tool/They want what is lost to be found.* These factions must be what Gran was referring to!

I kept reading about the affair. It also angered the Church—and the Court. Ultimately, Arthur had to put Guinevere on trial. According to legend, instead of sentencing her to death, the court sentenced her to life in the convent. She was allowed to bring only one item from Camelot. She chose to bring her Henge Piece.

Dr. Hasserin presented eyewitness accounts from nuns at the convent who described how Guinevere walked around in a trance, holding the Henge Piece and muttering strange words. The nuns were terrified of the Henge Piece, since they thought Guinevere was using it to conjure the dead or cast spells. Guinevere assured them she was not a witch and was using the Henge Piece to find solace during her distress. They eventually left her alone.

"YES!" I jotted my notes down in exuberance, grinning as I circled words in my journal. This was the first time in an archaeological text I'd read about the Henge Piece. Dr. Hasserin had provided the historical evidence for the children's story in Blane's book—the evidence I needed to show one of the Henge Pieces had belonged to Guinevere.

More importantly, I'd learned that Stonehenge and the convent were not too far away from each other. *Is this why Gran and Lydia had found the Henge Piece at the village near Stonehenge? Maybe it had been lost or stolen from Guinevere and didn't surface until Gran and Lydia's dig*. I took a long sip of tea. The lemon flavor was the right balance of sweetness and tart in my mouth. I began to put the puzzle pieces together.

Dr. Hasserin also analyzed Guinevere's diary, which was part of the convent's library. In her diary, Guinevere not only wrote about how the Henge Piece was an instrument Arthur made to bury treasure at Stonehenge, but also sketched a diagram of the Henge Piece—and the ruby! She showed how the Henge Piece aligned with Stonehenge—and how the ruby in the dagger's hilt aligned with the Altar Stone. The ruby had double dagger marks—exactly like the ones on the notes—etched in its center. Most importantly, her diagram had the Henge Piece's real name: the Grealmæp. I read the name to myself: *the greal maep, the greal map, the grail map, the Grail map*!

"BINGO!" I blurted out.

"What was that?" my mom asked from her desk. "What are

you so excited about?"

"Oh, nothing," I muttered, realizing I had to be careful around her. "I'm enjoying my book."

I had hit the jackpot. Guinevere's diary was the primary source I needed to understand what the Henge Piece was and how it was used at Stonehenge. Beaming in amazement, I took a picture of the page and wrote the page number in my journal. As I stared into our living room, I thought about what this revelation meant. I flicked my pencil in my fingers as I got lost deep in my thoughts.

"Well, whatever it is you're reading, you're so engrossed in it, it must be fascinating."

I smiled. "It is!" I tried to concentrate.

This meant the Henge Piece—the Grealmæp—was a map to locating the Grail at Stonehenge—and the Altar Stone was an important site. It meant we needed to find the ruby. It meant the Knights of the Dagger were linked to the ruby. It also meant Dr. Hasserin had done additional research on the Henge Piece, without telling Lydia, after the case was closed. *Why?*

By the end of *Getting the Grail*, I had seven pages of notes. I skimmed through them, reflecting on the new evidence. I had to figure out whether the Grail was still buried at Stonehenge. I closed my eyes and thought about everything I'd learned on Stonehenge, King Arthur, and the Grail.

I replayed the plots of all the legends and thought about the eyewitness accounts and the Grealmæp. *The legends weren't true*, I thought. King Arthur *had* found the Grail. By presenting concrete evidence for the Grail and the Grail locations, Dr. Hasserin's book showed exactly that.

Dr. Hasserin's book sounds exactly like the paper on the Grail that he and Dr. Wengaro never published. Why had Dr. Hasserin published this without Dr. Wengaro—and as a book, not as a journal article? What happened? I opened my eyes, grabbed my journal, and jotted down my questions.

"All right, my favorite scholar, are you ready for TV and dessert?"

I nodded. "Yeah, one second." I scribbled a few more notes.

"Look at you, you're totally in the zone. Gran would be so proud." My mom smiled and took a deep breath as she gazed at the couch. "Seems like yesterday you were jumping off that couch in Gran's boots, taking down monsters with her cane. Now you're a beautiful and incredibly smart young lady tackling your homework—and doing so well in your college courses."

I laughed as I remembered how Mom would find me battling the monsters in our living room. Since then, there was nothing more I wanted to do than fill Gran's shoes. I glowed with purpose to know Mom thought Gran would be proud of me.

"Thank you, Mom, that means a lot to me." I felt my pendant under my T-shirt. *I may not be jumping off couches fighting imaginary monsters, but I have a pendant that connects me to a very real adventure involving a dead professor and the Grail.* "This is my passion."

"A passion—and a real talent." She headed to the kitchen. "I always thought you were precocious, and that's paying off with your studies. You're so smart." She paused. "I'm listening. I'm grabbing some leftover cake from the fridge."

She emerged with the cake, two plates, two forks, and a knife. She picked up the knife and effortlessly sliced through the cake. As I looked at the knife, I thought of the Grealmæp's dagger—and the Knights of the Dagger. *Are the Knights of the Dagger the "evil ones all around" Gran mentioned in her poem?*

I needed to know what exactly Dr. Hasserin had said at the conference. Had he found the exact location of the Grail at Stonehenge? I also needed to learn what side the Knights of the Dagger were on—and whether they were good or evil.

††

I sat upright in bed, staring at the clock on my nightstand. Its red display jarringly contrasted with my otherwise dark room.

12:31 a.m.

I'd been rolling around all night, clutching my pendant, unable to sleep. Every time I closed my eyes, I'd open them what I thought was hours later, to see that only minutes had passed. Every now and then, a car would pass by on the road, its headlights shining through my curtain. Did the Knights of the Dagger know King Arthur buried the Grail at Stonehenge? Did they murder Dr. Hasserin because he had shared this discovery?

I had to get into Dr. Hasserin's house and look for more of the Knights of the Dagger's notes. Maybe these notes would have more clues that would help me answer my questions.

My phone lit up with an incoming text. *Hey babe. :) You up?*

I replied, *Yeah, why are you still up?*

Finished chatting with my family. I told them all about you. My mom says hi.

Tell her I say hi too. :)

Of course! I miss you. Sleep well. <3

G'night Blane. You too!

I put my phone back on my nightstand and smiled. I loved when Blane used emojis in his texts. I missed him a lot—it was hard to go from seeing him every day for hours at a time to not seeing him at all.

Our budding relationship felt much more real now that he had told his family about me. This made me happy. Blane was someone I was excited to date. My initial impressions of him as goofy and genuine were still true. The more I got to know him, from our very first Archaeology Talks to our dinner dates, the more I loved how intelligent and kind he was. I appreciated his perspectives and how he saw the world. We made a good team—

not according to ourselves, but also to Lydia and the panel of faculty who'd seen our presentation. As Dr. Pritzmord had said, we "pieced together the past like seasoned partners in the field."

I smiled as I remembered Dr. Pritzmord's words and closed my eyes. The more I'd gotten to know Blane, the more I thought there was long-term potential with him.

With these happy memories on my mind, I slept.

XII

The next morning, right after breakfast, I FaceTimed Blane. "Happy Thanksgiving!" I said to him.

I was sitting at our kitchen table, and Mom was in the living room, watching our town's Thanksgiving Day Parade.

"Happy Thanksgiving!"

"How are you? How's your family? What's on for today? Where are you—looks like you're outside!"

Blane laughed. "Whoa, someone is excited! What, did you put an extra shot of caffeine in your coffee? One question at a time, please."

I grinned. "Can't help it. I have something awesome to share with you."

"Well tell me!"

"I will—but after you tell me what's on for today!"

"Leave me in suspense then! All right, well, we're watching the parade—my sister is actually there—and I was chatting with my parents."

As I was listening, I put my dishes in the dishwasher and walked out of the kitchen and up the stairs to my room.

"My dad's working on the turkey, and Mom is cooking up the best side dishes you've ever had. Then she'll make an amazing cheesecake for dessert. We'll get my grandma, then have dinner, and that's about it. Oh—and I am outside. I'm sitting on the deck outside our kitchen." He flipped his phone around so I could see the deck. "What about you? What's on for your day?"

"That's awesome—sounds relaxing! Yeah, Mom's watching our town's parade, then we'll probably go for a hike, then order in, and watch a movie. Super low key. We'll go walk around town early tomorrow for Black Friday deals—and some yummy homemade baked treats."

"Nice! Exactly what you need to relax. What treats are you going to make?"

"Oh, no, we're not going to make them. We get them from a place in town. They always do fun menu items, and they're one of the oldest bakeries in town."

"That's so cool. Now, no more suspense—tell me about that 'something awesome.'"

I sat on my bed, crossing my legs and bringing my phone right in front of my face. "I have pretty good evidence King Arthur buried the Grail at Stonehenge."

Blane's face lit up. "Oh yeah? So, Dr. Hasserin's books had some good stuff in them?"

"You bet they did. One in particular. It had a diagram of the Henge Piece—and its real name. Guinevere called it the Grealmæp. Why else would she do that—"

"If it didn't map to where the Grail was buried?" Blane completed my question. "You're a genius! We need to figure out where exactly the Grail is buried—and if it's still buried at Stonehenge."

"Yep, and to do that, I have to go to Dr. Hasserin's house. Maybe whoever murdered him left some clues."

"As usual your mind blows me away. I love how you're piecing these clues together. Wow! Well done!"

I beamed, looking at Blane on the screen. "I couldn't have done it without my teammate!"

We virtually high-fived through our phones.

"Can I tell my mom and dad?" asked Blane. "I wanna brag about you to them."

I got quiet. I didn't want other people knowing what I'd

discovered until I had more conclusive evidence that pointed to the Grail's location.

"That's a sweet thought, but let's not say anything for now. I need more evidence, and I'd like to talk to Lydia. If the Grail is still buried at Stonehenge, and we figure out where, we might be headed there soon. And if Dr. Wengaro is also after the Grail, we can't let him get to Stonehenge first."

"Great thinking. As usual, you're thinking about the case, and I'm thinking about you and how smart you are."

I blushed. Blane's endearing lines got me every time.

††

I'd texted Lydia and wished her a Happy Thanksgiving. *I have something important to share with you after break*, I said. She hadn't texted back, but I knew she was probably with her family, so I figured she was busy.

After FaceTiming Blane, I finished Dr. Hasserin's book. By the end, I was intrigued with who Dr. Hasserin was. He'd seemed to balance history with science and evidence with emotion—carefully presenting his arguments, supporting them with relevant claims, and analyzing them through multiple perspectives. Dr. Hasserin was an incredible scholar who had significantly advanced research on the British Isles. Who would kill him? Surely it was someone who was jealous of him—someone who wanted the Grail and its glory for themselves.

"Are you ready for our hike?"

"Yep, one second, Mom!"

I closed my book and walked down the stairs to our back door. Mom had packed some trail mix and was already wearing her sneakers. I put mine on, and we headed out for our hike. The trail ran right behind our house.

"This was one of Dad's favorite trails," I said as we walked.

"Sure was," said my mom. "Remember when we hiked it

that one afternoon and it started pouring?"

"Of course—I got so upset that my shoes were soaked. They got completely ruined."

"And we bought you new ones, but you hated them." Mom chuckled. "You wanted your old ones back so badly."

I laughed. "I sure do have a thing for old shoes."

There were a few people on the trail—some were running and others walking in a group. Most were taking their time as they enjoyed the fresh air.

"So, how's Blane? I heard you FaceTiming him this morning."

"He's good. They have a nice Thanksgiving planned. His family seems really close."

"That's great. I'm happy you guys are dating."

A runner wearing only tights and a singlet sped by us.

"Oh gosh, looking at him makes me freeze," I said. "Why're you happy?"

"Well, Blane seems smart and like he stays out of trouble. You told me you got high praise on your midterm. It seems like you make a good team. You have fun together outside of the homework and projects. All that is important."

The trail had taken us into the woods. As we walked up the hill, we took bigger breaths to compensate for the changing elevation. Our breaths, now deeper and more frequent, were visible in the chilly November air.

I smiled. "We do."

"And he's also helping you with the Henge Piece mystery!" she blurted out, catching me off guard. "You haven't said a word about it, so I thought you gave it up. Have you been working on it this whole time?"

I froze. *How did she know about the Henge Piece mystery?* "Mom, I, I . . . There isn't any danger in it!" I lied. "It's only a pendant—"

"And a murder! Someone was *murdered*. Don't lie to me, Carlyle Elizabeth. I heard you talking to Blane. You said so yourself! How are you safe if there is a murderer on the loose?" Every ounce of my mom's anger hit me as she looked at me. "This is why I wanted you to destroy the Henge Piece in the first place. But you didn't—and worse yet, you lied to me. You promised me you'd stop if things became too dangerous."

My mom and I sat on a nearby boulder. I looked through the bare trees in the forest, watching a crinkly brown leaf blow by in the wind. My heart was still beating from exerting myself over the elevation change—and from my mom's confrontation.

I'd been caught in a lie.

I confessed everything, telling my mom about Lydia, Dr. Hasserin, the Knights of the Dagger, the notes, the missing ruby, and the Grail.

"And where is the Henge Piece—the Grealmæp—now?" she asked when I finished.

"I'm wearing it. Under my shirt."

"Carly! I hope no one knows you have it!"

"No one but Lydia, and Blane, trust me."

"But what if these knights come after you? They are dangerous." Her apprehension was evident.

"They don't know I have it!" I repeated, adamant. "Plus, I'm being careful."

Mom took out the trail mix and offered me some. "I only want you to be safe."

I nodded as I picked a few peanuts out and ate them. "I am, Mom."

"I don't think you're being safe enough. These Knights of the Dagger—these 'evil ones'—are out for blood. They seem to be everywhere. They want this Henge Piece. They targeted Gran, Lydia, and Dr. Hasserin—and they proved they will stop at nothing to get it. They will target you too." She paused, clasping her glove-covered hands together in front of her. "I know how much you want your own adventure, but you need to stop working on this mystery immediately. I don't want to lose another loved one. Two in three years is enough. Tell Lydia you wish her all the best, but you can't get caught up in this murder and mystery."

††

I couldn't bring myself to tell Lydia over text, so I'd texted her that we needed to talk. She hadn't texted back. I had barely been able to concentrate on anything other than the Grail and Stonehenge.

I wanted to respect my mom's wishes, but I wasn't ready to walk away from Gran's pendant and our case. *Mom certainly has the right to be worried, but she can't tell me what to do.* I understood where she was coming from, but I also felt she didn't understand how much solving these mysteries meant to me. If I could get one lead on the Knights of the Dagger, I'd be able to crack more of the case.

But I couldn't find anything on them, no matter how many times I searched Google or Rockfire's catalogues. I'd stayed up all night, pacing around my room as I mapped out my ideas. I needed to organize my thoughts, so I started a list in my journal: *Five Things I Need to Know for My Quest*.

First, I needed to figure out if Dr. Hasserin had discovered the Grail was still buried at Stonehenge. I needed Lydia to help me find Dr. Hasserin's journals, and I needed to find the missing ruby. To get Dr. Hasserin's journals, I had to get to his house, which was a lot easier than finding the missing ruby. Once I found his journals, I would be able to learn more about the phrase *etched in stone* and what it meant.

Second, I needed to figure out the exact location of the Grail at Stonehenge. If Dr. Hasserin's journals contained this information, then we wouldn't need the Grealmæp or the missing ruby. We could go to Stonehenge and dig. If Dr. Hasserin's journals didn't have this information, we'd need the missing ruby—and we'd have a whole lot more work ahead of us.

Third, I needed to know how we could get permits to dig at Stonehenge. I imagined Lydia and I couldn't show up and start digging at a World Heritage Site. If the Grail was buried there, we'd need to start planning the logistics of our trip.

Fourth, I needed to know why Dr. Hasserin was murdered—and who had murdered him. Judging from the note, the Knights of the Dagger were involved—and probably were at the conference. I suspected whoever had murdered him had also taken Lydia's books.

Fifth, I needed to know whether my passport was expired. If Lydia and I needed to go to Stonehenge at a moment's notice, then I had to know I'd be able to get there.

Once I'd written everything down, I felt relieved. Seeing how all my thoughts and questions converged into a logical, viable plan made me feel confident.

Pink and orange streaks filled the sky as the night turned to morning. I'd pulled my first all-nighter, and it wasn't even for my schoolwork. I opened my curtain, letting the sunlight stream into my room in the quiet of the morning. One ray lit a picture of Gran and me. In the picture, Gran and I were sitting on our couch as Gran told me her stories. The picture was taken from behind the couch. I liked that perspective because it was as though Gran and I were looking into the future as she told me her stories.

I'm doing the right thing. When I was little, I barely filled Gran's shoes. I was inspired by her stories and eagerly awaited the day I'd follow in her footsteps with my own adventures. As I slid my moccasins on and walked downstairs to make my coffee, I knew that day was today. Now, I wearing Gran's shoes—and pursuing the most important adventure of my life.

††

Mom and I were headed into town for Black Friday shopping. I'd told her that after reflecting on what she said, I had texted Lydia about my involvement in the case. Technically it wasn't lying—but it certainly wasn't telling the whole truth, either. I wanted to enjoy a peaceful day shopping without any residual tension from the confrontation on the walk.

"So what are you going to get from Tony's?" my mom asked, putting her blinker on and glancing behind her to see if there was anyone in the other lane. "They probably have delicious Thanksgiving pastries."

She exited the highway and navigated the downtown streets to find a parking spot. Tony's had been around since our town was founded—and was still operated out of its original location. It was one of the first establishments in our town, and it was a nationally recognized historic site. It even had a little plaque outside the entrance that described its history in the community, as a place started by immigrants pursuing the American Dream. The line at Tony's looped around the corner. It didn't matter how early or cold it was, people still waited.

"Here's a menu if you want to see what's on for today." The hostess handed us a laminated menu.

"Thank you," my mom said. I huddled around her as we looked at the menu. All the items had clever names or puns.

"I'm gonna have Tony's GOAT Hot Chocolate with almond milk base and America's Greatest Chocolate Chip Cookie Dough Dream," I said. "Or wait, should I get the Apple Sigh-Brrrrr and the Not Your Grandma's Apple Pie Breakfast Toastie?"

"That sounds delicious, I think I'll go for the Sin-a-mon Lot-T, and mind if we split the cookie or the toastie? I want a few bites," said my mom.

"Works for me," I said.

I ended up getting the Apple Sigh-Brrrrr, which was exactly what I needed on the cold November morning. With the Not Your Grandma's Apple Pie Breakfast Toastie, I was set with a delicious breakfast.

"Once a year, once a year," my mom said as she bit off a piece of my toastie and washed it down with a sip of her cinnamon tea. "This is so delicious."

Treats in hand, we headed down Main Street, looking at the window displays.

"Oh my gosh, look." Mom pointed to the display of Ogston's Toys. "That teddy bear is too cute."

I loved how each display featured something from our town's past, whether it was vintage teddy bears, recreated wintry scenes from one of our trails, or snapshots of shoppers of yesteryear. As I pulled out my phone to take a picture of the display, I noticed a missed call from Lydia.

"Hey, give me a minute. Lydia called me. I need to call her back." I stepped to the side of Ogston's, out of the flow of pedestrian traffic on the sidewalk.

Lydia picked up almost immediately.

"Carly, oh, Carly, I'm so glad you called me back."

"Is everything okay?"

"I went to my office this morning because I needed a book. I thought I'd had it at home but realized I'd left it on my desk. When I got there . . . the door had been pried open and someone had broken into my office. Nothing in my office had been touched—my books, the sofa, the pillows, the papers were how I'd left them. Whoever did this knew exactly what they were looking for—and found it."

"Oh my gosh, Lydia. Did you report it to campus security?"

"Yes, right before I called you."

"Okay, good. And what was missing?"

"My Stonehenge replica—it's gone."

XIII

Blane and I cut our Thanksgiving break short to get back before classes started, and now we stood in front of Lydia's office. The lock on Lydia's door was busted out. Her door looked like someone had taken a crowbar and yanked it open.

"I've notified Daniel, so the break-in is on university record. I need a whole new door, too, which means getting on the list for maintenance." Lydia sighed. "No way I can get any work done in this office in the meantime."

We walked into her office and sat down.

"To be sure, your Henge Piece wasn't stolen, only the Stonehenge replica?"

"Right, it's still here, safely hidden."

I breathed a little sigh of a relief. Whoever stole Lydia's replica didn't know she had the Henge Piece in her desk—and that was far more valuable than her replica.

"Who do you think did it?"

"No clue."

"What if the Knights of the Dagger are on to us?" I asked in a trembling voice. I thought about the conversation my mom and I had during our walk. *"But what if these knights come after you? They are dangerous."*

As the reality of how much danger we were actually in hit me, I got genuinely scared. The Knights of the Dagger had damaged and stolen property. Would physically harming us be next? Maybe my mom had been right—this case was too risky.

Maybe I should have told Lydia I needed to stop. But when she called about the break-in, I didn't have the heart to tell her.

Now, the Knights of the Dagger had escalated from warning notes to break-ins and robberies. Did they know about me? Would they target my dorm room for their next break-in? What if they robbed or hurt me? What about Lara? The questions swirled around in my head like a whirlpool gaining strength. *What type of person would put her friend at risk?* I thought, disgusted with myself. I couldn't imagine Lara getting hurt because of my desire to find the Grail! Was I becoming blinded by my own desire to find the Grail—the same desire that blinded every knight who had fought over it throughout time?

I shook my head as I stared into space. I was in danger—but not only that, I was putting Lara in danger without her even knowing! But if I gave up my quest now, the Grail would go undiscovered, leaving the door wide open for more nefarious deeds—and bloodshed.

"No," I blurted out. "No. I have a moral obligation to find the Grail and stop this once and for all." I clutched my pendant through my sweater. *Be brave.* "Lydia, there's something I need to tell you. I realized it over break. I think Dr. Hasserin discovered the Grail was—and is still—buried at Stonehenge."

"What? Sid was actively researching the Grail? He never mentioned this to me."

"But remember how he needed those books—your books—on the Grail? Right before the conference?"

Lydia nodded.

"Remember how you couldn't find them when you went to his house?"

She nodded again.

"I read some of his books over break. Dr. Hasserin had written a book on King Arthur and the Grail. He discussed the historical evidence for Grail locations—including places where Arthur might have buried it. He cited Guinevere's personal diary, and oh, the Henge Piece's real name is the Grealmæp—not the

Henge Piece. That's what Guinevere calls it."

"That's amazing. The Grealmæp." Lydia smiled. "So now we know what the Henge Piece does. And doesn't that sound like the paper—"

"The paper he and Dr. Wengaro never published. We need to find out *why*. Something must have happened between them. I'm not sure what. Maybe they had a falling out."

Lydia closed her eyes and put her hands behind her head. She arranged her bun, making sure not a hair was out of place. Leaning back in her desk chair, she took a deep breath. "Why would they have had a falling out?"

"Maybe Dr. Hasserin discovered something he wanted to keep a secret from Dr. Wengaro," Blane said. "Something like where the Grail was buried."

"Or maybe Dr. Wengaro got jealous he wasn't getting attention," I added.

"Or, do you think Dr. Hasserin found the missing ruby—and wanted to keep it for himself?" Blane asked. "He was one of the first people there when Dr. Ainsley fell."

Lydia opened her eyes. "I don't—because he never told me. He never brought it up. He knew how important the Henge Piece was. Wouldn't he have told me? If he found it, a scholar like him, he'd have said something. No—he was too much of a scholar to be a thief." Lydia tapped her fingers in the space on her desk where she'd kept her Stonehenge replica.

"That's a great question," I said. "Right now, we're asking a lot of great questions. Speaking of questions, over break I organized my next steps."

I took out my journal and opened it to my *Five Things I Need to Know for My Quest* list. I put my journal on Lydia's desk.

"This is great. This helps us plan our next steps. You're remarkably thorough."

"Thank you," I said. "It took me all night to write it down. Five is probably the easiest one to take care of," I said as I texted my mom to check that my passport wasn't expired. *Blane and I are thinking of taking a trip to Niagara Falls over Christmas break*, I typed.

"And three—let's cross that bridge when we get there. I'm sure Allister can help us with the permits. He knows all the guys at all the parks and societies."

"Excellent. What we really need to find are Dr. Hasserin's journals. I bet those would have his analyses and discoveries."

Lydia nodded. "I bet they're still at his house—maybe on his desk or in his office. I have the spare key."

"Can we go tonight?" I asked.

"Unfortunately, no, I promised my brother and his family I'd spend the weekend with them. I need to hit the road soon. Five-hour drives are really tiring when you're my age—and night driving is way too difficult for me."

"Monday?"

"Yes."

Lydia read the rest of my list.

"Number four. This is important. We have a developing motive for the murder—we need the evidence to identify suspects. I think you're right. Whoever murdered Sid also took those books. They were on very specific topics."

"What was Dr. Hasserin's conference talk on?" I asked.

"The Grail's status as a sacred artifact."

I leaned over Lydia's desk and jotted that down in my journal by my fourth point.

"Do you remember the titles of your books?" asked Blane.

"I sure do." Lydia got up and looked at one of her shelves. "*Grail and Glory: The Truth of Man's Quest for Eternal Life*; *Ancient Roman Crucifixion Stories: The Medical Evidence for the Death of Christ*; and *The Early Church: How the Early Christians Hid the Grail*."

"How did you remember those?" I asked.

"Because I organize all my books by country and century, then by their title."

"That's clever," said Blane. "That's a lot like—"

"Rockfire?" smiled Dr. Kells. "Yep. When you're building the Archaeology Research Room one book at a time, you need a good system."

I smiled. I was inspired by how Lydia had built the Archaeology Department and the Research Room. Her list of accomplishments was impressive, and she never bragged about anything she'd done. I admired her humility and could see why she and Gran were a great team. They were in the field for the right reasons and didn't get caught up in the glory and fame that accompanied their achievements.

My phone buzzed. My mom confirmed my passport hadn't expired. *You can get it when you come home. You'll love Niagara Falls! It's beautiful in the winter.* I felt a twinge of remorse for lying to her, but it was the only way to solve the case.

I grabbed my journal and checked off number five. I set my journal down in the empty space where the Stonehenge replica used to be. "Lydia, aren't you scared of the Knights of the Dagger? With a break-in and stolen property, they're showing us they mean business."

"Should I call the police?" asked Blane.

"Of course, I'm scared. But just because I'm scared, I'm not going to give up. That's what they want me to do. Until we have evidence that links them concretely to this case, we will not call the police. What will we tell them? That we think there is a dangerous person belonging to a secret order of knights we know nothing about, armed with a Stonehenge replica and seeking a mysterious pendant? What would we say when they ask what evidence—video footage, fingerprints, items left at crime scenes, or eyewitness testimony—we have? We don't have any—only a whole lot of speculation."

"And a broken-into office, and a stolen Stonehenge replica," added Blane.

"But that's not evidence—that is circumstance," Lydia corrected.

I'd been listening, twirling my curl, and gazing out Lydia's window. Lydia was right. We needed evidence.

"Who are the professors in the department working on anything Stonehenge related? Who might have a motive to steal your replica?"

"Well, with Sid gone, Kenneth is really the only one who comes to mind."

I nodded. "Do you think Dr. Wengaro is part of the Knights of the Dagger?"

Lydia opened her mouth as if she was about to say something.

"Carly . . ." She sighed as her voice trailed off. "I don't know what to think anymore—other than you and I need to be very careful. My office doesn't lock, and my replica is gone. Those are facts. We need more facts to help us solve this case. Finding the facts is our highest priority. If we think Kenneth is our top suspect, let's watch him. Watch him during your seminar, watch him at Archaeology Talks. Without evidence, we only have emotions."

††

On Monday, Lydia met with Dr. Pritzmord. After their meeting, she, Blane, and I met in her office.

"Daniel told me he and campus security would look for anything suspicious from the building's entry and exit logs. He also authorized my maintenance request." Lydia got up and started pacing around her coffee table. Her boots thudded on her hardwood floor in a measured, slow cadence. Every time she walked in one spot near her door, the floor creaked. "I told him it's high time they installed security cameras in our hallways. I can't keep coming to work every day feeling unsafe."

"Did maintenance say when they'd fix everything?" Blane leaned against one of Lydia's bookcases as he looked at her.

"No. They respond within forty-eight to seventy-two hours,

with a time frame based on the request."

"But this is an emergency!"

Lydia chuckled. "Not according to them. An emergency is a clogged toilet in one of the students' dorms."

"So, what do we do now?"

"We wait, Carly. One thing at a time."

"And we go to Dr. Hasserin's house," I added.

††

After dinner, I walked to Lydia's office. She closed her door and met me outside.

"Not much I can do about it, really," she said, motioning toward her door. "I've moved all my valuables to my house for the time being. Now I'm waiting. This whole thing probably won't be fixed till next semester. Ready?" Lydia wrapped her scarf around her neck and face and pushed her hat over her head.

"Ready as I'll ever be," I replied, feeling my pendant under my coat. I was apprehensive about going into a dead man's house. As we exited the building, even the gargoyles around the window seemed to be staring at us, adding to my uneasiness. I let out a big breath. My curls stuck out from under my teal woolen beanie, bouncing as we walked.

"I mean it's technically not breaking and entering. I do have the key," said Lydia.

"Why'd he give you his key?" I asked as we walked past Rockfire. The lights were on. All the tables in the front were packed with students.

"He didn't. He used to keep it under his doormat. He used to joke if he were ever late for work, he needed someone to come to his house and wake him up. He was brilliant, but eccentric."

We reached the main road that separated Nassauton's campus from the town. "How so?" I pressed the crosswalk sign.

"Oh, he'd spend hours and hours getting lost in his research.

He'd disappear into his office on the weekends, poring over manuscripts and texts. His mind was always working, always thinking, always connecting the dots."

The light changed, and we walked across the street, passing the Gardenia Theatre. A few moviegoers waited by the ticket booth, their breath forming little clouds in the cold evening air. One couple sipped hot chocolate as they checked their phones, waiting for their friends.

"When I went to his house to retrieve my books, I took his key and kept it with me. If someone else wanted to get in, the first place they'll look for a key is under the doormat."

"Good thinking."

She smiled. We kept a brisk pace as we walked down the streets, turning here and there in a maze of midsize houses and condo units.

"Here we are." Lydia pointed to a small house at the end of a cul-de-sac. "A lot of faculty members live on this street. The houses are the right size for a single person or small family, and it's close enough to campus that you can walk."

Dr. Hasserin's house was a small, two-story stone structure. It was set back a bit from the street, with a longer driveway lined with trees on both sides. As we walked up the driveway, an eerie feeling came over me. Though it had been months, going to a dead person's house was unnerving. I noticed Dr. Hasserin's garage door, which looked like it had recently been cleaned.

"His garage door is spotless," I remarked.

"Oh yes, Sid was a very clean person," said Lydia, pointing at the door. "He had a system for organizing everything, and his workspace needed to be spotless or else he'd get too distracted."

I chuckled as I nodded. I hated working among piles of paper and messes, and I could tell Lydia was the exact opposite of Dr. Hasserin and me.

"It looks cozy," I said as we walked around to the back door. Lydia reached into her pocket for the key.

"Yes. Sid was happy here." Lydia unlocked the kitchen door.

"That's odd," she said as we stepped in. She turned on the light. "I know it's cold, but I wasn't expecting it to be this cold in here. It's absolutely frigid!"

I followed her in, closing the door and looking around. Except for a few pots and plates that were in the dishrack, the kitchen was unsurprisingly tidy. I glanced around the rest of the kitchen, which opened to the living room and a hallway.

I pointed at one of the windows in the hallway. "Of course it's going to be frigid inside when there's a broken window."

Lydia turned around in shock. She gasped. Shards of glass littered the floor in front of the window. They glistened in the kitchen light. We both darted to the hallway.

"Someone broke into Sid's house!"

Lydia turned from the window. "Sid's office door is wide open. I swear I closed it. I wiped my handprints off the doorknob." She dashed into Sid's office, heading for his desk. "Oh my gosh. Oh my gosh." She held her hand to her mouth in fear. "The *etched in stone* Post-it note is gone! His journals are gone. His books are gone! Everything he had on his desk is gone!"

"Not everything," I added, my heart pounding with adrenaline. I joined Lydia. "The Knights of the Dagger note is still here." I pointed to the note, my head spinning. Someone had crossed out one line—and scribbled another next to it:

††

And so the scholar meets his fate
He thought he could get the Grail
~~*But alas—here he lies*~~ YOUR TIME IS RUNNING OUT
The Knights of the Dagger will prevail

The Knights of the Dagger knew about us! My eyes darted around Dr. Hasserin's office. I backed away from the desk and chair. I bit my lip. I tried to collect my thoughts but couldn't focus. Fear filled my stomach. A white plastic piece sparkled under Dr. Hasserin's desk. "Look at this." I squatted down and picked up the piece. "It looks like it's an iridescent chip."

"I wonder what it's from," said Lydia. "It's probably part of a button. It could be one of Sid's. Maybe it fell off and the chair crushed it. Whatever it is, I'm sure it's nothing. What matters is the Knights of the Dagger have been here—and recently. They could still be around campus."

††

All week, the one thing on my mind was the Knights of the Dagger note. They weren't only on to us; they were anticipating our moves. I was terrified. Every time I saw someone in the hallway, or walking around campus, or sitting in the dining hall, I bit my lip and watched my back.

Had someone overheard Lydia and me in her office? How soundproof were the walls? The severity of the break-ins overshadowed our progress—and shattered my confidence. My spirit of adventure and excitement at solving our case had instantly disappeared. The Knights of the Dagger were dangerous. Notes were one thing; break-ins and more stolen property—and messages written to us—were another. I should have obeyed my mom.

On Thursday evening, Blane and I went to Archaeology Talks. Dr. Vikaney Garison, an expert on the Shroud of Turin, was speaking.

"Thank you for coming tonight. Tonight's talk is brought to you by a very special guest, here to explain one of the most, if not *the* most, mysterious artifact on the planet." Dr. Wengaro looked around the Commons. "The Shroud of Turin has puzzled scientists, forensics experts, doctors, priests, pastors, and archaeologists for centuries."

Blane and I were sitting in the front row. The Commons was packed. The Shroud of Turin drew students from religion, archaeology, and even some science classes. When I walked into the Commons, I wasn't surprised to see my chemistry TA there—she really liked analytical chemistry. If there was any artifact that had intrigued chemists, it would be the Shroud of Turin.

Dr. Wengaro continued. "Is this really the garment that covered Christ's body? What does the genetic evidence tell us? Was the image really created by Christ's blood? Or, is the Shroud a fake? Does it even date to Christ's death? Or fourteenth-century Western Europe? Dr. Vikaney Garison, an expert in archaeology and chemistry, is here to reveal the history, science, and mystery of the Shroud of Turin. Please join me in welcoming him."

Dr. Wengaro lowered his microphone and applauded as Dr. Garison got up and walked to the stage. As Dr. Wengaro applauded, I noticed flashes of light coming from his hand.

"Blane, look!" I poked Blane's arm. "Look at Dr. Wengaro's hand!"

Dr. Garison grabbed the microphone. Dr. Wengaro walked off to the side, still applauding, as Dr. Garison set up his notes and water bottle on the podium.

"His ring!" I hissed in Blane's ear. "Is that his class ring? It is sparkling all over the stage. Look at it. He's never worn it before. I've never seen him with it in our class."

Dr. Wengaro walked down to the front row, a few seats away from us. The house lights dimmed, leaving only the stage lights, as Dr. Garison turned on the projector. I rested my hand on Blane's knee, barely concentrating on Dr. Garison. I kept my eyes focused on Dr. Wengaro's ring.

"It looks like a ruby! Look!"

Blane subtly turned his head and glanced at Dr. Wengaro. "It *is* a ruby," he said after a few seconds. "And it's huge."

How did Dr. Wengaro, a young professor who had been an academic all his life, get his ring?

"Do you think it's the missing ruby?"

Blane's eyebrows rose. "Sure could be. We need to get a closer look. If it's the ruby, it will have the double dagger marks."

"The Shroud of Turin is fascinating. The first mention of it was—does anyone want to guess?" Dr. Garison asked.

I texted Lydia. She had never seen Dr. Wengaro's class ring but couldn't recall for sure. I told her if she'd seen it, she wouldn't have forgotten it.

A few students raised their hands, and Dr. Garison started calling on them.

"First century?"

"Nope!"

"Fourth century?"

"Nope! The first mention was in 1355 A.D., in Lirey, France. It was found at a tiny church. This church was built by Geoffroi de Charny, one of the leading knights of the Middle Ages, also famous for writing *The Book of Chivalry*. But that's a topic for another time. According to the history textbooks, thousands of people—tens of thousands of people—flocked to the church to see and touch the shroud that performed miracles. They wanted to be healed by the sacred cloth that touched Christ's body."

Dr. Garison clicked to his next slide.

"How was this miracle-working artifact made? The research we have leaves a lot up for debate. Some research suggests ultra-high radiation emanating from Christ's body created the image. Produced spontaneously, in one singular moment—say, the moment Christ the Son of God died—this radiation would have generated an incredibly intense heat. It should have incinerated the cloth. But it didn't. What happened? Other research suggests the Shroud is a fake, has nothing to do with radiation or heat, and was stained with a special type of chemical resembling ink. Let's dig a little deeper."

Throughout Archaeology Talks, I kept trying to look at Dr. Wengaro's ring. Every time he shifted his hand or how he was sitting, I'd lose my view.

"That concludes Archaeology Talks. If this fascinates you, I recommend you check Dr. Garison's most recent book," said Dr. Wengaro. "We'll have it on sale at our post-talk discussion. Please join me in thanking Dr. Garison." He raised his hands and applauded. His ring glistened in the light. "We'll be heading to Winnie B.'s for our post-talk discussion and appetizers. Hope to see you there."

"I'm going," I whispered to Blane.

"You should go. I wish I could, but my economics group is meeting to finish our problem set."

"All good. I'll get the scoop. Hope your problem set goes well." I kissed Blane on his cheek.

"Ha, you know it won't. You know these problem sets are famously difficult, if not impossible. They purposefully try to weed people out. But we will try." Blane hugged me and kissed my forehead. "See you later."

††

Dr. Wengaro had booked the back room at Winnie B.'s. As other students trickled in, I walked up to him, trying to get a chance to talk to him and look at his ring. Dr. Garison was at the appetizer station, surveying a tray of little quiches.

"Hi, Dr. Wengaro, I attended the talk, and it was great."

"Hi Carly," said Dr. Wengaro. He extended his hand to shake mine. He wasn't wearing his ring. "I'm so glad you liked it. Great to see you here."

As I was about to ask about the ring, Dr. Garison approached Dr. Wengaro.

"Kenneth, are we ready? I don't want to miss my flight."

"Yes, we are," said Dr. Wengaro. "Well, Carly, we'll chat more later. I hope you enjoy the discussion."

Why had Dr. Wengaro taken his ring off? Where did it go?

When the discussion finished, Dr. Wengaro left to drive Dr. Garison to the airport. I returned to my room, disappointed I hadn't made progress on the ring.

I sat in my bed, reading over my journal. So far, we didn't have answers for the break-in, we didn't have Dr. Hasserin's journals, and we hadn't come any closer to figuring out who the Knights of the Dagger were.

††

On the last day of classes before Christmas break, Lara, Paul, Blane, and I went to Winnie B.'s to celebrate. As we walked in the entrance, I could have sworn the gargoyle with the mortarboard on his head was smiling at me, proud of my scholarly accomplishments.

After dinner, Lara and Paul met up with a few of their friends. Blane and I walked the campus one last time. Arm in arm, we strolled around our quad. The volleyball net had long since been taken down. The wintry evening was peaceful and quiet—as if the campus knew it was sending students home for Christmas. As we walked near Greenlor Hall, Blane pointed out how the light of the stained-glass windows added so much warmth to the cold December night.

"They really do," I said. "Nassauton is such a beautiful campus."

"It really is, and you know what's even more beautiful?"

Blane stopped and looked at me, the light from the stained-glass windows glistening in his hazel eyes. This was exactly where we'd had our first kiss. I blushed as my heart started fluttering. I could guess what he was going to say next.

"You are," he said, pulling me in for a long hug. "You, and your smile, and your heart, and your brains—and your love of adventure and desire to ask questions. You're beautiful, inside and out. That's one of the many reasons I love you, Carly."

I felt my whole face, from my chin to my ears, to the top of my head, turning red. Blane had said he loved me! He'd chosen the spot where we shared our first kiss to say it. It was one of the sweetest and most romantic things that he'd remembered where we'd had our first kiss. Saying "I love you" was a big step in our relationship.

My feelings for him had been intensifying, especially since coming back after Thanksgiving and hanging out with him every day. I didn't realize how much I'd missed him during the break, and how much better my days were with him. I loved him, but I was too shy to verbalize my feelings. I still got nervous butterflies around him and I wasn't sure how he'd respond. Being goofy around someone, and making them laugh, were not the same as saying "I love you." But now that he'd said it first, I felt more confident in sharing my feelings with him.

I hugged him back, my heart pounding as I tried to calm my nerves. "I love you, Blane. I love that we made it through our first semester with each other as teammates."

Blane grinned, looking at me as he held me in his arms. "I like that—teammate. Carly, there's something I was thinking."

"Yes, teammate?" I looked into Blane's eyes. His pupils were so big, I could barely see the hazel in his eyes anymore. He had a goofy grin on his face.

"Break is one month long. I was thinking, would you want to . . . would you want to spend a weekend visiting me and meeting my family? Maybe in January, after Christmas, before we come back for final exams? We live only a few hours north of campus. I remember you said you're not too far, either."

"Only about an hour and a half southwest of campus. I'd love to." I smiled.

"It's a plan, then. Can't wait."

We linked arms and walked back to our dorm, ready to say goodbye to Nassauton and the semester.

XIV

When I was little, Christmas was my favorite holiday. My dad, mom, Gran, and I had our own Christmas traditions.

The first week in Advent, we'd go to the mall and walk around, window shopping and looking at all the people and decorations. The second week, we'd drive out to the country and see a show—and go out for a fancy dinner afterward. The third week, we'd drive downtown and walk around Main Street, looking at the lights and decorations that dotted the parks and sidewalks. In the middle of the town square, down the street from Tony's, there was a giant Christmas tree with a nativity scene at the foot of it. Right next to the nativity was a collection box for toys. Our town's Ladies Association would make sure all kids in the county had at least one present to open on Christmas morning. We'd get hot chocolate from Tony's, walk around the tree, and drop off our presents.

On Christmas Eve, we always attended the Midnight Candlelight Service, and on Christmas morning, we'd wake up, make breakfast and Christmas cookies, sing carols, open presents, and play board games. For Christmas, each person got the others one present and picked a local nonprofit to donate to in each other's name.

When Gran and Dad passed away, Mom and I tried to continue our traditions, but each year, I was less and less interested. This year, I wasn't ready to celebrate any traditions. But I was ready for a break from schoolwork and some downtime.

Without any leads, the Knights of the Dagger would have to wait while I enjoyed relaxing with my mom.

The breakfast pancakes my mom made were still hot off the griddle as we talked.

"It's so great to have you back. I missed you so much. The house is empty without you." She hugged me. "I'm so glad you've dropped that case. I feel better knowing that you're safe. You're all I have in this life, sweetheart."

I hugged her again, overcome with guilt that I had disobeyed her. But I couldn't disappoint Gran, who had also disobeyed my mom in leaving me the Grealmæp.

"I know. I missed you too."

"So, what are you up to today?" Mom asked as she sat and cut into her stack of pancakes. The blueberries, still piping hot, squirted out a little juice on her plate. I poured syrup over mine before putting a giant forkful into my mouth.

"Whoops, sorry." She grinned. "Finish chewing."

"These pancakes are so good. I'm going to the mall to pick up your and Blane's presents and then to the park. And I'm going to make sure I put my passport in my bag."

"The one you and Dad used to hike?"

"Yeah. It's a nice day. I could use some alone time and a good, long, thinking walk."

††

With the figures of elves lining the walkways, the North Pole gift factory recreated in the entrance, and Santa's sleigh hanging from the ceiling, the mall had outdone itself with Christmas decorations. Shoppers scrambled to get their presents, and fortunately I was able to dart in and out. I wanted to get to the park as soon as I could, to catch the day at its warmest.

The park was the site of a pivotal battle in the Revolutionary War. On walks with my dad, I'd imagine how the soldier

exhausted from fighting during the day, would lay down their weapons at night. I'd picture the soldiers huddling together around fires for warmth on cold winter evenings, chasing sleep but having restless nights as they dreamed about home or had nightmares about the war. Then, they'd wake up the next morning to fight all over again. I was in awe of their bravery and determination to fight for the freedom in which they so strongly believed—no matter the conditions.

Every time Dad and I hiked, I'd get overwhelmed with gratitude for the men and women who had lost their freedoms—and their lives—in the war so centuries later, we could have our freedoms and enjoy our lives. They'd not only taken a leap of faith for themselves, but for our country in her earliest days. They had no idea if the experiment that was America would work, but they believed enough in the vision to fight for it. They'd left their families and loved ones, trading the comforts of home for life on the battlefield and in the barracks.

I drove through the visitor's entrance and continued up the road to the chapel, noticing that quite a few people were out on the trails. From the chapel, the whole park was visible: rolling hills, trees, and various monuments scattered around the fields. I hadn't been to many other places where I could stand in one spot and see so much land. My dad and I would always park at the chapel because the view was a peaceful way to start our hikes. I hadn't been back to the park since Dad passed away.

As soon as I parked in the same spot we used to park in, all my memories of our conversations and walks hit me.

I sat in the car, overcome with how much I missed my dad. He never got a chance to see me go to the prom, graduate high school, or go to Nassauton. *What would he think about Blane? Would they talk about science and faith?* As tears started streaming down my cheeks, I found a crumpled napkin and wiped my face.

When I was ready, I grabbed my earmuffs, gloves, and scarf,

and got out and locked the doors. Setting out for the leafless trees, I passed one of the memorials to the fallen soldiers. I thought about Stonehenge. Stonehenge had been built as a memorial to those killed in a gruesome massacre. Tension and conflict—and murder—were built into its history.

The history of the Grail, from Christ to King Arthur to Hitler, was one of bloodshed, with no shortage of violence and killing. I was sure the Knights of the Dagger, the Knights of Vanora, and many other factions had fought bitterly when Camelot fell apart. *Is Dr. Wengaro a Knight of the Dagger? Had he murdered his friend to get the Grail for himself? Had he broken into Dr. Hasserin's house and Lydia's office?*

I sat on a bench by the memorial, gazing at its gray stone and marveling at its height. Towering over me, the top of the memorial pierced the clouds. I wondered how many names were carved onto it—names of real people who had given their lives for their convictions. *Like Dr. Hasserin, who had given his life for his research.*

I sighed, thinking about Dr. Hasserin and Dr. Wengaro, who had been friends. I thought about Lydia, who had lost her best friend and partner. I thought about my mom, who, haunted by the back-to-back losses of her mother and husband, wanted nothing more than for her daughter to be safe. I thought about Blane, who was such a supportive boyfriend and teammate.

I thought about myself, who, as a six-year-old girl, delighted in wearing her grandmother's shoes and jumping off the couch to fight imaginary monsters. I'd wanted nothing more than to be brave enough to fill Gran's shoes.

I started college ready to find adventure. Now that I'd found it—and it had led me down a path with a murder, break-ins, and thefts—I wasn't sure I was prepared to pursue adventure anymore. I'd bitten off way more than I could chew with this case. I was a teenage girl—no match for the Knights of the Dagger. While I thought I cared about the missing ruby and the *etched in stone* phrase, I cared about my safety more.

As I sat in the quiet of the wintry park, more questions and doubts crept into my mind. I let out a long sigh and watched as my breath disappeared into the air. *Is the Grealmæp worth my life? Are my emotions getting the better of me, convincing me there is evidence when there is none? Is Dr. Wengaro's ring really the missing ruby? Is it all only legends from children's books, masquerading as history? What if Lydia and I found the Grail, then what—we'd take it to Nassauton's museum, or the Smithsonian, or the British Museum, or the Vatican? Would the museums of the world fight over it? Would governments devise plots against each other? Would evil ones—forces like the Nazis—steal it, killing all who stood in their path? Was the Grail better left lost to time?*

I took a deep breath and gazed at the memorial. In the names of each soldier, I saw each man's identity. I saw each man's story. Each man had gone to war, fighting for what he believed in. Each man had taken a leap of faith, bravely paying the ultimate price for what he thought was true—even if, in the moment, he couldn't see where the evidence was leading him. Each man had given his life to create a better world.

How many have died for the Grail—not only in trying to find it, but also as victims of bloodlust for it? What is it about the Grail that is so compelling and powerful? Is it the promise of immortality? Is the Grail even real? Or, as Lydia said, is it an abstraction? If it were real, could Lydia and I even find it—especially when so many throughout history hadn't? . . . And if we don't find it, how many more Dr. Hasserins will die questing for it?

I asked myself my last question again. Whether we wished for it or not, Lydia and I were the ones to pick up where Dr. Hasserin had left off. If the Knights of the Dagger were the evil ones, we were the good ones. If we didn't solve the mystery of the Grealmæp, we were giving up the chance of a lifetime to change history forever. Like the soldiers in the Revolutionary War, we had to make a choice. Did we abandon our quest in the face of danger, or did we summon our bravery and take a strategic, careful, and evidence-backed leap of faith?

I knew which choice the soldiers had made, and I knew which choice I, and Lydia, had to make. Either the Knights of the Dagger would get the Grail, or we would. Either evil would win, or good would.

I clutched my pendant through my coat and sweater. *Be brave.* I stood up to continue my walk. The path ahead would not be easy. It would be full of doubts and questions, to which we might never know the answers. And that would be okay. The path ahead was the only road worth taking.

On Christmas Eve, my mom headed to the Midnight Candlelight Service. I stayed home. I wasn't interested in going to church, and I had too much on my mind with the Grealmæp.

As I aimlessly flipped through the TV channels and texted Blane, I noticed a small wooden box with a metal clasp on the shelf near some of Gran's books. Intrigued, I took the box off the shelf and opened it.

Inside, there were letters addressed to Gran. Some of the letters were from her friends—friends I'd never heard of. Some were get-well-soon letters from around the time of her fall. One, dated three years ago, caught my eye. In some places, it was too tear-stained to be legible. I tried to make out the words.

††

Dearest Lyle,

I will try to be with you I can. This case is crazy. We are closing in on the Knights of Vanora—would you believe those devils changed their name!

They thought they could hide, but the Knights of the Dagger . In this battle between we must. The world doesn't know it, but it depends on us—we must usher in a new world order—and soon—by eliminating them. Only then will the Grail—and the world—be safe.

When your young explorer is old enough, you must . We both know she holds .

, till we meet again,

J. Car

Oh. My. Gosh. I trembled as I reread the note. *J. Car* could only be one person: J. Carmichael. *He didn't only know about the Knights of the Dagger, but he must also be one too.* The Knights of Vanora were the same as the knights that Dr. Hasserin had mentioned in his book, *Getting the Grail.* They were the ones who protected Guinevere. *Could the Knights of the Dagger be good?*

What was even more shocking were the last two sentences. *Young Explorer* was my nickname from Gran! Goosebumps rose all over my arms. What did Gran—and J. Carmichael—know about me that I didn't?

I needed to contact J. Carmichael—as soon as possible.

††

Mom and I finished opening presents and were enjoying a relaxing Christmas Day watching TV and reading. She loved her engraved mother–daughter necklace I'd given her, and I loved the whimsical Nassauton College pajama set she'd gotten me. It had little Christmas ornaments and snowmen wearing scarves in our school colors.

I had to figure out how to get J. Carmichael's number without my mom getting suspicious. After wandering around the kitchen and seeing the pot of lavender honey as I pretended to look for snacks, I hatched a plan.

"Mom, did we ever thank J. Carmichael for the getting us the honey from France?" I called to her from the kitchen.

"What's that?" She turned down the TV. "What makes you ask that now about the honey?"

"I saw it in the cupboard and remembered how delicious it was," I said.

"I can't remember. I'm sure I did though."

"I'd like to thank him myself."

"I can text him, no problem. I'll do it when my show is over."

"No worries, if you text me his number, I can do it."

"Oh, sure."

I couldn't believe how easy that was. As soon as I got J. Carmichael's contact information, I saved it. I texted him.

Hi J. Carmichael. This is Carlyle Stuart, Lyle Ainsley's granddaughter. I hope you're well.

He texted back almost immediately: *Hi Carlyle. How are you?*

I recently learned some shocking news. I'm still a bit

shaken. Do you have time to talk?

Sure, Carlyle. I'm on vacation, but call me anytime.

Now? I asked.

Sure, I have a few minutes.

With my mom engrossed in her TV show, I could bundle up and slip out the kitchen door unnoticed. My chest was pounding as I called J. Carmichael. After a few rings, he picked up.

"Hi Carlyle, how can I help you?"

I blanked, overcome with nervousness. I didn't know what to say. I stared at his note to Gran. "What was Gran supposed to tell me?"

As soon as I said that, I facepalmed myself. Why was talking to J. Carmichael so difficult?

"I beg your pardon. What do you mean?"

"The note, the note you wrote to Lyle, three years ago, about the case and the Knights of Vanora and the Knights of the Dagger and saving the world and how Gran had to tell me something and how I hold—" My words spilled out in one enormous breath. "What does it all mean?"

I heard a pause.

"I can't discuss those topics over an unsecured line. We'll need to talk in person."

"When can we meet?" I asked.

"After my vacation—first thing in the new year. Text me the time and place, and I'll be there."

XV

I arrived at Blane's house after my drive.

"Hi Carly!" Blane gave me a huge hug, picking me up and twirling me around as he kissed me. Even though I was wearing my beanie, my curls went flying all over the place. Blane's mom was standing at their front door, grinning.

"Meet my mom!" Blane beamed.

"Great to meet you, Mrs. Henley," I said, extending my hand and tucking some unruly curls behind my ear as Blane finally put me down.

"Please, give me a hug. Call me Stephanie. Let me help you with your bag."

She picked up my duffel bag and ushered me to the living room. I followed her in, holding Blane's Christmas present.

"Merry Christmas." I handed him his gift.

"Thank you," he said, kissing me. "Yours is in the living room."

"I made you and Blaney a dairy-free cheeseboard, with plenty of crackers, nuts, fruit, and jams. I figured you'd be hungry after your drive. We'll have dinner when Mickey gets home—maybe not for another few hours or so. And Mardsen is already home. She's upstairs in her room."

Mickey was Blane's dad. Mardsen was Blane's younger sister. Looking around the living room, I could see how Blane's parents' professions and interests influenced their design style.

Right next to me was a glass case full of collectibles and Ancient Egyptian urns.

"My grandfather's!" Blane exclaimed. "My grandfather brought everything on those shelves back from his digs."

I looked at the necklaces, bracelets, and brooches that were scattered among the urns. The brooches were beautiful. Some were cameo, with ornate designs. Some were silver, engraved with dainty monograms in elegant script. Others were gold, with dazzling gemstones arranged in creative patterns. A few were pearl-colored.

"That's cool!" I pointed out the pearl-colored one to Blane. "That's kind of like Dr. Pritzmord's brooch. It looks like the crests of ocean waves."

"Oh yeah! That's my granddad's. That one meant a lot to him—he always said it was the symbol of some prestigious archaeological society."

I loved how archaeologists were such a scholarly and quirky bunch. Only they would cherish brooches as symbols of respected societies. I walked over to the fireplace, noticing that on the mantel, there were only trinkets and no family pictures, except for a collage of Stephanie and Mickey's wedding day. In one corner of the room, a few renderings of buildings with rooftop gardens rested on an easel. The walls had paintings of trees and fields, mountains, and seascapes, with Stephanie's signature at the bottom.

Mardsen ran into the living room. "Hi Carly! It's so good to meet you. Blaney talks a lot about you."

I blushed. "Hi Mardsen, good to meet you too. I hope he says only the good things." I elbowed Blane playfully.

"Everything he says about you is a good thing. He's smitten!"

"Mardsen!" Blane poked her in the shoulder. "Quiet." He walked to a chair and picked up a little wrapped box. "Merry Christmas, Carly."

I grinned, taking the box from Blane, but still enthralled by the paintings around the living room. I'd stepped into an art museum. “Thank you!” My eye was drawn to one painting in the far corner of the room. “That one is beautiful, Stephanie,” I said. “That’s Stonehenge on the summer solstice.”

“Yes. One of my favorite places. We took Blane there when he was a kid—Mardsen was a baby—for the solstice. Mickey and I had always wanted to go, but not when it was cloudy.”

“Which was every year,” added Blane.

“It wasn’t exactly a cheap trip. But we caught it one year, and it was amazing! But Blaney—Blaney got lost in the crowd and got so scared.”

“Shh, Mom!”

“Aww, he’s embarrassed!” said Mardsen.

“Nah, I already told Carly that story. You don’t have to retell it!” Blane grinned at Mardsen. “I’m giving you a hard time, sis. Love you.”

“Love you, bro.” Mardsen galloped up the stairs to her room. “I’ll be back for dinner.”

“Aside from Blaney getting lost, it was a beautiful morning.” Stephanie turned to me as I gazed at the painting. “No rain, no clouds, only the sunrise. Incredible. Mickey and I watched it together. It was perfect.”

Stephanie had painted the solstice as though she were standing right on the altar. The blood-red sun was behind the Heel Stone. Its burnt-orange and pink rays streamed through the stones, illuminating the altar with a deep reddish light. It was as though Stonehenge were on fire, glowing with an ethereal energy.

I’d never seen a painting of Stonehenge and the summer solstice. I’d only seen pictures on Google and diagrams in Dr. Hasserin’s book. Even the videos I’d found on YouTube weren’t close to the stones and didn’t show the sun rising the way Stephanie had painted it. I thought about Gran’s poem, the missing ruby, and the Grealmæp’s alignment with Stonehenge.

“What made you paint the solstice from that perspective? I love it. It’s like I’m right there, on the altar, covered in sunlight.” I sat down on the couch next to Blane. He put his arm around my shoulder. I leaned back into him.

"Thank you. I'm so glad. I thought it was a cool perspective. I had been reading about rituals and altars as sacred places of bloodshed and atonement." Stephanie sat in an armchair across from me. "I knew if you stand in the center of Stonehenge on the summer solstice, you see the sunrise beyond the Heel Stone—the large stone outside the circles. I got that image in my mind of something on the altar as a sacrifice to the coming summer. Sacrifice rituals weren't neat and tidy. The animal was sliced open, and its blood bathed the entire altar. I wanted to capture that visceral, raw concept of blood spilled to atone for sin."

As Stephanie described her painting, I started getting paranoid. *Is Stephanie a Knight of the Dagger?* Their notes mentioned atonement and sins. I stared at Stephanie. There was no way. *She's Blane's mom!* My emotions were getting the better of me. *Operate from evidence, not emotion.* This must be what Lydia meant. My paranoia was leading me to places I shouldn't go. I took a deep breath.

"You captured it very well." I smiled. "It's powerful."

"She's a great artist," said Blane, looking at his mom. "And also, are you ready for some fun facts about Stonehenge's altar? It weighs six tons. How do you move a stone of that weight without a truck? Its composition is similar to the composition of stones from Ysgyryd Fawr, in Wales—which has a very interesting myth associated with it."

"Yeah? What's the myth?" I asked.

"Well, *Ysgyryd* means *broken* or *split*. Legend has it a massive landslide occurred there—at the exact moment Christ gave up His spirit on the Cross, and the exact moment the veil of the Temple in Jerusalem was torn from top to bottom. As the lore says, Christ had to do something with humanity's sin, so He sent it to Ysgyryd. The landslide destroyed everything in its path—forever. Ysgyryd is nature's literal way of showing us the cost of Christ's ultimate sacrifice. Very mysterious, right?

To add to the mystery of it, the Altar Stone was excavated some sixty years ago, but no records of the excavation survived."

"How'd you get to be such a walking encyclopedia?" Stephanie laughed.

"No records survived?" I asked. "How do you lose dig records?"

"Bad data collection, weather, misplaced, stolen. Anything can go wrong. Some even speculate the Altar Stone *didn't want* anyone to learn its secrets."

"What do you mean, didn't want? It's not a living thing."

"I wouldn't be too sure. Stonehenge, like Ysgyryd, is on one of Earth's ley lines. These are lines that make up a global grid of electromagnetic energy. Some physicists believe the ley lines hold the key to dark energy and dark matter, and since this grid connects every sacred place, these scientists are probably on to something. Stonehenge and Ysgyryd are linked not only by the Altar Stone, but also by these ley lines. Some say no records of the Altar Stone excavation survived, because Stonehenge needed to protect the Altar Stone's secrets."

I'd never heard anything about ley lines and made a mental note to look them up. Ley lines, dark energy, and dark matter sounded like something Lydia would dismiss immediately because they had no scientific basis. *Is there a link between the Altar Stone, the summer solstice, and the Grail?* Dr. Hasserin had suggested the Grealmæp's missing ruby aligned with the Altar and Heel Stones. With the Grail's association with the Last Supper and Christ's blood, maybe the Grail was buried under the Altar Stone. Maybe we had to be at Stonehenge on the solstice to use the sun's alignment with the stones to find the Grail.

"What would you like to drink?" Stephanie's voice interrupted my thoughts.

"Do you have sparkling water?"

"You bet we do, honey, I'll get you some. Blaney, I'll get you some too."

"She's a saint," said Blane as Stephanie left the room. "My mama doesn't have a selfish bone in her body."

I smiled. "I can tell. She's amazing."

"She is indeed. Speaking of amazing, what's going on in that big, amazing brain of yours? A penny for your thoughts?"

"They're that cheap?" I chuckled, teasing him for using a cliché. "I was thinking about the Altar Stone as a place of sacrifice and atonement. Dr. Hasserin showed how the missing ruby, with its double dagger marks etched into it, aligned with the Altar Stone. Do you think King Arthur chose a ruby—a red stone—to symbolize blood? What if he buried the Grail—the symbol of the ultimate communion and eternal life—under the Altar Stone?"

I nibbled on a few crackers and jam from the cheeseboard.

"Those are very interesting theories! Go on?"

"Those questions are really all I have now."

"Well, questions are a great start. If there's anyone who is going to answer them, it's going to be you! Speaking of questions, you wanna open your present?" Blane pointed to the box.

I was so enthralled by Stonehenge, I'd forgotten about my Christmas present. "Yes, but only if you open yours!"

I'd gotten Blane a book on King Arthur. He'd gotten me a gold chain-link bracelet with a little charm on it. Made by one of my favorite designers, the charm was a black crystal cross inside a gold circle.

"It's the Ailm! Like Lydia's!"

"It's the opposite of Lydia's. Hers is a gold cross on a black stone. I noticed hers in office hours."

"I love it!" I kissed Blane, picking up the card that described the charm. Blane grinned as he wrapped his arms around me.

The Ailm is a simple and powerful Celtic symbol. It is a cross inside a circle. The Ailm is connected with Yule Logs, which provided light and warmth to the Celts throughout the longest and darkest winter days. For this reason, the Ailm is a symbol of light overcoming the darkness—and also of seeing a clear path forward.

The Ailm charm reminds its wearer to have physical, mental, and spiritual strength; to be resilient; and to persevere through hardship.

The meaning of the charm was not lost on me. It was one of the most thoughtful presents.

"Help me put it on?"

Blane picked up the bracelet and clasped it around my wrist. Marveling at how dainty my new bracelet was, I kissed him.

"And thank you for my King Arthur book. How'd you know I'm a fan of his?" Blane winked at me as he laughed. "Seriously, this is the perfect present for a kid raised on Camelot!"

Stephanie returned with three cans of sparkling water, three glasses with ice cubes, and three cocktail napkins.

"You two pick whichever ones you want, and I'll have what's left."

We sat in the living room, sipping our water and chatting. Every so often, Stephanie would get up and check on dinner.

When Mickey arrived, he walked into the room and planted a big kiss on his wife's cheek before he even took his coat off. In every way Blane was tall and lanky, his dad was the exact opposite. Mickey looked like he had a very successful side gig moonlighting as Santa Claus at Christmas. As he was taking off one of his gloves, it dropped on the floor. I picked it up and handed it to him.

"Hello Carly," he said as he shook my hand. "Welcome to the Henley household. I see Stephanie is already sharing her stories with you. That's a good sign."

I grinned. Blane's dad's comment was reaffirming.

"Every time she tells her stories, I learn something new about her. You'd think after all these years, that's hard to believe, but it isn't." He looked at Stephanie adoringly. "I fall more and more in love with this woman every day. A whole lifetime is not enough days to show her how much I love her."

Blane squeezed my hand and winked at me. I was inspired by how much Mickey loved Stephanie. The way he interacted with his wife reminded me of the way my dad loved my mom. A pang of sadness hit me. I was sure my mom would never find a man like my dad again.

"And I love you, too, Mickey," said Stephanie as she hugged him. "But now it's time for dinner."

††

Exhausted from the day, and happily full from dinner, I headed downstairs to the guest room. I was excited for tomorrow: Blane was taking me on a surprise adventure. As I wondered where, I changed into my Christmas-ornament-and-snowman pajama set. Its fabric was warm and extra soft against my skin.

I brushed my teeth, gazing at my pendant in the mirror. I couldn't get Stephanie's Stonehenge painting out of my head. *Sacrifice. Bloodshed. Atonement for sins.* The sun looked like a ruby. *How are the missing ruby, solstice, and Altar Stone all connected to the Grail?* With Gran's poem and Dr. Hasserin's research, I was convinced not only that the Grealmæp led to the Grail, but also that the missing ruby, when illuminated by the sunrays on the solstice, held the key to where the Grail was buried. *The alignment of the Grealmæp and the sunrays must reveal the Grail's location!*

I finished brushing my teeth and opened my journal to write down my thoughts. As I flipped through the pages, I saw my questions on the Knights of the Dagger's notes to Gran and Lydia.

Their notes had specifically said to meet at Stonehenge's center and alluded to bloodshed and cleansing. *Could the Knights of the Dagger have meant stand at the Altar Stone?* I walked to my nightstand and got my phone. I swiped through the photos, looking for pictures I'd taken of Lydia's notes. In one of their notes, the Knights of the Dagger had indicated exactly how to use the Grealmæp!

The dagger points to the fallen,
You must see what's etched in stone
The world must be cleansed so it can heal
For past sins we must all atone

The day of atonement is not far
The fallen ones will rise again
For they will drink of the sacred cup
It's not a matter of if, but when

As I reread the poem, there was no doubt in my mind that the cryptic words and "sacred cup" referred to drinking from the Grail. *If the dagger pointed to the fallen ones, and the fallen ones rose again after drinking from the Grail, maybe the Grealmæp's dagger pointed to where the Grail was hidden.* I scribbled my questions down and underlined them. I was getting closer to knowing where the Grail was buried at Stonehenge!

††

Our breakfast conversation the next morning was mostly on Stonehenge.

"Your painting brought Stonehenge to life for me in a way I'd never thought about before," I said to Stephanie.

"That's so sweet of you to say, thank you. That's what art does."

"That's what *some* art does." I thought about the pictures of Arthurian monuments that Dr. Wengaro had shown us in Grail Times. "I wish our Grail professor showed us paintings like yours instead of stale diagrams."

"You mean that Wegro guy?" asked Stephanie. "Blaney told me about him. Sounds like a real full-of-himself jerk."

"Dr. Wengaro, and yup, that'd be him."

"So, what is your interest in Stonehenge, Carly?" asked Mickey.

I was thankful Blane had honored my request not to share the details of our case with his parents. It wasn't that I didn't trust them. But until we had more tangible evidence, I was uncomfortable discussing our case with others outside of our team.

"It's for some research I'm doing with one of my professors. We've got all sorts of speculations about Stonehenge. It has such a rich and mysterious history."

"I'd be happy to share a thing or two about Stonehenge if it helps you. Did you know it was important to the Druids?" asked Stephanie as she started clearing breakfast.

I shook my head. "Who were the Druids?" I got up to help her take dishes to the sink.

"They were kind of like Celtic aristocracy—religious leaders, legend-keepers, sorcerers, doctors. But they were prohibited from writing down any of their knowledge. So, a lot of what we know about them is from Roman observations and accounts—or pure guesses." Stephanie finished washing a bowl and set it on the drying rack.

"That's fascinating! Why was Stonehenge so important to the Druids?" I handed her a mug.

"We don't really know. It's speculative. The Druids thought Stonehenge was some type of calendar or way of marking the path of the sun and moon. The standing stones were carefully and precisely laid out to align with the summer and winter solstices—the longest and shortest days of the year. For example, on the summer solstice, the sunlight shines straight down a 'track' called The Avenue right onto the Altar Stone. The layout of the standing stones would have meant someone had been tracking the coordinates of the sunrise. It's like whoever constructed Stonehenge made it to align with the sun, the moon, the earth, and the heavens." Stephanie finished the dishes and sat down next to Mickey. "I was intrigued by how the mathematics of Stonehenge had shaped its art—because math and art are two sides of the same coin. It's truly a fascinating place. Its story is intertwined with England's history, which of course is tied to King Arthur and the Knights of the Round Table."

I nodded, thinking of Blane's book on King Arthur. "Didn't Blane have a book on King Arthur?"

"Yes, he loved it! He went through a phase where he always carried it around with him. He asked me to text him a picture of one of its pages a few months ago."

Blane laughed. "Yep, I told you I was fascinated by King Arthur."

"I'd love to see it," I said.

"Sure, it's in one of the closets. I'll get it for you. If you love Stonehenge and British history, you'd love it."

††

Blane ushered me into the car. "Are you ready for our most awesome adventure yet?" He grinned as I put on my seatbelt.

"Of course, but you haven't told me where we are going! You're keeping me in suspense!"

"Are you sure you want to know now?" He started the car and backed down the driveway.

"Yes!"

"I booked us a tour at the museum—the only one left was this time—and then I made us reservations for lunch at one of my favorite restaurants."

"I can't wait!" I said, squeezing Blane's arm in excitement. "Tell me about this museum!"

"It's one of the best art and archaeology museums in the world. It's half an hour away, near town. Every month, the museum features an artifact from an international museum. You get to see it up close. They do two guided tours a day, and ours is one of them."

"What are we seeing?"

"We are seeing the Antikythera Mechanism. It's an Ancient Greek artifact, and I know your gran was an expert. As soon as I learned it was coming here, I knew we'd have to see it together. The tours sold out in minutes. It's one of the reasons I wanted you to visit over break—but it was super hard keeping it a surprise!"

I gasped. Gran had told me about the Antikythera Mechanism! She told me one day after she noticed me wearing her gladiator sandals. Recovered over one hundred years ago from a shipwreck in the Mediterranean Sea, it was one of the oldest, if not *the* oldest, analog computers. It was a mechanical model of the solar system and was one of the most sophisticated devices ever found from that time.

Gran was on the team who studied it long after it had been recovered, bringing back renewed interest in the artifact. Her insights had been invaluable. She'd suggested the mechanism was used not only to predict solar eclipses and track months, but also to calculate the four-year cycle of the Olympics—the Greek athletic games. I couldn't wait to see the Antikythera Mechanism in person and was over the moon that Blane had booked the tour.

As we drove to the museum, I flipped through Blane's King Arthur book. I thought about how Stephanie said the math of Stonehenge had shaped its art. The whole monument was a beautiful and functional celestial calendar. I found the stained-glass picture of Arthur and Guinevere. There were their Grealmæps! Awestruck, I felt my pendant under my shirt.

"That's our mall. Before we had our driver's licenses, and cars, we'd all hang out there since it was so close to our neighborhood. Sounds pretty boring, but that mall food court has some of the best Chinese food you've ever had."

My head jerked up at Blane's voice. I looked out my window to see a sprawling parking lot and massive building. The mall must have been millions of square feet, with hundreds of stores. I liked that Blane shared the details of his childhood with me. But with all my thoughts on Stonehenge, its precise layout, and how the Grealmæp worked, the last thing I could concentrate on was the scenery.

As we passed the mall, I blurted out, "King Arthur made the Grealmæp not as a decorative ornament, but as a functional instrument to find the Grail. All the evidence points to that. The Grealmæp aligns with Stonehenge, and the ruby aligns with the Altar Stone. The mathematics of Stonehenge and the sun patterns are so precise. The Grealmæp was Arthur's way of guaranteeing the Grail could be found only if someone had the Grealmæp and knew how to use it—and only on the day of the summer solstice."

Blane turned and looked at me.

"Don't look at me. Look at the road, silly!"

"Hmm, I think you're on to something. But if finding the Grail was tied to the solstice, how would Guinevere—or one of Arthur's loyal knights—locate the Grail if it *wasn't* the solstice? Would they only get one chance per year to find it?"

As soon as I heard Blane's questions, I realized the flaw in my theory. He had a great point.

"You're right." I sighed, staring out the window at the cars. After a few moments, I said, "Here's another question. What if the solstice doesn't matter? What if you can use the Grealmæp *without* it being the solstice? What if the Grealmæp has a *different* alignment?" My voice trailed off, replaced by the sound of the tires on the road. "But why would Gran's poem be that specific about the sun rising behind the Heel Stone?"

"Gran's poem is one piece of the puzzle, from her to you. It's not a note from the Knights of the Dagger or a textbook. Maybe she put it in there because she knew Stonehenge was on your bucket list. Maybe she set it up so you would think of Stonehenge. Her poem didn't say you had to *use* the Henge Piece on the summer solstice, right? Have you come across any other research that mentions the Grealmæp and the solstice?"

I pulled my journal out of my satchel. "You're right. I haven't come across other research."

"So, maybe using the Grealmæp has nothing to do with the summer solstice—and everything to do with the missing ruby, the Altar Stone, and the way the dagger is positioned."

I sighed. "We really need to find Dr. Hasserin's journals."

"And we also need to figure out if Dr. Wengaro's ring is the ruby. If it is, and Dr. Wengaro knows about the alignment, he could be steps away from the Grail too." Blane said.

I reached for Blane's arm across the console.

"We'll figure it out, Carly. Don't forget, Dr. Kells has her half of the Grealmæp. There's not too much Dr. Wengaro can do without that."

I sighed. Blane was right, but I knew our time was running out. The Knights of the Dagger had reminded us of that.

"In a complete change of subject, there's my high school," said Blane as we passed a football field. "The number of football games I've gone to, I can count on—"

"Did you even go to any football games?" I laughed.

"Yes! I knew the whole cheerleading team," he said. "That's how I learned football."

"What else did you learn from the cheerleading team?" I teased.

Blane laughed. "Nothing. They were my friends."

I managed a half-smile. I couldn't believe a guy as handsome as Blane would be "just friends" with the entire cheerleading team.

"Okay," I muttered. "Just friends."

"Oh babe." Blane grabbed my hand. "I know you're bummed

because you don't have answers. We'll sort it. Hey, did you ever text J. Carmichael to meet up with him?"

"I haven't yet. He said first thing in the new year."

"Get it on the calendar from now. A guy like him is going to have a full schedule very quickly."

As we pulled into the museum parking lot, I pulled out my phone and texted J. Carmichael. *Can we set a date and time from now?*

Sure—how's January 15?

Works for me. I'll be back at Nassauton. Can we meet there?

Yes, but briefly. I'll be in and out between projects. See you then, he said.

With J. Carmichael's date secured, I felt a little more reassured and upbeat.

"See how easy that was?" Blane asked as he parked the car. We bundled up with our hats and gloves. "You ready?"

I smiled. "Of course. I can't wait!"

Blane locked the car and slipped his arm into mine as we entered the museum.

XVI

"The Antikythera Mechanism," said our tour guide, "has puzzled archaeologists for decades. At two thousand years old, it very well may be the first computer. The National Archaeological Museum in Athens has loaned us the Antikythera Mechanism, through our sister city relationship with Athens. My name is Marikeath. I will be your tour guide for today."

We clustered around a table with eight other people, as tours were strictly limited to ten. We'd filed into the museum's back office. The whole room smelled of old paper and folders that hadn't been opened since the 1970s. The ceiling was stained with cigarette smoke, and the windows barely let enough light in. If it weren't for the rows of fluorescent lights, the room would otherwise be completely dark. A yellow microfiber towel covered a lump on the table.

"Recovered in 1901 from a shipwreck off the coast of Antikythera Island, the Antikythera Mechanism was a type of calendar that predicted astronomical events, such as planetary movements, solar and lunar eclipses, and phases of the moon—what we would commonly call months. Until recently, we had no idea how it worked."

Marikeath put on white gloves and carefully rolled the microfiber towel back to reveal the Antikythera Mechanism. The group erupted in delighted murmurs. One woman took out her cell phone and leaned over the table.

"Sorry, no pictures, please," said Marikeath. "I'm going to

have to ask you to stand back. Please do not touch the Mechanism. It is comprised of thirty bronze gears and is split into eighty-two fragments. We think there used to be a knob or some type of handle on the outside to wind these gears. In front of us is Fragment A, which, with a diameter of about five inches, is the mechanism's largest surviving gear. Note the cross-shaped bars inside the circle."

Marikeath walked around the table and pointed out the different markings on the face with her gloved finger.

"Tony Freeth and his team have studied the Antikythera Mechanism, combining their observations, with their understanding of Babylonian astronomy, Ancient Greek writings, and mathematics from Plato's Academy. Freeth's findings present the Antikythera Mechanism as an incredible testament to the Greeks' precise understanding of celestial bodies—and how they could be used to mark time."

I looked at Blane, noticing he was enthralled by Marikeath's comments. I loved seeing him when he was learning new things. He gave his whole attention to whatever he was learning, and I could tell it made him happy.

"A penny for your thoughts?" I whispered to him, leaning into his shoulder and wrapping my arm around his back.

"They're not that cheap," said Blane as he winked at me. "It's amazing, the wheels in my head haven't stopped turning. I'm intrigued by the math. I see it, like Fibonacci's Numbers, as some code of the universe. That's what it is—the code of the cosmos."

"What do you mean?" I could tell he booked the tour as much for him, as he did for me.

"It's as though, in the positioning of every celestial body, God gave us the code of the cosmos. In the constellations, He's showing us how he structured His playground. As we explore more of the playground, we learn its rules and how it works. It starts with us looking up and seeing the heavens."

Marikeath's voice faded into the background as I concentrated on Blane's. "I'm sure you've caught yourself staring at the sky on a clear night—maybe those summer nights you and your dad would make s'mores. Weren't you utterly blown away that the same God who created the heavens and the Earth, created you? And the rules that govern how we work also govern how the stars work. There's something remarkable about that. Here is this instrument that helps us understand incredibly complex concepts. These concepts define our knowledge of reality—time, space, and matter."

His mind saw no separation between science and God. He saw science as evidence for God's existence. Blane's view helped me understand how I saw science and my own faith.

"If you look here," said Marikeath, "you can see the purposeful representation of the ecliptic longitude and phases of the moon. The Antikythera Mechanism helped the Greeks determine lunar cycles and understand the Metonic calendar. If we look at the gears and calculate their dimensions, ratios, and tooth counts, we realize these specific gears would have been synchronized with the Metonic and Saros dials on the back face."

Blane and I shuffled closer to see the gears.

"This would have helped the Greeks measure the duration of a month or predict, with surprisingly good accuracy, the number of days until a given lunar event—such as a full or new moon. This, of course, places the Mechanism alongside another very famous lunar calendar: Stonehenge."

My ears perked up.

"Over five thousand years old, Stonehenge famously marks solstices, acting as a solar calendar—but also, as Lloyd Matthews and Joan Rankin have studied, acting as a lunar calendar."

I clutched Blane's arm. I'd been so focused on Stonehenge's alignment with the sun, I'd never considered how Stonehenge could align with the moon.

"Matthews and Rankin painstakingly reconstructed two Stonehenge models, which are on display at the Maryhill Museum of Art in Klickitat County, Washington. Fun fact: Samuel Hill, the founder of the Maryhill Museum, was obsessed with Stonehenge—who isn't? I know I am! Hill constructed his Stonehenge Memorial—a life-size monument dedicated to the fallen soldiers of World War I and America's first World War I memorial. Back to Matthews and Rankin, who, in addition to their work on the lunar calendar at Stonehenge, identified three carvings on the Trilithon stones. Known as 'The Eye,' 'The Dividers,' and 'The Parallels,' these three carvings are etched in stone, on Stones 52, 53, and 59 respectively."

Etched in stone. I squeezed Blane's arm. Here I was, at a museum in Blane's hometown, learning about Ancient Greek lunar calendars—and Stonehenge! I had no idea about the stone carvings until now. These gave me brand new insights into our Stonehenge mystery. Was it possible that Dr. Hasserin referred to these carvings when he wrote *etched in stone* on his Post-it notes? Was the ruby related to these carvings?

"In addition to finding these carvings," Marikeath continued, "Matthews and Rankin might have also discovered the purpose of fifty-six holes—small, shallow pits—dug around Stonehenge during the first phase of its construction. Their research suggests these holes, known as the Aubrey Holes, could have been for posts that formed a calendar. This calendar marked not only the solar and lunar phases, but also the duration of each day. Counting days would have enabled astronomers to count the years with surprising accuracy."

I had never heard about the Aubrey Holes. Dr. Hasserin's books hadn't mentioned them. Maybe his journals contained information on them. I'd wished I hadn't left my journal in the car and hoped I'd be able to remember everything I was learning.

"Stonehenge, much like the Antikythera Mechanism, reveals humans' fascination with the earth—and the cosmos. Since prehistoric times, we have always been intrigued by the heavens above us, seeking to study what their secrets reveal about our planet—and us. Thank you for coming today. I hope you enjoyed learning about the Antikythera Mechanism. In the gift shop, we do have mini models of it on sale for a limited time only. Give the gift of history, and in this case, history, time, and space, to your loved ones—you won't regret it!"

††

Having entered Walt's and closing the door firmly behind us so it didn't blow in the wind, we took off our jackets and hats. The little bell on the handle jingled as the door closed.

"Hey Patty!" Blane called out as he hung his jacket on the coat rack.

A short, older woman stepped out from behind the bar, wearing a well-worn pink T-shirt that said *Walt's: Serving Up the Originals Since 1958* in faded, blue cursive writing. She looked like she'd been working all day, with her hair already frizzy and sweat beading up around her temples. She put her towel down.

"Great to see you, Blane!" Patty walked up to us. "Come on, I got your back booth ready. Who's this?" she said, pointing at me.

"Patty this is Carly. I met her at Nassauton. She's in my archaeology classes, she's my study buddy, and my girlfriend."

Patty smiled. "Carly, pleased to meet you. Welcome to Walt's. Blane is like family to me. He and his mom would always come here for lunch when he was a kid. Stephanie's great. They'd sit in that booth right there and order sloppy joes." She pointed to the back booth to which we were walking. It already had menus on the table.

"Best sloppy joes I've ever had! Mom says hi and says she's way overdue for one."

Patty's smile widened. "She can come in anytime."

Blane and I sat in the booth as Patty left to get us water glasses.

"Here's some water while you look at the menus. Let's see, what other dirt can I spill on Blane?" She paused, then looked at Blane with a teasing glance. "In high school, he would come here Friday nights with the whole football and cheerleading team. They'd always sit at that table"—she pointed to a spot in the middle of the restaurant—"and Blane would sneak his way back here to this booth with his book. There came a point when I stopped counting the books he was reading. Always reading about digs or quests or legends. He'd tell me one day, he wanted to lead a dig of his own. Sorry, Blane, hope I'm not embarrassing you, but she's gotta know at least a little bit about you."

I laughed. "Thanks Patty. He's definitely the archaeology nerd—and I love it."

"He sure is. He's a good guy, Carly."

Blane smiled.

"Let me know when you're ready to order." Patty left our table.

Walt's fare was mostly salads, sandwiches, and soups. I decided on a house salad and chicken noodle soup.

"The Antikythera Mechanism was so cool! Thank you for planning that."

"I knew you'd love it! How about that Stonehenge bonus?"

"Heck yeah! It got me thinking, do you think we're missing something if we're only focusing on Stonehenge and the sun?" I reached into my satchel and took out my journal and pencil.

"What do you mean?"

"Well, you know how Marikeath was talking about the lunar calendar, the carvings in those stones, and the Aubrey Holes?"

Blane nodded, reaching for my hand and holding it while we talked.

"I was thinking, what if Dr. Hasserin's phrase—*etched in stone*—referred to the carvings that were etched in Stones 52, 53, and 59?"

"Now that's interesting! It's even more reason to find his journals."

I nodded. "Marikeath mentioned Stones 52, 53, and 59: 'The Eye,' 'The Dividers,' and 'The Parallels.' I'm thinking these stones are important. What do we know about them?" I asked as I jotted down my thoughts.

"Hmm," said Blane. "I don't know anything off the top of my head." He took out his phone. "But Google might."

A few minutes later, Blane handed me his phone. "Whoa, look at this."

I read the website Blane had pulled up.

> *Richard J. C. Atkinson studied Stonehenge, bringing theories about the monument to the public, In 1953, he noticed the outline of a dagger and axe blades carved into Stone 53, one of the trilithon uprights. The shape of these carvings suggests they date to the Bronze Age—somewhere between 1750 and 1500 BC.*

"Matthews and Rankin weren't the only ones to discover the carving on Stone 53!" I scribbled the URL in my journal. "And it's a dagger!"

"That can't be a coincidence," said Blane. "All these daggers—the double daggers on the notes, the dagger on Stone 53—"

"And the dagger in the Grealmæp?" I added. I gave Blane's phone back to him and pulled out my own. I swiped through my pictures until I found the picture of Guinevere's diagram of the Grealmæp and its alignment with Stonehenge. As I studied the diagram, I realized I didn't know where Stone 53 was.

"Where is Stone 53?"

"Not sure, but I'm sure we can find a picture that has the standing stones numbered."

Blane put his phone in the middle of our table. After making sure no one was around, I pulled out my pendant. The diagram Blane found was too small compared to my pendant, but it had the numbered standing stones, and it also showed the Aubrey

Holes and fallen stones. As I aligned my pendant with Stonehenge, like Lydia had done with our pendants and her Stonehenge replica, I gasped. The dagger pierced through Stone 53, with its tip ending right at the fallen stones on the edge of the outer circle. I noticed that the fallen stones seemed to block one of the Aubrey Holes. Then it hit me. *The fallen ones*! I picked up my phone and swiped to my picture of Gran's and Lydia's Knights of the Dagger note.

The dagger points to the fallen,
You must see what's etched in stone
The world must be cleansed so it can heal
For past sins we must all atone

The day of atonement is not far
The fallen ones will rise again
For they will drink of the sacred cup
It's not a matter of if, but when

I knew exactly where the Grail was buried.

XVII

Blane and I sat on the sofa in Lydia's office. Her door had still not been fixed, so as we chatted, we kept our voices low and made sure no one was in the hallway to eavesdrop. With students trickling back to campus for final exams, there weren't too many people in the building. Regardless, we weren't taking any chances.

The three of us discussed my discoveries and theories about the dagger etched into Stone 53. I suggested the Knights of the Dagger subtly alluded to this in the notes they'd sent. As Lydia listened, she arranged her bun.

"So, you think the Grail is buried under those fallen stones?" She asked.

I nodded. "Yes. And I also think the Knights of the Dagger need the complete Grealmæp to be able to get the Grail. We need the missing ruby to be able to understand why."

"So, what's our next move?"

"Blane and I are going to Archaeology Talks tonight to keep an eye on Dr. Wengaro. We need to see if his ring is the missing ruby, and we must find Dr. Hasserin's journals. And we should call Dr. Leith to work on getting us our permits."

"Good thinking. Go for the evidence, not for the emotion. Let's meet after Archaeology Talks. I'll call Allister and see what he can do about the permits."

††

Dr. Wengaro hadn't missed a beat in scheduling Archaeology Talks. The featured speaker, Dr. Ray Rapalmo, had recently returned from his Easter Island dig and was discussing the mysteries of the moai. Easter Island had always fascinated me. Visiting it was also on my bucket list. I got to the Commons early and chose a spot in the front row. Blane texted me: *Running late with the econ group. Save me a seat. Love you!*

No worries, I already did! See you soon, love you! <3

As I waited, I pulled out one of my Arthurian legend books. I was so engrossed in reading, I didn't even notice Blane walk in and sit next to me.

"You'll never believe what happened to me."

"Hey!" I said, putting my book away and reaching up to give him a hug. "What's going on?"

Blane leaned in and started whispering in my ear. "I think Dr. Wengaro broke into Dr. Kells' office. I'm pretty sure he has her Stonehenge pieces!"

"What?" I couldn't believe it! "How do you know?"

"I bumped into Dr. Wengaro and Dr. Rapalmo as they were walking out of Dr. Wengaro's office. Dr. Wengaro had his papers, folders, and blazer balanced on his arm. When Dr. Rapalmo reached to hold a few things to help him lock, Dr. Wengaro dropped everything. All his papers went flying. I stopped to pick them up."

"That was nice of you," I commented.

"As I picked up his blazer, something fell out of the pocket—these little, brightly colored pieces. They looked like they were part of a board game, like they were part of a set."

"They've gotta be from Lydia's replica!"

Blane nodded. "As soon as they fell out, Dr. Wengaro scooped them up so quickly and stuffed them back in his pocket. He mumbled 'Thank you' and walked away so fast, you'd have thought he'd seen Dr. Hasserin's ghost."

"How do we get to his blazer and the pieces?"

"Good evening, ladies and gentlemen." Dr. Wengaro's voice boomed across the theater. His ponytail was neatly tied behind his back. "We are thrilled to kick off another Archaeology Talks. Tonight's speaker, Dr. Ray Rapalmo, is an expert on Easter Island and its mysterious moai. Who made them? How did they get there? What are they? Why are they arranged the way they are? All these questions and not a lot of answers. Please join me in welcoming Dr. Rapalmo. Don't forget, afterward, we'll head to Winnie B.'s for the post-talk discussion."

As Dr. Rapalmo walked to the podium, my mind wandered. How could I get to Dr. Wengaro's blazer? If the pieces in his pocket were indeed Lydia's, that would be the proof we needed to link Dr. Wengaro to the break-in of her office.

After the talk, Blane and I headed to Winnie B.'s, strategizing a plan to get the pieces. Dr. Wengaro usually had the same setup for every discussion—tables in the back room around the appetizer station—and tonight was no different. Dr. Wengaro and Dr. Rapalmo stood by the appetizer station. Dr. Wengaro had draped his blazer on the back of a chair near the appetizer station, saving himself and Dr. Rapalmo a seat.

Blane and I sat at a table on the other side of the appetizer station, then walked up and surveyed the spread. We had a very risky mission ahead of us. I had to keep my cool without letting my nerves get to me, or else our mission would fail. After I piled up my plate, I squeezed Blane's hand.

"You got this."

"You do too." He squeezed my hand back.

I walked up to Dr. Wengaro as Blane walked away. The whole room blurred in the background. I focused on only Dr. Wengaro and Dr. Rapalmo. My heartbeats were the only thing I heard.

I took a breath. "Hi Dr. Wengaro." I held a French fry and

dipped it in the ketchup. “Tonight was awesome. I have a ton of questions for Dr. Rapalmo.”

I chewed my fry, barely able to hide my nervousness. Our plan was risky—but it was the best we could come up with.

“Hi Carly,” said Dr. Wengaro. “Great to see you, and yes, ask away! Ray, let me introduce you to one of my star students, Carly Stuart. Her paper on chivalry and the Knights of the Round Table was superb—one of the best I’ve read.”

I noticed Dr. Wengaro wasn’t wearing his ring. I smiled. “Thank you, Dr. Wengaro. Great to meet you, Dr. Rapalmo.”

I started asking my questions. I made sure Dr. Wengaro and Dr. Rapalmo were paying attention to me. This would give Blane a chance to go to their table and take the pieces out of Dr. Wengaro’s blazer. My hands were shaking, but I tried to pick up my fries and stack them on my plate, using them to represent the moai.

“Here, maybe it’s easier if I draw it. Can you come to my table? We can sit down?”

I made sure Dr. Wengaro and Dr. Rapalmo sat so their backs were to their table. I had to stall for time for Blane. All he needed was five minutes. I didn’t want to take any chances. I wiped my fingers before pulling out my journal and pencil. I started sketching. My fingers were shaking so much, I could barely draw.

“Look at this, am I sketching this right? You said this moai layout is currently incomplete. Can you elaborate on that? Why does that matter? What does that tell us?”

I handed Dr. Rapalmo my pencil. We could not afford for Blane to get caught. They had bumped into Blane in the hallway and knew he had seen the pieces. If Dr. Wengaro suspected anything, it was game over.

“That’s a great sketch.” Dr. Wengaro studied the paper. “I didn’t know you could draw like that.”

I smiled, surprised that my lines amounted to anything.

Dr. Rapalmo filled in more of the sketch. “You need to

consider this moai would have gone here. If you're on the island, it's easy to see there is another behind it. Have you ever been to Easter Island?"

"No, but I've always wanted to go."

"You have? Dr. Rapalmo's dig is still active. One of the reasons why I brought him here is because . . . can I spill the beans, Ray?"

I was terrified Blane hadn't gotten the pieces yet. I couldn't turn around and look at him. I had to trust him. Beads of sweat formed around my hairline. I brushed them off and wiped my fingers on my pants. I hoped Dr. Wengaro didn't see how nervous I was.

"Yes, Kenneth," Dr. Rapalmo grinned. "Spill away!"

"I am organizing a dig to Easter Island over spring break for students in my seminar. The former professor required students to go on a dig. This trip could count for that requirement."

"Oh my gosh, that would be great," I mumbled, still in suspense about Blane. I hadn't even paid attention to what they were saying.

"Hi Carly!" Blane's voice pulled me back to the room. "There you are. Thank you for saving us seats! Hi Dr. Wengaro, thanks for a great Archaeology Talks tonight."

Dr. Wengaro smiled. "You're welcome, Blane. Thank you for coming."

"Let me know about sign-ups," I said to Dr. Wengaro.

"Sure." He looked around the room. Most students had gotten their appetizers and took their seats. "Shall we get started?"

Dr. Wengaro and Dr. Rapalmo headed back to their seats.

"Let me see!" I whispered as soon as they had cleared the appetizer station.

"Here you go." Blane dropped two pieces in my hand.

The pieces were the exact ones from Lydia's replica. They clinked together as they landed in my palm. Dr. Wengaro had broken into Lydia's office. I was holding the proof.

††

Lydia's new office door was even nicer than her old one. Since we last saw her, she'd called Allister. He agreed to help us apply for a permit.

"This certainly does not look good for Kenneth." Lydia sat at her desk, dropping the two pieces from one hand to the other. "Do I confront him? Do I go to Daniel? Do I go directly to the provost? Or do I go to the police? Do we continue to monitor him until we get the ruby?"

"If you confront him now, he'll know you know something. He'll be more careful to cover his tracks. There's no telling how he might retaliate or what harm he might cause," I said. "We need to learn what he knows about Stonehenge, Dr. Hasserin's research, and the Grealmæp. We need the ruby."

"I agree. I don't think we should do anything until we get those answers, since obviously he knows something," Blane chimed in.

"You two are right. If we go to the university, they'll put the break-in through their process. While he might get punished, we might not get our answers."

"And answers are far more important to us at this point," I said. "We need to get to his office."

"We need to be smart." Lydia stared out her window.

Blane smiled, his hazel eyes lighting up with an idea. "I could go for office hours," he said. "I'm in his seminar, but he doesn't really know me. I'm sure he's seen me at Archaeology Talks and Winnie B.'s for the discussions. The closest I've come to him is bumping into him in the hallway. I can ask him about his CV and accomplishments, or a question on Archaeology Talks. Maybe, say . . . Oh, I got it!" Blane got up and took a few steps around the coffee table. "I tell him I had a question on Easter Island, from Dr. Rapalmo's talk. Then, I turn the conversation to his career. I tease out of him what he knows about Stonehenge and the Grail—and the Grealmæp—without asking him directly, of course."

I smiled. "I love it," I said. "Maybe you can ask him about his ring too." I paused. "But are you sure you'll be safe?"

"I'll be fine! He's not going to try anything crazy on a student."

I nodded, still a little apprehensive, but at the same time, confident in Blane and his plan.

††

Blane and I had been in the Archaeology Research Room for the better part of the day. The plastic cover on the fluorescent light was finally fixed. We'd spent most of the time chatting and working—or listening to music. Blane loved sharing his favorite songs. I loved hearing them. We'd even play air guitar or drum along, laughing over our nonexistent careers as musicians.

"I think we should stick to archaeology," I said. "I don't think I would make a good musician."

Blane laughed. "You can be whatever you want to be! You can be an archaeologist-guitarist. How many of those do you think there are? We could have our own band: Diggin' It. Or, The Rock Stars. We could have guitars in the shape of shovels."

I burst out laughing. "We could do open-air concerts at famous places! I can see the headline now: *The Rock Stars: Live from the Rocky Mountains.*"

Our conversation had meandered from Stonehenge to our courses, to Blane going on the Easter Island dig, to silly, serious, or scholarly topics. I loved how Blane and I could talk about anything and everything—and laugh, and ask questions, and then ask more questions.

"I'm so excited for the dig," Blane said. "To prepare us, Dr. Wengaro is hosting mock excavations over the next two months. We'll learn how to use the instruments and follow dig protocols."

"That's such a smart idea—giving everyone some practice in a supervised setting before you go."

Blane grinned his big goofy grin. "Wish you could come, but I know you and Dr. Kells have to coordinate the Stonehenge logistics. How's studying for your literature final going?"

"It's going well—almost at a stopping point. These authors were absolute legends—some of the world's most brilliant thinkers."

Blane smiled. "You're very intellectually curious. I love that about you."

I grinned. "Thank you. There is so much I don't know. The older I get, the more I realize how much there is."

Blane started laughing. "The older you get? You're not even twenty-one. You are *not* old."

"Maybe not, but I'm an old soul. When I was young, I used to disappear to my grandmother's closet and wear her shoes. I loved her boots the most. Everyone would say I had big shoes to fill. I always pictured myself as an expert archaeologist, like Gran." I smiled as I gazed at the books on the shelf.

"Go on?" Blane put down his book and gave me his full attention.

"I love how archaeology brings mythology and history to life. You see the artifacts. You imagine people using the bowls and dressing up in the clothes. The artifacts bring the past to life. It's different from reading about history. The books are good—they're good starters—but they're so . . . two-dimensional, I guess. The artifacts are the actual proof, the evidence, that the stories are true."

"That was beautiful. You have the mind of a scholar and the spirit of an explorer. You're taking Dr. Kells' musings on evidence to heart. It's easy to get wrapped up in the emotion of it all. It's not like you can go back in time and ask people what they did or why they did it. You have to go artifact by artifact, piecing together the past."

There was a knock on the Research Room door. A librarian

walked in, heading straight for one of the shelves.

"Hmm, that's odd," she mumbled. "It should be right here. It's not. The catalogue shows no one has checked it out."

"Huh? What do you mean?" I asked her, curious as to why there was a discrepancy between the catalogue and the shelf.

"The catalogue shows the book is here, but it's not here on the shelf."

"What book are you looking for?"

"It's a book on Stonehenge. A professor is looking for it. It's called *Unearthing the Secrets of Stonehenge's Aubrey Holes*. I don't suppose it's on the table, is it?"

"No ma'am," Blane said, scanning the table.

"Hmm. I'll double check our system to make sure it's not already checked out," the librarian said as she walked out, closing the door behind her.

"A book on Stonehenge, missing?" I asked as soon as the door closed.

"If it has to do with Stonehenge, knowing what we know," Blane said, "I think Dr. Wengaro took it."

"But why would he take it without checking it out? He's on faculty. It's not that suspicious."

"Maybe he doesn't want to advertise that it's checked out in his name," said Blane. "Maybe he's starting to feel he's not the only one getting close to finding the Grail. You do have Dr. Hasserin's books on Stonehenge and the Grail still checked out. Everyone can see that catalogue. Odds are he knows you have them."

††

Lydia sat at her desk, sipping tea out of her porcelain mug. Blane and I were sitting on the sofa. "Close the door. This is gonna be epic," he said.

"How did office hours go?" Lydia could barely contain her

curiosity. "What did you find out?"

"Well, he wasn't wearing his ring. So that was a bummer. It didn't really come up in the conversation. But here's what did."

Blane got up and started pacing in front of Lydia's coffee table.

"I told him I'd been thinking about the Easter Island moai and how and why they got there. It was perfect. He was all in. I told him I learned the Rapanui people believed the moai were important for agricultural and food growing. I asked him what additional evidence there was for this belief, and whether it influenced how the monoliths were arranged. Were the Rapanui people aware of sunray patterns, lunar cycles, markers for the optimal start of the harvest, things like that?"

"What'd he say?" I sat on the edge of the sofa in anticipation.

"He said of course. He said many places around the world were built like this, as seasonal calendars, including—and he brought this up—Stonehenge!"

Blane was beaming with excitement and pride.

"As he was talking, I noticed he had this stack of brown leather journals and books on Stonehenge on his desk. The journals and books had tons of Post-it notes sticking out of them. I asked if there was any evidence Stonehenge was important for agriculture or crop cycling. He was blown away by my questions. He said I was making very good connections. I talked to him about the ley lines. He was very surprised I knew about Earth's energy grid. 'Most people don't believe in the ley lines,' he said. 'But I do because I've experienced them—at the Hill of Tara.'"

"This is amazing!" I said, springing up off the sofa and high-fiving Blane.

"Wait, wait, it gets better!" Blane grinned. "He said he was very interested in Stonehenge because it is a ley lines nexus. It has incredible energy, and like the Hill of Tara, it is an extremely sacred and protected site. He said there is an artifact that aligns with the ley lines and maps which ones go through what stones."

"He must be talking about the Grealmæp!" Lydia said.

"Yep!" Blane paused as he looked at Dr. Kells and me. "He said he knows Dr. Kells found this instrument—because he was at the dig. I played dumb the whole time. He said he hadn't seen the artifact. He also said Dr. Kells and Dr. Ainsley asked his best friend about it. Then he got quiet and directed the conversation back to Easter Island and lunar cycles."

"No way!" I fist-bumped Blane. "Great work! How did you respond?"

"I said it must have been difficult for him to have all the attention on his friend. He didn't comment but changed the subject again."

"So clearly something happened between them!" I said. "He won't talk about it!"

"He quickly changed the subject to how he had the connections to Dr. Rapalmo and was excited for the dig. As he was talking, I started looking at the books on his desk." Blane tore a piece of paper out of his notebook. "Dr. Kells, don't these titles look familiar?"

Lydia and I gasped as we read the titles: *Grail and Glory: The Truth of Man's Quest for Eternal Life*; *Ancient Roman Crucifixion Stories: The Medical Evidence for the Death of Christ*; and *The Early Church: How the Early Christians Hid the Grail.*

"Kenneth has my books," she whispered. "The same books I let Sid borrow."

"But how do we know they're not his own copies?" I asked.

"Because all three titles? Together? Even if they were his own copies, that's too much of a coincidence. And he has my replica pieces! I think Kenneth knows where the Grail is buried, and needs the Grealmæp to see Stonehenge's ley lines and find the Grail."

††

I'd been waiting in the back booth at Winnie B.'s for twenty-five minutes. There was no sign of J. Carmichael. He hadn't texted to tell me he was running late. I stared at the table as I waited. My phone rang. Relieved, I picked it up.

"Walking in now. Where are you?" J. Carmichael's voice was breathless.

"Back booth. By the big painting of the football stadium at Nassauton Homecoming," I said. "You'll see me."

After a few moments, a man who looked like he was in his late sixties, carrying a black leather briefcase and sporting a pastel pink bowtie, walked up to the booth. He wore khaki pants, a tweed blazer, and a crisp white shirt.

"Hi Carlyle. Sorry I'm late."

I could tell he was genuinely apologetic. He seemed wise—like a kind and compassionate grandfather. At the same time, he also seemed like a no-nonsense, to-the-point businessman.

Instinctively, I slid out of the booth and stood up. I reached my hand out to shake his. "I'm glad you made it." The last time I'd seen J. Carmichael was at Gran's funeral.

"I am too. Flight was delayed, cab took the wrong exit, had my phone in the trunk, you know." He looked down at my Atlas heels. "Nice shoes by the way. One of Lyle's favorites."

"They're one of my favorites too." I sat down as J. Carmichael slid into the booth.

"I haven't got much time, I'm afraid. Next flight leaves in two hours. But we can talk through some things."

I pulled out J. Carmichael's letter and held it in my hand. "First, how do you know my grandmother?"

"She was one of my first friends in grammar school. We were kids back then—we've had a whole lifetime of adventures since then."

I smiled. Picturing Gran, the poised and professional

archaeologist, as a schoolgirl was amusing. I had so many other questions for J. Carmichael, but I still was wary of him. "When was the last time you talked to my mom?"

"Must have been months ago. Let's see, I got her the honey from France. I was in Switzerland for Thanksgiving. Haven't really spoken to her since then. Why?"

"I'm wondering. She mentions you every now and then. Did you tell her you were meeting me?"

"No. Why would I? That's between you and me."

I exhaled. I could trust J. Carmichael. I looked at the letter he'd written Gran. "Do you know Gran's partner?"

"Yes, Lydia Kells. Lyle adored Lydia. They were quite the team."

"What do you know about the Knights of the Dagger?" I handed J. Carmichael the letter, staring intently at his reaction.

He was stoic while he read it—a reaction I didn't expect from him. When he was done, he folded the note and looked up at me. I couldn't read what he was thinking, and his poker face didn't put me at ease.

"Carly," he said as he unbuttoned the cuff on his left sleeve. He rolled his shirt up and showed me the inside of his left wrist. In barely visible red ink were double dagger marks, exactly like the ones on the letters. I gasped as shivers ran up and down my arms.

"Shh, it's okay. I think it's time you knew a few more things about the Knights of the Dagger. I can't tell you everything, not here at least." He looked around. "You never know who is listening. I'm sure at this point, you've found the Henge Piece. Lyle told me she'd left it for you, with a note, but she couldn't remember where."

I nodded. "It was in one of her shoeboxes, with a poem she'd written for me."

J. Carmichael smiled. "Clever Lyle, leaving you a poem."

"And a riddle!"

"The Riddle of the Ages, right?"

I nodded again. “How’d you know?”

“Because the one thing Lyle and I ran out of in the end was time.” I saw him try to hide a few tears from his eyes. “Sorry, it’s—”

“It’s okay, it’s hard for me too.”

“It will always be hard for me.” He paused. “What do you know so far about the Knights of the Dagger and the Henge Piece? Do you know how it works to get the Grail?”

I told J. Carmichael about Lydia’s and my case—and how all we needed were permits to dig at Stonehenge.

“If you keep your woman’s intuition and wits about you, you’ll be okay. First, we’re not the ‘bad guys.’ The bad guys are the Knights of Vanora—who now go by the Knights of the White Wave. That’s a story for another time. They’ve been trying to find the Grail since King Arthur banished Queen Guinevere to the Amesbury convent. If they find the Grail, they will use it to secure immortality for themselves and usher in a world over which they rule—forever.”

J. Carmichael must have seen me roll my eyes, because he said, “I didn’t believe the supernatural relic-y stuff either, until I saw it. It’s real—very real—and very powerful.”

I looked at him. “What do you mean?” I asked skeptically.

“That’s for another time. You’ll need to experience it for yourself to believe it.”

J. Carmichael looked at the note, then back at me. “The Knights of the White Wave are ruthless. They will kill anyone who opposes them. Their goal is to rule the world. The Knights of the Dagger’s goal is the opposite. We want to find the Grail so we can destroy it. It’s too powerful a relic for mankind to keep. Destroying it is the only way to usher in a new world order, a world that is peaceful and free from the terror of the Knights of the White Wave.”

I was stunned. The Knights of the Dagger notes were true but, like J. Carmichael had written in his note to Gran, their new world order was not evil. I realized that atonement and cleansing must relate to cleansing the world of the Knights of the White Wave.

"Were you the one who sent Gran and Lydia the Knights of the Dagger notes?"

"No—she told me about them. I risked my life to try to help her—technically we're not supposed to talk about the Knights with outsiders. Even within the Knights of the Dagger, we must be secretive. It's for our own protection. But, it was Lyle, my best friend—and love of my life. How could I not?"

As soon as J. Carmichael said that, I felt an unexplainable connection to him. I looked right into his eyes. *Was J. Carmichael Gran's lover?*

His phone buzzed. "I need to go, or I'll miss my flight. Please promise me you'll be careful. Don't tell anyone you met me—or both of us could be in more danger than we are already. Text me if you need anything. I will try to help you."

He handed me the letter, grabbed his briefcase, and slid out of his booth. "Please. The Knights of the White Wave are very dangerous. Your professor could be part of them. Your mom would be devastated if she lost you."

I clutched my pendant through my blouse. *Be brave.* I closed my eyes, inhaled, and exhaled.

Is Dr. Wengaro a Knight of the Dagger or a Knight of the White Wave? More questions. I was sure there was more to Gran's and J. Carmichael's story—and mine. Our time was running out. We had to figure out how the Grealmæp worked and get the missing ruby before Dr. Wengaro found the Grail.

††

Our answer to the missing ruby came the second week in February when Blane went to one of his mock excavations for the Easter Island dig. As soon as he told me what he learned, I texted Lydia to meet.

"Drumroll, please." Blane flicked his fingers like mini drumsticks. "Ready?"

"Ready!" exclaimed Lydia. "Let's hear it!"

"Dr. Wengaro's ring *is* the Grealmæp's missing ruby."

Lydia gasped. "After three years," she exclaimed. "The ruby appears right here on campus, worn by none other than the man who suspiciously shows up after Sid is murdered, steals my Stonehenge replica, and my books. How do you think he got it? Do you think he stole it from the dig?"

"No clue how he got it, only that when we were practicing how to clean artifacts, I saw it. It has the double daggers etched into it, like Guinevere's journal shows it does."

"We have to act fast, Lydia. He is chasing the Grail as hard as we are. Do we have an update from Dr. Leith on the permits?"

Lydia dialed Dr. Leith, but the call went to voice mail. "We still need to figure out where around the fallen stones the Grail could be buried. It would have to be buried pretty deep for it not to be disrupted after all these centuries."

"I'll bet the library has books on the fallen stones. We could start there," I said.

"Great idea," said Lydia. She pulled up the library catalogue. A few minutes later she looked at Blane and me. "Looks like they have a few: *Excavating the Past: Stonehenge's Stones*; *Fallen Angels: Making Sense of Stonehenge's Fallen Stones*; and *Unearthing the Secrets of Stonehenge's Aubrey Holes*."

"I'm gonna go get them," I said. I grabbed my ID from my satchel and threw on my coat. "With these books, we'll be one giant leap closer to determining the Grail's precise location. I'll be right back!"

A sliver of bright fluorescent light beamed through the crack under the Archaeology Research Room door. As I opened the door, I noticed a man squatting down in front of a shelf, intently focused. He was tracing his finger along the book spines and mumbling to himself. Upon hearing the door open, he jerked his head around and looked at me.

"Hi, Carly. You startled me."

"Dr. Wengaro! What are you doing here?" I was as startled as he was. My heart pounded with fear.

"Looking for a book. Isn't that what people usually do in libraries?" He looked back at the shelf, tracing his finger along more books.

"What's the book?" I was instantly curious. I squatted down a few feet away from him and started scanning the titles on the shelf.

"*Unearthing the Secrets of Stonehenge's Aubrey Holes*."

I froze. Could Dr. Wengaro hear my heart pounding? My eyes widened. I tried to take a deep breath. All I managed was a shallow one.

"That's an interesting title. Why that book?"

"I need it for my research. I'm on the cusp of a great discovery. This discovery will change the world. I'm one book away from piecing it all together. The catalogue says it's here. But I don't see it on the shelf."

"I'm sure it's here," I said, sitting as I scanned the titles. I knew I had to find *Unearthing* first. We couldn't afford not to. "Or it's on the table."

"Already checked—it's not there."

Where could this book be? Dr. Wengaro and I scanned the titles. I skimmed past other books on Stonehenge. I didn't even see the other ones we needed. As I saw a group of Dr. Hasserin's books, I had a realization: *What if Dr. Hasserin had* Unearthing *at his house? What if he borrowed it right before the conference, without checking it out, and never had a chance to return it? What if it wasn't with the other books on his desk, but in another room in his house?* I had to go back to Lydia. We had to go to back to Dr. Hasserin's house.

"Well, I hope you find the book." I leaned over and pushed myself up from the floor. As I did, my pendant popped out of my button-down shirt. I immediately brought my hand to my chest to hide the pendant.

But it was too late. I could feel Dr. Wengaro staring at the Henge Piece as I hastily tried to stuff it back under my blouse. *I really should have listened to my mom and to Lydia when she told me to keep it in the Tupperware box.*

"Nice pendant," Dr. Wengaro said. "Very nice pendant."

XVIII

I raced back to Lydia's office. As soon as I closed her door, I collapsed into Blane's arms. I started shaking as I told her and Blane what happened. I was too terrified to cry.

"He saw it! He knows."

"It's okay." Blane hugged me. "Now we know he's searching for the Grail. He might have the ruby, but we have the two pieces of the Grealmæp."

"We need to go to Dr. Hasserin's house tonight," I said. "I think Dr. Hasserin has *Unearthing the Secrets of Stonehenge's Aubrey Holes*. Maybe not on his desk, but in his bag, or kitchen, or somewhere else. Maybe his room. We need to get that book before Dr. Wengaro finds it."

††

The morning sunlight poured in through Lydia's window. We'd come up empty-handed after searching Dr. Hasserin's house for *Unearthing*. I stared at Lydia's bookcases, thinking through where the book could be.

"These old windows are pretty but don't keep heat in well," said Lydia as she pulled her coat closer around her. The wind howled outside. "They won't let us have space heaters, so I'm afraid coats and blankets are all I have." She pointed to the sofa at a stack of three neatly folded blankets. "This month and March are the worst, and by April, usually, we're in the clear."

"Thank you." I grabbed a blanket and wrapped it over my coat. "Do you want one?"

"I'm fine for now."

As I pulled the blanket around me, Lydia's office phone rang.

"Hello, Lydia Kells."

I couldn't hear anything on the other end of the line.

"Allister, great to hear from you." Lydia put the phone on speaker. "Yes, I'm here with Carly."

"Hi Carly," said Dr. Leith. "I'm afraid I have some interesting—and bad—news for you. Which one do you want first?"

"The bad?" I asked. The wind kept howling outside, causing the windowpanes to rattle. I pulled my blanket closer, preparing myself for what Dr. Leith had to say.

"Can't get you permits for Stonehenge until next August. That's the next available opening. I'm sorry."

"What?" I was crestfallen. We couldn't wait until next August, not with Dr. Wengaro actively on the case. We were so close! But without the dig permits, we couldn't get the Grail. "What do you mean, Dr. Leith?"

"I can't get you permits to dig at Stonehenge. I've tried everything. Beth even rang her friends at the conservancy too."

I looked at Lydia as tears started falling down my face. My mouth trembled. I buried my face in my palms.

"I don't believe it," I mumbled through my tears. Lydia tapped me on my arm, offering me a tissue from the box on her desk. I took it and dabbed my eyes. "We've worked so hard for this. Isn't there any other way?"

"I'm afraid not," Dr. Leith said. "I've tried everything."

I sighed and shook my head as I grabbed another tissue.

"Well, what's your interesting news?" Lydia asked.

"Ahh, right, one of the administrators of Stonehenge's dig permit office said someone else applied for a permit in the same spot you want to dig—around fallen Sarsens 8 and 9."

My sadness turned to curiosity. "Who?"

"They can't say. It's a breach of data privacy."

"Come on!" I clenched my fists in frustration. "Can't they understand? This one time, can't they give us something that will help us?"

"Rules are rules, Carly. They're paid to keep them, not to break them," said Dr. Leith. He paused. "But, here's the interesting bit. Clara, a friend in Beth's Bridge Club, is on one of the Stonehenge conservancy boards. She reviews all permit applications. Beth was talking about how I was trying to do an old friend a favor. Clara said she remembered an application from Nassauton last summer—early or mid-July or so—wanting to dig under the fallen Sarsens 8 and 9, to find the Z8 Aubrey Hole and an artifact buried there. Of course, the application doesn't identify the artifact name or the professor—they anonymize them so it's somewhat of a blind review."

"But why not include the artifact name?" I asked.

"Because, sometimes, Carly, archaeologists don't want to reveal what we're looking for—until we can wow the world when we find it. It's a pride thing."

"So what happened?" I asked as I twirled my loose curl.

"It took the board two months to review all the applications and approve the permit. But they couldn't get ahold of the guy who'd applied. They never got responses to their emails. They eventually stopped trying."

"Dr. Leith, do you think . . ." I paused. "Do you think that was Dr. Hasserin's application?"

"Yes," said Dr. Leith. "I do. As soon as Beth told me that, I tried to line up the dates. Sid applied, went to the conference, and then was murdered shortly after."

"That checks out," Lydia said.

I nodded, smiling at Lydia. I had an idea forming. I motioned for her to hang up, so we could talk.

"Thank you, Allister, you've been very helpful."

"Keep me posted, Lydia. I'm always here to help. If I can help with getting to the bottom of Sid's death, that would give me some closure."

She hung up the phone and smiled at me.

I grinned back, feeling the weight of my pendant under my sweater. "If Dr. Hasserin applied for the permit, that would mean he was sure of the exact location of the Grail."

"We need to know for sure. We need to get his journals."

"I bet Dr. Wengaro has already beat us to that. He broke into your office. He stole your Stonehenge replica—I bet he doesn't even realize two pieces are missing—and he has the Grealmæp's ruby."

"If he does have the journals, how are you going to get them?" Lydia sighed.

"I'm going to schedule office hours with him."

"Do you really think that's safe? He's seen your pendant."

"I know. I don't think he's going to try anything on a student in a campus building. Plus, Blane went to office hours with him."

"And Blane didn't have the Henge Piece! If he's evil enough to murder Sid, there's no telling what he would try!" Lydia retorted. "Carly, you can't risk your life for the Grail."

"Do you think Lyle Ainsley would give up now?" I pointed at Lydia's picture of her and Gran. "If anything happens to me when I'm in his office, all the evidence would point immediately back to him. Not a snowball's chance in hell he would risk his reputation for that."

"You may be right, but it's still dangerous. I can't let you go alone."

"I'll be fine!"

Lydia was having none of it, and I was adamant. I knew Dr. Hasserin's journals would have the information we needed.

"Tell you what," said Lydia. "I'll go with you. I'll stay in an empty office or classroom next door, within earshot. The moment you feel unsafe, or you discover new evidence, say, 'It's about time for the Riddle of the Ages,' and I will be there."

I smiled as I looked at Lydia. "A secret phrase to help me in times of trouble."

††

I was about to open the Archaeology Department door and walk down the hallway to Dr. Wengaro's office when my phone rang.

"Carlyle Elizabeth Stuart, we need to talk." I knew that tone. I was terrified of it. My mom only used it when she needed to discipline me. "Did you or did you not give up your Grail case like I asked?"

"Mom, I, the, what Grail—"

"Carlyle Elizabeth Stuart. It's a yes or no answer."

"No." I paused. "No, I did not."

"I knew it. I knew it! You lied to me! What did you take from my mom's letter box?"

"Nothing," I lied.

"Don't lie to me, Carlyle. I was in the living room the other day, sitting on the couch, staring at the shelf. The clasp on Lyle's box was open. At first, I thought my eyes were playing tricks on me. What did you take from there?"

"A letter." It was futile to lie to my mom at this point.

"Carlyle Elizabeth Stuart, you don't know what you're up against. I'm en route to Nassauton. When I get there, I'm leaving with the Grealmæp and the letter and the poem and whatever else I can find that is tied to this case. I'll be there in an hour." She hung up.

My face flushed with anger. My mom wouldn't tell me anything about the Grealmæp or Gran and the Grail. Yet, she had taken it upon herself to stop my quest. She had no right to interfere with a case she hadn't worked on and didn't understand! There was no way I was going to let her stop me.

I stuffed my phone in my satchel. I opened the Archaeology

Department door. As I walked down the hallway, passing the artifact display cases, I felt all the faculty members staring at me from their portraits. Some seemed to look at me skeptically, making me doubt if I knew the severity of the danger I faced. *Exactly like my mom.* Some cheered me on, reassuring me I'd come this far with my wits—and giving me the confidence to trust my intuition. *At least these professors believe in me and want me to keep going.* I kept walking, knowing Lydia would shortly be within earshot in an empty seminar room.

The hallway was quiet. With the cold weather, my peers were holed up in their rooms or hunkered down at Rockfire. Barely six months ago, I'd overheard Lydia and Dr. Pritzmord talking about Dr. Hasserin in this same hallway. As I passed the case with the burnt-orange bowl, I paused.

I inhaled and exhaled. Here's where it all began. I had submitted my course registration paperwork. I'd moved into my dorm room, like every other freshman. I'd found the pendant, which led me on a quest that only Blane—not even Lara—knew about. My quest had united me with Gran's partner. Our case had thrust us into a mystery that was deeper than Dr. Hasserin's death. The Grealmæp pointed the way to the Grail, a relic that archaeologists, secret societies, clergy, commoners, and even the Nazis had chased throughout the centuries.

The burnt-orange bowl glowed in the winter sunlight, reminding me of the burnt-orange hues of Stephanie's Stonehenge painting. As I stared at the bowl, I noticed a little number next to it. I found the number on the plaque by the case. *Roman bowl, Provenance: Amesbury, England, United Kingdom. Discovered by: L. Ainsley, L. Kells.*

I smiled. I knew Gran was smiling with me too—from wherever she was. Even if my mom didn't want me working on the case, I knew Gran did. That mattered more to me than what my mom wanted.

I took another breath and stepped back from the case. I was

ready for office hours. Over the last two days, I'd thought through countless directions in which our conversation could go. My priorities were locating Dr. Hasserin's journals and getting more information from Dr. Wengaro, without him becoming suspicious. I wasn't going to let whatever he might throw at me derail me. I clutched my pendant through my T-shirt. *Be brave.*

I turned the corner. My heart was pounding as I walked up to Dr. Wengaro's office. His door was open.

"Hello, Carly, come in," he said from behind his desk. His ponytail was neatly tucked behind his left shoulder.

I felt like I was entering a cave, with the only light coming from a small lamp on Dr. Wengaro's desk. I walked in, passing a bookcase by the door—and making sure to leave the door open. It had three books on the top: *Grail and Glory: The Truth of Man's Quest for Eternal Life*; *Ancient Roman Crucifixion Stories: The Medical Evidence for the Death of Christ*; and *The Early Church: How the Early Christians Hid the Grail.* As I read the titles, a shiver ran down my spine.

"Good afternoon, Dr. Wengaro. How's your day?" Offering mindless questions helped mitigate my trepidation. I scanned his office—the same office that was Dr. Hasserin's. Did Dr. Wengaro feel strange being at his dead friend's desk? I took a deep breath.

Dr. Wengaro didn't get up from his seat. He'd placed his desk in the far corner of the room, so he could see whoever was at the door. The rest of the office was sparse, with only a few wooden chairs on the other side of the desk. Three half-empty bookcases were pushed against one of the walls.

"Take a seat." Dr. Wengaro pointed at one of the empty chairs.

Until now, I'd managed to control my fear. I didn't know if I imagined it, but I heard a sinister tone in Dr. Wengaro's voice. The hair on the back of my neck stood up. I started shaking.

"Sorry you're cold. These windows don't do much to keep the heat in. Even having the blinds down is a fool's errand."

"It's okay," I chattered, anxiously trying to focus on his office and not my fear. I quickly changed the subject. "I wanted to discuss one of the Arthurian legends," I stammered, "with Sir Lancelot."

"Sounds great. But before we start, I had a question for you."

"What's that?"

"Your pendant, the one I saw in the Research Room, where is it from?"

I froze. Anticipating Dr. Wengaro would ask me about my pendant, I'd rehearsed my response. I took a deep breath. "I found it in a box."

"A box? What box?"

"A box with old shoes."

"That's fascinating. It reminds me of an artifact I saw on a dig a few years ago, in England. It broke, and I'm not sure where all the pieces are."

"I see. Sorry to hear that."

"Yeah, and the thing is, I have one of the pieces. I've been trying to find the others." He opened his drawer. "This beauty fell out when the artifact broke," he said as he laid his ruby ring on his desk. "Your pendant looks a lot like one of the missing pieces."

I nodded. My heart was pounding. I was looking right at the Grealmæp's ruby! No matter what, I couldn't reveal how nervous I was. "That's very interesting. But I'm sure it's merely a coincidence. You never know where jewelry designers get their inspiration. How would I have gotten that piece, anyway? I've never been to England."

"I know, I know, I'm not an expert in jewelry." Dr. Wengaro chuckled. "I guess you're right. I got excited. I thought maybe I'd have a lead. What was your Lancelot question?"

"I want to know more about Lancelot and Guinevere's affair. Why, if Guinevere was happy with Arthur, in Camelot, would she have an affair?"

"That's a great question. To answer it, we'll need to go to a few texts." Dr. Wengaro picked up a stack of books from his desk. As he picked them up, I noticed several brown leather journals under them. He opened his book. I scooted my chair closer. The initials *SH* were printed in gold letters at the bottom of the journal. I blinked. It was unmistakable. SH had to be Sidney Hasserin. I'd found Dr. Hasserin's journals!

"Is everything okay?"

"Uhh, yeah, a lot of dust," I mumbled.

"Oh yes, these are old books. The poor ventilation certainly doesn't help. This text is one of the most important ones in the Lancelot–Guinevere cycle."

There was a knock outside Dr. Wengaro's office. I turned around to see Dr. Pritzmord.

"Kenneth, sorry to interrupt."

"No worries, Daniel." Dr. Wengaro closed the book, got up from his desk, and walked to the door.

"I thought you might want this book, given the topics you are discussing in your seminar." Dr. Pritzmord handed Dr. Wengaro a book.

Dr. Wengaro looked at the cover as he took the book. "*Unearthing the Secrets of Stonehenge's Aubrey Holes*! Fabulous, that's the book I was looking for! Rockfire didn't have it, even though the catalogue showed a copy."

"Yes, that was my bad. I'd borrowed it and forgot to return it. When I got the missing books report, I called the library. They said you'd called requesting it. I figured I'd give it directly to you."

With Dr. Wengaro away from his desk, I'd looked at the double daggers etched into the ruby and confirmed the initials on the journal spelled *SH*. When I heard Dr. Wengaro exclaim that Dr. Pritzmord had *Unearthing*, I shifted my attention to their conversation. *What was Dr. Pritzmord doing with a book on Stonehenge?*

"Thank you, Daniel. I appreciate it."

Dr. Pritzmord walked away, leaving me alone with Dr. Wengaro.

"Sorry about that." Dr. Wengaro chuckled. "Where were

we?" He walked back to his desk and set *Unearthing* on top of the journals.

"It's fine, no problem. Lancelot and Guinevere. You were showing me the book."

"Right, right." Dr. Wengaro opened his book again. "So here, in this chapter, it discusses Lancelot's birthplace. While many people think that's not an important detail, it ends up forming the basis of the affair."

Dr. Wengaro kept reading from the book. His words buzzed in the background as I thought about how to get the journals. As I stared at them, I noticed something even more shocking. Sticking out from under the journals was a paper with the distinctive double dagger marks on it. This could mean only one thing: Dr. Wengaro knew about the Knights of the Dagger! I needed Lydia. I had to act fast.

"This is so interesting," I muttered, "but I think it's about time for the Riddle of the Ages."

"What?" He looked up from his book.

"It's about time for the Riddle of the Ages!" I said again, much louder. There was no sign of Lydia. My legs started shaking. Had she not heard me?

"The Riddle of the Ages? I don't understand what this has to do with Lancelot."

"Yes, it's about time for the Riddle of the Ages!" I said a third time, desperately hoping Lydia would arrive soon. I was shaking uncontrollably. I darted my gaze to the door. There was no sign of her. With every passing second, our whole plan could be blown.

Lydia knocked on Dr. Wengaro's door. I sighed audibly.

"Hi, Lydia. Can I help you?" asked Dr. Wengaro. Lydia glanced at me, then Dr. Wengaro, then Dr. Wengaro's bookcase. She strode up to his desk, grabbing her books from the bookcase.

"Hello, Kenneth, let me tell *you* how you can help me. It's time you shared some information with me." She slammed her books on his desk. "First of all, what are my books—the books I lent to Sidney Hasserin, the books he had at his house—doing on your bookcase?"

Dr. Wengaro looked at the books, then at Lydia, then at me, then at the books again. He shrugged. "First, Lydia, calm down. Take a seat. Second, Sid's books, and his journals for that matter, were on my desk when I moved in. This was his office, after all."

"They were here?" I asked. "But Lydia said Dr. Hasserin had them at his house."

"That's what Lydia said. Did she ask him? Did she confirm it with him? I'm telling you, they were here when I moved in. Why is that so unbelievable to you?" Dr. Wengaro responded.

"Because we thought whoever murdered Dr. Hasserin took them from his house."

"Wait." Dr. Wengaro looked at Lydia, then at me. "You think Sid was murdered too?"

"Too?" I blurted out.

"What do you mean, 'too,' Kenneth?" Lydia straightened her back in her chair.

"Oh Lydia." Dr. Wengaro stared at his desk and sighed. Then, he looked up, right into Lydia's and my eyes. "I've been trying to figure out how Sid died since the moment I got to Nassauton." He looked around his office. "Maybe you two can help me." He peered behind his blinds and glanced at the hallway. "Close the door, Carly. Even the walls have ears. We can't risk anyone hearing our conversation."

I did as Dr. Wengaro asked and darted back to my chair.

"You both must promise me no matter what I say, you cannot turn me in—not to Daniel, not to the police, not to anyone. You can't share anything we discuss. We could get killed for it."

"I can't promise that," Lydia said flatly. "How do I know what you're going to say? How do I know we can trust you?"

"Because I have the Henge Piece's ruby, and I want to work with you to unite it with the missing pieces."

Have we been wrong about Dr. Wengaro the whole time?

"How do I know you're not lying?" asked Lydia.

"Here's the ruby." Dr. Wengaro held his ring up.

She gasped as she stared at the gemstone. "How did you get this, Kenneth?"

"I found it in a box at the bottom of one of Sid's drawers when I moved into his office. When I saw the double dagger marks, I knew it must be the ruby from the Henge Piece."

"Go on?" asked Lydia.

"Do you promise not to repeat anything I share with you?"

Lydia and I looked at each other. "Yes," we said in unison.

Dr. Wengaro took a deep breath. "Sidney Hasserin wasn't the man the world thought he was. He wasn't a gentleman, and he *maybe* was a scholar. He certainly was a thief."

Lydia gasped again as Dr. Wengaro continued.

"Three years ago, you and Lyle Ainsley found an ancient artifact. Solid gold. An incredibly large ruby. The thing was priceless. Sid didn't know what it was—but someone on the dig sure did. They offered Sid a whole lot of money to steal it. So, he pushed Lyle when she wasn't looking, hoping he could scoop it up. But he didn't anticipate Lyle collecting the two gold pieces so quickly. All he managed to get was the ruby."

"What a crook!" said Lydia as she shook her head. "That's why he didn't say anything when he knew we were looking for it!"

I scooted to the edge of my seat and leaned onto Dr. Wengaro's desk. "How do you know this?"

"Sid told me. We'd published a paper on the Hill of Tara. We were supposed to start our paper on historical Grail locations. He showed me the ruby, saying that when he saw it for himself, he backed out of the deal. He told me after this paper, after people forgot about the dig, he'd sell it and pay off his debt—and we could start the archaeological consulting firm we'd always wanted to start. I told him I didn't want anything to do with stolen artifacts. I wanted out."

That's why they never published their journal paper!

"He said fine—and he threatened me if I told anyone, he'd kill me. We used to be best friends, but I couldn't be friends with a thief—and someone who'd deliberately harmed Lyle."

"Wow." Lydia whispered in disbelief. "Sid sure fooled me." She shook her head. "I even adopted him as my mentee."

"Sid fooled a lot of people," said Dr. Wengaro. "He didn't start out bad, but once he saw the ruby, he changed. I don't even know how he got out of his deal, either—I'm sure that person wasn't too pleased."

I couldn't believe it. Dr. Hasserin's real character was that of a felon. He wasn't as scholarly or good as I'd thought he was. He was a criminal, hiding behind his career, relationships, and reputation. He stole a priceless ruby. He lied to Lydia to cover up his tracks. He threatened to murder his best friend. He pushed my Gran, which ultimately made him responsible for her death. I clenched my fists as my face flushed with disgust.

I hate you, Dr. Hasserin. I drew a sharp breath in. *I hate you, Dr. Hasserin.* I tensed my jaw. *I hate you, Dr. Hasserin.* I clenched my fists. I needed to channel my hatred into solving our case. Getting the Grail wasn't any quest. Now, it was even more personal. I had to do better than Dr. Hasserin. Gran's death at the hands of a cheating thief couldn't be in vain.

The more I realized how much I'd been fooled by Dr. Hasserin, the more I thought about how Dr. Wengaro wasn't as evil as Lydia, Blane, and I thought he was. We'd completely misjudged him, letting my suspicions and emotions—and admiration for Dr. Hasserin—get the better of me. I stared at Dr. Wengaro's desk in disbelief as I reflected on what I'd learned.

"Dr. Wengaro, how did you know what the double dagger marks mean?"

He looked at me. He rolled his chair around his desk, so he was sitting with Lydia and me. He pulled up his shirtsleeve. Fresh, bright red double dagger marks were tattooed on the inside of his left wrist. *Like J. Carmichael's!* I gasped, immediately covering my mouth with my hand. Shivers ran up and down my body as I looked at Dr. Wengaro. "You're a Knight of the Dagger?"

"Yes." He rolled his shirtsleeve back down. "I only recently was recruited. I'm still in my Quest Phase. Just had my imprint." He pointed at his wrist.

"Quest Phase?" I pulled out my phone. I needed to text J. Carmichael to confirm whether Dr. Wengaro was telling us the truth.

"Every new member has a year and a day Quest Phase. It's a probation period until you prove yourself worthy to become a full knight. During this period, and until you are initiated as a full Knight, you're really only permitted to communicate with your sponsor."

I was more and more intrigued by the Knights of the Dagger, especially since J. Carmichael had told me they were good. I wanted to learn more. I glanced at my phone. Nothing from J. Carmichael. "How'd they find you?" I asked.

"Not too long ago, I'd keynoted a conference. I'd blocked Sid out of my memory and had poured myself into my research. After my talk, a man asked me if I'd ever considered applying my research to actual field work—work that involved finding and securing ancient relics. He said he'd been following my research for a long time and was very impressed with it. He gave me a card with a number written on it."

I started twirling my curl as I listened.

"Intrigued, I called him. We met up after the conference. He said his group could really use someone with my skills. That's when I first learned of the Knights of the Dagger."

My phone buzzed. *KW checks out. My boss heard his keynote and recruited him. All clear. Proceed.*

I smiled. A massive sigh of relief flooded over me. *Thank you, J. Carmichael!* I put my phone back in my satchel.

"What do the Knights of the Dagger do?" asked Lydia. "Other than write threatening notes?"

"We're a secret society, sworn to find and protect the Holy Grail. We keep track of anyone excavating sacred places or researching ancient artifacts—especially the Grail. We've prevented people like Hitler, for example, from finding it. We've never actually found it."

Lydia smirked. "Because the Grail doesn't exist. All the research is based on legend and fan fiction, not evidence and fact."

Dr. Wengaro continued. "All the research, except for Sid's. The Knights of the Dagger have been tracking Sid for quite some time. Last August, we learned he'd announced he found Arthur's buried treasure at Stonehenge. Through monitoring him, we learned it was the Grail—and that he applied for a dig permit. I was called in since I'd known Sid and could vouch for the historical validity of his research. We started by sending him notes, hoping he'd stop. Notes, like the ones they sent you and Lyle. You stopped. But he didn't—he doubled down his efforts. So, the Knights of the Dagger sent me here, to talk to him and convince him to stop."

"So, you ended up murdering him?"

"Lydia, please, as much as Sid had wronged me, I would never kill him. The Knights of the Dagger take an oath never to kill unless it's self-defense. They'll blacklist us if we disobey."

"If you didn't kill him, who did?"

"That's what I've been trying to figure out since my first day here. That's why I applied for Sid's job. There is a mystery here that is far greater than the death of Sidney Hasserin. Sid got caught in the crossfire—because he let his Stonehenge discovery slip. Someone else is after the Henge Piece and the Grail. I have the ruby. I need you to help me unite it with the piece you have."

"Why didn't you tell me this from the first day, Kenneth? Why all the secrecy?"

"You'd think I murdered Sid, and you'd turn me in to Daniel! I had to get the lay of the land and do more research. We are racing against time. Whoever murdered Sid is still around. The longer it takes the three of us to get to the bottom of this, the more danger—possibly even death—awaits us."

††

I had three texts and four missed calls from my mom, and one text from Lara.

Your mom is banging on our door. Where are you? What is going on?

I called Lara. "Is she at our room?"

"Yeah, she said she's not leaving till you come here. I calmed her down quite a bit and gave her some snacks."

"Did she say anything to you?"

"No, only that she needed to talk to you, and it was important."

"Tell her I'm on my way, and please keep her in a good mood. Thank you!"

I was grateful that Lara had been in our room and worked her magic to make my mom calm. When I got to my room, I saw Lara and my mom sitting on the couch, talking about interior design and furniture like they had known each other for years. My mom seemed in good spirits.

"Lara, it's been so great chatting with you. You're so smart and have such a knack for good design."

"Thank you, Ms. Stuart." Lara smiled. "It was great meeting you!"

"Carlyle, you and I need to go for a walk." My mom looked at me, her tone instantly changing. "Seems like you have some explaining to do."

She got up and put her coat on. We headed out the door, to the quad with the volleyball court.

"What's going on with you and your pendant? Why do you keep lying to me?" Her tone was one of concern, rather than anger.

Unable to look my mom in the eyes, I stared at the volleyball court. "I'm sorry, Mom. I needed to follow my heart. For Gran. She left me this poem. She left me the Grealmæp. It had to be for a reason. How can I, as a young explorer, not follow in her footsteps?"

"But I told you you're putting your life in danger. My mom wouldn't have wanted you to do that."

"I think she knew I'd be able to keep my wits about me," I replied. "And I have. Like Gran would have done. I learned Dr. Wengaro is searching for Dr. Hasserin's murderer too."

My mom looked at me in surprise. "He is? He's not bad?"

"No. If I'd have given up the case when you wanted me to, I never would have learned that. We're both trying to find who murdered Dr. Hasserin. Dr. Wengaro is helping Lydia and me. We're also going to find the Grail." I caught my mom up on some of Lydia's and my conversation with Dr. Wengaro, telling her how Dr. Hasserin was the one who pushed Gran.

"That's a surprising turn of events, but how do you know he's not double-crossing you?" My mom paused in the walkway.

"Because I asked J. Carmichael."

"How you'd get his—" My mom interrupted herself with a loud chuckle. "The honey. You asked me for J. Carmichael's number to learn more about Dr. Wengaro, not thank him for the honey."

"I thanked him too." I grinned as I looked at her. "And I learned that even though there is danger, J. Carmichael—and Dr. Wengaro—are on our team."

My mom smiled at me. "You're clever, Carly. You get that from your dad. And you sure are a young explorer who loves adventure."

"I get that from Gran, don't I."

"Yes, you do. I guess nothing I can say will make you give it up."

I shook my head.

"I'll ask J. Carmichael to keep an eye on you. Promise me you won't lie to me again. There can't be more secrets in this family."

I nodded. I was so relieved I wasn't keeping my Grail quest a secret from my mom anymore.

"I promise," I said, stepping into my mother's open arms.

XIX

Lydia, Dr. Wengaro, Blane, and I were in Lydia's office. Lydia had her half of the Grealmæp. I had mine. Over Valentine's Day dinner, which Blane and I celebrated at Pi's, I'd caught Blane up on Dr. Wengaro.

"Do you have the ruby, Kenneth?"

We'd cleared Lydia's coffee table and put a placemat in the center. Lydia smoothed the placemat as Dr. Wengaro reached for his ring. He placed it on the mat. The double dagger etchings were clearly visible on its face. I put my pendant next to Dr. Wengaro's ring.

"You have your part of the Henge Piece, Lydia? Oh, and before I forget, I have your Stonehenge pieces." Dr. Wengaro took a plastic bag out of his briefcase and handed it to Lydia. "I found them in the trash outside Dr. Pritzmord's office."

Blane and I looked at each other.

"Dr. Pritzmord?" I asked.

"Yeah, I'd needed to ask him a few questions about finals. I saw the pieces in the trash can—they looked like little board game pieces. I'd remembered them from Lydia's office. I had no idea how they got to the trash can, but I wanted to return them. I hope all the pieces are there."

I wondered how the pieces might have gotten thrown away. *Was Dr. Wengaro embarrassed to admit he broke into Lydia's office?* Lydia put the plastic bag on her desk and turned back to the coffee table. She unsealed a Tupperware container and took out a palm-sized object wrapped in a microfiber towel.

"Here she is," she said as she laid the object on the placemat and put on gloves. Her bracelets clanked around her wrists. I smiled as I saw her Ailm charm, which glistened under her office light. I looked at my Ailm charm, finding comfort in our similar bracelets and, with the soon-to-be-complete Grealmæp, our clear path forward to the Grail.

Dr. Wengaro's eyes lit up. Blane and I were riveted as Lydia took off the towel, revealing the gold circle that popped onto my horseshoe and dagger. As I looked at the three pieces, about to be reunited for the first time in three years, I felt like I was on my first excavation and had found my first artifact.

All the intrigue, mystery, and curiosity I felt when I first opened Gran's shoebox came rushing back to me. Then, I had no idea what the pendant was or why it was significant. All my questions had led me to answers I never imagined. They'd taken me on a journey that went beyond—far beyond—a mysterious poem and a gold pendant. *How had Gran felt when she found the Grealmæp?* I wondered. *And where exactly had she found it?*

I grabbed Blane's hand. He squeezed it, reassuring me as the significance of this moment hit me. Lydia snapped the two pieces together, like she had when she first showed me how her piece and mine fit together. All that was missing was the ruby.

"Wow," whispered Blane. "I feel like Indy."

Lydia glared at him, as if to say, *Indy? Is that the best archaeologist you can come up with?*

He put his arms around my shoulders as all four of us leaned over the coffee table.

"Kenneth, the ruby."

Dr. Wengaro put on his gloves and picked up his ring. He popped the ruby out from the prongs that were holding it. In the light, the ruby gleamed with a magical, otherworldly, vibrant brilliance. I saw the double dagger marks etched on one face and double dagger marks set as a relief on the other.

"That's cool," I murmured as Dr. Wengaro picked up the

Grealmæp. "It has double daggers on both sides—one etched in stone and one rising up from the stone." He placed the ruby into the gap on the dagger's hilt. The ruby rested there, as if it were floating.

"Wow," whispered Dr. Wengaro, grabbing a journal from the pile he'd brought. "It's complete."

"It's a perfect map of Stonehenge," whispered Blane as he marveled at the Grealmæp's precise craftsmanship.

"I never thought I'd see this whole again." Lydia teared up as she looked at the picture of her and Lyle on her desk. "Lyle, I wish you were here. I wonder what you'd have to say about all of us picking up where you and I left off."

I smiled as Lydia and I hugged. Blane and Dr. Wengaro fist-bumped.

Lydia picked up the Grealmæp and held it in front of her window. The sunlight illuminated its gold metal and ignited the ruby. The double dagger marks floated in a sea of blood-red light.

"She's as beautiful as the day I met her." Lydia sighed as the four of us looked at the Grealmæp. I grinned. It amused me how Lydia referred to the Grealmæp as a she.

"She is indeed," said Dr. Wengaro, taking the Grealmæp out of Lydia's hands and placing it on the coffee table. He studied it more closely. "She's very delicate. We'll need to be extra careful. She's certainly more fragile—and beautiful—than in the legend."

"What legend?" asked Blane.

"There's a book I read as a kid once. It had a picture of a stained-glass window with King Arthur and Queen Guinevere wearing these beautiful pendants. The book said the pendants led to treasure at Stonehenge. It got me thinking, even though this was a children's book, what if this legend were true?"

Blane grinned and looked at Dr. Wengaro. "They're never merely kids' books, are they?"

"Never," said Dr. Wengaro, with a whimsical twinkle in his eye.

"Is that how you got interested in King Arthur?" I asked.

"Yeah. I did a lot of research on Merlin. He's one of my favorite people. One of the best seminars I've attended was on Merlin, his magic, and the British Isles. We studied one of his spell books. In this book, I learned about the Henge Piece."

Lydia rolled her chair closer to the coffee table as Dr. Wengaro continued.

"As the legend goes, after Arthur—well, more specifically, Sir Galahad—found the Grail, Arthur asked Merlin to make an enchanted instrument to keep the Grail safe. He made one for himself and one for Guinevere. Arthur and Merlin thought long and hard about where to bury the Grail, and how. Finally, Merlin suggested Stonehenge. As a hub of Earth's ley lines, Stonehenge was one of the most sacred places in the world. It is a vortex of dark energy and dark matter, which has been confirmed by scientists and spiritualists. It was a deeply held belief that disrupting the sacred ground would bring curses for generations to whoever dug there."

"No way," said Blane. "I knew the ley lines were part of it!"

I high-fived Blane and smiled at him.

Dr. Wengaro continued. "So, Stonehenge it was, and Merlin made the Henge Pieces. In doing so, he specifically chose rubies that belonged to Joseph of Arimathea—the same Joseph who brought the Grail to Britain. Merlin made each Henge Piece as a map—and as a key. The map pointed to where the Grail was buried—and the key opened the box in which it was kept. The double dagger marks on the face of the ruby corresponded to their complement on the top of the Grail box. When pressed into the top, the marks acted as a key that unlocked the box."

"Whoa, so that's why we need the actual Henge Piece!" I exclaimed. "It's a key."

"Yes—and it wasn't until I saw Sid's ruby that I realized it was real. I don't know how to use the Henge Piece to find the location of the Grail."

I started twirling my curl as I listened. "The dagger," I said. "The dagger points to the fallen stones and the Aubrey Holes in which the Grail is buried. I read about it in Dr. Hasserin's book. He found Guinevere's diary, which describes how the Henge Piece works—and gives its real name. The Grealmæp."

Dr. Wengaro nodded. "Yep, Sid found Guinevere's diary. He must have published what would have been our Grail paper as a book."

I nodded.

"So, that's why Sid, Allister, Lyle, and I couldn't find any records of the Henge Piece in the *archaeology* literature," said Lydia. "Because the Henge Piece—the Grealmæp—was part of Guinevere's private jewelry collection—and documented only in her diary."

"Precisely," said Dr. Wengaro. "And in Merlin's spell book. After taking my seminar, I realized Lydia and Lyle found one of the Grealmæps. I realized the significance of the ruby Sid had stolen."

Dr. Wengaro picked up one of Dr. Hasserin's journals. "Sid had done some remarkable research on the Grail and the Henge Piece, corroborating what I'd learned in Merlin's spell book. His journals describe Guinevere's diary and a poem in an obscure Arthurian legend. He even translated the poem, which I'm sure wasn't easy."

Dr. Wengaro opened the journal and flipped to a page with a Post-it note. He put the journal on the coffee table. We leaned in to read it.

The dagger points to life eternal with the Lord
The ruby red, a blood sacrifice for the world
Sacred energy flows through the sacred stones
The Grealmæp unlocks the box, breathing into
old bones

The blood floweth forever: the source of eternal life
The chalice of Christ is found at the point of the knife
Sealed in a gray stone box with the double dagger mark,
The Grail rests protected, preserved in the dark

"Sacred energy flows through sacred stones," I read aloud. "That's Stonehenge—the place of sacred energy."

"Yep." Dr. Wengaro nodded. "But the more I researched Stonehenge and the Grail, the more I realized Sid was wrong. While King Arthur had buried the Grail at Stonehenge, I don't think the Grail is there now. There's no way, not after all the excavations."

"Excavations?" I asked, looking at Dr. Wengaro.

"Most of the Aubrey Holes have been excavated, and over sixty years ago. The odds the Grail is still at Stonehenge are incredibly small. Even with the Aubrey Holes that haven't been excavated—and even with the missing Z8 Hole. They're pretty shallow pits to begin with, hardly deep enough to hide a box."

I nodded. Marikeath had said the Aubrey Holes were small and shallow.

"I'd needed one book, *Unearthing the Secrets of Stonehenge's Aubrey Holes*, to be sure. The library didn't have it, but Carly, it's the book Daniel gave me when we had office hours."

"The book we thought Sid would have," said Lydia. "Why would Daniel have it?"

"No clue. He said he'd had it and forgot to return it."

Dr. Wengaro reached into his briefcase and pulled out *Unearthed*. He scanned the table of contents, then flipped to the index. "Hmm," he muttered aloud. "I thought it would surely be in here." He put his finger in the index and started flipping back and forth, searching the pages. "Ahh! That's it. Here!" He turned to a page near the back of the book and put the book on the coffee table.

The Aubrey Holes are fifty-six pits located around the Sarsen Circle of Stonehenge, known as the Z Holes and the Y Holes. They date back to Stonehenge's original construction. Their original purpose is unknown. The pits were probably the last structural activity at Stonehenge. Some say these pits were originally for posts around the stones, to aid in the construction process. Others say they were posts that held a tarp of sorts, which enabled Stonehenge to be covered like a tent. However, as recent re-excavations have revealed, the Aubrey Holes contain human bone fragments. This leads us to believe they were also used as shallow graves, containing everything from bones to relics.

In 1666, John Aubrey, a philosopher, discovered these pits. He recorded information about them, but, for over 250 years, nothing came of Aubrey's discoveries. In 1920, William Hawley and his team excavated twenty-five pits. The team was fascinated by their size and spacing. Each pit is about three feet in diameter and one and a half feet deep. In 1924, the Hawley team uncovered seven more, unearthing some answers—and digging up more secrets. Hawley's team named these holes for Aubrey, paying homage to his work. When Hawley shared his findings, interest in these strange pits spiked. Permits to dig at Stonehenge increased by a hundred-fold, as archaeologists and looters wanted in on the Aubrey Holes.

By 2008, most of the Aubrey Holes had been re-excavated, by various teams, including the Stonehenge Riverside Project. For the better part of the 2000s, a team of two hundred researchers and students descended upon Stonehenge, building from Richard Atkinson's excavations in 1950. One of the major findings of the Riverside Project was that Stonehenge was a prehistoric cremation cemetery. This advanced Atkinson's work.

Atkinson developed close relationships with museums, schools, and historical societies around Amesbury, including the Amesbury Museum. Located near the site of Amesbury's oldest priory, this museum contains numerous artifacts and books on Stonehenge's history. In fact, most of the items—cremation-related boxes, urns, and bone fragments—found in the Aubrey Holes have been given to the museum in effort to keep Stonehenge's secrets close to the mysterious monument.

"That's it," said Dr. Wengaro. "I bet the Grail box must have been found on one of those excavations. If Sid had read this book, instead of only going from the legends, he would have arrived at this conclusion too. He got too swept up in his own pride while forgetting to think through all the facts."

"Evidence, not emotion," murmured Lydia. "Evidence, not emotion."

"So, if the Grail box isn't at Stonehenge, where is it?" Blane asked. "How do we find it?"

I'd been twirling my curl and listening. As I gazed at the Grealmæp, Dr. Hasserin's journals, and *Unearthing*, I thought about Stonehenge. Atkinson had excavated most of the Aubrey Holes and the Stonehenge Riverside Project had come after him. The Aubrey Holes were very shallow. With that many excavations, had someone found the box—and been unable to open it?

"Let's call the Amesbury Museum," I finally said. "If most of the excavated items were brought there, maybe there's a chance the Grail box is there. If not, maybe they can tell us where it is."

††

The Amesbury Museum had confirmed they had rooms of Stonehenge artifacts. The receptionist was happy to work with us to schedule a visit.

"Dr. Kells and Dr. Wengaro, you're more than welcome to come in and look, under supervision. That's a courtesy we do give to archaeologists, especially through our reciprocity with universities. How's tomorrow?"

Lydia chuckled. "I'm afraid we can't get there tomorrow—we're in the States. What do you have next week?"

"Afraid we're all booked through, but how's the week after?"

"Perfect," said Lydia. "We'll take it!"

††

I'd needed to go home before we flew to England, to pick up some sweaters and my travel backpack. In the spirit of no longer keeping secrets from my mom, I'd told her we needed to fly to England to find the Grail. She, of course, told me to be safe and stay with Lydia, Kenneth, and Blane at all times. She even offered to help me buy my flights. I appreciated this gesture, because it demonstrated that my mom was at peace with, and supportive of, me making my own decisions. I also appreciated that my mom was willing to pick me up from Nassauton.

"Flights are not cheap," she said as we drove home. "Let me pitch in a little bit, and you can pay me back when you have your summer job."

"No worries, Mom. The cool thing I learned about Nassauton is that we have funds to support student research. Joyce and Lydia helped me apply. My entire trip is covered."

"How does your Grail quest count as research?" My mom chuckled.

"As long as a faculty member and student are going, it's research." I grinned. "And in our case, we have two faculty members and two students."

"Clever. You all are a bunch of skilled researchers indeed. I'm amazed by how much you've already learned at Nassauton. Seems like yesterday I was dropping you off." She smiled as she pulled into our driveway.

I nodded. "And it's not even the end of my first year! Time certainly flies by."

"Of course, time flies—even though it doesn't have wings," said my mom, chuckling.

"What did you say, Mom?"

"That time flies, even though it doesn't have wings. It's from my favorite riddle."

"The Riddle of the Ages!"

"Yep, how'd you know that?"

I smiled. "Gran."

I walked in the door and changed into my slippers. "I'm gonna go look for my travel backpack. I'll be in my room."

"Sounds good. Let me know when you want dinner."

I headed up to my room and opened the door. Gran's boots—the knee-high, brown leather ones with passport stamps embossed on them—were neatly placed along my closet wall. My mom had left a Post-it note on them: *Found these while cleaning. You'll need sturdy boots for your England adventure—and to fight whatever monsters you might find there. Be safe and text me or J. Carmichael if you need anything! Love, Mom.*

Mom had come full circle. Her change of perspective meant a lot to me.

I grinned. The last time I'd worn these was jumping off the couch, trying to fight imaginary mythological monsters. I laughed as I remembered how the boots were so big, they swallowed my legs. I picked up the boots and walked to my bed.

Kicking off my slippers, I slid my right, then left leg into the boots. They slid on effortlessly. I stood up and wiggled my toes. There was the perfect amount of room in the boots. I took a few steps around my carpet, noticing how the boots had been broken in. The well-worn leather had cracks and nicks on it here and there and had shaped to Gran's calf. The more I walked around in them, the more I realized how comfortable I was in them. Gran's boots fit me perfectly.

I walked to a picture of Gran and me from my middle school science fair. She seemed to be smiling even more as she looked at me. *"All a woman needs to conquer the world are her curiosity, her research, and her faith—and shoes that make her smile dazzle like a thousand diamonds,"* I heard Gran say as my smile lit up my room.

I looked back at her. "I love you, Gran," I whispered to myself, closing my eyes.

When I was little, I couldn't wait for the day I would fill Gran's shoes. And today, as I stood in my boots—I knew Gran would be proud of me for doing so.

XX

Our flight to Heathrow was smooth and arrived early. This gave us time to grab breakfast before Dr. Wengaro's friend Jude picked us up. The whole flight over, Dr. Wengaro wouldn't stop talking about Jude, saying how Jude makes things happen and Jude gets things done. "We've been friends for a long time," said Dr. Wengaro. "I trust him with my life."

"Welcome to England!" Jude helped us load our bags into his car. "Kenneth has told me a lot about you. This is so exciting, what you are doing. I'm happy to help; let's say I owe Kenneth a favor." Jude looked at Dr. Wengaro and grinned. "I'll never forget your kindness, Kenneth, thank you. And she won't either."

"You're welcome." Dr. Wengaro winked. "Glad it's working out for you!" He hopped in the front seat and closed the door. "And of course, happy to help."

As soon as we got on the highway, my jetlag hit me. That, and the hum of the tires on the road, lulled me to sleep.

Before I knew it, I was waking up in Amesbury. Only a few miles east of Stonehenge, Amesbury was the closest town to the monolith. Most of the industry was based on Stonehenge tourism, and the town took immense pride in its association with the World Heritage Site. Surrounded by rolling fields and farms—that even in the winter had a peaceful stillness to them—Amesbury had a bustling town center with shops and pubs.

As Jude drove into town, we passed by stone houses with

thatched roofs and little gardens. We stopped at a pedestrian crossing, as parents with two young daughters in matching woolen peacoats sauntered to the other side of the street. I smiled as their mom waved to thank us.

I noticed the buildings, from the two-story terraced houses, with rows of windows, doors, and chimneys, to the church with its orange-red roof tiles and cemetery. Little cars were parked neatly alongside the cemetery's stone wall. I grabbed Blane's sleeve.

"Look, their driver and passenger seats are flipped." I chuckled. It was funny to me how Britons drove on the other side of the road, and the configuration of their cars was flipped to accommodate that.

Amesbury, with its centuries-old churches and sidewalks and its modern-day houses and shops, mixed past and present in a way that gave me the vibe that one of the Knights of the Round Table might pop out from around any corner and walk up to me. The Amesbury Convent couldn't be too far away from the city center. I was sure King Arthur, maybe even Queen Guinevere herself, had walked these streets.

Our cottage was across the street from a local pub. The Courtly Robin was a brick-and-stone building with a gray slate roof, white windows, and a small wooden door. How many centuries of Amesbury residents had the pub served?

"I feel like I've stepped into a postcard," I blurted out as Jude parked the car. "It's charming!"

Blane winked at me. "Amesbury is a quaint, romantic town, that's for sure. Maybe after we get the Grail, we'll have time to grab dinner—the two of us."

I grinned as I squeezed his hand. "I'd love that."

Jude parked the car in front of our cottage. It had a royal-blue door with a wrought iron handle and big bay window. As I looked through the window, I saw a study full of books. Jude helped us unlock the door and bring our bags in. I plopped my backpack and satchel down in the study and walked down the hallway to the kitchen.

"Look at this cute kitchen setup!" I said. The kitchen, dining room, and living room were open, making the whole cottage seem bigger. Near the dining table was a couch, coffee table, and TV. A big, sliding glass door with long, pastel yellow curtains took up one of the walls. Beyond the glass door was a small patio with a wrought-iron table and chairs. "It's perfect!"

We settled in and spent most of our day bundled up walking in and out of shops and getting groceries. Well into the evening, couples, groups of friends, and families walked around the main streets, finishing their errands, shopping, or having dinner.

"Come on, Noah-Jordan, hurry up dear," I heard one mom say to her son as they walked briskly past us. She grabbed his hand and walked faster. "Don't want to keep everyone waiting." Her son turned and looked at us. He waved, as though welcoming us to Amesbury, then obediently followed his mom. I grinned as I waved back. They disappeared ahead of us into the sea of pedestrians. Even in the chilly March night, Amesbury had a cozy and charming vibe.

††

That night, I could hardly sleep. Would we be able to identify the Grail box? The Grail box hadn't been opened for centuries. What if the Grealmæp didn't work?

I still couldn't wrap my head around the Knights of the Dagger. *Who exactly are they?* J. Carmichael was one. Dr. Wengaro was another. What other cases had Dr. Wengaro been on? What cases had J. Carmichael been on? Had Gran known J. Carmichael was a Knight of the Dagger? How dangerous were the Knights of the White Wave?

I took a deep breath. Since the moment I first heard Lydia's murder speculation, there were so many times I could have turned back. When my mom told me to destroy my pendant. When Lydia's office was broken into and her Stonehenge replica was stolen. When I distracted Dr. Wengaro and Dr. Rapalmo so Blane could get Lydia's Stonehenge pieces. When Lydia and I saw the crossed-out line in the Knights of the Dagger's note on Dr. Hasserin's desk. When Dr. Wengaro saw my pendant. When I first found Gran's mysterious poem and gold pendant—I'd barely started college and was in the middle of organizing my shoes!

I heard Blane's breathing in the bed next to me. The cadence of his breaths was calming. Without Blane, I wouldn't have taken the leap of faith that brought me here—the leap of faith to push through my doubts and questions, accepting them as important parts of the process, rather than dismissing them.

Without his reassurance, I wouldn't have had the courage to walk in Gran's shoes as I took my first steps on this path to the Grail. He never once thought I, as a college freshman, was silly to be chasing the Grail. Through our teamwork, he helped me find faith to keep going, collect the evidence one piece at a time, think through my questions, and follow where my path led.

Evidence, not emotion, as Lydia would say. I'd learned what she meant when she said that. There had been times when sifting fact from fiction seemed impossible. But we did it. The evidence had led us to the truth—about Stonehenge, Dr. Hasserin, and Dr. Wengaro. The evidence was leading us to the Grail.

My Ailm charm glistened in the moonlight streaming in through the curtains. My quest had been one of inner strength, bravery, and purpose. I knew Gran would be proud. I thought about my pendant, safely wrapped in Lydia's Tupperware with its other half. *Be brave*. I closed my eyes and inhaled and exhaled.

Tomorrow was the final challenge. It was going to be the most exciting day of my life.

††

As promised, Jude picked us up on time and drove us to the Amesbury Museum. He navigated the roads with ease, effortlessly driving past the church with the cemetery and several clusters of terraced houses. Despite the rain and dreary skies, the stone of the museum looked stately. I'd imagined the museum had seen hundreds of years of drizzly days—and could certainly handle one more.

A jovial woman with short hair done perfectly in voluminous curls—the kind that only someone with decades of styling experience could pull off—lowered her mug. She swallowed her tea. I marveled at how her curls stayed in their shape given the morning's drizzle.

"Good morning. Can I help?" She smiled as she looked up from her desk. She was wearing a maroon vest with her museum ID clipped to one side. A big pop-up banner behind her desk read: WELCOME TO THE AMESBURY MUSEUM, WHERE HISTORY AND LEGEND MEET. Dr. Wengaro finished shaking out his umbrella and looked around for a rack.

"Hi Paige. We have an appointment with Dr. Gellmane," said Lydia. She grabbed a mint from a bowl near the brochures on the desk. "These are my favorite. I've never found them on my side of the pond." She unwrapped her mint and crumpled up the wrapper in her hand.

Paige smiled. "Here, I'll take that. Dr. Gellmane insists we put the mints out for guests. I'm glad you like them."

Dr. Wengaro found the umbrella rack by the security guard's desk. He dropped his umbrella there as the security guard, barely looking up from watching his cameras, nodded to Dr. Wengaro. I looked around the room, wondering if someone had turned an old estate into the museum. I'd imagined even on a sunny day, its two windows didn't let in a lot of light. The room had a few wooden benches against the walls and wooden chairs arranged around small coffee tables. Other than colorful pop-ups and posters on the walls, the room's colors were neutral.

"Right, just a moment. Let me pop to the back and let Dr. Gellmane know you're here. In the meantime, please complete these forms. We need your Amesbury address in case we need to reach you." Paige handed Dr. Wengaro a clipboard and disappeared behind a door. Dr. Wengaro and Lydia walked to the bench and began completing the forms. Blane and I walked up to one of the pop-ups, which had a schedule of events.

"Donuts and Druids?" My gold bracelet with the Ailm charm slid down my arm as I pointed at one event that recurred every Wednesday. "It's a breakfast discussion led by experts on the Druids. That sounds really cool."

"You should start that next semester at Nassauton," said Blane, leaning his chin on my shoulder and grabbing my hand. "You'd be the perfect person. Maybe Dr. Kells will be your faculty sponsor. Can you imagine Café Naiviv hosting a roundtable breakfast every Wednesday? That would be awesome."

I smiled. That was a really good idea.

"Plus, you have your marketing logo right there," said Blane as he pointed at my charm. "The Ailm. It would be perfect."

After ten minutes, Paige reappeared with Dr. Gellmane. She looked about the same age as Lydia. Her platinum blonde hair was braided and wrapped in a bun at the top of her head. Dr. Gellmane had a lithe, strong build, like she'd been a ballerina in a previous career. We grouped around the front desk, eagerly anticipating our next directions.

"Hello, you must be Dr. Kells and Dr. Wengaro. I see you have your students with you! How can I help?" Dr. Gellmane offered each of us a handshake.

"We have an appointment to visit your Stonehenge artifacts," said Dr. Wengaro. "Here's our paperwork."

"Right, of course," said Dr. Gellmane, glancing at the clipboard. She flipped the pages over, scanned the form, and nodded. "Right this way. We have a short orientation before we go to the collection."

I grabbed Blane's hand and grinned as we followed Dr. Gellmane behind Paige's desk. Paige opened the door for us. "Right then, have fun! You'll love seeing everything."

We walked down the hallway. The soles of my boots—Gran's knee-high, brown leather ones with passport stamps—barely made any noise on the wooden floor. It felt like I was walking on air. I noticed old pictures and posters on the wall. Some showed the museum's blueprints. Others showed pictures of groups touring the collections.

"This used to be an old manor," said Dr. Gellmane. "In 1935, the National Trust bought it and built the museum. We're lucky because we're the first stop for artifacts found at Stonehenge." She unlocked her office door and ushered us in. "In 2015, we received funding, generously given by Lord Breekson, to build a proper facility, with climate-controlled storage rooms and actual workstations. This enabled us to host school groups and classes."

"Who is Lord Breekson?" I asked.

"He's a globally renowned, locally based politician. He's also a philanthropist and advocate of science, art, and archaeological education."

Dr. Gellmane gestured to the sofa and chairs around a glass coffee table in front of a wall-size glass window. "Take a seat." The morning drizzle had turned into a steady rain. "I'll be with you in a moment."

The wall behind Dr. Gellmane's desk was covered in framed plaques and awards. The museum had been recognized as "best tourist museum," "best access to artifacts," and "most community education programs." Dr. Gellmane picked up a few papers, walked over to us, and sat down.

"One of our post-docs will supervise you. It's not that we don't trust you alone with the artifacts, it's that if you have questions, you can ask the post-doc." Dr. Gellmane paused, then chuckled. "I mean they are priceless, so I guess we don't really trust you."

Dr. Gellmane continued, placing a piece of paper with the blueprint of several buildings on the coffee table. "You'll be in the Examination Room," she said as she circled the biggest rectangle. "It's a few minutes' walk away. It has our workstations and storage rooms. Only the post-docs are allowed in the storage rooms. The artifacts are housed by type—such as bowls, utensils, boxes, and garments. The workstations are set up with tools and gloves. You'll tell your post-doc which artifacts you want, and your post-doc will bring you up to four at a time. You're lucky. Usually, there are several groups in there, but today it looks like only a few people made appointments. Any questions?"

We shook our heads.

"Right, follow me." Dr. Gellmane grabbed a big golf umbrella.

We followed Dr. Gellmane down the hallway to the exit.

"Should have brought our own umbrellas," Blane said to me as Dr. Gellmane opened hers. The five of us tried to cram under it as we walked between buildings.

"Hopefully it will stop by the time we're done," I responded.

"These days are always rainy," said Dr. Gellmane. "They're best spent with some hot tea and a good book."

"Or spent looking at Stonehenge artifacts." Blane smiled as Dr. Gellmane unlocked the Examination Room door. The lights were already on.

"Here you are. Head to Workstation 1. Your post-doc will be with you shortly." Dr. Gellmane closed the door behind her. I shook the rain off my jacket and hung it up on the coat rack near the lockers. Workstation 1 was by the door and had four stools. The hum of the air conditioning units, for climate control, filled the air. My teeth started chattering as I adjusted to the cold air.

"We're here," I whispered to Blane. "This is awesome!"

He winked at me and hugged me. "Sure is, teammate."

"Lydia, you have the Grealmæp, right?"

"Of course, Kenneth." Lydia patted her satchel. "You think I'd forget it?"

"No, but I'm making sure. Maybe it's the nerves. Maybe it's the excitement." Dr. Wengaro smiled and looked at Blane and me. "Big day for us. Not sure how many students get to say they found the Grail before they graduate college."

I beamed as I held Blane's hand. My Ailm charm sparkled under the workstation's light.

"Hello everyone. Welcome to the Examination Room!" A chipper post-doc wearing black pants and a white lab coat with brushes and towels stuffed into the pockets greeted us. She held a clipboard. "My name is Tiffdill Parks. Which artifacts would you like to see first?"

"Hi Tiffdill. We're here to see a box. It's gray stone and has a special insignia on it. The insignia looks like Stonehenge with a dagger at the bottom," Lydia said.

"Right, one moment, let me check for you. Anything else?"

"No," said Dr. Wengaro. "Only the box."

"Right. Please leave any food or drink in the lockers. Then put on your gloves. I'll be back shortly."

Tiffdill walked across the Examination Room, her heels clacking on the stone floor as she disappeared among the other workstations. Soon the clacks were less audible. We heard a door click shut. I turned to Lydia and smiled. "Don't you wish Lyle were here?"

"She is," said Lydia, looking at me. "She is."

Twenty minutes later, Tiffdill was still gone.

"Do you think she's having a hard time finding the box?" Blane asked. "How many gray stone boxes with a strange insignia on it can there be?"

"Not sure," said Dr. Wengaro, "but we'll give her ten more minutes. Then I'm going to find her."

After ten minutes, there was still no sign of Tiffdill.

"I'll be back." Dr. Wengaro got up from his stool. He adjusted his ponytail, perfectly positioning his long, curly hair. "It shouldn't be taking her this long. Not with all the information we've already given them and how well their collection is organized." He headed across the Examination Room. We heard the door click shut after him.

A few moments later, I heard him scream. "Lydia! Come here. Fast!"

We raced across the Examination Room in the direction Dr. Wengaro had gone. Gran's boots were certainly not made for running. Blane got to the other side first and opened the door. It led to a long hallway with storage rooms on either side. Dr. Wengaro was at the end of the hallway, kneeling.

Blane and I ran toward him, ahead of Lydia. Tiffdill was lying on the floor, blood dripping from what looked like a broken nose. Her white lab coat and clipboard were spattered with blood.

"Oh no!" I gasped. I buried my face in Blane's shoulder. "What happened?"

"She's still alive," said Dr. Wengaro. His hand was on her wrist. "She'll need ice and stitches for sure. But she'll live."

Still panting, I nodded as Lydia arrived. She crouched down by Tiffdill's head. "Should we call someone?"

"I can run back to the office," said Blane.

"Who did—"

"I wouldn't ask any more questions if I were you," said a man, cutting Lydia off.

I turned my head toward the voice.

"Dr. Pritzmord?" I gasped. He was standing in the middle of the hallway. His hands were covered in blood. He was holding a revolver.

He looked at me with a chilling stare, and my stomach turned in fear.

He reached for his pocket square and slipped the barrel of his revolver into his breast pocket. He calmly wiped his hands, bunched up the blood-smeared pocket square, and threw it on the floor. He reached for his revolver.

"Collateral damage, of course," he sneered. "Plenty more

where those came from."

"Daniel! What are you doing here?" Lydia blurted out in shock.

Dr. Pritzmord looked at us. He chuckled, a calculating and cruel laugh that made me feel like throwing up. He stepped over the pocket square and walked toward us, the squeak of his shoes echoing throughout the hallway.

"What am I doing here, Lydia? I'm getting the Grail. Or, I suppose, I'm thanking you all for getting the Grail for me."

"But you're the dean of Nassauton's Archaeology Department." Dr. Wengaro looked at Dr. Pritzmord in astonishment. "You're also seeking the Grail?"

"For quite some time, yes," Dr. Pritzmord sneered. "You all made my task that much easier. And the best part is that I had no idea that Nassauton hiring you would result in this surprise ending! A lovely bonus after what has proved to be a long and difficult quest!"

"A surprise indeed to find you here, with a gun and a battered post-doc. Why did you do this to her?" Lydia asked.

Dr. Pritzmord shrugged. "She served her purpose. I couldn't take chances."

"You evil monster." Dr. Wengaro spat out his words. "Who are you? Wounding an innocent post-doc like this? I thought you were a respectable dean and scholar. Heck, was I wrong."

Dr. Pritzmord shrugged again. "To many, I am. I try to dress the part at least." He sneered.

He was wearing khaki pants, a button-down shirt, a navy-blue-and-white-striped tie, and a black blazer. Bright spatters of red blood dotted his white shirt and pearl-colored brooch. I noticed it was in the shape of a row of iridescent ocean waves. One wave was broken, like a chunk had snapped off.

The sparkling white chip from under Dr. Hasserin's desk, I realized. It wasn't a button. It was a chunk of Dr. Pritzmord's brooch!

My pulse surged. Dr. Pritzmord smirked as he looked at his revolver, then at us. My heart started pounding even more. Apprehension filled my stomach.

"It sure is so much better when all you have to do is hop on a flight and have the Grail handed right to you." Dr. Pritzmord hovered over us, cornering us against the wall and blocking our only hope of an escape.

"We're not handing you anything!" I blurted out. Surprised by my audacity when I was this terrified, I added, "It's our research and our Grail."

"*Your* Grail?" Dr. Pritzmord scoffed. "It might be your research, but it is not your Grail." He walked up to Lydia, who'd been gently caressing the post-doc's head. He kicked her. She lunged forward, grimacing in pain as she caught herself with her hands before she hit the floor.

"What was that for?" Lydia asked between labored breaths.

"I've always wanted to watch the mighty fall. You're not the only top archaeologist here, Lydia."

Dr. Pritzmord held the barrel of his revolver to Lydia's head. "Carly, you don't have to hand me anything. I don't have to let Lydia live." Dr. Pritzmord traced Lydia's face with his gun. "Ladies and gentlemen, the great Dr. Lydia Kells! Is this how her illustrious career ends? With her cowering in a hallway in some small-town museum? Watched by two freshmen wannabe Grail archaeologists and some professor who thinks his research is actually interesting and unique?" He enunciated his words in a mocking way.

I narrowed my eyes and scowled at him. I did not appreciate him talking about Lydia—Gran's and *my* partner—like this.

"You wouldn't kill me," spat Lydia, looking Dr. Pritzmord in his eyes.

"What makes you so certain?" he sneered. He shoved his gun to the back of Lydia's head. "Funny, Sid said the exact same thing, from the exact same position."

"Sid?" asked Dr. Wengaro. He tried to walk up to Dr. Pritzmord, but Dr. Pritzmord jerked his revolver from Lydia's head to Dr. Wengaro's direction.

"Don't try anything, Kenneth. Wouldn't want to kill you too."

"You murdered Dr. Hasserin?" I asked.

Dr. Pritzmord trained his revolver back on Lydia's head. "Collateral damage," he said. "He was a brilliant researcher who got very far. He would have gotten even farther had he cooperated with me. He got in way over his head and didn't understand that he was dealing in matters darker than anything he'd ever encountered."

"You murdered Dr. Hasserin?" I repeated. The fear in my stomach was pulsing in waves. I had never seen a gun in person before. Watching Dr. Pritzmord hold it against Lydia's head and train it on Dr. Wengaro was making me nauseous. I was standing in the presence of a murderer—a murderer who was none other than the dean of Nassauton's Archaeology Department! *Dr. Hasserin's murderer had been on campus, right next to us, the whole time!*

Dr. Pritzmord shrugged. "He didn't cooperate. In the end, I still got what I wanted."

"How long have you been tracking us?" asked Lydia.

Dr. Pritzmord beamed. He lowered his revolver from Lydia's head. She turned around and sat on the floor, rubbing her wrists as she looked up at Dr. Pritzmord. "Since you suggested Sid had been murdered. I knew you wouldn't let it go. Not with your Henge Piece—or as I've come to learn, Grealmæp—case never fully closed. Not with Sid's teaser Stonehenge discovery at the conference. And when Carly Stuart—Dr. Lyle Ainsley's granddaughter—signed up for Sid's seminar, showed up in your class, started meeting with you for hours on end, I knew something was up. Lydia and Lyle's granddaughter, closing the door and meeting. Sneaking around in Sid's house. The last time the great Lydia Kells was up to something, she'd unearthed the Henge Piece itself—the instrument that attracted the Knights of the Dagger."

"You know about the Knights of the Dagger?" I asked.

"Of course. They sent notes to Lyle, Lydia, and Sid. They want the Grail. Why else would they want the Grealmæp? Do you know how long I've been searching for the Grail? Now, it's almost mine, thanks to Sid—and thanks to you!"

I clenched my jaw. There was no way Dr. Pritzmord was getting the Grealmæp—or the Grail.

"Well done," he said mockingly. "Carly Stuart's first case, and she hands me the Grail!"

I wanted to retort, but my mouth was too dry to form words. I looked at my Ailm charm and took a deep breath.

"So, Sid didn't share his research, so you didn't let him live," spat Dr. Wengaro. "How do you justify killing a man because he wouldn't work with you? Sid wasn't perfect—he surely wasn't perfect—but did he deserve to be murdered? Yet another death associated with the Grail?" He lunged at Dr. Pritzmord and shook him by his blazer. "You evil, conceited piec—"

Dr. Pritzmord interrupted Dr. Wengaro with a swift, strong punch to his jaw. Dr. Wengaro reeled back, clutching his face. His ponytail, already loosely tied, came undone.

"Anyone else in the class care to share their opinion?" taunted Dr. Pritzmord. He rolled his shoulders back and smoothed out his blazer. "Who's next?"

"Blane—get help!" I screamed. Blane sprang up to run down the hallway.

"Don't think so," said Dr. Pritzmord, sticking out his leg and tripping Blane. Blane crashed down, smashing his shoulder on the stone floor.

"Blane! Are you okay?"

Blane looked at me with pain in his eyes. "My shoulder."

"Did you hit your head?" I caressed Blane's face, checking for bumps and bruises.

"No, I don't think so." Blane winced in pain as he touched his right ankle. "It hurts pretty bad. I think I tore the tendon."

I tried to prop Blane up and rest him against the wall. "Sit here for now. Don't put weight on your ankle."

Dr. Pritzmord cut me off. "He'll be fine. He's a big boy. He can handle a little pain." Dr. Pritzmord pointed his revolver at Lydia. "Where's the Grealmæp?"

"I don't have it," Lydia responded calmly.

I didn't take my eyes off Lydia or Dr. Pritzmord. I was terrified he would shoot Lydia. I didn't move.

"We'll never give it to you," said Lydia. "You'll never get the Grail."

Behind Dr. Pritzmord, I could see Dr. Wengaro stumbling forward. He held his hand to his face. "Daniel, put the gun away. We can work this out."

"One punch wasn't enough, Kenneth?" He struck Dr. Wengaro a second time. "Back for more?" He laughed as Dr. Wengaro crumpled in pain. "And one more, for good measure." He delivered a third punch, sending Dr. Wengaro against the wall. He collapsed to the floor. His once perfectly coifed curls were now completely disheveled.

Dr. Pritzmord's eyes were gleaming. He held his revolver to Dr. Wengaro's temple. "I'm not leaving without the Grail. Give me the Grealmæp, Kenneth."

"I don't have it." Dr. Wengaro gasped for air. Blood gushed out of his nose.

"I'll give you one last chance. *Give me the Grealmæp.*"

"I told you I don't have it." Dr. Wengaro spat out words and blood. Fresh droplets of blood landed on Dr. Pritzmord's shirt.

"Have it your way." Dr. Pritzmord kneed Dr. Wengaro in the stomach, sending the man to the floor. Dr. Wengaro lay motionless on the ground, unconscious. Blood pooled next to him, pouring from his nose.

Dr. Pritzmord turned to Lydia. "Where is it?" He pointed his revolver to her face.

She stared at him defiantly, not speaking.

He lunged at her and threw her on her knees—she cried out in pain—then he stood in front of her and grasped her by her throat. "Don't know what to say? I know what will help." Taking the gun, he rammed the barrel into her bun and jerked it around, causing it to come undone.

She stared up at him without breaking her silence.

Dr. Pritzmord released Lydia, sending her onto the floor. She undid her bun and redid it, perfectly positioning her hair.

Dr. Pritzmord leaped at me, prying me from Blane. He twisted my arms behind me and stuck his revolver to my cheek. Searing pain tore across my shoulder. The cold metal barrel made my heart stop. I couldn't fight or escape. I froze in fear. "How about now, Lydia? Where is the Grealmæp?"

"Don't shoot Carly," said Lydia. "I'll give you the Grealmæp."

"How do I know you're not lying?" Dr. Pritzmord's gun pressed into my cheek. I couldn't feel my heartbeat, but something told me I was still alive.

"It's in my satchel, at Workstation 1."

"Excellent." Dr. Pritzmord released his revolver. I stretched out my shoulders as I felt my pulse. My whole upper back was numb with pain. "Let's take a walk, shall we?"

Holding Lydia's arm and pointing his gun at me, Dr. Pritzmord marched us down the hallway. I looked back at Blane.

"Keep an eye on Dr. Wengaro. See if Tiffdill wakes up. Don't try to move. You'll hurt yourself more."

"Shut up, Carly." Dr. Pritzmord jammed the gun's barrel into my ribs. I winced in pain. "Walk!" he said. "Do as you're told."

I kept walking. There were no security cameras in the hallway. Our chances of escape—or for someone to come into the Examination Room—were lessening. I could feel the barrel poking me in the side, sending shooting pain down my rib cage every time I took a breath. The only thing stopping Dr. Pritzmord from shooting me was that he needed me or Lydia to work the Grealmæp. *What if the Grealmæp doesn't work? Will he kill us anyway?* Our only chance of surviving was opening the Grail box in the presence of Dr. Pritzmord—and giving him the Grail. *What would Gran do if she were here? Had she ever encountered danger—or been outsmarted—like this?*

Dr. Pritzmord had outsmarted us. I never saw that coming. He was a respectable dean! And yet here he was, pointing his gun at his colleagues and Nassauton students! I never suspected him when Lydia and I considered the evidence. I shook my head.

As we entered the Examination Room and headed to our workstation, the reality began to sink in. We were steps away from handing Dr. Pritzmord the Grail. I had failed Gran. Lydia and I both had. I was angry and frustrated. Where did I go wrong? But most of all, I was disappointed. I'd worked so hard. I clenched my fists as though that would absorb some of my anger. It only made me angrier.

We arrived at Workstation 1, and Lydia rushed ahead to grab her satchel. The shape of the Tupperware container was visible under the leather. I wanted to throw myself over Lydia's satchel and scream, *"NO! DON'T DO IT!"* I knew that would have been futile.

My anger was turning to despair. The only thing left to be done was to escape, before handing over the Grealmæp. At least in that case, neither Dr. Pritzmord nor Lydia or I would get the Grail.

"At last!" said Dr. Pritzmord. "The complete Grealmæp!"

I bit my lip, fighting back anger and tears. Dr. Pritzmord was going to get the Grail. I wiped my face with the palms of my hands. It was over. I didn't know what to feel, other than emptiness. My first quest hadn't resulted in triumph—it had resulted in failure. I stared at Dr. Pritzmord as he gloated over the Grealmæp.

"Where's the Grail box?" Lydia asked.

"Follow me." Dr. Pritzmord picked up Lydia's satchel, led us across the Examination Room, and down the hallway. Blane, Dr. Wengaro, and Tiffdill were still there. Dr. Wengaro was passed out. Blane alternated between nudging Dr. Wengaro and Tiffdill and rubbing his ankle. I tried to talk to Blane, but Dr. Pritzmord jabbed his revolver into my side. "Don't even look at him. Walk into that storage room."

Lydia and I stepped over Tiffdill. Dr. Pritzmord flicked on the lights.

The storage room had a concrete floor and white painted walls. Two of the walls featured metal floor-to-ceiling cabinets. In the center of the room was a wooden table and a few chairs. A few fluorescent lights illuminated the table. There, on the table next to a box of gloves and some brushes, was a gray stone box. The Grealmæp insignia was unmistakable.

"Whenever you're ready, Lydia." Dr. Pritzmord placed Lydia's satchel on the table and closed the door. He pulled a chair up and sat down, with his back to the door. He set his revolver in front of him, keeping his grip on the trigger as he watched us. "Don't try anything funny."

I walked to the opposite side of the table. Lydia opened her satchel and slid her Tupperware container out.

"Lydia, a Tupperware? The great Dr. Kells keeps the Grealmæp in a Tupperware?" Dr. Pritzmord taunted her.

"It's airtight." Lydia slowly started popping the lid off, corner by corner. "It does its job." She set the lid off to the side.

"Can't you move any faster?"

"I need gloves." She pulled two gloves out of the box. She tried to put them on. "Too small."

Dr. Pritzmord rolled his eyes. "Come on!"

"Daniel, I have a process. I need gloves. You need to be patient."

"Can't you wear the small gloves?"

"No."

"Fine." Daniel got up, walked to one of the metal cabinets, and started searching for more gloves. He found a box labeled LARGE and tossed them across the table to Lydia. "Here, Carly and I will wear them too," he said as he pulled gloves out of the box. "Would that make you feel better?"

Lydia replied by squinting at Dr. Pritzmord. We put on our gloves. Dr. Pritzmord sat down, with his back to the door and eyes fixed on the Grealmæp. He rested his hand on the gun. Lydia reached for the Grealmæp, then carefully placed it on the table. Dr. Pritzmord stared at Lydia's hands as she began to unwrap the Grealmæp.

Her eyes were focused on the towel with her lips pursed in concentration. As she unwrapped the Grealmæp, her lips curled with the slightest smirk. *What is she smirking at, at a time like this?* I caught her eye as if to ask, *What is going on?*

Careful not to let Dr. Pritzmord see her, she nodded her head ever so slightly to the door. My eyes darted from her to the door. Dr. Wengaro held a finger to his lips as he slowly opened the door a fraction of an inch more.

An anxious shiver ran down my spine as I blinked to acknowledge to Dr. Wengaro I'd seen him. I looked at my Ailm charm. *Inner strength. A path forward.* I took a deep breath. With Dr. Wengaro sneaking in, I was starting to see a path that would lead us to keeping the Grail—and to an escape. It started with the biggest leap of faith I would take. I would need to make sure Dr. Pritzmord kept his focus on the Grealmæp and didn't look behind him.

"Dr. Pritzmord." I took a deep breath and prayed my plan would work. "Look at the Grealmæp. You know King Arthur made it to help him hide the Grail, right? How did you become interested in the Grail in the first place?"

He looked at me, then at the Grealmæp, loosening his grip on the revolver. Lydia kept unwrapping the microfiber towels. "Of course I know about King Arthur. He, like so many before and after him, was fascinated by the Grail. I've been fascinated by it ever since I realized it was real. Ever since I first read about it. It's an elusive artifact that brings its owner the incredible power of eternal life."

"Dr. Pritzmord, that's so interesting. Something I was also wondering is, do you think microfiber is the best way to keep these artifacts protected? I mean, look at this towel and how it has these marks." I picked up one of the towels Lydia had put off to the side. "How clean do you think the Grealmæp really is? Do you think dust gets trapped in here? What if the Grealmæp doesn't work because this towel isn't all that clean?"

Dr. Pritzmord put his revolver on the table and picked up the towel. "Hmm. It is kind of dirty. The Grealmæp better work. I'm not leaving here without that Grail."

"Oh it better!" I chimed in, then remembered to curb my faked enthusiasm. I was talking about anything that would keep Dr. Pritzmord's focus on the table, and not the door. "Wait, you were saying the Grail brings whoever has it eternal life. How?"

Dr. Pritzmord looked at me. His eyes gleamed as he described the Grail's power.

"It's an ancient relic, like the Spear of Destiny, the Crown of Thorns, St. Peter's Bones, the Ghent Altarpiece, the Ark of the Covenant, and the Shroud of Turin. The Ark of the Covenant, and the ones Jesus Christ touched, seem to have more otherworldly power than the others—which makes them especially desirable. That's why Hitler was obsessed with finding these relics, especially the Grail. He who finds them will be able to control access to eternal life."

He has no interest in archaeology for the sake of scholarship or advancing the field, I realized. He had deceived everyone at Nassauton. He was a con man and a killer, chasing immortality—and murdering those who got in his way.

Dr. Wengaro had successfully snuck into our room, behind Dr. Pritzmord. My heart skipped a beat. We were one step closer to escape. I glanced at Lydia. I tried to control my breathing.

"Dr. Pritzmord," I replied flatly, "do you really believe that? That sounds like a whole lot of legends. Where is the evidence for that?" I looked at Lydia. "I was trained to operate from evidence, not from emotion. The evidence is what matters, not how you feel about it."

Dr. Wengaro leaped at Dr. Pritzmord from behind, wrapping his hands around his throat. "And the evidence always leads to consequences for the killer."

Lydia pushed Dr. Pritzmord's revolver off the table. It

clanked as it hit the floor. Dr. Pritzmord's eyes bulged out of his head as he gasped for air, clawing at Dr. Wengaro's hands. Dr. Wengaro's grip tightened.

Dr. Pritzmord elbowed Dr. Wengaro deep in the stomach, and he reflexively dropped his hands to clutch his stomach. Dr. Pritzmord spun around, smashing Dr. Wengaro into the concrete wall. Blood spurted from Dr. Wengaro's nose, splattering on his hair. He crumpled to the ground.

"Kenneth!" Lydia screamed. She grabbed the microfiber towels and raced around the table. "Kenneth, no!"

Dr. Pritzmord and I stared at one another. Cold sweat dripped down my neck. Paralyzed in fear, I stared at the Grealmæp in the Tupperware. It blurred in and out of my vision as the room spun around me. I leaned on the table, trying to steady myself. *I am going to be next. Dr. Pritzmord is going to kill me.*

Lydia's scream echoed in my ears as my body hit the floor.

"Open your eyes!" roared Dr. Pritzmord, as if from miles away. "I told you I'm not leaving without the Grail."

I blinked my eyes open. I gasped for my breath. *The gun.* The barrel of the gun jabbed my ribs.

"The only reason I haven't killed you yet is that you know how the Grealmæp works. Either you finish the job or tell me how to." He twisted the gun in my ribs.

I swallowed. My mouth was too dry. I stumbled to the Grealmæp. Lydia was holding the microfiber towels up to Dr. Wengaro's head, trying to stop the bleeding. Dr. Pritzmord kept his gun in my ribs. I put new gloves on and picked up the Grealmæp, my hands trembling. Its ruby and gold gleamed in the fluorescent light. I traced the double dagger etchings on the ruby. *Etched in stone.* I looked at the insignia on the top of the box. *Etched in stone.*

"That's a good girl, Carly." Dr. Pritzmord's voice gave me chills. Even if he didn't shoot me, he could still hurt me. I had to comply.

I stared at the insignia on the box. It was the mirror image of the Grealmæp. I had to invert the Grealmæp and place it on top of the insignia.

Double dagger marks were etched into the stone box. I looked at the Grealmæp's ruby. *We have to use the ruby's back face—the face with the relief of the double dagger marks, not the face with the etched dagger marks*, I realized. Dr. Hasserin had been wrong about etched in stone. It didn't refer to Stonehenge or the ruby. It referred to the double dagger marks etched in the stone Grail box.

I grinned as I nodded. I knew what I had to do.

I carefully lifted the ruby out of the Grealmæp and flipped it around. *The double dagger relief on the ruby is a key that unlocks the stone box.*

"So that's how it works!" Dr. Pritzmord exclaimed. "Move. I can take it from here." He set his revolver on the table, then pushed me back and grabbed the ruby.

As he placed the ruby on top of the Grail box, I heard heels clacking down the hallway. Dr. Gellmane and the security guard burst into our room. The security guard trained his gun on Dr. Pritzmord. Startled, Dr. Pritzmord looked up, clutching the ruby. Blane, supported by Tiffdill, limped in after them.

"Stop him!" I pointed at Dr. Pritzmord.

"Drop it." The security guard kept his gun aimed at Dr. Pritzmord. "Put your hands above your head."

As Dr. Pritzmord raised his arms, he tried to swing them up to tackle the security guard. But the guard was too quick—he punched Dr. Pritzmord in the face. The impact sent Dr. Pritzmord reeling backward away from the table.

"When I said drop it and put your hands above your head," the security guard hissed, "I meant drop it and put your hands above your head!" The guard trapped Dr. Pritzmord in a body lock on the floor. "Do you think you're above the law now?"

"Hand over the ruby." Lydia stepped toward Dr. Pritzmord.

He tightened his grasp on the ruby. The security guard stuck his gun in Dr. Pritzmord's ribs. Snarling, Dr. Pritzmord released the gem. Lydia grabbed it.

"Don't think you've seen the last of me, Carly Stuart," Dr. Pritzmord sneered as the security guard whipped out handcuffs and jerked him off the floor. "Watch your back, Carly Stuart. When our paths cross again, you won't be as lucky. Watch your back. The Grail will be mine yet."

Dr. Pritzmord's threat echoed in my head as he and the guard disappeared down the hallway. I closed my eyes and took a deep breath. Shaking my head, I opened them and looked at Lydia and Dr. Gellmane. Blane and Tiffdill were crouched around Dr. Wengaro.

"How'd you know to find us?" I asked Dr. Gellmane.

"Your boyfriend." She smiled.

"When Tiffdill came to," said Blane, "she helped me hobble back down the hallway to her office. We called security."

"And the ambulance. The medics should be here by now." Dr. Gellmane glanced at her phone. We'll have to get Tiffdill, Blane, and Dr. Wengaro to the hospital."

Dr. Wengaro groaned as he came to.

"I, I, what happened?" he asked. "Where's Daniel?"

"Shh, shh, it's okay," said Lydia. "Daniel is gone. You're safe now."

Dr. Wengaro managed a small smile. "Did we get the Grail?"

I shook my head. "We haven't even opened the box!"

"Well, what are we waiting for?" Blane asked. He grinned impishly and added, "We came all this way. It's been a long—and painful—journey. Come on, let's see it!"

I grinned as we gathered around the table. Tiffdill got Blane a chair. Lydia gave me the ruby. "You want to do the honors, Carly?"

"You should, Lydia."

Lydia smiled. "Lyle would want you to."

Oh Gran. What would you do if you were here? Carefully placing the ruby on top of Grealmæp insignia, I took a deep breath. The double daggers fit perfectly in their marks on the stone box, exactly like a key going into a lock. I lifted my hand. I looked down at my Ailm charm as I turned the ruby to the right.

Nothing happened.

I pushed the ruby in deeper and turned it even more. *Click.* The stone lid popped up an inch.

Trembling with excitement, I opened the lid all the way. Inside the box was a small, dark-gray felt bag, tied with a thick rope.

"Go on, open it." Lydia beamed.

My chest swelled with pride as goosebumps appeared on my arms. "Are you sure?"

"Yes. Lyle would want you to."

I wiggled my toes in my boots. I took a deep breath and picked up the felt bag. It felt full—and heavy. My hands were shaking as I tried to unknot the rope. I finally unknotted the bag and slid its contents onto the table.

Tears filled my eyes as I stared at the contents. I took a deep breath and looked at Blane, then Lydia. I closed my eyes, taking another deep breath before I opened them. "Well," I said, my voice trembling. "I'm pretty sure that's not the Grail." I didn't know what else to say.

I let out a long sigh as I looked around the room. *Where's the Grail?* I shook my head in disbelief. We'd worked so hard for this moment—and I was so sure the Grail would be in this box. I stared at the mortar and pestle in silence—and in despair.

"How did those tools get in the Grail box then?" Dr. Wengaro asked, breaking the silence.

"Someone must have the other Grealmæp," said Blane. "You know, like how my book said there are two."

I looked at the box's lid and Grealmæp insignia. The box wasn't broken or tampered with. Who had the other Grealmæp? I shook my head. *Maybe Lydia is right, and the Grail isn't even real.* I couldn't control the tears that gushed from my eyes.

Blane grabbed my hand. "Oh Carly. I know you're upset." He

let go of my hand and wiped my eyes with his sleeves. "But look at how far we've come! We might not have found the Grail, but we found artifacts with a history of their own." He paused, then added, "The Grail remains lost to time—lost, like it has been for centuries—but this mortar and pestle look super cool too!"

Even though I was disappointed, I knew Blane was right.

"What do you think they were used for?" Lydia asked as she pointed to the contents of the felt bag.

I looked at the table. The mortar and pestle had pale pink residue on it. "No clue," I mumbled.

"Carly," said Blane. "You know what this means?"

"What?" I could tell he was trying to make me feel better.

"It means I think we've lifted the lid on a whole other adventure for us to pursue."

Adventure for us to pursue. I looked at Blane. He had a goofy grin on his face. I loved how my teammate was already ready for our next adventure. I cracked a smile as I chuckled at his bad pun.

I stared at the mortar and pestle. We hadn't found the Grail, but we had found something else that was leading us to another quest. I looked inside the box again.

"Whoa," I said as my eyes widened in amazement. "There's something else in here." I pulled out a journal, noticing the swastika embossed on its cover.

"A Nazi journal." Dr. Wengaro gasped. "Maybe Hitler found the Grail."

Blane grinned. "Evidence that Indy wasn't too far off, after all."

"Oh my gosh," Lydia exclaimed. "Mr. Henley, what is with you and Indiana Jones?"

"He taught me how to use the evidence to take a leap of faith. Evidence might get you to the finish line; faith is what gets you across."

I grinned. Faith had indeed gotten us across this finish line. As I flipped through the journal's pages, I realized its entries were chemistry equations, experiment lists, and notes.

"Speaking of finish lines," said Dr. Gellmane, "now that you've crossed this one, your next destination is the hospital."

As I closed the journal, I noticed its cover page, surprised that the writing was in English and not in German:

††

Notes and Experiments, Volume IV:
Making Grealia Eternae, Part II

by KAvG

XXI

Six weeks of rest and care, and Blane would be fully healed. He could relax around town, provided he didn't go overboard with too much activity. His doctors had even given him a wheelchair so he wouldn't have to walk around on crutches. The hospital wanted to monitor Dr. Wengaro more closely, since he'd sustained injuries that put him at risk for internal bleeding. Tiffdill had needed stitches, and she would make a full recovery.

"Guess when we get back to campus, I'll have to ask you to go to all my classes in my place," Blane jokingly said to me. "Or maybe you'll wheel me around to them."

"You're in that much of a rush to get back to Nassauton?" I asked. "We should stay here without worrying about the stress of a trans-Atlantic flight."

"Carly's right," said Lydia. "I'm sure your professors will work with you to get you what you missed."

I hoped Lydia was right. Despite the circumstances, I was looking forward to being a tourist in Amesbury. I knew exactly what attraction I wanted to visit first.

Blane smiled at me. "You ready?"

I grinned. "You bet, teammate!" I squeezed Blane's hand. "Are you?"

"Almost."

"Almost?" I looked at him skeptically.

"Just need one thing." He grinned his big, goofy grin.

"What's that?"

Blane leaned in and kissed me.

The bus driver pulled into the parking lot. "All right everyone, welcome to Stonehenge."

Lydia had stayed behind, opting to explore the town. "I've seen it before," she said, "with a person who was very dear to me." She smiled as she pointed to her Ailm charm bracelet. "I think Lyle would want you two to see it together."

As the wintry sunrays hit Stonehenge, I grinned. I felt the Tupperware container with the Grealmæp in my satchel. I had made sure to bring three pairs of gloves—one for me, one for Blane, and one extra, just in case. The very first thing I was going to do when we got closer to the monument was see how the Grealmæp aligned with Stonehenge.

"Shall we?" I asked Blane as we exited the bus.

"Yes." Blane grinned. His hazel eyes sparkled with excitement as he took out his phone. "But first, let's document this so we have evidence we were here. As they say, selfie or it didn't happen."

He positioned himself with Stonehenge in the background and stretched his arm out in front of his face.

"Come here, Carly. This is one of the best days of my life. I've got my teammate and Stonehenge. Our first archaeological adventure is in the books. Here's to a whole lot more ahead of us."

He pulled me close to him, pressed his lips on my cheek, and snapped our selfie.

ACKNOWLEDGMENTS

I owe a debt of gratitude to my parents. Thank you for encouraging my pursuit of adventure and quests. I have always been able to see myself as Nancy Drew, Hermione Granger, Lyra Belacqua, and our beloved Lucy Pevensie, because you encouraged me to. More than encourage me to read about worlds in which these female adventurists exist, you empowered me to follow my own adventures and quests so I honored these heroines' fearlessness, bravery, and spirit in my own real-life journeys. And, thank you for letting me have Granddad's cool pens that he collected from his international travels. Perhaps they are for me what Gran's shoes are for Carly . . .

To my brother and sister, who constantly inspire me with their passion, intelligence, and humor. Never stop creating, and believing you can change the world through music, film, and being who you were created to be. I love you endlessly and love seeing you achieve your dreams.

To SMA, whose insights on King Arthur and his court, countless Irish legends, Narnia, and of course, our old friend Chaucer, have had an indelible influence not only on my research and writing, but also on the way in which I see our world and our place as pilgrims (or knights?) in it . . .

To Giselle Harrington: The cover is gorgeous and lets me look right into Carly's world of archaeology, academia, and mystery. The title font is beautiful and makes me feel like I'm about to open a Celtic spell book. Your eye for detail, from the filigree to the Grail to the daggers, makes the cover a unique and beautiful work of art. What a privilege and joy it is to work with you again!

To Kristen Hamilton: I am so lucky that Holly Spofford put us in touch (thank you Holly). You have made this entire process so easy and manageable, providing the attention, guidance, feedback, and direction that *Etched in Stone* needed to get to where it is now. Wow, what a journey. It takes a team to produce a book, and I'm so thankful you are part of mine! Thank you for everything.

To Cayce Berryman and Crystal MM Burton: You are experts at what you do. Listening to how readers engage with the layout of *Parables* has been so rewarding, and whenever someone comments on *Parables*, I respond with, "This is why you work with the professionals." I stand by those comments and am over the moon with the quality of *Etched in Stone*.

To every fearless woman who has gone before me as a trailblazer and role model . . . thank you.

ABOUT THE AUTHOR

Archaeology, the Holy Grail, and Arthurian legends have always fascinated Christine Galib. Christine writes to empower the knight in each of us to pursue our quests with grace, courage, and faith. She loves getting lost in a good book and can be found at christinegalib.com.

CPSIA information can be obtained
at www.ICGtesting.com
Printed in the USA
BVHW080744010622
638416BV00004B/13

9 781955 824026